*More acclaim for C.D. Payne's*
# Youth in Revolt: The Journals of Nick Twisp

"This American cult 'Adrian Mole' is an altogether rougher, sexier, and funnier tale. . . A rollercoaster ride through the nemesis of adolescent angst." —*London Mail*

"A sussed, silly and energetic account which literally bulges with Nick Twisp's hormonal excitations. . . Faster and funnier than 14 ever felt before." —*The Punter* [UK]

"In the course of 499 pages, Nick falls in and out of favor with his divorced parents; he looks for love in all the wrong places; he invents; he schemes. He even burns down half of Berkeley. But throughout, this novel—or three novels—is extremely readable. For while Nick searches for the joys of sex, he finds a great deal more—a general *joie de vivre* and compassion that prove addictive." —*L.A. Reader*

"A hilarious six month journey through the thorny underbrush of sexual desire, frustration, and (occasionally painful) discovery. . . Payne does not offer up his characters to the altar of hackneyed change or growth. He gives us instead a wonderfully original refugee from parental cynicism and the 'gulag of the public schools' whose scorn, bad attitude, and unflagging horniness persist in a way that is engagingly real. . . There is a refreshing frankness and celebration in the writing that elevates it above the mere silliness of much of today's comic fiction." —*New Haven Advocate*

"*Youth in Revolt* . . . [is] a hefty coming-of-age novel which actually lives up to the publisher's comparisons to *A Confederacy of Dunces* and *Portnoy's Complaint*, and in many ways surpasses them. . . One of the funniest novels I've ever read." —*Hypno Magazine*

"Payne's ability to constantly introduce new characters and new plots while interweaving the old ones is like watching an aerialist interrupt his highwire act to take out a lawn chair, then do a headstand on it and start juggling with his feet. And then just as you're wondering how he can get out of that predicament, he sets fire to the juggling balls. It's hard to say which are more satisfying: the twists you can tell are coming or the ones that take you by surprise." —*Berkeley Express*

"It's a high honor and distinct privilege, then, to introduce C.D. Payne's totally unsentimental and extremely funny first novel, *Youth in Revolt: The Journals of Nick Twisp*. It's the antidote to Salinger's tale of the teenage saint Holden Caulfield." —*The Oregonian*

"*Youth in Revolt* is an unstintingly hilarious black comedy, almost certainly the funniest book you'll read this year. . . Nick is irresistible, for his first encounters with adult phenomena always seem to bring out an appropriately warped response or an almost-brilliant insight. . . Nick's voice is unique and indelible, Payne's language rich and inventive. C.D. Payne has set a high standard for himself." —*Los Angeles Times*

"A genuinely funny book, one that will have many readers laughing out loud. . . Nick is an inspired chronicler of his inner life and philosophy . . . Payne captures the trials of adolescence in these perilous times, dealing with far more than just the pangs of hormonal upheavals." —*Sonoma County Independent*

# Civic Beauties

"A witty, inventive, unique, engaging,
laugh-a-minute novel of pure delight."
—*Midwest Book Review*

*Also by C.D. Payne*

Youth in Revolt: The Journals of Nick Twisp

# Civic Beauties

*a novel with songs*

C.D. Payne

AIVIA Press
www.nicktwisp.com

Sebastopol, California

CIVIC BEAUTIES. Copyright © 1999 by C.D. Payne.
All rights reserved.

Manufactured in the United States of America.


10 9 8 7 6 5 4 3 2


No part of this book may be used or reproduced in any manner whatsoever without written permission except in the case of brief quotations embodied in critical articles or reviews. For information, address Aivia Press, P.O. Box 1922, Sebastopol, CA 95473

Data from *Jane's Fighting Ships* are reprinted with the kind permission of the publisher.

Library of Congress Cataloging-in-Publication Data:
Payne, C. D. (C. Douglas), 1949-
    Civic beauties: a novel with songs / C.D. Payne. -- 1st. ed.
        p.    cm.
    ISBN 1-882647-20-3
    I. Title.
    PS3566.A9358C58  1999
    813'.54--dc21                                                        99-
24473
                                                                        CIP

*To all the pals of Nick*

Reality is what you make up.
—Nick Twisp

*Chapter 1*

When I heard my father was being mentioned as a possible candidate for the Republican nomination for Vice President, my first impulse was to slash my wrists. Why shouldn't I take these things personally? How would you like some shadowy Secret Service agent in sunglasses snooping through your underwear drawer and following you around day and night? It would be like having multiple sets of extra parents to cope with. My life was impossible enough when Dad was just pastor of the First Baptist Church and mayor of Rocky Pike, Ohio. Now that he's a United States Senator, my friends look at me like I'm a freak.

Of course, my twin sister Carissa (age 15$^1$/$_2$) is thrilled by the whole thing. She wasn't even disturbed when I pointed out that one consequence of 24-hour-a-day Secret Service protection could be the prolongation of her virginity for four, if not eight more years. Boys, even the really slaggy ones, are only willing to go so far while under government surveillance. As usual, she pretended not to care. Perhaps she's taken to heart Dad's message that all a teen really needs to know about sex can be summarized in five words: Total Abstinence or You Die. I sure hope she's not a lesbian. If by some chance she is, I pray to God she announces it to the press before the convention.

I see from the morning *Plain Dealer* that before leaving for the Republican national convention, Senator Horace B. Mason (Dad) introduced legislation declaring that life begins at the moment of conception and compelling everyone to add nine months to their ages. Helpful in some respects for my sister and me, but it still won't get us into R-rated movies. Damn.

Dad takes a somewhat narrower view of the world than our mother. She spent her junior year abroad in Florence, and loves all things Italian, including the names Antonia (that's me) and Carissa. Like Dad, she is of mongrelized WASP extraction; her maiden name was Gloria Drucker. Only in the Midwest is the bestowing of such horrible names still actively encouraged. Dad contributed our freckles and wretched middle names: Esther for Cara and Rachel for me. Once at the Cuyahoga County Fair I had my monogram engraved on a bracelet, and it looked like a brass anatomy label or instructions for where to wear it (ARM). My third marriage (for love) will be an artful alliance with a guy from the "T"s, maybe one of Ted Turner's handsome grandsons.

Lately the consensus seems to be that we look like Doris Day, a fellow Buckeye who went to Hollywood and got famous for just saying no to Rock Hudson. I guess maybe it's our freckles and perky noses and Cara's wholesome personality. In any case I'm planning on having my nose fixed; perhaps some disastrous boyfriend choices will selectively darken my sister's persona—God knows I've tried. The freckles I think will fade or can be chemically erased. Thankfully our figures and all-important bone structure show promise. With a little work, at least one of us could develop into a marginally captivating beauty.

Pay attention now, Cara wants to take over the narrative. We're going to swap back and forth, so you have to stay alert.

※ ※ ※

This morning brought rare blue sky and sunshine (nearby Lake Erie is a prodigious generator of clouds). Since we were—as Toni put it—"whiter than our stepmother's soul," my sister and I lay on our beach towels in the back yard until Dan the Picketer showed up, when Toni suggested we transfer to the front yard. A dedicated member of the Sierra Club, Dan Wyandot is a forestry major at Cleveland State and quite good-looking. We stretched out our towels on the grass near the tall sycamore tree and chatted up the protester as he marched back and forth with his angry, hand-lettered sign: "God Save Our Forests from Senator Mason."

"Is your father home today, Toni?" he asked. "Er, which one of you is Toni?"

"I am," replied my sister, sliding her bikini straps down her shoulders like a dissolute Malibu beach-goer. In Ohio straps are worn UP. "He's in there, Dan," she lied. "He hasn't left for the convention yet. He's tremendously embarrassed by your courageous actions."

"Well, he should be. He wants to sell off our national forests to timber companies to help retire the national debt. He wants to log Yosemite, for God's sake!"

"We're appalled, Dan," replied Toni. "We're on your side. Aren't we, Cara?"

"Not entirely," I replied, feeling somewhat self-conscious sprawled in Toni's old red bikini in front of such an extraordinarily cute guy. (He has the most piercing blue eyes that go through you like a chain saw.) As you might expect, Toni's swimwear left very little to the imagination. Fortunately, Dan, like most of his sex, only had eyes for my sister.

"Toni, could you ask your father to come out? I'd like to speak to him."

"Oh, he'd never do that, Dan. He hates confrontations with informed constituents. If you'd like, perhaps you and I could go out to lunch sometime to discuss the crisis in our forests. I could make sure your concerns reach my father's attention."

"Really, Toni? That'd be great. How about today?"

"Perfect! I'll go change."

My sister pushed up her straps, picked up her towel, and dashed into the house.

Dan looked at me and my body. His looming presence was much scarier without the defensive distraction of my sister. "I can't believe Senator Mason has such intelligent and aware daughters."

"He, he can't either," I stammered.

"I guess you must be twins."

"That's right."

"You're quite . . . identical."

"Well, you're in a good position to know."

Dan reddened and gripped his sign.

"Not exactly identical," I continued, nervously blurting out the first thing that came to mind. "I have this scar on my right knee from the time I fell out of a car when I was little."

Dan studied my legs sympathetically. "Do you mind if I ask how old you are?"

"We're 15."

"Boy, you look considerably older."

"No, we're . . .uh, somewhat young."

"Thanks for mentioning that."

"Have a good time, Dan. Keep up the good work."

He smiled, convulsing several of my internal organs and causing my right hand to reach up involuntarily to pull down a strap. I intercepted it just in time.

\* \* \*

Being a twin is rewarding in so many ways. My sister Toni and I have always felt sorry for the unlucky people who don't have a twin. How lonely that must be. We were as alike as two peas in a pod when we were kids, and lots of people still get us confused. (Though these days Toni tends to go a little heavier on the blusher and mascara.) Even our dreams are similar. Recently we compared notes and discovered we'd both had disturbing menstruation dreams in which we hadn't changed our sanitary napkins for three weeks and were beginning to panic.

At the age of eight, Toni and I made a joint vow that someday we would marry twin brothers. Our dearest dream was a big double wedding in Father's church with twin bridesmaids and best men. All through grammar school we were active in the Rocky Pike Twins Club, where we met and discreetly evaluated many sets of potential husbands. We eventually concluded our dream wasn't very practical as we always seemed to develop a crush on the *same* brother, and then had to endure a distressing period of not speaking to each other while the fortunate sister (usually Toni) enjoyed the attentions of the boy in question. It does seem to be generally true among male twins that one brother gets all the personality. (I trust that's not the case for females too.)

Toni is the vocalist in the family, but I hope you will bear with me as I attempt this song. Those of you who are musical can make up your own tune.

Me, myself, and I—
  The world is o'errun by ego;
Individuality is the cry
  From Boise to Oswego.

But better far than oneness
  Is a measure of duality;
It verges on the wondrous—
  Our state of double reality.

How lucky to be a twin,
  To know this duplication:
To have as next of kin
  Your true self's bifurcation.

For she is me and I am her,
  And that's not silly sophistry;
For from the science you'd infer
  We're just the same genetically.

And if an interlude of solitude
    Permits the mind to flower,
Consider the magnitude of the amplitude
    When *two* are joined in power.

How lucky to be a twin—
    An accident of germination;
Too bad everyone can't win,
    But that would swell the population.

It's ducky to be a twin—
    A consequence of conjugation;
How sad that you can't join in,
    But that was God's determination.

❄ ❄ ❄

The doorbell rang as I was watching a CNN convention update. I opened the front door and said hello to Thom Kirkwood, who stepped around the screen door, gripped me in a tight embrace, and hungrily pressed his open mouth against my famished lips. Thom smelled faintly of motor oil and strongly of a citrus cologne. Immobilized, I diplomatically kissed him back, and he parked a large warm hand on my right breast.

"I'm sorry I didn't call, Toni," he said, coming up for air and slipping his unoccupied hand down inside the back of my bikini bottoms. "I was working on my car and before I knew it, it was after midnight."

"That's OK, Thom. I don't mind."

Thom withdrew his hands and stepped back. "You're not Toni!"

"Er, what makes you say that?"

"You look like Toni, but you're being nice. You're Cara. Hey, I'm sorry!"

"No offense, Thom. It happens all the time."

It was true. Most of my limited experience with boys has resulted from similar incidents of mistaken identity. Perhaps that's why I often linger around the front door dressed only in Toni's cast-off bikinis.

"Where's the other Mason babe?"

"She's not here right now."

A dark cloud passed over Thom's ruddy, boyish face.

"Where is she?"

"She went shopping with my mother," I lied. "You're in the doghouse."

"I figured I would be. What can I do, Cara?"

"Take the abuse like a man. It's better if you don't wimp out. Just call every hour on the hour."

"OK. Tell her I dropped by."

"Will do."

"Thanks for the kiss, Cara. You feel just like your sister. Maybe better."

I could have kissed him again for that remark, but he trotted back to his shiny yellow Ford Probe and "laid a patch" with his oversized tires. I don't know if my sister has slept with Thom, but it was clear they had worked past the awkward hand-holding stage.

⁂ ⁂ ⁂

Now commences an actual twins conversation, such as graduate students in linguistics get lucrative grants to study instead of working at Starbucks:

Cara, I just shared a pizza with the mother of all tree-huggers!

I think he's cute, Toni.

Dan is tremendously cute, Cara. That point is not at issue here. All those soft blond hairs curling around those tanned legs in those khaki forest ranger's shorts with the funny pockets and flaps. A Fashion Don't if ever there was one, but still the guy is devastating. Too bad he has such a one-track mind.

Are you seeing him again?

Cara, I just sat through a three-hour seminar in forestry management. The guy can't see the girl for the trees.

Did you tell him Dad doesn't live here any more?

Of course not, silly. I do enjoy being picketed by him.

That reminds me, Toni, your boyfriend Thom stopped by and was very apologetic.

That's not getting him off the hook, Cara. The guy hasn't phoned for two days. He's going to grovel.

I know. I warned him. After you've finished tormenting Thom, invite him over for dinner. I'm making spaghetti.

OK, this once. But I'm not letting him get the idea I'm a cheap date.

By the way, CNN had a pre-convention report on Dad. They said he has the solid support of the Southern Baptists. Why *is* Dad a Southern Baptist, Toni, when we live in the north?

Oh, something to do with the Civil War and a lingering snit over Lincoln freeing the slaves. At least the church leaders have apologized formally for six generations of racial bigotry. Now they merely discriminate against gays and unsubmissive women. Thank God, religion never stuck with me. Just as the shoemaker's children have no shoes, the minister's kids demonstrate no piety.

Speak for yourself, Toni.

Look at it this way, Cara. If Dad worked in computers, would society demand that we worship Bill Gates? I think it's so unfair. Cara, to make amends for our religious upbringing, I think our first husbands should be African-American atheists.

OK, Toni, but the blacks at Rocky Pike High are so narrow-minded and suburban.

We'll marry inner-city Cleveland men, Cara. Big twin brothers—with burly physiques and police records.

Dad would die. And Mindy would shit a brick.

Our stepmother doesn't shit, Cara. She's much too refined. Her colon terminates in a lovely picnic area set with coordinated linens. I tell you she's Barbie come to life: pneumatic breasts, flawless vinyl skin, artificially chiseled nose, and never a golden Dynel$^R$ hair out of place.

At least Dad married Mindy. It wasn't just a fling. He did the honorable thing, Toni.

Two-timing our mother while preaching the sanctity of marriage is not exactly doing the honorable thing, Cara.

Mom didn't love him any more anyway.

Still, it was hardly pleasant for her to read in the *Plain Dealer* that her husband was touring Cincinnati on a campaign trip with the reigning Miss Ohio.

※ ※ ※

While we were having dinner, Mom came home dead on her feet from the battered women's shelter she founded and runs in downtown Cleveland. She said hello, nibbled a piece of garlic bread, then excused herself and went to her bedroom. After dinner I washed up while Toni and Thom watched a safe-sex video in the family room.

"They really should call it 'Safe Sex with Vegetables'," observed my sister.

"What's that green pepper supposed to be?" asked Thom. "Oh, I get it. Yeah, it does kind of look like that, especially with the parsley."

"See, then you put the plastic wrap around it."

"It's kind of like you're making a sandwich. What's he doing now with that carrot?"

"That's supposed to be his tongue, idiot."

"That's a relief. I thought it was his . . ."

"No, Thom, you're not paying attention. See, the carrot doesn't have a condom on it."

"Oh, right. I'm glad they're not expecting me to put a rubber on my tongue."

"Who says they're not? We may not have come to that part yet."

"Maybe they should just make us guys wear NASA space suits."

"The jet thrusters might be fun. Oh, here comes the part where they put the condom on the cucumber. I can't watch. Tell me when it's over."

"Boy, that cuke is really built. No wonder the announcer is smiling."

"Don't be gross."

"OK, it's over, Toni. But I'd say that green pepper is in for a really wild time."

After the video concluded, Mom came out to give her speech.

"Thom, have you watched and understood the video?"

"Yes, Mrs. Mason."

"Antonia, have you watched and understood the video?"

"Yes, Mother. Several times, as you know."

"Thom, Antonia, do you understand the importance of practicing safe sex and the need to prevent the transmission of communicable diseases?"

"Yes, Mrs. Mason."

"Yes, Mother."

"Thom, will you give me your word that if you choose to be intimate with my daughter that you will always practice safe sex?"

Thom gulped. "Yes, Mrs. Mason. I promise."

"Will you always use a condom?"

"Yes, I will."

"Antonia, will you reaffirm the promises you have made in the past to practice safe sex exclusively?"

"I promise, Mother. As usual."

"Thom, I would prefer that my daughter wait until she were older to be sexually active. But since she has chosen otherwise, I have given her my permission to have boys in her bedroom. I would rather be a technical accessory to a crime than watch my daughter die of a wasting disease. Do you understand?"

"Gee, I guess so, Mrs. Mason."

"Good. There are condoms and dental dams in the drawer of her night stand. Use them in good health. You may not stay here overnight without your parents' permission. End of lecture. Have a nice time, you two."

"We'll try, Mother. But it won't be easy."

\* \* \*

More than once Toni and I have threatened to place a personals ad for Mom. We think she should cut back a little on her work and put some effort into meeting a nice man. Toni's afraid she's getting permanently soured on men, what with Dad having been a cad and all the creeps and sadists she has to get restraining orders against down at the shelter. Mom says she doesn't have the time, but I think that's just an excuse. As Toni says, it's time for our mother to put her first marriage behind her. "The first one's just for practice anyway," says my sister. "It's just to get your marital feet wet."

Mom met Dad when they were students at Muskingum College, a pretty conservative school in those days. She says sociology majors are often attracted to divinity students, falsely sensing complementary values. Toni thinks they should put warning notices about this in the sociology textbooks. It *was* hard for a person with her ideals to cope with the politics of being a minister's wife, especially after Dad started running for public office and cheating on her. Mom is still nicely packaged for her age and has a lot to offer a man if she would only put herself out there.

CNN reports that since there's no clear front-runner, the Republican Presidential nomination process might go beyond the first ballot for the first time in decades. At least it should prove more interesting than the Democratic convention, where the selection of Vice President Greer as the nominee is a foregone conclusion. No sightings of Dad on TV since this morning. I don't care what my selfish sister says. I think it would be wonderful if Father were picked for Vice President. Or maybe even President!

*Chapter 2*

I love Sundays. Thom and I have the whole house to ourselves. Mom and Cara are down at the shelter; our husky blue-collar boarder Lizzie and her biker boyfriend are off rocking Cleveland. Naturally, I am taking advantage of this privacy windfall to get better acquainted with my friend. Thom is the first athlete I have gone out with. He's a football player, though in the off-season to improve his mind he works out with the wrestling team. I thought I would give him a try after burning out on intellectuals. The smart boys in my school are so jaded. I find it enervating to associate with people who have given up on Western Civilization (not to mention the human race) by age 16. They are so nihilistic, they refuse even to make an effort to acquire a car. Sorry, I do not date by skateboard.

Thom says he is light for a defensive end, but I would have to rate him fairly heavy as a bed partner. He is a well-fed six-footer with his own muscle-building equipment at home. I feel like the filling in a Godzilla and mattress sandwich. Despite the reputed sensitivity-deadening properties of the latex condom, Thom is remarkably quick off the line. Ten seconds after play commences he sacks the quarterback and hustles back to the huddle for a time-out. He does revive quickly and is able to resume play frequently. Still, the constant interruptions can put a girl off her game. The score this morning: Thom 3, Antonia 0. He *is* extremely cute and has a laid-back, self-deprecating manner I find refreshing after my former boyfriend Jeff's dour pomposity. But the big lug can be dull at halftime when backed against the conversational wall. The last book he read was a biography of Knute Rockne.

I just slapped Thom. The guy had the nerve to suggest a three-way with my sister.

* * *

Like it or not, everyone comes into this world entwined in a web of connections. Sometimes a little newborn baby is already someone's Aunt Florence. But being an identical twin, you're really ensnared. You're linked, spliced, conjoined, commingled, and anchored by your feet for eternity in a large block of sibling cement. As a tiny toddler you already have a significant other. Birthdays are always joint celebrations. You must unwrap your package quickly, because someone else—your best friend and worst enemy—is receiving the same gift and may beat you to the surprise. Eventually, of course, you tire of the competition and decide to eliminate your twin.

I tried it at the age of four. I pushed my sister out of a moving car. Dad was driving back from his weekly trip to Scio and Sons Printers for the church bulletins. I was miffed because Tyrone Scio (the attractive son) had let Cara flip the start switch on the offset press and smear a gooey dollop of "angel honey" (gold ink) on the rollers. That was the last straw.

So I popped open her seat belt, yanked up on the door handle, and gave her a shove. Out went my twin onto the grimy slush of McKinley Avenue at 42 miles per hour. I remember watching with amazement as her thin legs, white knee socks, and pink snow boots (identical to my own) flew up and then disappeared out the door. At that moment I was swept by a sense of profound remorse.

"My sister!" I screamed. "She fell out of the car!"

Dad slammed on the brakes, my head whammed forward into the seatback. Then I remember screeching brakes, skidding tires, doors slamming, people yelling, Dad screaming. The loudest sound, though, was the thump, thump, thump of my little heart. Total juvenile terror. I was carrying on so hysterically, the ambulance crew thought *I* was the trauma victim. Luckily for my future relationship with my sister, I had pushed her from the passenger-side door. The cars behind managed to swerve out of the way. Tumbling along through the dirty snowbanks beside the road, she suffered only major kiddie road rash.

Good thing for me Cara had no memory of how she came to exit the car so abruptly. Having sustained nearly identical forehead bruises, we were able to share a warmly bonding convalescence. And best of all, I didn't even get in trouble. For many years after the incident, though, I was convinced it was the Vinyl Hand of Jesus that had smote me in the face with the Chevrolet upholstery for my evil deed. Anyway, it's my deepest, darkest secret—besides the usual adolescent erotic fumblings, which I'm sure certain unnamed boys have already blabbed all over town.

You're not hearing things—those massed violins are leading into my first song:

For some, childhood evokes nostalgia,
   While mine induces a vile neuralgia:
The throb of deep subconscious traumas
   Inflamed by dark preconscious dramas.

My natal day was strangely crowded,
   My early years perversely clouded,
By an obstetrical irregularity
   That deprived me of my singularity.

What an imposition by my mother:
   I shared the cradle with another!
The trespasser was not just fraternal,
   But by consensus absurdly identical.

My needs alone were not the priority;
   Fate had stuck me in a damn sorority.
For dining there always was a queue:
   Mama's breasts were ever set for two.

And snuggles, and coos, and vital caresses—
   I got mine—I did!—but only under duresses.
On me alone Ma couldn't dote; a
   Second tot had to get her quota.

I lacked supremacy in the pram,
   My "only childhood" was a sham.
Even Daddy dear I had to share—
   It was all too much, too much to bear!

Since our sistership was my ruin,
   My only twin I resolved to do in.
Yes, I put my infant qualms aside,
   And tried a sibling homicide.

The incident was rather disturbing,
   The gore alone most unnerving—
Quite unlike the tidy terminations
   Pictured in my morbid ruminations.

Please don't be angry, sister dear,
   I've since reformed, never fear.
You're now an ally on my team
   In circumventing the parental regime.

I'd take up smoking to get a little more character in my voice, but all those carcinogens really play havoc with a girl's looks.

❖ ❖ ❖

Vaudeville is not dead; it is semiretired and touring the old folks' homes of Cuyahoga County for the minimum wage. This Monday morning it was on the road in a rusty van, driven by Mrs. Gerda Melmore, a garrulous grandmotherly volunteer from Cleveland Heights. She has lived a long and remarkably uneventful life—even for Ohio—and is determined to tell us all about it.

She's a very pleasant woman, Toni. I enjoy listening to her talk about her craft projects and numerous relatives. I only wish she'd concentrate a little more on her driving.

On the contrary, Sister, I find the periodic highway terror pleasantly distracting from the conversational tedium.

Our fellow performers are also very nice, Toni, if somewhat reserved.

They hate us, Cara mia. I could sense their hostility the moment we climbed into the van and Mrs. Melmore made the introductions. Those two snobs turned their noses up at us.

They were just shy, Toni. And I think nervous about their first performance. I was shaking like a leaf. You seemed quite calm.

I have a infallible cure for stage fright. If I start feeling nervous, I just remind myself that I'm toiling for $5.75 an hour. And that I'm absolutely indifferent to the impression I'm making on the audience.

Oh, Toni, I know you don't mean that.

No, come to think of it there were some cute orderlies on duty. I appreciated their applause. Can we help it if they liked us more than Rosemary and Renk?

Opening the show today was Rosemary Hudnall, a tall, stolid redhead who can juggle four balls at once if the audience remains perfectly still and I don't crack my gum and she's not starting her period and the gods of manual coordination are with her. She was better at spinning plates on a stick, but Mrs. Melmore made her stop after she beaned that World War II veteran with a soup tureen.

He shouldn't have parked his wheelchair so close to the stage, Toni.

And he should have worn his helmet, Cara. Second up on today's bill was Renk Pohlsohn, a skinny, hawk-faced boy with a camel-hump nose and painfully prominent cheekbones like his skull wanted to come out and say hi. He whistled Western tunes and performed an original dramatic oration, "A Trip

Down the Ohio and Erie Canal by Mule-driven Packet Boat."

Renk wrote it himself. It's a fascinating evocation of the pioneer transportation scene circa 1835.

We started off on the wrong foot with the cowboy whistler right after our driver made the introductions:

"Renk. What's that short for?" I asked pleasantly.

"Renk."

"It's an usual name."

"You don't remember at all, huh?" he asked.

"Oh, have we met? What school do you go to?"

"Chagrin Falls. We haven't met, but I thought the name Pohlsohn might ring a bell."

"I don't think so. Do you know a Pohlsohn, Cara?"

"The name sounds familiar."

"It should. My dad used to teach biology at Rocky Pike High. He was the man your father campaigned to have fired because he refused to teach creationism."

"Oh, right," said Cara. "That was back when Dad was an ambitious school board president. We were just little kids then. I'm sorry your father lost his job."

"That makes us even. I'm sorry your father was elected to the senate."

"Where does your dad teach now?" I asked.

"He doesn't. He sells real estate downtown. Say, why are you girls stooping to this low-wage public service job? With your connections, I'd have thought you'd score some really cushy summer jobs. You know, belly up to the public trough."

"We didn't take this summer job for the money," I replied coldly. "We're doing it to bring some happiness into the lives of those less fortunate than ourselves."

Cara coughed. "That's right."

"I'd do anything so's I don't have to be flippin' burgers this summer," remarked Rosemary, nervously squeezing her repertoire of colorful rubber balls. "Even this."

\* \* \*

OK, I admit it. I did experience some slight twinge of anxiety, sitting in that first fluorescent-lit activities room, dressed in my claret satin slip dress, as Renk's round and vibrato-rich whistle faded away on the last plaintive notes of "Colorado Trail." Now it was our turn to perform. In her effusive introduction, Mrs. Melmore emphasized the audience's extreme good fortune in being entertained by the talented offspring of so prominent a man as Senator Horace B. Mason, R-Ohio.

"I know you're not too thrilled by the way he's been slashing our Medicare," she said, "but let's give his lovely daughters a nice big Parma welcome."

As we stepped up to the microphone, I sensed some confusion among the seniors.

"It's Doris Day!" one woman cried. "In her underwear!"

"Boy, her career must really be on the skids," replied her tablemate, crocheting feverishly.

"Is that her daughter playing the accordion?" asked an elderly man, finger-painting.

By then Cara (my elder by eleven minutes, let me note) was squeezing out the familiar melody of our first blockbuster tune, "It's Magic."

It wasn't.

My music, I discovered, was turned to the wrong page. So I smiled, snapped my fingers to the beat like Tina Turner, and let Carissa set the mood with a rousing instrumental solo.

"Her voice must be gone," remarked a heavy-set woman busily weaving pink potholders. "It's that wild Hollywood life-style."

I located the correct music for our next song, and belted out "A Guy Is a Guy" as if the point were a medical certainty. From there, we launched into the confessional "Secret Love," journeyed into the realm of the occult with "Bewitched," and concluded with the fatalistic "Whatever Will Be, Will Be." Our first encore featured the politely ambiguous "You Brought a New Kind of Love to Me." Encouraged by a smattering of applause, we segued into our modest finale, "I've Got a Feeling You're Fooling." I'd have preferred a lively medley of Young Dickheads' hits, but was overruled by the always-tasteful Cara. Then the canal-boating whistler returned to end the program with his mournful "Bury Me Not on the Lone Prairie." I looked at my watch. Already I had earned over six dollars. I was a professional singer!

* * *

We ate our bagged lunches at a rest stop on I-271 while Mrs. Melmore consulted her map and rested her vocal cords. Her billowy print dress snapped like a spinnaker in the humid breeze.

"Where did you learn to whistle like that, Renk?" asked Cara.

"Where do you think—the Rochester Conservatory of Music? They don't teach whistling anywhere. I picked up myself. I used to whistle on my paper route."

"On your skateboard?" I asked.

"As a matter of fact, yes."

"Maybe you should put it in your act. You could pretend it was a packet boat."

"Maybe you should learn the words to your songs, Toni. You don't look very professional on stage reading them."

"Renk has his entire dramatic oration memorized," noted Rosemary.

"Very impressive," I replied. "But I wonder if we have to visit every single lock between Cleveland and Akron? All that water sluicing through the gates keeps giving me a powerful urge to go to the bathroom."

"I loved your oration, Renk," said Cara. "I really feel like you've turned back the pages of time."

"Thanks, Carissa. Your accordion playing is first rate. It's by far the high point of your act."

"I like the mules best in yours, Renk," I said. "You have a true gift for plodding quadrupeds."

"Eat up, artists," said Mrs. Melmore. "My Lord, look at the time! We're due in Medina in 20 minutes. I'll have to floor it."

"I hope I can juggle on a full stomach," moaned Rosemary.

"Why not juggle with fewer balls?" suggested Cara.

"Only amateurs do it with three balls," she replied.

"That will be our thought for the day," I said, folding up my lunch bag.

※ ※ ※

When we finished our performances and returned to Rocky Pike, little Amy Czerkoffski from next door was waving Dan's sign and chanting "Save the forests!" in our front yard. Thom and the Picketer were inspecting the engine of the gleaming yellow Probe parked at the curb. They waved as we de-vanned and wished our fellow troubadours a good night.

"Tune for power, Thom, not speed," said Toni, walking over and kissing her boyfriend. Dan glanced up and gave me a friendly, stomach-churning smile. The late afternoon sun lit up his coppery sidewalk tan.

"How's show business?" asked Dan.

"Fun, but tiring," I said. "Tomorrow Toni has to play the heavy accordion and I get to sing."

"No, Cara, we'll leave the squeezebox at home and make it an all-whistling concert."

"Dan figured out I had my plug wires crossed," said Thom, slamming the hood and wiping his hands on a rag.

"That's nice, honey. Keep the boy talking about cars. Don't let him get started on trees."

"That reminds me," said Dan. "I've been talking to your neighbor Amy. She says your father hasn't lived here for years."

"What does that kid know?" demanded Toni. "She's only six. Excuse me, it's time for our prayer hour. I have to go give my dad a nice big hug."

"Me too," I said, picking up my accordion case. "He doesn't like to be kept waiting, the sweet dear."

* * *

Speaking as a Southern Baptist, I think Catholics have the right idea. If you want to join their management team, you have to sleep alone (more or less). I pray those misguided reformers agitating against priestly celibacy never succeed. The whole point is to prevent priests from having children, thus sparing their offspring the acute anguish of listening to Dad sermonize every Sunday. It's so embarrassing. Whatever the topic, the message always boils down to "I'm OK, you're a rotten sinner." So we're all bound for hell—could it be any worse than suburban Ohio on a grey Sunday morning?

The biggest problem for me wasn't the content, it was the performance anxiety. I'd sit there tied up in knots worrying that Dad was going to flub his lines or dribble spittle or cross the line into true rhetorical ickiness. Of course, I could never look at any of my friends who'd show up occasionally when their parents dragged them to Sunday school or they were interested in some boy in the choir. Oh God, I'd think, deliver me from this evil.

After church Cara and I would have to tell Dad how much we enjoyed the sermon. For being a semi-dynamic man of the cloth, he's always been pretty needy in the ego department. Yet words of praise from his lips are as rare as hundred-dollar bills on the collection plate. I don't think I've every heard him compliment Cara for her accordion playing. I suppose it's his way of inoculating us against the sin of pride.

It could be worse though; I know kids whose parents are both ministers.

* * *

My sister has a date!

It's not a date, Toni. I said I would go to the movies with Renk.

Have you looked up the definition of 'date' lately, Cara mia? After just four days and 23 languid trips down the Ohio and Erie Canal, my sister has captured the heart of the cowboy whistler.

Hardly. We're just friends. I told Rosemary she was welcome to come along if she wanted. I regret she reacted so childishly.

What I can't understand is why my sister turned down a dinner invitation from our handsome tree-hugger to go out with young Pohlsohn.

I explained to Dan that if we went out together I'd probably fall in love with him. And there is no future in love when you're only 15, except prolonged and needless heartache. Therefore, although immensely flattered, I was obliged to decline his invitation. He seemed to think my response was eminently sensible.

You're both nuts. And how is the whistler proposing to transport you to the movies for your Friday evening non-date?

He's borrowing his father's car.

Renk has a driver's license?

Of course. He's older than we are, Toni. He's 16.

The lonesome whistler is 16? He doesn't look a day over 12!

You're being unfair. He's a nice, intelligent person and I look forward to getting to know him better.

Don't tell me you intend to sleep with him?

I've told you before, Toni, my lovelife is my own business.

Yes, I know, Cara. I just wish you hadn't incorporated it as a sole proprietorship.

Renk and I share an interest in current events. Observing and discussing the dramatic events of this week's Republican national convention have deepened our friendship, Toni.

Is that what you've been huddled together over in the back of the van? I thought you were plotting against poor Rosemary. She certainly thinks so.

Rosemary has no reason to adopt that attitude. Renk is relieved and I'm naturally disappointed that Dad won't be on the ticket, even if he did make that inspiring speech to the convention last night.

Renk is relieved? I'm ecstatic. Who'd have ever imagined that after 14 ballots the exhausted delegates would hand the mantle of their party to so obscure a leader as Governor Claude D. Flunch of Michigan? You could tell the man was stunned. I've never seen anyone look so bewildered on national TV. Now he has to go and learn the names of all those obscure African countries to be prepared for reporters asking sneaky foreign policy questions. They might do better to ask the man where to find good kielbasa in Lansing.

So now the party has to balance the ticket with someone from the South or the West.

Yes, Cara, to balance Governor Flunch, I understand they're looking for a liberal black lesbian abortion-provider from San Francisco.

Dad doesn't have a chance, poor dear.

*Chapter 3*

We're in shock!

They picked Dad!

The Christian right called in their chits. It's an all Rust Belt ticket.

*Time* magazine headlined it "Claude and God," which I feel may be somewhat irreligious.

*USA Today* was just as irreverent, Cara. They're calling the ticket, "the Bag Baron and the Baptist." I can't believe it—our own father, a guy I've seen unshaven and hung over in his underwear at the breakfast table, is now being swarmed over by the world media. Worse, you can't turn on the TV without being subjected to Mindy's vacuous pronouncements on God, her wonderful husband, and her inspiring family life. What a disaster! I feel like crawling under a rock. Why couldn't we have an agnostic, apolitical, decently dressed, semi-together but easily manipulated, normal dad like other kids? Oh, and rich too. Cara, our worst nightmare has come true.

Speak for yourself, Toni. Personally, I'm thrilled. Two nights ago Renk and I came back from the movies and found three large men in dark suits sitting in the living room.

The Secret Service had arrived. They'd already taken me prisoner and carded Thom, who got intimidated and left. The wimp.

They made Renk produce his I.D. and asked him to explain his exact relationship to me. He said he was hoping to recruit me into White Slavery, which did not make the situation any easier.

Secret Service agents have no sense of humor—or style. Some of them are quite cute, but they dress abominably. They must buy those suits off the rack at some insurance salesmen's outlet store.

They made Renk leave immediately.

I hope he wasn't anticipating a good night's kiss, Cara. The entire might of the federal government is poised to guarantee our chastity.

At least they're only protecting us, the immediate family. They're not bothering Mom.

No, except for installing four phone lines in her house, and parking a large communications van in her back yard, and mounting a satellite dish on her roof, and forcing her to evict Lizzie so the agents can use that bedroom as their command post to spy on us night and day.

They *are* paying Mom for the room and the backyard space, Toni. It's considerably more money than she was getting from Lizzie. And Lizzie's boyfriend Ed was very nice about letting her move into his trailer. Anyway, it's all your fault.

How is it my fault, Cara?

You were the one who was always complaining about the absence of men in this household. Well, now we've got an occupying army of them.

Yeah, well I just hope they're not all third-stringers.

What do you mean, Toni?

Cara, this can't be a very choice assignment—guarding the older daughters of a remarried man who is merely a *candidate* for Vice President. There may be somebody out there with lower priority than us, but I can't imagine who. Let's face it, they didn't send in their top team on this job. Some of these guys probably have black marks in their personnel records. They must have pissed off their superiors in some major way to be exiled to Rocky Pike, Ohio. This must be their equivalent of Siberia. Would you want to spend your professional career watching a couple of teenage girls hang out in their bathrobes and answer the phone all day?

That is pure speculation, Toni. The agents seem very nice and competent. I feel quite safe.

Cara, it's creepy. They're not even allowed to read a magazine. They have to pretend they're not bored out of their skulls sitting around watching us.

At least you've been walking about half-undressed. That seems to perk them up.

Cara, we have to keep these guys awake. It's our duty. One more slipup, and they're out on their ears.

⁕ ⁕ ⁕

The phone continues to ring. We've heard from both sets of grandparents, most of our girlfriends, some old twins club pals, two former grammar school teachers, and several of Toni's former boyfriends.

But not the present one, the rat. For some reason people feel the need to call up and congratulate us. You can tell they're really impressed that we're related to a person who in fifty years may appear on some bored seventh-grader's American history quiz.

We also got a call from a reporter for the Rocky Pike *Mall Advertiser*, which may do a feature story on us.

No call so far from the candidate himself.

Well, I'm sure Dad is very busy, Toni.

He's probably trying to figure out where Botswana is.

CNN just ran a profile of Dad and Mindy at their new farm in Sagamore Hills.

We've only seen it on TV; they haven't invited us out yet. Must have slipped Mindy's mind. Notice, Cara, that CNN made no mention of Dad's *other* family.

Well, it wasn't an in-depth report, Toni. Their farm looks quite grand. The house is buff-brick Tudor with stained glass doors leading to a vast terrace overlooking the swimming pool and deer park.

CNN also featured a brief shot of our twin half-sisters. Little Fawn and Colt were seen running toward the camera, followed by violent shaking, then the camera tilted straight up at the sky, and muffled grunting could be heard.

I pity the Secret Service agents assigned to that household. Who was that on the phone, Toni?

Mrs. Melmore. She offered her sincere congratulations and asked if we would be resigning from the tour. I said certainly not. Even though we are now protected day and night by the Secret Service, we're still mired in abject poverty.

We are! I need a new strap for my accordion, but I'm completely penniless.

How unfortunate, Cara, to be both strapped and unstrapped. At least our jobs are secure. Mrs. Melmore said the aged and infirm shut-ins will be even more thrilled to see us tomorrow than usual.

✳ ✳ ✳

Still no call from Dad. Cara has written him a congratulatory letter, enclosing our phone number in case he misplaced it. Yeah, I grudgingly signed it too. Mom was busy down at the shelter, so we invited Special Agent Graham and Special Agent Tompkins to dinner. They said they weren't permitted to eat with us and sent out for cheeseburgers. With their sedentary jobs, I don't see how they expect to stay in fighting shape loading up on greasy road food. Cara had made her low-fat vegan eggplant lasagna too.

At my suggestion, Cara opened a window and called out an invitation to Dan the Picketer, who had spent the day out front discussing Dad's candidacy with curious neighbors and Secret Service groupies. My sister's gesture of hospitality caused the special agents to leap up from their french fries in alarm.

"Miss, do you propose to fraternize with that demonstrator?" asked Special Agent Graham.

"Why yes," said Cara. "He's our friend. And he looks hungry."

"How well do you know this person?" demanded Special Agent Tompkins.

"Very well," I replied. "He's a forestry major at Cleveland State and a member of the Sierra Club."

"Sierra Club. Is that on our list?" Special Agent Graham asked Special Agent Tompkins.

"I think so," grunted his partner. "We better get a full I.D. on this character."

Dan came in and stoically spread his arms and legs against the living-room wall while his T-shirt, multi-pocketed hiking shorts, athletic socks, and sports sandals were frisked brusquely. Then the agents forced him to produce for their inspection the entire contents of his braided leather wallet. He had only two dollars in cash, which Cara informed me later had almost made her cry. He also had a small color photo of an attractive brunette holding two pompoms above her head. After the grilling, we sat down to dinner informally in the breakfast nook; the special agents returned warily to their burgers in the family room.

"Good lasagna, Cara," remarked our guest listlessly to me.

"I'm Toni, Dan. She's Cara."

"Oh, sorry! How do people tell you two apart?"

"It's not easy," I admitted, "unless one of us is seen holding an accordion. Even Mom gets us confused."

"Having an identical twin is like being able to see yourself from outside your body," said Cara. "Most people know their appearance only from their reflection in a mirror, which is reversed. They don't know how they really look to others. Being a twin gives you this amazingly close connection, but also a heightened sense of your own identity."

"And we can share each other's clothes," I pointed out.

"Do you ever dress identically?" asked Dan.

"We used to," I replied. "Grandmother Drucker especially was into sartorial redundancy. She still buys us matching outfits for holiday gifts. I never wear them though."

"Why not?"

"Grandmother's tastes are different from ours," said Cara.

"Right," I agreed, "hers are rotten. So, Dan, who's the cheerleader in your wallet?"

"She's not a cheerleader, Toni. That was a party costume."

"Bullshit," I said. "Dan's hung up on Suzy cheerleader and doesn't want to admit it. He doesn't feel it's politically correct to lust after someone in charge of fomenting team pep."

"I'm not hung up on anyone. And I'm not sleeping with her. Cheryl and I used to go out."

"She broke your heart, huh?"

"Not exactly."

"Toni, we shouldn't pry into matters that don't concern us."

"Hey, this guy's picketing our house and eating our groceries. We've got a right to pry. Besides, I know he's going to start lecturing us about Dad. I was just hoping to delay the inevitable."

"This nomination is a disaster," said Dan, right on cue. "I hope you realize that."

"I know," I said. "We're the ones whose dinner guests are being frisked. I haven't heard from my boyfriend in nearly two days. And my sister missed out on a dreamy good-night kiss from her hot date Friday night."

"Oh, really," said Dan. "Who was that?"

"It wasn't a date, Dan," said Cara, blushing. "He's just a friend."

The lecture continued: "Of all the Republican officeholders in the country they had to pick the one Neanderthal who actually owns a paper mill. Flunch's family has been denuding the forests of the upper Midwest for four generations. And I don't need to point out your father's sorry environmental record. I suppose you'll be out there campaigning for him?"

"Oh, I don't think so," I said. "We're busy with our jobs and then school starts. Cara is thinking of trying out for the Zydeco Polka Band, and I'll have my Italian Club duties."

"We'll be keeping a low profile, Dan," said Cara comfortingly.

"You could join the other side," he urged. "And fight against them."

"Oh, we couldn't do that," replied Cara. "He *is* our father, after all. We're very proud of him."

"Even if he never calls," I pointed out. "And seems determined to ignore our very existence."

❖ ❖ ❖

Confession time: Don't tell Cara, but I've been endeavoring in my modest way to light a small cherry bomb under Dad's campaigns for years. Lots of politicians' kids resort to petty sabotage—at least among the ones I've met in D.C. and Columbus. Disloyal, I suppose, but it makes for a nice change from all the hypocrisy.

In Dad's last race for the senate he plastered the state with photos of his All-American family, never mentioning that Mindy, drooling babies, and pure-bred cocker spaniel were Chapter Two in his life. So when I was manning the campaign phones, I'd do things like call up elderly voters and tell them their ride to the polls was scheduled for 4 a.m. Or inform them that they'd have to submit to a drug test and strip search before they could vote. Boy, did that piss them off.

Then there was that well-publicized incident with the visiting Boy Scout color guard from Grove City. We were just kidding around, what can I say?

Not that any of it did much good. Trouble is the voters are so damn jaded in this post-Watergate, post-impeachment, post-you-name-it era.

This next song I dedicate to my dear old dad:

> When Father to office aspires
>   As the candidate Republican,
> His daughter rebellious conspires
>   Daily contretemps to scheme and plan.
>
> In a spirit distinctly Libertarian,
>   A rally is reset for Angkor Wat,
> The mail finds its way to Siberia an'
>   Even to places more obscure than that.
>
> Big-shot callers I place on hold
>   To vex with melodies jangling;
> Vital messages I simply withhold
>   To occasion vicious staff wrangling.
>
> For guests strictly vegetarian
>   I order knackwurst with extra suet,
> And if I hear any words contrarian,
>   I tell them exactly where they can screw it.
>
> Our ads that attack so raucously
>   Reveal a curious photo selector,
> The rival is flattered most mawkishly,
>   While Dad looks like a wanted molester.

And the mother's milk of our endeavor:
    The checks from rich fat cats
Slip unseen into the shredder. Never!
    You'd almost suspect the Democrats.

I suppose it's not so politic
    To indulge in such machinations,
But I must confess I get a kick
    Out of foiling ambitious relations.

*Chapter 4*

Back among the stalagmites of the Swing Era. Special Agent Holgate accompanied us in the van today, tailed closely by shy Special Agent Conover in the unmarked but glaringly obvious official sedan. Special Agent Holgate is the youngest and handsomest of our guardians; I naturally sat next to him in the middle seat. Renk and Cara cuddled together in the back; Mrs. Melmore and unhappy Rosemary occupied the front.

Special Agent Holgate has pale grey eyes, thick black hair, a blue-hued shaven jaw that could cleave granite, and an intimidating automatic lodged in a discreet shoulder holster. After much coaxing, I got him to admit he was only 26 and to divulge his first name which is Ryan. Don't you think Ryan is the perfect name for a man? Notice, for example, how smoothly "Hello, I'd like you to meet my husband Ryan" rolls off the tongue.

Ryan is from East Gaffney, South Carolina and speaks with an accent that makes you want to muss his hair while playfully removing his boring suit. He is, in short, a total dreamboat—with a good government job too.

Mrs. Melmore spent the first ten miles shouting questions to Ryan about his family, and why he joined the Secret Service, and was he married (no!), and how long had he had a hearing impairment? Ryan explained that the small instrument in his left ear was a radio earphone, connected by a thin wire to a transceiver he wore on his belt. A tiny microphone was clipped to his watch. He was in constant communication with Special Agent Conover, who had just radioed to inquire if our driver was inebriated.

"I'm a total teetotaler," replied Mrs. Melmore, breezily running a red light. "I like to be in control of my faculties at all times!"

Daphne Piqua, feature writer for the Rocky Pike *Mall Advertiser*, was waiting for us at our first venue, a tree-shrouded Methodist old-folks home with the over-manicured pall of a ritzy private school. Heavy smoking and 20 years of deadlines had withered Daphne's former prettiness. She had interviewed us twice before during Dad's previous campaigns, but Cara and I went over the familiar story again while Rosemary fumbled her balls and Renk prodded the mules down the dusty towpath.

"Thanks for giving me this exclusive, girls," she said, snapping shut her notebook. "Frankly, I'm surprised no other reporters have contacted you."

"Well, we're keeping a low profile," I said.

"My, I can't believe how you both have filled out. May I ask what you're wearing, Toni?"

"It's my grandmother's satin nightgown from her honeymoon in the Poconos. All the singers are wearing them these days."

"Very Joan Crawford. And what do you have on underneath?"

"Hardly anything worth mentioning."

"That's what I thought. Well, you girls must be so proud of your dad."

"It's a great honor," said Cara.

"We're thrilled," I lied.

"And will you be traveling around the country and campaigning for him?"

Cara glanced at me. "Well, we really don't. . ."

"That is, Miss Piqua," I said, "the campaign doesn't get underway until after Labor Day. And we'll be back in school then. But we'll be following it closely on the news."

"That's right," said Cara. "Dad feels our schooling must come first. He's a strong believer in education."

"Of course," I added, "without excessive federal bureaucratic intrusion or funding."

"You're sure you don't mind if I snap a few photos while you're performing? It won't make you nervous?"

"Oh, no, Miss Piqua," I said. "We never get nervous."

* * *

I was a wreck. Special Agents Holgate and Conover were sitting in the front row, the aged and infirm Methodists were restless from having been kept waiting, and Cara made me leave my music behind. My mind went blank. I sang whatever came into my head; some passages, I noticed, seemed to recur more frequently than the lyricists had intended. Only rarely did anything rhyme. At one point, during the middle section of "Bewitched," I found myself trilling "Que, sera, sera." Toward the end, I feared Daphne's popping electronic flash would trigger an epileptic seizure. At last, we took our bows and retreated forcefully past the thronging oldsters toward the rusty refuge of the van.

"You ladies did really well, all of you," said Special Agent Holgate, sliding in beside me. "And Renk, you're the best darn whistler north of the Pacolet River. You whistle my kind of music too. What was that second song you did?"

"Whoopie Ti Yi Yo."

"Right! It brought chills to my spine. I thought I was back in Cherokee County."

"That would be spine-chilling," I said. "Perhaps it's only a summer cold. Maybe should take some vitamin C and lie down."

"Miss Mason, I'm on duty. I feel fine. Besides I want to hear about that neat canal boat trip again."

"What about my juggling?" demanded Rosemary.

"Four balls at once!" exclaimed Special Agent Holgate. "How on earth do you manage that?"

Of course, a girl would not wish to become engaged to just any Ryan she happened to meet. Some discretion must be shown, even for a first marriage.

* * *

After a rocky beginning, my sister settled down and sang beautifully. I think her lyrics, on the whole, worked nearly as well as the composers'. The audiences certainly were enthusiastic. What a revelation to discover this huge unsuspected population of elderly people. There seem to be institutions full of them in every town. I hope old age is not as dreary as it looks. Toni says she prefers to think of these homes as sedate fraternities and sororities. "It's like being in college," she says. "You have your own room, you eat in the cafeteria, you take some classes, read a few books, and go to a concert now and then. In a few years you'll be graduating. It's all very collegiate, except there are no tests, football games, or sex."

* * *

Renk pretends to be blasé about Dad's nomination, but I think even he was impressed to be traveling with a Secret Service escort.

"Did you hear from your father yet, Cara?" he asked during the rainy drive to Lorain after lunch.

"No, but we called his house and left a message on the answering machine."

"You should have said you wanted to donate $50,000 to his campaign. He would have called you right back."

"Dad's a whiz at fund-raising, Renk. CNN reports he hopes to receive

$10 each from ten-million Christian families."

"Boy, Vice President Greer will have trouble matching that from the Satanists and devil cultists. Speaking of Hollywood, Cara, would you like to go to another movie on Saturday night?"

"I thought you were going to write some patter for Rosemary."

"That won't take long. It's only light patter, intended to make her act less desperately anxious-making for the audience and the performer. It's a very heavy act to follow now."

"All right, Renk. But the Secret Service will want to accompany us. We'll have to pick a film they haven't seen."

"Maybe we can ditch them, Cara," he whispered.

"Oh, no. We can't do anything to get them in trouble. Toni is convinced they're all on probation."

"I believe it," he whispered. "Both of these guys have been ogling your sister like a couple of paroled sex offenders."

"I saw you looking at her too."

"Only in disbelief, Cara. I'm amazed she has the nerve to leave the house dressed like that."

For being such a liberal, Renk is exhibiting signs of a disturbing narrow-mindedness.

✲ ✲ ✲

Thom has reemerged, groveling, from under his rock. The sun came out after dinner, so I let him take me to his parents' country club for a swim. Special Agent Holgate did everything he could to humiliate my beau, including checking his I.D. twice, sneering at his back seat upholstery, ridiculing his latest cam modifications, belittling his taste in FM radio stations, and—most mortifying—requiring him to observe the posted speed limits.

When we arrived, Thom refused to acknowledge Ryan and Special Agent Conover as his guests, but they flashed their badges to the club secretary and were graciously admitted. Then Ryan caused a great hubbub by making the towel girl evacuate the women's dressing room so he could inspect it prior to my use. Fortunately, Thom belongs to an exclusive club whose elite membership is almost entirely Republican. The ladies bustled out in a good-natured display of patriotism.

While the special agents guarded the door and blocked all entry, I changed quickly into my suit, accepted a towel from the awestruck attendant, and hurried out. The waiting agents felt a professional obligation to scrutinize my swim apparel, as did my date. I smiled at Thom, Thom glanced at Ryan, and the special agents exchanged looks. None of the fellows said anything, but the body language could have sparked a bloody skirmish among hostile tribesmen.

The special agents, not inconspicuous in their dark wool salesmen's suits, sipped ginger ales at a poolside table, while Thom and I paddled languidly back and forth in the warm, spotlight-illuminated water.

"I feel like punching out that guy's high beams," he said, fondling my most buoyant curves under water.

"I wouldn't try it, Thom, if I were you. They're both armed to the teeth and trained in every major martial arts discipline. I have reason to believe Special Agent Conover's briefcase contains an Uzi submachine gun."

"I could handle that Holgate guy—in a fair fight."

"They're professionals, Thom. They don't fight fair. They're trained to kill. So be nice."

"I'm sleeping with you tonight, babe. I'm going to jump your bones with that Holgate guy listening in on the other side of the door!"

Men are so weird.

"I have to get up early tomorrow, honey," I replied, patting his hand. "Let's order hot fudge sundaes at the snack bar and call it a night."

※ ※ ※

Mom handed me the phone this morning while she was making cappuccinos for Special Agent Troy Pulaski and Dan the Picketer—the first time in memory she had plugged in the espresso maker on a weekday.

"This is Toni. May I help you?"

"Hello, Toni. This is Mindy."

"Who?"

"Mindy Mason. I'm married to your father."

"Oh, Mindy! I thought you said middling. Hi, Mindy. What's up?"

"Your father has received the Republican nomination for Vice President."

"Yes, the Secret Service agents here mentioned something about that. Congratulate Dad for us."

"Your father and I are very disturbed about the article concerning you and your sister in today's *Mall Advertiser*."

"Oh, it came out, huh? We haven't seen it yet. We can't afford newspaper subscriptions."

"What on earth could you have been thinking of? Talking to the press like that and letting yourself be photographed in such scandalous attire."

"Hardly scandalous, Mindy. Your husband's mother wore it on her wedding night. They were married in a church."

"You were practically naked in public!"

I glanced over at the tree-hugger, who was sipping his cappuccino and peering down my robe. I gave him a withering look and pulled my collar tightly closed.

"Mindy, do you recall the swimsuit competition during a certain Miss Ohio pageant? I do. I remember one contestant in particular whose suit was cut so high she mooned an entire statewide television audience."

Silence on the phone, then a loud crash that sounded like something metallic being hurled violently.

"Are you there, Mindy?"

"I'm remaining calm, Toni. I refuse to permit you take control of my emotions. You have no power to affect my inner peace."

"Mindy, is this a tape recording?"

"Toni, as a spiritual and political leader, your father must set the highest moral tone."

"Yes, I know what a burden that can be."

"Naturally, we would not wish for the media to dwell on his divorce."

"Why not? Lots of voters ditch their wives to marry bimb—I mean, younger women."

Another loud crash, followed by faint rhythmic sounds. Teeth gnashing? Hair pulling? Ritual chanting? Just when I was about to hang up, Mindy returned to this astral plane. "After considerable discussion, Toni, your father and I have decided that it would be best if you and your sister did not take part in the campaign or invite notice by the media."

"I see. You decided that, have you?"

"Yes. You must not give interviews or appear in public. You must stop this ridiculous singing in rest homes. You must live quiet lives well out of the public eye."

"Perhaps Cara and I should enter a convent?"

"Baptists do not have convents, Toni. You must strive to make yourself as invisible as possible. That is a direct order from your father."

"I get it: The Incredible Invisible Twins. OK, Mindy, whatever you say."

"After your father is elected, perhaps you can visit the Vice Presidential residence in Washington. I believe they have tours for the public."

"Thanks, Mindy. Say hi to Dad for us, and our dear half-sisters. We look forward to seeing you all on TV."

"I'll tell Horace he has your cooperation. Good-bye."

Cara came into the kitchen and blushed when she saw Dan. I've noticed my sister does this frequently in his presence—even when fully clothed.

"Morning, Dan," she mumbled. "Toni, why aren't you dressed? The van will be here any minute."

"I was talking to Mindy."

"Oh, what did she say?"

"We're joining the campaign, Cara. A full-bore, all-out sprint to November. Nationwide tours. Maximum publicity."

"I don't believe it!" exclaimed Dan, slamming down his cappuccino mug.

"We're on our way to the top, Cara mia. We're going to be famous!"

"Well, I don't know about that, Toni," replied Cara, calmly sponging up the spilled coffee. "But I'm glad you've finally decided to accept Dad's candidacy."

How little my twin sister knows me if she believes that.

*Chapter 5*

On our way to Elyria we stopped at a mini-mart for six copies of the *Mall Advertiser*. A bold headline across the front page read, "Local Musical Twins in Race for Second Family."

"We've already got that title nailed down," said Toni, nearly spilling her Flam Cola as Mrs. Melmore floored it. "Cara, what on earth happened to our eyes?"

"They turn red like that because of the flash," explained Special Agent Conover, riding today beside my sister while his handsome partner followed in the unmarked car. He is a husky man around 30, with a surprisingly diffident manner for a fellow with several automatic firearms concealed about his person.

"Too bad they printed the photo in color," said Renk.

"Yeah, you look like outer-space aliens," observed Rosemary. "And one looks like a musical Martian without a bra."

"That's the last exclusive we're giving Daphne," declared my sister. "Cara, you look like you're surgically attached to your accordion. No wonder Mindy was livid."

"The article is very flattering though," I pointed out. "Toni, Daphne says you have the potential to be a talented singer."

"Sort of like bread has the potential to be mold," observed Renk.

"Good news, Cara mia," Toni replied. "Your accordion playing is praised as 'lively and infectious.' Sounds like some of your recent dates."

\* \* \*

"I've been thinking it over," said Renk, watching with us from the wings as Rosemary struggled with her unruly balls. "What you girls need is a good press agent. Without a pro managing your media relations, these press embarrassments will spiral out of control."

"Do you know any press agents?" I asked.

"Cara, have you ever heard of the Chagrin Falls Chess Club?" he replied.

"No, I don't think so."

"You're joking."

"No, Renk. I never heard of it. Did you, Toni?"

"Sorry, I like games where big muscular guys smash into each other."

"Cara, they won the national high-school championship! They toured 23 cities in Russia. They played a game against a cosmonaut in space. The press and media coverage was amazing!"

"I'm sure it was a big story, Renk," I said. "Sorry I missed it."

"I take it, Renk, you have some connection with this celebrated team of Buckeye chess phenomenons," said Toni.

"Yes, I'm the club media manager."

"I suspected as much."

"Renk, would you be willing to serve as our press agent?" I asked.

"Sure, Cara. If you want me to."

"Excuse me, Renk," said Toni. "But I was under the impression you despised our father."

"I do. What's that got to do with it?"

"Why would you want to work to help get him elected?"

"I'd be working for Cara, not your father. I want to help see she's treated fairly."

"Thank you, Renk," I said, profoundly touched. "That's very nice of you."

"It's nothing," he replied. "Besides, Cara, I don't think your father has a prayer of winning. Therefore, I can assist you without moral qualms."

"The source of Renk's campaign fervor is no mystery," said my sister. "Once again biology has triumphed over ideology."

* * *

Another day. Another near-verbatim twins conversation:

Renk has been making phone calls for us all day, Toni.

The guy is motivated, I'll say that.

How will we ever pay him back?

Don't worry, Cara. I'm sure he'll think of a way.

We have to raise some campaign funds, Toni. Renk deposited over eight dollars of his own money in pay phones today. I feel terrible. I wish we knew some wealthy people.

Me too. Our zip code is embarrassingly down-scale, even for Ohio.

Isn't Thom's family rich?

Well off, but hardly rich. The guy had the nerve to ask me to go dutch on our sundaes the other night.

Call his father and ask for $500.

OK, Cara. Should I say I'm pregnant?

Are you?

Of course not.

Then don't say it except as a last resort. We don't want people to think we're extortionists.

I'd better call him today. I may be breaking up with his son soon.

I expected it, Toni.

Why, may I ask?

Well, you have been going out with him for over a month.

I've explored every dimension of his soul, Cara. The only part of him I really like is his car. Is that shallow?

Not excessively—for your age. Are you in love with someone else?

I'm always at least partially in love with someone else, Cara mia. A girl should never put all of her eggs in one basket. Look at our unhappy mother.

She seems more cheerful now. Have you noticed the gleam in her eye when she hands Special Agent Pulaski his morning cappuccino?

A small glimmer perhaps. Troy *is* good looking for a man in his late forties. But Mom could never fall for a guy in law enforcement, especially the shift leader of a Secret Service detail. He's much too establishment and un-Italian for her. Besides, he wears a wedding ring.

Oh, darn, I didn't notice that.

You're hopeless, Cara. That's the first thing you should notice!

I'm sure it's not the first thing you look at, Toni.

Maybe not, but I do get around to it eventually.

＊ ＊ ＊

Thom's father was out, but I was able to reach Mrs. Kirkwood, who had read about us in the paper and offered me $200 in cash if I would disappear forever from her son's life. I informed her that such a meager sum barely covered my weekly expenses for diet pills and rap albums. Aghast, she raised the offer to $300, and we finally settled on $375 in small bills to be delivered no later than 6 p.m. by her gardener. The fellow roared into the driveway at 5:59 and was almost shot by Special Agent Bradford, returning from a burger run. Agent Smyrna Bradford is a well-built black woman with a no-nonsense manner and an amazingly fast draw. She confiscated the envelope from the frightened gardener (now spread-eagle on the asphalt), examined its contents suspiciously, and handed it to me without comment.

"Oh good," I exclaimed. "My baby-sitting money at last. I thought they'd never pay off that tardy debt."

"Miss Mason, if you're running dope," she replied, releasing her prisoner, "try to let us know in advance when your bagmen will be arriving. We don't like to shoot people unnecessarily."

"Thank you, Agent Bradford. I'll let you know when my next shipment is landing from Caracas. Actually, it was a generous campaign donation from a person who wishes to remain anonymous."

"I can certainly understand that," she replied, walking into the house with her burger bags.

Needless to say, Dad has never been an outstanding vote-getter in African-American precincts.

Later, Thom called and I picked a fight.

"Well, why do you think I'm angry?"

"I don't know, Toni. Is it your period?"

"I might have expected you to say that. It's no surprise from a guy who tells someone he's going to 'jump her bones'."

"I only said that because I was pissed at that Secret Service asshole."

"I saw the true you, Thom. And I was shocked. All you care about is using my body for your own base pleasures."

"I like you, Toni!"

"It's too late, Thom. You've shattered my hopes and dreams. Have a nice summer."

"Gee, Toni. Give a guy a break!"

"Good-bye, Thom."

Not very nice, I admit, but a good lesson for the boy. In these small ways are men sensitized to the emotional needs of women.

* * *

Our campaign officially got underway Saturday morning. What a madhouse getting ready: Renk and his friend Howard Archbold (said to be one of Chagrin Falls High's best chess players) nailing up red, white, and blue crepe paper bunting over the garage. Ear-splitting feedback as Dan the Picketer fiddled with the rented sound system and delivered an impromptu address on the decimation of our old-growth forests to the empty driveway. Mom and Lizzie, our ex-boarder, setting up the tables, arranging the refreshments, and making gallons of coffee in giant chrome urns. Amy and Bobby Czerkoffski blowing up patriotic balloons and tying them to the house, shrubbery, sycamore tree, and neighborhood dogs. Secret Service agents stringing up crowd control tape and surreptitiously radioing intelligence to reserve units inside. Toni and I rushing to dress and trying to decide which wholesome matching outfits from Grandmother Drucker to wear for our media debut. We finally settled on cornflower blue party frocks with starched white sailor collars, puffy sleeves, and oversized cuffs.

"That's perfect," said Renk, when we emerged at last. "That's just the look I was hoping for."

"I'd have thought you'd be hoping for a look of love-struck adoration," said Toni, touching up her eye-shadow.

"You girls look great," said Howard. "Like a double dipping of wholesome Americana, circa 1952."

"Yes, we're going after the Eisenhower vote," said Toni.

"Renk, where did all these baked goods come from?" I asked.

Lined up across the front of the garage were three cloth-draped tables laden with cakes, pies, cheesecakes, fruit tarts, trays of brownies and cookies, cupcakes, Viennese pastry, candied watermelon rind, and other attractive confections.

"Officially you baked them all yourselves," he replied.

"How busy we must have been!" exclaimed Toni, sampling a brownie.

"Unofficially," continued Renk, "they came from area bakeries, mostly donated. Some were supermarket returns Howard refurbished with canned frosting."

"Very resourceful," said Toni, depositing the rest of her brownie in a plastic trash bag. "And how adulterated is the coffee?"

"It's OK," confided Howard, "but I'd stay away from the lemonade."

"It was a stretch getting all this together on our budget," explained Renk. "But we should make back our investment and more from the sale."

"It's the capitalist system at work, Cara," said my sister.

\* \* \*

The Channel Four news van arrived at 10:45, disgorging glamorous Celina Lagrange in person and her muscular Korean cameraman. Then, in rapid succession came Channel Five, the *Plain Dealer*, Channel Nine, WUCK-FM, the *Beacon-Journal*, Channel 16, WAKO-AM, the *Mall-Advertiser* (Daphne again), ALIVE-95 FM, and—most thrilling—CNN's roving Midwest news ace Monty Bellefontaine, looking dapper in his tan trench coat despite the scorching August heat. While Mom and Lizzie sold pastries and Renk and Howard manned the beverage table, Cara played her accordion, I sang, we posed for photos, mingled with crowds of enthusiastic voters, kissed slobbering babies, were shadowed by ever-vigilant special agents, and answered reporters' probing questions.

"This bake sale of yours—isn't it an obsolete method for raising campaign funds?" asked a gaunt young man with a ponytail from ALIVE-95.

"That's why we decided to have one," replied Cara. "We'd like to see a return to traditional values in this country."

"And we love to bake," I added. "It was one thing we knew we could do to assist Dad."

"Will you be campaigning for him this fall?" asked a black woman from Channel Nine.

"Oh, yes," I replied. "We hope to tour all 50 states, Puerto Rico, and the Virgin Islands."

"Our bags are packed and we're ready to go," said Cara.

"Do you always dress identically?" inquired Celina, honing in on her area of expertise.

"As often as possible," lied Cara. "It's so much fun to observe people's reactions to us!"

"Being a twin is a total ball," I bubbled. "I guess it runs in our family. We love that our half-sisters are twins too."

"Yes, I encountered those two last week," said Monty. "How do you feel about your father's new family?"

"We were thrilled when he told us he was getting remarried," said Cara. "We do so want both of our parents to be happy."

"And we love our new stepmother," I added. "Mindy is my role model now. I want to be just like her when I get old."

"What do your boyfriends think about your being away so long on the campaign trail?" asked Daphne.

"Oh, we don't have boyfriends," replied Cara.

"Not at all," I blushed. "We're too young."

"Dad and Mom are very strict," said my sister.

"But we realize it's for our own good," I added, observing Special Agent Holgate in the distance clamp a headlock on a familiar figure and muscle him toward a double-parked yellow Probe.

\* \* \*

After the last news van and pastry customer had departed, we invited the Secret Service agents to help themselves. Mom brewed a fresh pot of real coffee, and everyone sat around on folding chairs in the garage and picked at the remains of the sweet buffet.

"I'm annoyed the Youngstown *Vindicator* never showed," said Renk. "I called them four times and sent them our on-line media packet."

"When we assume power, we will terminate all federal funds to Youngs-town," declared Howard, counting the wads of bills in the cash box. "The steel mills will be confiscated."

"Good luck," I said. "They were all torn down years ago."

"I hope your father appreciates all the effort you've gone to today, girls," said Mother.

"I'm not worried," sang Toni into the rented microphone, "'cause my heart belongs to Daddy." Toni flipped on the rental amplifier. "Hello, ladies and gentlemen," she said in a breathy Mindyesque whisper. "I'd like to thank you all for coming here today. I'd like to thank the garage for providing such lovely shade. I'd like to thank the driveway for connecting us day and night to the street. I'd like to thank Renk and Howard for personally poisoning half the neighborhood. But most of all, I'd like to thank Special Agent Ryan Holgate for ejecting a boorish party crasher named Thom."

"My pleasure, Miss Mason," Ryan replied, sipping his coffee. "I informed the young man you did not wish to see him, and he tried to get frisky on me. I was obliged to subdue him."

"Thank you for defending my honor," said Toni.

"What's to defend?" muttered Special Agent Bradford.

"OK, I've got the total!" announced Howard, punching keys on his pocket calculator. "We took in one thousand, two-hundred twelve dollars and eight-four cents."

"Not bad," said Renk. "After expenses, that's over $800 profit."

"It's great!" exclaimed Toni. "We can do this every week. We'll get rich!"

"I don't think the neighbors would stand for it, Antonia," said Mom. "And neither will your mother."

"This is small potatoes," said Renk. "We've got bigger fish to fry."

"Almost makes a person hungry for power," commented Dan.

"Shut up, Dan," said Toni. "Be diplomatic, or I won't let you take me to the movies tonight."

I glanced over at Dan in surprise. His blue eyes twinkled as he returned my sister's seductive smile.

※　※　※

We're stunned. Not only were we featured on all the local 6 p.m. news programs, we even made the ABC network news! Here's how handsome weekend anchorhunk Keene Rumley introduced us: "In this era of corporate PACs and thousand-dollar-a-plate campaign dinners, our next report may come as a surprise. Today in Rocky Pike, Ohio—a Cleveland suburb—the elder twin daughters of Vice Presidential candidate Horace Mason hosted an old-fashioned bake sale for their father's campaign. Dressed alike, 15-year-old Antonia and Carissa Mason entertained the crowd and sold pastries they had baked themselves . . ."

The segment segued through quick shots of Cara and me performing "I'm for a Flunch from Kalamazoo," Mom selling Mrs. Melmore a peanut butter cupcake, a little boy puckering up after a big gulp of lemonade, me explaining why Dad is an inspiration to the youth of America, Dan somberly waving his signs, Cara demonstrating polka riffs on her accordion, Renk whistling "I Ride an Old Paint," and Cara and me in rented gingham aprons pulling trays of molasses cookies from the oven without the benefit of potholders.

We appear remarkably insensitive to heat, Toni.

People don't notice those minor details on TV, Cara. It's the emotions that register. And we were registering very positive emotions today.

Uh-oh, Mother says Mindy's on the phone.

I took the last call, Cara. It's your turn.

She's screaming for you specifically, Toni.

Oh, all right.

* * *

"Hello, Mindy. What's up?" I asked in my perkiest voice.

General apoplectic raging.

"Oh, did you tell me that, Mindy? I must have misunderstood you."

Bellowing and hysterical name-calling.

"Really, Mindy, I doubt if we cost Dad the election. We got lots of nice publicity and raised $800 for his campaign."

Abusive vituperation.

"No, Mindy, we're keeping the money. We'll need it for our campaign expenses."

Scurrilous imprecations.

"I'm sorry you feel that way, Mindy. I don't think you're being at all reasonable."

Minacious execrations.

"Well, this is a free country after all. That's why we have elections."

Scatological fulminations.

"Really, Mindy, get a grip. Take a pill. Chant your mantra."

Maledictory invective and ranting.

"I've got to go, Mindy. It's been lovely talking to you. I have to get ready for my date with a liberal young Sierra Club member. Good-bye. See you on the campaign trail!"

*Chapter 6*

Would you like to come along on our date, reader? Everyone else is.

Not everyone, Toni. Mother, for example, is staying home.

She's being personally guarded this evening by Special Agent Troy Pulaski. I've been looking at his ring, Toni. I don't think it's a wedding band. It's got some kind of inscription on it.

What does it say?

Well, I can't get close enough to read it. One has to be discreet about these things.

Cara, you're so polite. And why on earth did you invite Howard Archbold? I like Howard, Toni. He's very intelligent.

He's a monstrously huge brain in a small, repellent package. And I don't think Renk wants him along.

I thought we could all discuss campaign strategy after the movie.

Renk doesn't want to discuss campaign strategy, Cara. He wants to discuss putting his hand under your blouse.

No, he doesn't. And why did you invite Dan? I know you don't really care for him.

I may, I may not. I haven't sampled him yet. Parts of him look quite delectable.

Then why did you sit next to Special Agent Holgate on the drive to the movies? Dan looked miserable crammed in the back seat with Howard and Smyrna, while you rode in the tail car with Ryan.

Cara, when one goes out for an intimate evening with a party of seven in Renk's father's rusty Honda Civic and an unmarked government sedan, one must take the seating accommodations as they come.

Then why did you spend the whole trip flirting with Ryan?

I didn't!

Yes, you did. Special Agent Bradford was listening in on the radio and repeated everything you two said.

That was a clear breach of ethics on Smyrna's part. She repeated everything?

Yes, Toni, word for word.

Well, then—like me—you have learned some new and curious facts about the dating habits of the young women of Cherokee County, South Carolina.

I can only hope Ryan was exaggerating. Well, we should be getting back to the film. I'm sure Smyrna must be tired of guarding the ladies' room door.

Renk has probably regained the feeling in his arm.

I hate it when boys you like as a friend put their arm around you in the movies. It's so distracting.

Don't complain, Cara. I've been holding hands with Dan *and* Ryan. It was completely immobilizing. I missed out entirely on the popcorn.

✳ ✳ ✳

"This is the largest plate of fried chicken I have ever seen," said Toni. "I feel like Wilma Flintstone."

"I told you to order the child's plate," said Renk, gnawing on a leg bone. "This restaurant is famous in Chagrin Falls for its big portions."

We were dining after the movie in a local eatery selected by Renk.

"I am *not* a child," replied Toni, "and neither is my sister, as you may discover sometime, though probably not this evening."

"Toni, please!" I said.

"Cara, eat your nine pieces of chicken and don't mind me," said Toni. "Why do they stack the pieces in these precarious piles? Why don't they just get larger plates?"

"It's part of the presentation," explained Howard. "The human race evolved through eons of privation. This bountiful display is intended to trigger our most primitive impulses to gorge savagely."

"Well I think it's cute that Dan's a vegetarian," said Toni, patting his hand. "This restaurant must be a nightmare for you, honey."

"I'm thankful, at least, that the Secret Service is dining separately," he replied, slicing into his massive day-glo yellow brick of macaroni and cheese.

Toni glanced over at a nearby table. "Ryan has the biggest plate of chicken of all. The barnyard must be completely decimated!" She turned back toward her date. "Tell me, Dan, is Cheryl the Pom-Pom Queen also a vegetarian?"

"Cheryl is not a pom-pom queen and not a vegetarian."

"How disappointing for you both."

"I'm disturbed that no one has recognized us," said Renk, gazing around at the other diners.

"Perhaps cowboy whistling is not the route to fame that you imagine," replied Toni.

"After today's media blitz, people should be mobbing you girls," he said, ignoring the sarcasm.

"They shouldn't have changed out of their Pollyanna outfits," said Howard. "They're muddying their image."

"You're right, Howie," said Renk. "Girls, I'm appointing Howard your personal image czar. From now on, he's in charge of the way you look in public."

"You're fired, Howard," said Toni, gesturing with her fork. "And you're fired too, Renk."

"No, they're not," I said. "Toni, they're doing a great job for us. We're public figures now. We have to put more thought into our dress. Come over tomorrow, Howard, and you can go through our closets."

"Cara mia, a girl's closet is a very private thing."

"There's no such thing as privacy in politics," said Howard, sucking on a wing bone. "Just ask Teddy Kennedy."

* * *

It's nearly midnight, reader, and this interminable double date refuses to end. We're all sitting around in the family room digesting poultry and watching Dan and Howard play chess. So far, Dan is holding his own—as opposed to holding me, for example. Beside me on the sofa, romantic Renk has again maneuvered his restless arm around my sister.

"Cara, why don't we go into the living room?" he asked.

"We can't, Renk. Mother is in there having a brandy with Special Agent Pulaski."

"Uh, why don't we go out on the front porch?"

"We'd be eaten alive by mosquitoes."

"Oh. Well, would you like to go for a drive?"

"Renk, I think the Secret Service agents have been inconvenienced enough this evening."

"Why don't you two go to Cara's bedroom?" I suggested. "It's ever so neat. She could show you how she individually wraps her sweaters in scented tissue paper. It's something no one should miss."

"Shall we go to that room and talk, Cara?" Renk proposed hopefully.

"Sorry, Renk. I'm not allowed to entertain boys in my bedroom."

"That's not quite true, Cara," I pointed out. "Such visitations are permitted, if Renk watches the tape."

"What tape is that?" he asked, intrigued.

"It's a video about vegetable reproduction," I explained.

"Toni, shut up. Why don't you go to bed?"

"With whom, Cara? Everyone seems to be engrossed in cerebral combat."

"Go to bed by yourself!"

"I believe that is what is known as preaching what you practice."

"Check and mate," announced Howard.

Dan slapped his forehead and groaned; Special Agent Holgate smirked.

"Don't worry, Dan," I said. "You can still win big this evening if you apply yourself."

"Up for another game, Howard?" asked Dan.

"Sure," replied his bespectacled adversary.

That was not the sort of application I had in mind. I excused myself and went to bed.

* * *

The phone rang early this morning. It rang and rang and rang, until blind fury compelled me to roll over in bed and lift the receiver.

"Yes!"

"Hello, who's this? Toni?"

"Oh, hi, Dad. What time is it?"

"It's almost seven. Sorry to call so early, Toni. I wanted to reach you before you left for church."

"Oh, right."

"It's been a tumultuous week, Toni. Forgive me for not telephoning sooner."

"That's OK, Dad. Congratulations."

"It's an immense responsibility and very humbling. With God's help, I know we shall succeed."

"Right, Dad."

"Thank you so much, Toni, for your wonderful bake sale yesterday. And thank your sister for me too."

"Oh, you didn't mind?"

"Of course not. Mindy suggested it might be counterproductive, but I got a call last night from Claude, who loved it."

"Claude?"

"Governor Flunch."

"Governor Flunch heard about it?"

"Oh, yes. CNN carried quite a long segment about you girls and your friend who whistles. Monty Bellefontaine was most enthusiastic."

"Monty's a sweet guy. He's been all over the world and has shrapnel scars from Serbia."

"He was surprisingly complimentary for being a tool of the liberal media conspiracy. Anyway, Toni, I've been asked to invite you and your sister up to the island next week."

"What island?"

"Bag Island. It's a private island in Lake Michigan where the Flunches have their summer house. We're meeting there to introduce the families and brainstorm ideas for the fall campaign."

"And you want Cara and me there with you?"

"Yes, of course. We want you to participate in the campaign as well. The Governor was most insistent."

"Gee, that's . . . unexpected."

"The travel coordinator will messenger over your itinerary this week. Be prepared to leave on Friday. And could you tell Cara to bring her accordion?"

"OK. We'll be ready."

"One more thing, could you ask that whistling boy if he could come too?"

"You want Renk?"

"Yes, Governor Flunch loves Western music."

"OK, Dad. My guess is wild horses couldn't stop him. He also does dramatic readings."

"Good. I understand the Flunch family has a tradition of amateur theatricals. We'll all be expected to entertain. I'm thinking of preparing a sermon for Sunday morning—not that its purpose will be one of entertainment."

"Right, Dad. Well, we'll see you next weekend."

"I have to run, Toni. God bless."

"Why didn't you ask him if I could come too?"

Startled, I pulled up the comforter and turned toward the voice. From the adjoining twin bed, Howard stared at me through his thick glasses.

"What are you doing in here?" I demanded.

"The chess match ran pretty late last night. Your boyfriend Dan was not satisfied until I had whipped him five times. It got to be pretty late. Your mother said Renk and I could crash in the family room, but the sofa was so uncomfortable I came in here."

"Why weren't you intercepted and shot by Secret Service agents?"

"I don't know, Toni. You'll have to ask them that. I'm pretty sneaky. Do you always sleep in the nude?"

"That's none of your damn business."

"I do. I don't have any clothes on under these covers."

"That's disgusting."

"Don't worry, I'm not going to make any physical advances toward you."

"That's a relief. Why not?"

"I'm gay."

"No, you're not. You don't dress well enough to be gay. And you're too young."

"That may be. But I'm gay."

"Do you mean to tell there's a naked gay male in my bedroom?"

"In the flesh, as it were."

"Have you made it with other guys?"

"Made what?"

"Don't be dumb. Have you done it?"

"Not really. I'd certainly like to though."

"Then you're not really gay. You're just confused."

"Shall I come over to your bed and see if I get turned on?"

"Ah, I thought so. You're right, Howard. You are sneaky."

"I'm sneaky and I'm gay."

"Well, regardless of your alleged sexual orientation, you'll have to get up and get me my robe."

"Why don't you get up and get me my clothes?"

"Because this is my room, and you are the uninvited nude interloper."

"Are you going to look at me if I get out of bed?"

"Certainly."

"OK, I was afraid you were going to shut your eyes."

Howard got up and walked over to the closet. "I can see no robe amid this chaos."

"Of course not. It's on the floor by the dresser."

Howard picked up my robe, placed it beside me, and strolled casually back to his bed. He has a compact, but surprisingly well formed and muscular body.

"Howard, you look much better with your clothes off."

"Thanks, Toni. I know. I'm thinking of having that fact printed up on cards that I can pass out to attractive young men."

* * *

What amazing news about our trip to Bag Island. At first I thought Toni was making it all up. Renk just went home to try and persuade his parents to let him go. It won't be easy. He and Howard spent the night in the family room, and Dan slept in his VW bus in the driveway. Suddenly everywhere you look there are men in the house. The atmosphere is extremely stimulating; I am trying to keep busy and not obsess about one person in particular. It's silly to get so worked up over a person I hardly know and who is considerably older than me. But it's true: I find it almost painful to be in his presence. This trip away will be a fortuitous separation from Dan to help quell these unsettling feelings and regain my equanimity.

The *Plain Dealer* featured our bake sale in a big presentation on the front page of the Sunday "Style" section. Their creative photographer snapped a cupcake's view of Toni and me across the entire length of the sweets display. The photo was cropped vertically and filled two full columns of the page. A real eye-grabber according to Renk, but I wish they'd taken the time to airbrush out several flies, unappetizingly reproduced in full color. The reporter said we were "animated and charming" and "much more charismatic" than the "lumpen Flunch brood." Flattering to us, but I hope the article does not find its way to Bag Island.

Oh, there you are, Cara. I've been looking for you.

Toni, for the past hour a yellow Probe has been circling the block and squealing its tires in front of our house.

I know, Cara. It's some sort of automotive version of the male plumage display. I'm ignoring it.

I hope Thom's emotional distress does not result in premature tire wear.

That is how boys cope, Cara. We mustn't interfere. Jocks like Thom seem to take these breakups more personally than intellectuals. My old boyfriend Jeff just got stoned, slipped a rap tape into his Walkman, and rolled off into the sunset on his skateboard.

Why don't you quit toying with Dan and give Jeff a call?

I'm an optimist, Cara. I don't look back, I stride forward. If you stop, life will snare you in a net of regrets. Speaking of which, Howard—our fashion czar—is here and wants to rifle your closet. By the way, he seems to be under the impression he's gay.

He is gay. Renk told me.

I'm glad. I feel slightly better now about his taking command of our appearance, though he's already extracted six hideous Grandmother Drucker outfits from the back of my closet. I told you we should have burned them. And he's confiscated all of my swimsuits.

Oh, is he opposed to our swimming?

Only in contemporary beach attire. He's threatening to bring over some of his big sister's old bathing suits.

Oh dear.

I can imagine the press coverage now: "The Young Flunches Host the Twin Frumps." I hope our sudden dowdiness doesn't impair Renk's ardor.

I should be so lucky. He knocked on my bedroom door last night.

How polite. What did you do?

I told him I was tired and shook his hand.

Only your second date, and already you're shaking hands. Cara mia, where will it all end!

* * *

If you don't have a driver's license, being protected by the Secret Service is the next best thing. The agents get so bored sitting around watching the wallpaper fade, they leap at the chance to drive you places. You travel in a roomy if utilitarian unmarked sedan, and Uncle Sam chips in the gas money. In case of traffic altercations, your escorts are fully armed. Should you pass people you know, you can nod gravely and wave like Henry Kissinger. That part is especially gratifying.

After Special Agents Holgate and Bradford (Ryan and Smyrna) left with Cara for the shelter, Special Agents Pulaski and Tompkins (Troy and Ken) drove Howard and me to the mall. Howard suggested this excursion after Cara and I—citing sanitary issues—rejected his sister Tallmadge's jumbled rag bag of expired bathing suits.

"Then we'll have to buy you some new ones," he said. "Let's go to Marion's Refinements Shoppe."

"How do you know about that horrible store?" I demanded.

"I called your grandmother and she recommended it."

"Howard, you are the sneakiest person I have ever met. What are we supposed to use for money?"

"Image polishing is a legitimate campaign expense, Toni. Renk gave me $400."

"OK, but we're not going to buy anything too revolting. Paparazzi may be helicoptering over Bag Island with powerful telephoto lenses. I don't intend to wind up on the cover of *Time* looking like some rube from the sticks."

Marion herself greeted us as my fashion czar was pawing through a rack of one-piece horrors.

"Hello, miss," she said. "Aren't you one of the Mason girls?"

"Yes, I'm Cara," I lied.

"I know your grandmother. She's very proud of you girls. We have some lovely bathing suits in your size."

"Oh, where are you hiding them?" I asked.

Maintaining her gracious smile, Marion scanned the rack and selected an emerald green suit that a young Esther Williams might have worn if she were color blind.

"That's perfect!" exclaimed Howard. "Go try that one on."

"Is this your young man, Cara?" inquired Marion.

"Hardly," I said. "He's gay."

Marion's exotically manicured eyebrows rose several notches. "You young people are so amusing these days."

The suit was even worse than I imagined. It fit.

"Let's see, Toni," called Howard over the dressing room wall.

"Didn't she say her name was Cara?" asked the shop owner.

I opened the door and bravely walked out. Marion smiled. Howard studied me with professional detachment and straightened a strap. Special Agent Pulaski scratched his neat Polish nose and looked away. I turned and pondered my reflection in a full-length mirror. Down my front ran a riot of bold sunflowers. The iron-banded built-in bra molded my breasts into geometrically perfect cones. Below my modestly covered navel, flounced a perkily ruffled skirt, trimmed in sunny yellow rickrack.

"Somehow I think not," I said. "I look like a Special Olympian preparing to swim the English Channel in 1933."

"We'll take two," said Howard. "Wrap them up!"

※　※　※

Thom and three of his football buddies confronted us in Badlands for Men, where I was advising Howard on the purchase of stylish casual clothing.

"Step back, you," warned Special Agent Tompkins.

"I don't want any trouble," said Thom, raising his hands and retreating one step. "Toni, what's the story?"

"Thom, go away," I said. "It's over."

"It's not over, damn it," he insisted. "Who's the raisinette?"

"This is Howard, if you must know. He's an international chess champion."

"Are you sleeping with that twink?" demanded Thom.

"Why, yes," I admitted. "I slept with him last night as a matter of fact."

"But only technically," my Image Czar hastened to add. "And not in the same bed."

"You're history, dude!" shouted Thom.

"OK, let's move on," said Special Agent Pulaski. "All of you, move it!" Thom and his friends reluctantly moved back.

"Keep on going," commanded Pulaski. "Out of the store."

When they were gone, Howard turned to me. "Toni, why did you tell that brute you had slept with me? He did not appear rational. Steroids may have destroyed his mind."

"Sorry, Howard, I wasn't thinking. How could I? It's not every day a girl gets such a flattering new bathing suit. Oh, aubergine trousers. Perfect. It's *the* color in menswear this fall!"

"I can't wear purple pants," he gasped.

"Don't be a fashion coward, Howard. This color is a universally recognized siren call of erotic longing. And it's twenty percent off today too."

# Part Two

## Chapter 7

Located 17 miles due west of the Michigan shore, Bag Island can be approached several ways. Tradesmen and laborers motor over in the supplies boat that embarks every weekday morning at 10 (summers only) from Petoskey. Captains of industry dock their imposing yachts at the guest pier in Sack Cove. VIPs touch down on the helicopter pad mowed into the meadow behind the tennis court. And special guests of the family, like our party of four (plus two Secret Service agents) arrive by private seaplane from Cleveland. Our handsome pilot, Kent Stow, smiled reassuringly as the twin pontoons clattered over the splintering green waves and the welcoming spray fell away to a soft foam as we slowed.

"Toni, this is the most exciting moment of my life," I whispered to my sister. "The sunset over the lake was breathtaking."

"Lake Baikal was more dramatic, Cara," noted Howard, unfastening his seat belt and peering out the window. "It's the deepest lake in the world."

"Are we supposed to swim to shore?" wondered Toni. "I don't see a boat."

"Don't you worry, miss," said Kent. "We'll tie up at the end of the dock."

"Damn, I don't see any reporters," complained Renk. "Just some fat girl in a sunsuit."

The girl was Dola Flunch, the only daughter of our hosts, Claude and Lima Flunch.

"Hello, hello, hello," she called, as we trundled down the old wooden dock with our bags. "I'm Dola. You missed dinner. Hamler caught a mess of big-mouth bass, but we devoured them. O-o-oh, you brought cute boys too."

After quick introductions and handshakes, Dola hoisted my case and led us up a sandy path that wound between tall spruces. "The house is all filled up, so we're putting you in the lab. Don't worry, it's not too bad. I'm out there too. So's Forest, he's 17. He was supposed to come down to the dock, but he gets shy fits. Hamler is my big brother. He's out eel hunting. Boy, what did you pack in here, your boat motor?"

"No, it's an accordion."

"Good. I hear you girls have quite the act. On the island everybody's got to perform, that's Mom's rule. Your bee-u-tiful stepmom put Fawn and Colt in my room in the house. What a couple of monsters. Forest wants to drown them. If you see guys prowling around in the dark, don't get scared. It's just the Secret Service or Hamler. Forest calls them the Secretive Disservice. He built a radio to monitor their communications. My code name is 'Barracuda.' What's yours?"

"I don't know," I replied. "I didn't know we had one."

"Oh, you've got one all right. They give one to everybody they guard. Forest will find out yours. His is 'The Sphinx.' He hates it. Hamler's is 'Tarzan's Lawyer.' Man, you have a lot of twins in your family. We'll have to make you girls wear name badges. I can't tell you apart. How old are you?"

"Eighteen," replied Toni.

"She may be," I commented, "but I'm fifteen and a half."

Dola smiled. "Almost my age. I'm 16. Where are you from in Ohio?"

"Rocky Pike," I replied. "It's a suburb of Cleveland."

"Have you been to the Rock and Roll Hall of Fame?" she asked.

"Not yet," said Toni. "We're still working our way out of the Swing Era."

"Did anyone ever tell you you look like what's-her-name, Doris Day?" asked Dola.

"Why no," lied Toni. "No one's ever mentioned it."

"I like your purple pants, Howard," said Dola, overlooking the sarcasm.

"It's aubergine," he replied.

"Big hot-shot designer, huh?"

"No, it's a color. French for eggplant."

"Oh. Well, we don't go in much for snappy dressing on the island. We like to strip to the basics and run free. The house is just over that hill. The Secret Service keeps the path lit all night. We didn't used to. We can find our way around this island blindfolded. It's our own private kingdom. There's lots to do. The swimming is great and you'll want to see my uncle's boat. Here's the laboratory. The dog is Mr. Tiro. If he gets in your way, just give him a push."

Mr. Tiro was an elderly low-slung dachshund mix with a shuffling gait and a graying snout. He wagged his tail and hopped unnaturally like a low-rider's chopped Chevrolet. Our guest house was a large one-story red-brick building lined with steel-sash industrial windows. Through the trees to the east, Lake Michigan shimmered in the fading light.

"It looks like an old factory," said Renk. "Was this your family's first paper mill?"

"Nah, it was built as a laboratory by my great-grandfather. He fooled around in here for years. They'd be calling him the Thomas Edison of paper if he'd ever invented anything."

"Didn't he invent the paper bag?" asked Renk.

"Nope, just got rich making them. When I was little the lab was abandoned. Hamler busted out every single window. Mom had it remodeled into guest rooms about ten years ago when Dad got into politics. Of course, all the glass makes it a killer to air-condition, but Dad writes it off on his taxes."

Dola set down my accordion with relief and held open the door. A wide hallway lined with pastel-painted flush doors bisected the long building. Mismatched metal tables and folding chairs straggled down the center to suggest an impromptu common room.

"Choose your color and take any unoccupied room," she announced. "Girls on the right, boys on the left. There are no locks on the doors. Dad says we Republicans have nothing to hide—at least not from each other. There are two bathrooms at each end. First come, first served. Try not to dawdle if people are waiting. Drink the water out of the tap if you like straight lake water, or there's filtered well water in the plastic bottles. I'll go see if I can find Forest."

Toni and I took adjoining rooms near the door, but Howard and Renk could find vacancies only far down the hall. The small rooms were identical: red-painted concrete floor, crudely Sheetrocked white walls, and a roll-down plastic shade across the big factory window. Each was furnished with a narrow single bed with a flat mattress, plastic lamp on a three-drawer pine dresser, and a high shelf above an exposed closet pole. On each door was stenciled the name of a famous Republican.

"I'm in the Oliver North room," I said.

"I'm in the Spiro Agnew cell," announced Toni.

"I'm in the Dick Nixon cell," said Howard.

"See, there is justice in this world," said Renk.

"What room are you in?" asked Toni.

"Pardon me," he replied.

"I asked what room you were in. Cara may wish to know for later."

"Toni, please!"

"Pardon me," repeated Renk.

"Oh, I see," said Toni. "You are an undeserving occupant of the Gerald Ford room."

*　*　*

Stars twinkled overhead at a unnaturally bright, deep-boondocks wattage as we gathered outside the lab building.

"Should we go over to the house and say hi to Dad?" suggested Cara.

"Everyone's in meetings," replied Forest. "They will be for hours." Forest has the smoothed-over, streamlined features of a Flunch, but on him they looked much better than on Dola. An inch or so under six feet, he was lean and tanned, with deep-set Nixonian eyes and thick sandy-brown hair like a golden retriever.

"But we could probably track down your bee-u-tiful stepmom Mindy for you," added his sister.

"Don't bother," I said. "Let's get something to eat. I'm starving."

"Me too," said Howard.

"You mean you didn't bring food?" asked Forest.

"No," said Cara. "Were we supposed to?"

"You didn't bring any cookies, dried fruits, protein bars, canned clams, Spam, crackers, or chocolate?" asked Dola, incredulous.

"Of course not," I replied. "I know we missed dinner, but surely someone can fix us a sandwich."

Dola exchanged grim looks with her brother.

"Even under the best of circumstances," explained Forest, "there's a very narrow window of opportunity for meals here."

"And the portions are pretty meager," added his sister. "I lost 12 pounds so far this summer."

"Things have been totally chaotic on the island since the convention," continued Forest. "Dad's trying to gear up for a presidential race from his skeleton statehouse staff. People have been coming and going in droves. We only have one cook and a helper in the kitchen, and they haven't had a day off in two weeks. Mother had to put down a kitchen mutiny yesterday."

"Did she use a whip?" inquired Renk.

"Dad offered Forest a nice summer job helping out in the dish room," said Dola.

"I told him my investment portfolio was up 43 percent so far this year," said Forest.

"That's a spectacular return," commented Howard. "Mine is only up 37 percent. Are you in mutual funds?"

"No, I buy and sell directly. I've had some fair success with South American communications stocks this year."

"Could we get back to the matter at hand," I said. "What are our chances of getting something to eat?"

"Hamler might've caught some eels," suggested Dola.

"Maybe," said Forest, "but Hamler's a profiteer. If he senses they're hungry, his prices will skyrocket. Do you have any money?"

"Not much," admitted Renk. "We thought everything would be provided."

"Welcome to the real world," said Dola.

"Wait a minute," I said. "I'll bet the Secret Service has some food."

"Too late," said Forest. "We raided them all last week. They've posted armed guards by their provisions tent."

"Couldn't we take a boat to the mainland?" suggested Cara.

"Dad's cruiser is locked," replied Forest. "You could charter Hamler's boat, but he'd probably require that you sleep with him."

"What does your brother look like?" I asked.

"He gets pretty feral on the island," said Forest. "He spends the whole summer in a scummy deerskin loincloth, which is bad for his skin allergies."

"What does he do the rest of the year?" asked Howard.

"He's a junior at Dartmouth in pre-law."

"I guess we starve," said Cara.

"There's one other possibility," said Forest. "The press fleet is anchored in Big Bag Bay. Reporters are banned from the island grounds after dark. They've got food. And booze."

"Lead the way," I said. "It's time to meet the press."

\* \* \*

Big Bag Bay was a long march south through dark thickets of scratchy pines.

"Why hasn't your family logged this island?" I asked, feeling my way around a bramble patch. "There must be paper bags by the millions in all these trees."

"These woodlands are off-limits, Toni," replied Forest. "We only denude land other people have to look at."

"It's nice to know there'll be at least one green spot left up here in this part of the world," said Renk.

"Too bad you won't be invited back to see it," said Forest.

"I'll invite you, Renk," said Dola. "And you too, Howie."

"Are you guys the boyfriends or what?" asked Forest.

"Renk is our media manager," said Cara.

"And Howard is our fashion consultant," I added. "That's why he's wearing purple pants and we're dressed like Mamie Eisenhower."

✳ ✳ ✳

"Good God," said Howard, "it sounds like the world's largest frat party."

More than a dozen brightly lit motor yachts were anchored in the broad, moonlit bay. We could see figures moving about on the decks and hear peels of laughter above the amplified rock music.

"See that big eighty-footer in the center with the satellite dish?" said Forest, pointing. "That's Ted Turner's boat."

"Is he here?" asked Cara.

"No, just Monty Bellefontaine and Adena Zoar," said Dola.

"Oh, we know Monty," I said, my heart fluttering as it always did at the mention of that name. "He did a report on us in Ohio—a highly flattering profile of our bake sale."

"Yeah, we heard about that," said Dola. "Monty's a pest. He keeps asking questions about our Uncle Maximo."

Forest directed a warning glance at his sister.

"But we don't mind," she added hastily. "He's really cute. Do you think he's sleeping with Adena?"

"Certainly not," I replied. "Monty's a professional. He'll give us some dinner. How do we get out there? Where's the boat?"

"Who needs boats?" said Forest, stripping off his shirt. "We swim."

"I didn't bring my bathing suit," said Cara.

"Who needs bathing suits?" said Forest, unbuckling his belt.

"I can't swim that far," I said, observing the disrobing process with interest.

"It's less than 200 yards," said Forest, pausing with his fingers on the waistband of his boxer shorts. "Renk, Howard are you with me?"

"I guess so," said Howard, reluctantly removing his glasses and slipping them into his shirt pocket.

"Sure," said Renk, kicking off his shoes.

"Cara," I said, "you are about to get a preview of coming attractions."

"Toni, please!" she protested.

* * *

"Now this is what I call a Tupperware party," said Dola, spreading French goat cheese with her finger on a baguette and offering it to Mr. Tiro. He sniffed it suspiciously then swallowed it gravely.

We were gathered in a circle on the sand around a large plastic container filled with savory CNN delicacies. The naked buffet raiders had dressed and were passing around a bottle of vermouth.

"Howard, I told you to go for the gin," said Forest. "This stuff is rank."

"Sorry, Grove. I didn't have my glasses on," said Howard, taking a swig. "You're lucky I didn't grab the teak polish."

"This black forest ham is delicious," said Renk. "Did you get some, Cara?"

"Yes, thank you, Renk. What are those lights bobbing out there in the distance?"

"Tourist boats," replied Dola. "We're a magnet for curiosity seekers."

"The Secret Service has imposed a two-mile exclusion zone around the island for water craft," said Forest. "That's considered beyond the range of a sharpshooter with a scope."

"Well, that's a comfort," I said uneasily.

"There's a Coast Guard cutter on patrol day and night," said Dola. "With radar!"

"I wonder if they're watching us," said Cara, looking around.

"I just assume I'm under constant surveillance," said Forest.

"Adena Zoar had me under constant surveillance," said Howard, slurping down an oyster. "I can't believe a famous TV personality saw me naked."

"Too bad she'll be too drunk to remember it," said Forest. "Say, how did you get that impressive washboard stomach?"

"Nice of you to notice, Copse," said Howard. "I guess from leaning over a chess board."

"Oh, do you play?" asked Forest.

"I fool around with it."

"So do I. I have a board in my room. We'll play a game tomorrow."

"Sure," said Howard. "Let's."

Cara startled me by putting an arm around Renk. "Whistle us a tune, Renkie," she said.

"Oh, I don't know . . ."

"Do it, Renk," said Forest. "It's egotistical to have to be coaxed."

Renk took a tote of vermouth and whistled "The Old Chisholm Trail."

His sagebrush vibrato rolled across the silvery sand and rose toward the blazing stars. Mr. Tiro cocked his head and soberly studied the whistler as if Renk had lost his marbles.

When he finished, Cara kissed him.

"I've got goosebumps," said Dola. "Do us another, Renk."

Renk performed "Red River Valley" and "Streets of Laredo."

"It makes me feel sad," said Dola.

"That's the idea," said Forest. "People like to wallow in sentiment, the sadder the better. Happiness is boring. Dad's right. You'll be good for the campaign, Renk."

"How's it going?" asked Cara.

"Terrible so far," said Forest. "Things are in complete turmoil. Dad's just about disappeared off the radar screens. He was most impressed with the coverage you girls got for your bake sale."

"It was Renk's idea," said Cara proudly.

"Good work," said Forest. "Dad's got to hire pros to run his campaign. He's no manager. He couldn't manage a bowel movement if it wasn't orchestrated by his gut."

"Then why on earth does he want to be President?" Renk demanded.

"All politicians want to be President," explained Forest, swigging from the bottle. "It goes with the territory."

"It must be great being power mad," observed Howard, feeling his wine. "Megalomania can be such a turn-on."

"Howie, you're so wowie," giggled Dola. He forgot to duck when she zoomed in to kiss him.

Renk embraced Cara and kissed her passionately.

I glanced uneasily at Forest and gazed out across the water. I thought of dear, shrapnel-scarred Monty suavely sipping a cocktail in his trench coat. I sensed that the ace reporter was on the trail of something big, and I knew it wasn't Adena Zoar.

*Chapter 8*

We caught a brief glimpse of Hamler Flunch—an unshaven, scabrous, nearly nude rustic—when he stopped by the laboratory to pick up breakfast: one individual-size box of cereal, one half-pint of warm milk, and one cellophane-sealed midget donut. He skipped the one Styrofoam cup of weak but corrosive coffee. A bigger and coarser version of his brother, he has a thick red neck, meaty thighs, and the same sandy dog's hair gone long and tangled.

While staffers of all ages and sexes buzzed in and out of the pastel doors, Dola showed us how to slice open our tiny boxes, fold back the flaps, and pour in the precious milk. We ate with used plastic spoons at the wobbly metal tables.

"I'm saving my donut for mid-morning break," said Cara, slowly chewing her cornflakes.

"Take some extra of those little creamer packets," advised Dola. "You can suck on 'em if you start to feel faint."

"I thought your family was loaded, Clear Cut," said Howard. He had dressed us this morning in pink culottes, white middy blouses, and pink hair ribbons. Our Fashion Czar himself had coordinated a champagne T-shirt with baggy orange beach shorts tailored with oddly positioned rear seams.

"The Flunches have been comfortable for two centuries," admitted Forest. "But Mother comes from a family of prosperous cherry farmers, who taught her the value of thrift. She still insists upon her small economies."

"How early do you have to get up to enjoy hot water in the shower?" asked Renk.

"Oh, the water's piped straight into the baths from the lake," replied Forest. "The supply at least is inexhaustible. I find it rather bracing."

"I find it rather prison-like," I said.

"You must be Toni," said Forest. "I'm beginning to tell you girls apart.

You're the one who doesn't kiss Renk."

Cara blushed.

"I don't kiss a lot of people," I said, "especially boys who whistle."

Renk put down his coffee and began to whistle "Cattle Call." Howard joined in, and then Forest. Disgusted, Mr. Tiro left through the open door.

"My, we're a merry bunch this morning," said Columbus, the elderly black food rationer. "Maybe I better tell Mrs. Flunch to go easy on the eats!"

* * *

After breakfast Toni and I walked over the hill to the main house with willowy Gilboa McComb, Dad's young assistant press liaison. She had gone native in a long tropical-print dress accessorized with a necklace of chunky, primitive beads. In her long brown hair was a fresh-picked marigold.

"I could live forever on this island," she said, inhaling the piney sunshine.

"No, you couldn't," said Toni. "You'd starve."

"We're in an enchanting setting, Toni, being served a slimming diet of low-calorie meals. I try to think of it as one of those expensive health re-sorts—only without the mudbaths and compulsory workouts. It's wonderful. I've lost four pounds since last week."

"We should quit grousing and emulate Gilboa's positive attitude," I said. "We're lucky to be here."

"We're lucky to be alive," replied Toni.

The Flunch summer house was a bulky three-story box, stark white and nearly square, with a shallow hip roof and irregularly sized windows set at random in the plain clapboard facade. The porch-less front door faced west toward the lake. On a raw new deck of greenish wood, several groups of VIPs were dining at umbrella-shaded tables. At one sat the two nominees, their wives, and our half-sisters (dressed identically in striped playsuits). I also recognized the cereal boxes, milk cartons, and donut wrappings.

"Mrs. Flunch is scrupulously fair," said Gilboa. "The menu is the same for everyone—except the house residents dine on real china and are allowed one refill of coffee."

"Is it OK for us to go over to them?" I asked.

"Oh, sure," said Gilboa. "The Flunches are dying to meet you."

At least one person at the table did not seem anxious to see us. Our step-mother Mindy sipped her coffee and looked away as we approached. She was professionally tanned and painstakingly made up. Despite the morning breeze off the lake, every golden hair was rigidly in place.

"Good morning, girls," called Dad. As he stood up, little Fawn kicked him sharply in the bare knee. Like the governor, Dad was dressed casually in a short-sleeve sport shirt and plaid Bermuda shorts. Dad's calf-length socks were conservative black; Governor Flunch's were sunflower yellow to match his shirt. Wincing in pain, Dad gave us his customary peck on the cheek.

"Claude and Lima," he said, "I'd like you to meet my daughters Toni and Cara. Please don't ask me which is which." Still smiling, he flinched as little Colt rapped his other knee smartly with her cereal spoon.

Looking exactly like their now world-famous selves, Governor and Mrs. Flunch stood up, smiled, and extended their hands.

"Welcome aboard," said the governor. "You're doing great work, great work."

Tall and sun-reddened, Gov. Flunch *did* look presidential, being (as my sister points out), "white, bald, middle-aged, and inclined toward corpulency."

Dad was thinner, with wavy salt-and-pepper hair, still youthful features, and his familiar air of good-natured but no-nonsense piety.

"I can't wait to hear you girls perform," said Mrs. Flunch, a stout, plainly dressed woman in her early fifties. Her thick orange hair fell straight and unstyled to the puffy shoulder pads of her well-washed print dress.

"Your island is lovely," said my sister. "Thank you for inviting us."

"I hope you have everything you need," she said graciously.

"Oh, yes," I assured her. "And Forest and Dola have been most kind in showing us the sights."

"Glad to have such pretty distractions around the place for young Forest," said Claude. "It's time that boy got interested in somebody's bottom line besides his own."

"You must meet my son Hamler," said Mrs. Flunch. "He's an extraordinary young man."

"Yes, he seems like it," said Toni.

"Please, Fawn honey, you mustn't pinch," I said, removing a small sticky hand from my right leg.

"Don't touch my child," snapped Mindy. "I will discipline my children myself!"

"I have never disciplined my children," said Lima. "They've always known how to behave. Fortunately, social poise is a hereditary trait in my family. And the Flunches too, except for Claude's brother Maximo."

"CNN is looking for him," remarked Toni.

"Everyone is looking for Max, missy," said Claude. "But no one is going to find him. I'm seeing to that."

The presidential nominee jumped.

Mindy wrestled the fork away from Colt and slapped her. My half-sister howled.

"I'm glad you did that, Mindy," said the governor, rubbing his Bermudas. "Otherwise, I would have had to do it myself. And it would be just like the press to snap a photo of me cold-cocking a three-year-old."

You could have knocked us over with a feather when Gov. Flunch began to sing:

> Mild and moderate you must be,
>   When you become the nominee.
> A sanctimoniousness you must display,
>   An incorruptibility you should convey.
>
> Pose you must for veneration
>   By the citizens of the nation;
> Inspired by you youth must be,
>   Lest we descend into anarchy.
>
> Urges low must be subjugated,
>   And all carnality expurgated.
> Spotless must your character be—
>   Burnished by a native prudery.

Father joined in on the chorus:

> *Libertines, rakes, and voluptuaries*
>   *Shall not serve as our functionaries!*
> *Lechery, lust, and debaucheries*
>   *Never shall besmirch our dignitaries!*

Snapping his fingers, Governor Flunch continued:

> Straight ahead you must stare
>   While the press strips you bare;
> Chin up, chest out, head held high—
>   Show the voters you're their guy.
>
> You're the man to lead the nation
>   From its swamp of degeneration.
> You're so clean it's nearly boggling,
>   No bare harlots have you been ogling.
>
> Abnegation total is your creed,
>   You're so bloodless you don't bleed.

Blinding must your purity be,
   When you become the nominee.

*Temperance, prudence, and sobriety,*
   *These we'll bring to the Presidency!*
*Vice, dissolution, and obscenity,*
   *These we'll exclude from our residency!*

\* \* \*

Inside, the Flunch mansion was just as boxlike as its exterior. Large square rooms led maze-like to more large square rooms. Each was crowded with ponderous, ornate furniture inexpertly painted to resemble wood.

"The house was built entirely without a plan," declared Forest, giving us a tour. "Great-grandfather Foraker, the famed inventor, landed a party of mill hands on the island in 1893 with two barges loaded with lumber and salvaged windows. He told them he would be back in a month with the curtains, rope beds, and Mrs. Flunch. So they went to work. The house was ready when great-grandfather returned. It's now regarded as one of the region's foremost examples of naive domestic architecture."

"It's a marvel," agreed Toni. "And where did you get all the unusual furniture?"

"Foraker Flunch designed it," replied Forest. "That's what great-grandfather was working on all those years in the lab. What do you suppose this furniture is made from?"

"Some sort of carved material?" I guessed.

"Fairy dust?" speculated Toni.

"Paper," announced Forest proudly. "Molded paper pulp."

"I think it's hideous," said Dola. "Mom made Dad dump the stuff out of our Kalamazoo house. He donated it to the Governor's Mansion in Lansing for a big tax write-off."

"It seems old-fashioned to our modern tastes," agreed Forest. "But it's a technological triumph. It was years ahead of its time."

"What time was that?" asked Toni. "The dark ages? I guess it didn't catch on, huh?"

"Alas, people refused to accept varnished paper furniture," explained Forest. "So great-grandfather had to train young women to paint on the imitation woodgrains. At the time a table made from solid white oak retailed for about three dollars; these could be profitably marketed for no less than fifteen."

"That doesn't sound very competitive," I noted.

"It nearly bankrupted the family," said Dola. "Worst of all, we've been stuck with it ever since."

"It's very durable and quite valuable now," said Forest, leading the way up a tricky staircase built with irregularly spaced steps. "The Henry Ford Museum is dying to acquire some pieces. They've already got most of the lab's old molding machinery. Be careful, you could break your neck on these stairs."

The broad staircase opened on a long second-floor hallway lined with illuminated gun cases, also apparently molded from paper. A solid wall blocked the continuation of the staircase to the third floor.

"Are you anticipating an invasion from Canada?" asked Toni, surveying the lethal weaponry.

"These are Uncle Max's guns and rifles," said Dola. "He's got lots more in the basement. The island used to be crawling with deer and badgers and muskrats and squirrels and skunks and such, but Uncle Max shot them all. We don't even have mice any more."

"Uncle Max always kept the cases unlocked and his guns fully loaded," said Forest. "He believes in an alert and strong defense. The first thing the Secret Service stormtroopers did when they landed was confiscate all the ammunition."

"Thank God for that," said Toni. "And where is your uncle Maximo?"

"I don't know," said Forest with apparent casualness. "I haven't seen him."

"Me neither," said his sister. "Here's my room. Fawn and Colt are wrecking it."

Dola pushed open the door and we peered past her into the large square room. She was right.

"Your dad and Miss America are in my room," said Forest, opening the next door and walking in. We followed.

"She was only Miss Ohio," said Toni, threading her way around great piles of teal leather luggage.

"I know," said Forest. "That's her Secret Service code name. Your father's is 'Vice Preacher.' The brats are 'Hiroshima' and 'Nagasaki'."

"What are ours?" I asked.

"Well, I don't know which is which," he replied. "One of you is 'Dream Date' and the other is 'Desolation Doris'."

"Both are equally offensive," said Toni, opening the lid of a teal cosmetics case. "Don't you agree, Cara?"

"I don't know, Toni. Since you're the singer in the family, I must be 'Dream Date.' I find it rather flattering."

"You are presuming too much, Sister," said Toni, removing a tube of lipstick from the dozens on display. "Remember, we share the Doris curse equally. Come, Mr. Tiro!" The dog shuffled in from the hallway, sniffed the offered cosmetic, and licked it solemnly. "Thank you, Mr. Tiro." Smiling, Toni recapped the lipstick, returned it to its appropriate slot, then closed the case.

"What's up on the third floor?" I asked.

"Not much," replied Forest. "By the time the builders got up that high, they were running out of wood. The floor joists were dangerously undersized. They've weakened so much over the past century the entire floor has been condemned and the staircase closed off. There's nothing up there now except some old packing crates and a few of the lighter pieces of Foraker's furniture."

"There's hardly more in this room," said Toni. "Forest, your room is lacking in personality. Where are all your boyish souvenirs? Where are your pinups of busty babes ripped from cheesy magazines?"

"Oh, my brother is much too serious for that," said Dola.

"Then, Forest, you have no personal interests at all?" asked Toni.

"I have my books and my saxophone and my chess board. I have my computer and my investment files and my electronics equipment."

"You're wasting your time on youth," said Toni. "You should skip the prologue and enter a retirement home immediately. You'd be a sensation in the activities room."

"You know nothing about me," he replied calmly.

"No one does," said Dola proudly. "He's the family enigma."

✳ ✳ ✳

After lunch (one thin slice of bologna between two pieces of white bread, small Rome Beauty apple, and paper cup of watery punch), Howard and Renk suggested a swim in the lake. Cara and I retired reluctantly to our rooms and changed into our abominable sunflower swimsuits. Oh well, at least we're more tanned than some of our pasty companions, who could be models for *Basement Life* magazine.

On his pallid, wiry body with its baby-smooth legs and one lonely hair sprouting from the center of his hollow chest, Renk had draped baggy blue trunks. Howard had clothed his slight but well-formed body in baggy red trunks. Rounding out the patriotic trio, Forest appeared in baggy white trunks. His sister filled out a black two-piece suit, allowing the considerable leftovers to remain in public view. Carrying a towel and portable chess set, Forest led the way to their preferred swimming beach in Shopping Bag Cove. We followed behind with a huffing Mr. Tiro.

"You girls look stunning," said Howard.

"I'm glad all the important people are locked away in meetings," I said. "It would be mortifying to be seen dressed like this. I hope the press continues to ignore us."

"I think those suits are cute," said Renk, taking my sister's hand. She didn't resist.

"I love your little skirts," commented Dola, plucking her Spandex from a crevice.

On the way to the swimming beach, we trooped past the Secret Service encampment with its inflatable command post building, satellite dishes, and portable latrine. Our cute Cleveland agent Ryan Holgate was sizzling something delicious-smelling in a skillet on a Coleman stove. He waved, but did not invite us to lunch.

"Did you call your parents, Renk?" asked my sister.

"All the house phones were locked, Cara," he said, "so I called them collect from the pay phone in the laboratory. I told them I was learning a lot about the American political system at work. They're still not too happy about my being here."

"But it's so educational," insisted Cara. "It's the chance of a lifetime."

"And it only comes along once every four years," I noted.

"Look," said Forest, pointing.

In the distance across the lake, the silvery Flunch seaplane swooped down in a graceful landing (laking?).

"Who do you suppose is arriving?" asked Howard. "Your uncle Maximo?"

"I hear it's Essex Kennard," said Forest.

"Essex Kennard!" exclaimed Renk.

"And who is Essex Kennard?" I demanded.

"Essex Kennard," said Howard, "is the most astute and highest priced political consultant in the country."

"In the world," said Forest. "And completely without scruples. Dad's finally decided to bring in the top gun."

"I thought Essex was working for Vice President Greer?" said Cara.

"Money talks," said Forest, turning back up the trail. "The bucks are flooding in for your dad."

"We Masons have always been popular," I said. "It's our winning personalities."

"I thought it was your vicious right-wing agenda," said Renk.

"Be nice," said Cara.

"Co-optation through sex," I observed. "It's one of our more insidious tactics."

\* \* \*

The beach was a pleasant crescent of rippled sand in a private wooded cove near the northern tip of the island. We spread our towels on the virgin sand and splashed into the blue water. Mr. Tiro waded out six inches and plopped down in the sun-warmed shallows.

"Shouldn't we wait an hour after lunch to go swimming?" asked Howard.

"Not after that lunch," I replied. "Thirty seconds should be more than adequate."

"This really is a paradise," said Cara, floating on her back.

"It is," agreed Renk, dog-paddling beside her, "as long as you don't think about the dioxins and chlorine contaminates pouring into the lake from the Flunch paper mills."

"And what do you carry your lunch to school in, Mr. Ecology?" asked Forest.

"In a metal, recyclable lunch pail," replied Renk.

"No doubt with Mickey Mouse embossed on the lid," said Forest.

"Remember when we used to decorate lunch bags with hearts in school and tape them to our desks?" asked Cara. "Then classmates would put Valentines in them."

"Those were probably Flunch bags!" exclaimed Dola.

"The people I liked never gave cards to me," confessed Howard.

"Who were they?" asked Forest.

"Oh, nobody special."

"I'd deliver a Valentine to you, Cara," said Renk. "Even if I had to put it in a Flunch bag."

"How sweet," said my sister, kissing him. Only one day out of Ohio and she had already turned into a libertine.

"Hey, Forest," I said, pointing east, "there's a boat out there. Much closer than two miles."

Forest glanced toward the trespasser. "Oh, that's Hamler in his sloop. The Coast Guard monitors his movements by radar—or so they claim. The Secret Service gave up insisting an agent accompany him; such an extended intimacy with my brother is not to be endured. Looks like he's spear fishing. Let's hope he catches something. The reports from Columbus about dinner are not encouraging."

\* \* \*

After our swim Toni and Dola stretched out in the sun by the beach to read their books. Renk watched as Howard and Forest played chess. I decided to explore a path along the shore and search for wildflowers or edible plants. I was gathering some gay toadflax when I was startled by a voice.

"You come."

I stood up and turned around. "Oh, Hamler. It's you."

"You come," repeated the husky native.

"I'm Cara. Horace Mason's daughter."

"You come."

"Where?"

Without reply, Hamler turned and strode west along the trail. Gripping my flowers, I followed.

"You know you really should put some lotion on that rash," I said. "And with your fair skin a sunblock is really a necessity."

Hamler plodded on silently in his bare feet, his loincloth bouncing with every step. He led me to a narrow inlet where a small white sailboat was beached under some high weeds. Hamler untied a rope on the stern and pulled from the fecund water a string of large, white-bellied fish.

"You cook," he said, displaying his catch.

"Of course, Hamler. Let's take them back to the others and we'll have a barbecue on the beach."

"We no share. You come."

Hamler darted up the steep slope; I struggled to follow. The faint path let to a thicket of trees and the ruins of a small brick building. Inside was a rudimentary stone cookstove, a blackened frying pan, and some basic food-stuffs. Hamler already had a wood fire going in the stove.

"This is very nice, Hamler. You fillet the fish and I'll get the breading prepared. After we've eaten our fill, we can take the rest to the others."

Grunting, Hamler pulled a hunting knife from the sheath on his loin-cloth, and skillfully scaled, gutted, and deboned the fish. I dipped the fillets in beaten egg, dredged them in spiced cornmeal, and slid them into the sizzling oil.

"What was this building, Hamler?"

"Steam powerhouse."

"Oh, where does the electricity come from now?"

"Cable under lake."

He watched attentively as I flipped the fillets to brown on the other side. I noticed a blanket rolled up in a corner.

"Is this where you sleep?"

"Sometimes. Sometimes on boat."

"Your brother tells me you're studying pre-law at Dartmouth."

"Fish done now, woman."

"Oh, so it is." I transferred the first batch to absorbent paper towels and added the second batch to the smoking oil. Hamler grabbed a hot fillet with a soiled, scratched hand and began gobbling it hungrily.

"Be careful, Hamler, you'll burn yourself. Do you have any plastic forks?"

"No."

I wrapped a fillet in a paper towel and nibbled a corner. It was delicious.

"This is wonderful. It's very nice of you to invite me, Hamler. We're all very hungry, as you may know. How do you like Hanover?"

"What?"

"Hanover, New Hampshire. I'm told the Dartmouth campus is quite wooded and beautiful."

"Turn the fish."

"Oh, OK." I flipped the fish. Hamler popped the top off a warm can of beer and drank deeply. He paused, wiped his mouth with a musky arm, and held out the can to me. "No thanks, I don't drink. I'm 15. What do you think of your father being nominated for President?"

"Fish is done."

I removed the rest of the fish and placed the skillet on a rock to cool. With much grunting and belching, Hamler devoured three more pieces of fish. I finished my first and reached for a second.

"We mate now."

"I beg your pardon?"

Crouching on his haunches, Hamler unrolled the ratty blanket on the concrete floor.

"We mate now."

I put down my fish. "We what?"

The savage lunged toward me and gripped me in his strong arms. He had bad b.o. and fishy beer breath.

"You strip, woman."

"I don't think so, Hamler. You behave yourself!"

Hamler groped my left breast and attempted to kiss me. I pushed him away.

"We mate now," he insisted.

"I'm leaving!"

Hamler grabbed me and tried to pull me toward him. I struggled and kneed him hard in the groin as I had seen on TV. He gasped and released me.

"Jesus Christ!" he moaned, doubling over. "You didn't have to do that!"

"What do you take me for?" I demanded, incensed. "You're lucky I didn't pour that scalding oil over you."

Hamler clasped his hands under his loincloth flap and groaned.

"Are you OK?"

"I'm dying!"

"I doubt that. You're quite obnoxious, you know."

"I would have stopped," he said, gingerly sitting upright. "This seduction technique has often worked in the past. Many women have fantasies of making it with strong, primitive men."

"This one doesn't, I can assure you of that. You mean women have permitted you to paw and slobber on them like that?"

"Certainly."

"Name one."

"Gilboa McComb. Yesterday at two o'clock."

"You raped Gilboa?"

"I had sex with her."

"Did you use a condom?"

"Of course, Cara. I may be primitive, but I'm not reckless."

Hamler removed his hands from beneath his loincloth and gazed at me.

"What are you looking at?"

"You look extremely silly in that ridiculous bathing suit, Cara. Silly but sexy."

"You look quite absurd in that repulsive loincloth, Hamler. I only followed you here because I was hungry."

"Now I'll have to seduce you the hard way—with my charm."

"Yes, I can see how for you that would be a nearly insurmountable challenge."

Then, to make matters worse, the uncouth youth broke into song:

When a man retreats
    From the city streets
And ventures back to nature,
    His mind is freed
    So he has no need
For an urban nomenclature.

*I hunt, I grunt,*
    *I prowl, I growl,*
*I trap, I yap*
    *In a patois unrefinéd.*

When a man discards
    Society's shards

And shrinks from civilization,
   Hygiene drains
   And etiquette wanes
From rapid trivialization.

*I catch, I scratch,*
   *I sneak, I reek,*
   *I snare, I bare*
   *A nudity undisguiséd.*

Though a man recoils
   From the polite turmoils
Of love's gentle blushing,
   He may not purge
   A baser urge
To mate with lustful rushing.

*I spear, I leer,*
   *I lurk, I smirk,*
   *I trail, I wail*
   *Of an ardor unrestrainéd!*

"Good grief," I exclaimed, heading toward the door. "Let me out of here!"

❊ ❊ ❊

Good news, voters. It's time for another twins conversation:
Howard is the toast of the island!

He's been personally congratulated by Essex Kennard, who invited him to sit next to him at the gala Saturday night barbecue.

Where he dined, like the rest of us, on one blackened hotdog and an ice-cream scoop of warm potato salad. Thankfully, you had provided us with some fish, Cara, so starvation was momentarily averted.

Howard has succeeded where teams of political staffers laboring around the clock had failed. He's created the slogan for the fall campaign.

This latest triumph came on top of winning all three hotly contested chess matches against Forest this afternoon. That boy is still sulking.

Howard's slogan is a masterpiece of brevity. They wanted something that conveyed Gov. Flunch's extensive business experience and his zealous commitment to remaking government according to his Republican ideals.

Howard's brilliant synthesis: "Your Change Is in the Bag."

Actually, he proposed "Your Change Is in the Bag, Amen," but Essex Kennard edited it slightly. Howard says the famed strategist is a fascinating man who knows everybody in Washington and is full of stories about the latest political intrigues. By the way, you appeared to be fascinated by your dinner mate as well, Toni.

Monty Bellefontaine was telling me about his exploits in Bosnia and Oklahoma City. He's a fearless reporter, Cara. The man has ice water in his veins.

Is that why he is never seen without that tan trench coat?

He has to wear it, Cara, even in the stifling Michigan heat. A million dollars in cash is sewn into the lining for his expenses. Besides, I heard a rumor it's bulletproof. Monty says Howard's success is making us look very good, Cara. After all, he is our protegee.

And they loved our performance after dinner, Toni. Especially your rendition of "If I Give My Heart to You." And Renk's whistling was a complete sensation. Another point in our favor.

Forest was surprisingly competent on the saxophone, but I thought the erotic imagery in Dola's poetry was pretty pedestrian.

Yes, I noticed Howard squirming through most of it. What tune did Forest play?

"Body and Soul," I think. What did you think of Hamler's magic act, Cara?

Well, I liked his finale where he pulled six yards of dental floss out of his ear. Poor Mindy. Too bad she kept dropping her baton.

Mindy has always been weak in the talent area, Cara. It was her Achilles' heel in Atlantic City—that and her crummy artificial looks. I'm surprised the pageant officials there still permit baton twirling. It's so passe.

She wasn't helped tonight by Fawn and Colt running out and trying to grab her baton. It disrupted her concentration.

I know, Cara. We should have done a better job keeping those twins restrained. I don't know why Mindy entrusted them to us in the first place.

Everyone else refused, Toni. Still, I feel terrible.

Yeah, I'm riddled with guilt. So what's with you and Renk?

What?

You and Romeo of the Western Plains. I thought you didn't like him that much?

I don't know . . . islands are so romantic. It's something in the air.

You're warming up to him, huh?

Sort of. Ever since he took his clothes off on the beach last night, my feelings have changed. It seems like he's let his guard down. He's more accessible.

That is the compelling appeal of nudity, Cara mia. It's a marvelous aid to accessibility.

*Chapter 9*

Except for the red glow of a digital clock, the small room was entirely dark.

"Who's there?" a sleepy voice asked. "Is that you, Howard?"

"It's me, Forest," I replied, feeling my way toward the bed. "Cara."

"Oh, hi, Cara. Are you looking for Renk's room?"

"Not particularly."

"Oh. . . Here, let me turn on the light."

"That's not necessary. I prefer the dark."

"Oh." Another pregnant silence. "Uh, how may I assist you?"

"Forest, when a girl enters a boy's room at night, she expects that her intentions will be discerned with a minimum of controversy."

"Oh."

"Would you like me to leave?"

"Not at all. Come, sit on the bed. You've taken me by surprise."

"Push over, Forest. These beds are very narrow."

"Cara, you have removed your robe. And your nightgown!"

"Nice of you to notice, Forest. You may remove your elaborate sleeping apparel if the mood strikes you."

"OK," he whispered, "but we'll have to be quiet. There's very little soundproofing in these walls."

"Forest, what are you doing?"

"Unbuttoning my pajamas."

"What's that horribly obscene sound?"

"That's Mr. Tiro under the bed. I expect he's cleaning his bum."

"Oh. Why did you ask if I were Howard? Were you expecting him?"

"Not at all. I thought perhaps he couldn't sleep and wanted to play another game of chess. You have taken me quite by surprise, Cara. I thought you liked Renk."

"He's OK. He's a nice boy, but young."

"I had no idea you liked me."

"I had very little indication that you liked me, Forest. Do you?"

"Why, yes."

"In that case, feel free to touch me."

"All right."

"What do you think of my sister?"

"Toni? Oh, I think she's quite opinionated."

"In an objectionable way?"

"Sometimes. I prefer your quiet dignity, Cara."

"Really? What do you think of her singing?"

"Well, she's no Doris Day."

"No, she isn't, I suppose."

"I like your accordion playing better, Cara."

"Thank you, Forest. You're a first-rate saxophone player."

"I'm adequate. My intensity of expression is weak. Columbus attributes it to my being a white upper-class Republican. Cara, I have no condoms."

"Relax. I have some in the pocket of my robe. So you don't like Toni's singing?"

"I didn't say that. She's very expressive. And she generally sings in tune. That distinguishes her from the great mass of popular vocalists. Cara, you do that so well."

"You kiss like a Boy Scout, Forest. Hmmm, that's better."

* * *

Thirty-one minutes later by the clock.

"That was marvelous, Cara."

"I hope we didn't disturb Mr. Tiro."

"He seems to be resting peacefully. Is my arm hurting you?"

"No, it's fine. So tell me about your uncle."

"What?"

"Your uncle Maximo. Tell me about him. Renk says he's rumored to be hiding out in the Flunch forests of the Upper Peninsula. They say he's leading a band of revolutionary militia gun fanatics."

"That's absurd, Cara. Uncle Max simply likes to tramp through the woods on weekends with his hunting buddies."

"Is he up there now?"

"I have no idea. I haven't seen him since Dad was nominated."

"What's he like?"

"Maximo is the elder son, Cara. All the firstborn Flunch men are difficult, Hamler being only the latest example of this phenomenon. Dad is the second son, and so was Foraker, the inventor. The second sons are the reliable, intelligent ones. Uncle Max has always imagined himself a romantic figure, a 20th century knight if you will. He's never been interested in the paper business, and just flits about spending his inheritance and striking heroic poses. He's a pretty dull fellow after you become inured to the bombast."

"Could he be lying low on the island?"

"I doubt it. Keeping a low profile is not his style. And why this dogged interest in my uncle?"

"Just idle curiosity. You have a fascinating family."

"Thanks. Now I have a question for you about Howard."

"The answer is yes."

"Then he has played chess competitively?"

"What?"

"I want to know if Howard is a ranked chess player. Does he compete in tournaments?"

"I don't think so, Forest. Renk says he just took up the game last month."

"Damn! He must be a natural prodigy. I've been playing since I was nine, and he whipped me three straight games."

"I'm sure it's just a case of beginner's luck. Uh-oh, Forest," I whispered, "someone opened the door!"

"Who's there?" called Forest.

"It's me. Howard."

"Oh, hello, Howard. I have someone here with me."

"Who?"

I shook my head.

"The person declines to be identified."

"OK, Foliage. I was just restless. Thought you might be up for a game of chess."

"Sounds great. How about tomorrow?"

"Fine. Sorry to disturb you. Well, good night."

"Good night."

The door closed.

"You seem to be very popular this evening, Forest. Perhaps your saxophone playing is more expressive than you imagine."

* * *

OK, let's make one thing perfectly clear. When I slipped into Forest Flunch's room, I wasn't actually planning on making it with the guy. I don't even like him. I certainly don't find him attractive. No way is he my type. I was just intending to ask him some questions. But his supercilious attitude was so irritating, I felt an obligation to prove to the pedant that he wasn't as aloof and superior as he pretends to be. And don't think the fact that I had a marginally satisfactory time makes me any more kindly disposed toward the creep. Sometimes for the greater good a girl has to do things she'd rather not. And don't go striking any moral poses either. It's not like I was using the guy. He is a teenage boy after all, and let's face it, even the ones trying to play it cool can always use a little relief in that department. You can tell from their body language—all that leg twitching and crotch scratching. Boys Forest's age are drooling beasts, the lowest rung on the sexual food chain. OK, that's a broad generalization, but don't kid yourself—it's true. At least Forest doesn't have a clue who he actually slept with. Thank God I'm spared that mortification at least.

\* \* \*

Howard dressed us for church Sunday morning in rosebud-print pinafores with Peter Pan collars and Captain Kangaroo pockets. At 8 a.m. we were served bowls of mucilaginous oatmeal on the lawn beside the main house, and Dad preached a sermon from the deck titled "Why a Carpenter from Nazareth Would Vote the Straight Republican Ticket." Then Essex Kennard passed out official "Your Change Is in the Bag" buttons that had been stamped out overnight in Detroit and fl own to the island by Kent Stow. Next, Mrs. Flunch sang several Methodist hymns in a high raspy voice, accompanied by Cara on the accordion. After that, the congregation filed by the deck and received paper cups of coffee and small sticky buns from Columbus.

"Did you see that?" I said, downing my bun in four famished bites.

"See what?" asked Cara, sipping her acrid beverage.

"Lima Flunch took three sticky buns from the basket and sneaked them to Hamler."

"Mom's always doing stuff like that," said Dola. "Hamler's her favorite. He wraps her around his little finger."

"We'll just see about that," I said.

I took my coffee and followed the loinclothed youth around the north side of the house.

"Hey, Hamler," I called, "wait up."

"Hello, Cara," he said.

"It's not Cara. It's Toni."

"Follow me to woods, woman."

"Cut the crap, Hamler. I got the whole story on you yesterday from my sister."

"Damn. You people are interfering with my efforts to sustain a serious performance work."

"Too bad, Hambone. Hey, I'll take one of those sticky buns."

"You had yours already. Why should I give you one of mine?"

"Because if you don't, I'll tell your mother who tried to rape her favorite minister's daughter."

Hamler handed me the smallest of his three pastries.

"Thanks. Let's go have a chat under that tree."

We sat on a fallen log overlooking the sun-glazed lake.

"I'm going to seduce you too," he announced, scratching something under a flap. "In some ways, you're more attractive than your sister. I have a feeling I wouldn't be your first."

"My first Neanderthal, at any rate. Sorry, Hamler, I like guys who bathe."

"I swim three miles every day in the lake."

"Well maybe you should skip the post-swim wallow in the dirt. Hamler, I'm looking for your uncle Maximo."

"Why? He bathes even less frequently than I do."

"Where is he?"

"I haven't seen him."

"Do you know where he might be?"

"Haven't the foggiest. I'm more interested in tracking the movements of sexy babes. I'm going to be keeping my eye on you, Toni."

"Just keep everything else to yourself. What can you tell me about your uncle?"

"Uncle Max is Dad's older brother. All the firstborn Flunch men are brilliant—a radiant incandescence that flames only once every generation. Succeeding sons are plodding, turgid fellows like Forest. Max is a born leader of men, with intense personal magnetism—traits you may have already noticed in me."

"Right. So let me get this straight: Your uncle, your father's only brother, is leading his own private army up in the woods."

"Is he? I hadn't heard that."

"If Maximo were on the island, where would he be?"

"Most likely in your bed, Toni. Assuming he could fight his way past me."

* * *

Itching oddly after my interview with Hamler, I took a wrong turn on a path and ran into Mindy garbed for the beach. Her skimpy teal bikini was fastened with many dangling ties, perhaps designed to intrigue passing bondage fetishists. Her breasts kaboomed out from her rib-cage like two termite mounds on the Serengeti Plain. I can't believe men lust after something so transparently artificial. They resemble actual breasts like a $9.95 CrumpPak housedress resembles a Chanel suit.

"Which one are you?" she demanded, pausing and straightening a strap.

"I'm Toni, your special favorite," I replied, beaming.

"Toni, your father and I don't want you talking to the press. You are not authorized to give interviews. If I had my way, you wouldn't be here at all."

My eyes kept straying to her chest. Of course, they are rather fascinating. I found myself wanting to reach out and give one a squeeze. Now I know how those aforementioned teenage boys must feel.

"And what am I authorized to do, Mindy?" I asked, still maintaining my politely perky smile.

"You are here to demonstrate our commitment to the family. You and your sister are to remain discreetly in the background, say nothing, and gaze respectfully toward your father at public gatherings."

"Even when he's wearing black socks with Bermuda shorts?"

"Your father is a minister of the church, Toni. Try to remember that."

As if I could ever forget.

* * *

Twin sisters can always find each other. It must be our inborn radar.

There you are, Toni. I've got some tremendous news. I just called home and Special Agent Ken Tompkins answered. Guess where Mother is?

Volunteering at a Greer for President rally?

No, silly. She's in Toronto. She went there for the weekend with Special Agent Pulaski!

Really, Cara? But let's not jump to hasty conclusions. There could be some other explanation.

I doubt it, Toni. It sounds like love to me. I told you Troy wasn't married.

We don't know that for certain, Cara. Maybe they went with his wife— just the three of them.

Now you are being ridiculous, Toni. I tell you it's love! Which reminds me. Forest Flunch has been acting most peculiar this morning.

How so?

First he smiled at me all through Father's sermon. I thought perhaps he was experiencing some sort of religious revelation. Then on the way back to the laboratory to change into our swimsuits, he patted me in an unexpectedly intimate way. I was shocked.

Did Renk see him?

No, fortunately. Renk was engaged in another difficult phone conversation with his parents. They're disturbed about some reports on CNN concerning Governor Flunch's brother. It was all Renk could do to calm them down. Liberal parents are fine until you start challenging their cherished left-wing dogma.

Maybe Forest likes you, Cara.

Do you think so? He's very attractive. This is so confusing. I was just warming up to Renk too. Are you coming swimming with us, Toni?

In a minute. You guys go ahead. I'll catch up later.

* * *

Lurking behind the storage shack on the boat dock was Monty Bellefontaine. He was pacing back and forth in his trench coat and smoking one of his famous little cigars. A small speck of egg glistened on his pencil-thin Douglas Fairbanks mustache. He was wearing more makeup than I usually find attractive on men, but I knew that at any moment a sudden scoop could send him dashing in front of an unforgiving camera.

"Hello, Toni. You're right on time. Did you get any information?"

"Not much, Monty. All the Flunches seem to have acquired bad cases of amnesia about their uncle Max. No one has seen him or knows where he is—or so they claim."

"Damn. He must be on the island. This is the logical place to hide someone. Access is completely restricted."

"I have a few more ideas, Monty. Let me follow them up. I'll get back to you."

"I appreciate your efforts, Toni. And so does Ted."

"Thanks, Monty. That means a lot coming from you. Do you really think this Uncle Maximo angle is a big story?"

"The biggest, Toni. It could blow the whole election sky high."

I winked at him. "Then just call me dynamite."

Monty tossed his cigar in the lake and gave me an affectionate hug. As he pressed me to his chest, the cash in his lining crinkled erotically against my breasts. He gazed down at me and smiled. I smiled back and wondered if the camera really demanded eyeliner in such Elvis-like proportions.

\* \* \*

Toni, Dola, and I enjoyed another leisurely swim at our private beach, while Howard beat Forest mercilessly at chess, and Renk reclined on his towel in the sun and wrestled with his conscience. I hope parental pressure does not spoil this summer idyll for him. We waved as the Coast Guard cutter motored past on patrol. Then Hamler cruised by in his sailboat with Gilboa McComb, who shockingly had removed her swimsuit top.

"She's got very nice ones," announced Dola, shading her eyes with her hand.

"Too bad her Sunday school class isn't here," said Toni. "I understand she's very active in youth outreach work."

"Looks like she's reaching out for my brother," said Dola. "In a big way."

After our swim we spread our towels beside the boys and watched the game.

"How did you sleep last night, Cara?" asked our Fashion Czar.

"Very well, Howard. Moments after my head hit the pillow I dozed off in a deep, satisfying slumber."

"And how did you sleep, Toni?"

"Extremely well, Howard. Unlike my insomniac sister, I was asleep even before my head hit the pillow. I slept soundly throughout the night."

"You did not get up and venture out of your room?"

"Not to my knowledge. And there is no history of sleepwalking in our family. Why do you ask?"

"Oh, no special reason."

"Howie," said Dola, "how come you don't ask me how I slept?"

"I know you slept well, love. I could hear your snoring from across the hall."

"That's a lie. I was awake all night, pining for you."

"If you don't mind, Howard," said Forest testily, "could you at least pretend to devote some of your prodigious intellect to this game?"

"Sorry, Woodlot," he replied, casually moving a knight and neatly pinning Forest's queen and king. "Check."

Forest sighed and tipped over his king.

"Why not play for a draw?" asked Dola.

"That's like asking Adolph Hitler why he didn't stop with Czechoslovakia," replied Forest.

"Your brother is out for world domination," explained Howard. "It seems to be a fetish with you Flunches."

\* \* \*

A shocking development! Thom Kirkwood has been detained by the Coast Guard, who alertly thwarted my ex-boyfriend's attempted assault by rented jet skis on our island sanctuary. While we were eating lunch (grilled cheese sandwich, one ripe banana, and cup of Tang), the cutter docked at the pier and turned over its captive to the Secret Service for interrogation. Four special agents with guns drawn hustled the soggy, handcuffed prisoner up the hill to the laboratory. I at once recognized his bulked-up physique and minimalist swim attire.

"Miss Mason, this trespasser claims to know you," said Special Agent Smyrna Bradford.

"Hello, Thom," I said coldly.

"Toni, I had to see you! I went AWOL from football practice. Coach Granger is going to have my ass!"

"He's welcome to it. Thom, you shouldn't have come here."

"Toni, you're my girl! I want to invite you to the homecoming dance."

"Thom, that's not for months. You could have been shot."

"I want you, Toni. I need you. I know you don't really like that twerp."

Howard bristled. "You wouldn't say that if four large agents with guns weren't protecting you."

Thom lunged for our Fashion Czar. "Hey, guy! I'll take you on handcuffed and blindfolded!"

"That's enough," warned Smyrna, restraining him. "So you know this person, Miss Mason?"

"Yes," I confessed, "I used to go out with him."

"Did you invite him to the island?"

"Certainly not."

"Do you wish to press charges against him?" asked another agent.

"No, just make him leave."

"Toni, you're being awfully heartless," said Cara. "Thom came all this way to see you. He crossed 17 miles of lake on jet skis. That had to be a treacherous journey, even on a calm day like today."

"I want to be with you, Toni!" implored the prisoner.

"Thom, we have nothing to say."

"Just let me stay here," pleaded Thom. "I won't bother you. Or that twerp. I promise! I'll sleep outside on the grass. I'll pay for my food. I'll even work!"

"What did you say?" piped Forest.

"I said I'd work," admitted Thom.

"You're in luck," Forest replied. "At the moment we've got an acute manpower shortage in the kitchen. Are you willing to wash dishes?"

"Just lead me to them!"

"OK, officers," said Forest, "I'll vouch for this person. You can take him over to the house and introduce him to Mrs. Flunch as the new dishwasher."

The agents exchanged glances, shrugged, and began to remove Thom's handcuffs.

"No, leave those on until he meets Mother," said Forest. "It will make a better impression. She puts a high premium on docility among her workers."

"This is exciting," bubbled Dola. "Another cute boy on the island and a blood feud brewing with Howard. Toni, are you sure you don't want Thom?"

"He's yours, Dola."

"He won't be sticking around long," said Howard. "I've seen that dishroom. It's 112° in there, grease-encrusted dishes are stacked to the ceiling, it's crawling with flies, and under the vile-smelling sink burns a perpetual propane flame. The dishwater is scalding!"

※ ※ ※

As we were helping Columbus clean up after lunch, Essex Kennard strolled over the hill from the house in the largest pair of plaid Bermuda shorts I'd ever seen. He's a stout man with a graying beard and enormous bags under his eyes as if his face were melting. He smokes continuously and huffs painfully when he walks. He invited Howard and Renk to an afternoon strategy meeting, so Toni suggested the rest of us explore "the mysteries of Bag Island." Dola excused herself to go spy on the dishwasher at work.

Before commencing our trek, we applied a thick layer of sun block and borrowed a basket from Columbus in case we encountered edible berries. Forest led our party of three north toward the highest area of the island. We followed a well-worn path through green groves of towering pines. While pointing out the sights, our guide touched me occasionally on my bare, oily elbow in his new familiar way.

"Here's the old water supply cistern," said Forest, hiking toward a large, moss-covered cedar tank on a terrace cut into the slope. "It's empty now, of course. We have a deep-water well with a jet turbine pump. Hamler hopes to turn the old tank into the world's largest hot tub. He thinks he could get naked with at least 20 girls in there."

"Could someone live in this tank?" asked Toni, inspecting it closely.

"They could if they were a slug," said Forest. "Inside there's a two-inch layer of green slime on the walls."

Farther on we came to a tall aluminum mast, triangular in cross-section and tapering as it rose dizzyingly into the blue sky. Perched at the top was a tiny plywood room.

"My grandfather Deshler Flunch erected this TV tower in 1949," explained Forest. "He was trying to pick up the Friday night fights from Detroit. Unfortunately, the picture was too snowy to see much. Now we have a satellite dish. Mom's a big fan of professional wrestling."

"Yes, I read that in *Parade* magazine," I said.

"What's in that little shack up there?" asked Toni.

"Just some old tube electronics stuff and Hamler's toy binoculars."

"Could we go up there?" asked Toni.

"It's not safe any more," said Forest. "We used to climb up years ago, but the guy-wires are rusting out. It'll blow over in a storm one of these days."

"I'm going up," announced Toni, gripping the ladder and starting to climb.

"Toni, don't!" I shouted.

"Come down, Toni!" called Forest.

Hand over hand, my sister continued to climb, the skirt of her bathing suit fluttering in the breeze.

"Forest, you've got to stop her!" I cried.

"There's nothing I can do," he said, putting his arm around me. "The tower won't support two."

I struggled to control my panic. The tower groaned and swayed in a sudden gust. Far overhead my sister pushed open a hatch and disappeared into the plywood structure.

"Come down, Toni!" I pleaded.

At last, her legs reappeared on the ladder and she began the slow descent. I held my breath as, rung by rung, she made her way down.

"Toni, you gave us a terrible fright!" I exclaimed, as my sister hopped nonchalantly off the ladder and brushed off her hands.

"Oh, did I? Sorry. It's really disgusting up there. The bats have moved in *en masse*."

"Why did you go up there?" I demanded.

"Just to look around. I saw some interesting things too."

"What?" I asked.

"Well, over there by a small brick building Hamler and Gilboa are sunbathing in the buff."

"That must be the old steam plant," I said.

"That's right," said Forest. "Hamler's homesteading it as his trysting pad."

What else did you see?"

"I saw a ship!" Toni replied.

"A ship on the lake?" I asked.

"No, a ship on this hill. Under the trees!"

We both stared at Forest.

"That would be the Battleship Flunch," he said. "It's our destination this afternoon, ladies. All the visitors to Bag Island want to see it."

\* \* \*

As big as a house, with its faded battleship-gray paint starting to peel, the Battleship Flunch was moored in a meadow overlooking the lake. Its mighty guns pointed toward distant Wisconsin—oblivious to the enemy ivy creeping silently up from below. Dry leaves littered its high decks and an opportunistic aspen was sprouting from a forward gun turret.

"It's amazing," I exclaimed.

"It's weird," said Toni. "It's like a folly."

"It's Uncle Max's folly," said Forest. "When he hit middle age, he went through a rare period of introspection and decided what he really wanted in life was to own guns, shoot game, and build a model of a World War II battleship. Unlike the great lot of humankind, my uncle has realized all of his aspirations."

"What's it made from?" I asked, running my fingers over the coarse surface of the curving hull.

"Stucco over chicken wire nailed to a pine and spruce frame. It's built to 1/18th scale. The guns are iron pipe, the portholes are the bottoms of baby food jars. Back then, infant Hamler was eating strained peas by the carload."

"Your uncle built it himself?" asked Toni.

"Not hardly. Uncle Max supervised. He hired high-school kids from Petoskey for the labor. Took them four summers to build it. The local newspaper heard about it, and sent over a reporter to check it out. Uncle Max shot him."

"Did he die?" I asked.

"No, he recovered, but the paper still holds a grudge against our family. They've never endorsed my dad in any of his political races."

"Was your uncle prosecuted?" I asked.

"Of course not," said Forest. "We own this entire island, all 328 acres. It was an obvious case of trespass."

"Oh, look," said Toni, walking around the great prow. "There are windows on the other side. And a door!"

Forest and I made our way through the tangled undergrowth to the starboard side. Under a rickety porch roof, my sister was peering in through a crumbling window.

"There's a pinball machine in there," she called. "And a bar!"

Forest lifted the rusty latch and forced open the small door; we followed our host into the musty interior. As my eyes became accustomed to the gloom, I could make out dusty tables and chairs, a decrepit pool table, a gangrenous refrigerator with its door ajar, and an ornately carved bar inset with grimy rose-tinted mirrors. Small circles of light glowed high up the wall from rows of tiny portholes. Arrayed along the wood-paneled wall under the portholes were decaying stuffed animal heads, mounted sport fish, and a large dartboard with a rusty ax stuck in it.

Toni spronged the broken pinball plunger. On the faded pinball backboard silkscreened biplanes harried a Zeppelin placidly bombing London. "Looks like the party's over," she said, wiping her hands. "What happened?"

"Uncle Max gave up trying to keep the rain out," said Forest. "This was his personal retreat for entertaining his buddies, but there's no real roof on the structure. Winter ice cracked the stucco, then the frame started to rot."

At that moment a sound like a door slamming was heard overhead.

"Somebody's up there," whispered Toni.

"I don't think so," said Forest. "It's just the wind."

A ceiling board creaked.

"How do you get up there?" demanded Toni.

"The stairs are behind the refrigerator," sighed Forest, leading the way. "I should caution you there are no windows up there, just the little portholes. It's a big unfinished space—full of hornets nests and spiders."

Toni gulped and peered up the narrow, dark staircase. "You first, Forest. You're the guy."

"No, thanks. I'm staying right here. Have fun, you two."

"Come on, Cara," said Toni, taking my hand.

I pulled back. "Toni, let's at least go back for a flashlight."

"No, Cara. They might leave. Come on!"

Sighing, I followed my reckless sister up the dusty, creaking stairs. Somewhere very close I heard what sounded like an owl hooting or a rapist sniffling. Toni paused at the top of the stairs; I crept up close behind her. I could make out a dim network of wooden beams far over head, illuminated by amber porthole moons and tiny stars of daylight blazing through perforations in the stucco skin. I touched my sister's arm; she started, then clutched at me.

"Hello!" called my sister. "Maximo Flunch, are you here? We'd like to speak with you."

No reply. Water dripped, winds moaned.

"Let's go back, Toni," I whispered. "Please!"

Toni edged out from the stairs; I followed behind like the coal-tender on a steam locomotive.

"Yoo-hoo, Mr. Flunch," called Toni, shuffling forward into the profound gloom. "We'd just like to talk to you for a moment. We're Republicans too. And gun aficionados."

"We love your battleship," I lied, puzzled why my sister was so determined to meet up with Forest's elusive uncle.

A board creaked in the distance. Toni madly altered coarse toward the sound. I clung to her waist and closed my eyes. Toni ducked under a beam, pushed open a door, a figure rushed out of the darkness, knocked us away, and lurched toward the stairs. I fell against a filmy material and felt something cold and bristly crawling on my arm. I screamed. A many-winged flapping blackness fluttered close by our heads. Toni screamed. I screamed. Forest rushed up the stairs and pulled us to our feet. Somehow we made it down the stairs and out of the building and into the blinding sunshine.

"Who was it, Forest?" demanded Toni, desperately pulling cobwebs from her face and hair. "Who was it?"

"Who was who?" he asked, calmly closing the door.

"You saw him," insisted Toni. "Who was it? Was it your uncle Max?"

"I didn't see anybody," said Forest. "I was outside taking a leak. Why? Was there someone in there?"

"You're lying, Forest Flunch!" declared my sister. "You're lying and I'm going to discover the reason why."

"Fine," said Forest, unconcerned. "Clue me in when you find out."

\* \* \*

The following twins conversation took place shoulder deep in North America's second-largest freshwater lake:

Cara, I'm glad this water is so murky. As long as we stay out here our horrible bathing suits are completely hidden.

Toni, something's bothering me.

I know what you mean, Cara. Just try to think of the muck oozing between your toes as soft silt and not slimy, disgusting mud.

Toni, why are you hunting for Maximo Flunch?

Who says I'm looking for him? I don't even know the man.

Toni, I know you're up to something. I think you should stop. I don't think all this media controversy about Governor Flunch's brother is at all helpful to Father's campaign.

Of course it's not, Cara. That's why we have to get it out into the open as soon as possible.

What do you mean?

Cara, American voters have very short memories. If Claude's brother is involved in any shenanigans, it should come out now. That way, people will have forgotten all about it by election day.

You really think so, Toni?

Of course. Cover-ups always end disastrously—except for Iran-Contra and they only got away with that because everyone felt so sorry for poor, addled President Reagan. Cara, it's our duty to find Max and expose him, warts and all.

You're not just doing this because you're stuck on Monty?

Of course not, silly. I'm doing it for Father. You know that.

My sister sighed pensively and adjusted a strap.

Toni, maybe we should ask Renk's opinion on this. Or Forest's.

No way, Cara. We've got to keep our involvement in this affair a secret.

But why?

Maximo's men, Cara mia. Monty tells me they're absolutely ruthless.

You mean . . . we could be in danger?

Not if we're careful. Just leave everything to me. And promise me you won't breathe a word of this to anyone.

Oh, all right. But you have to promise me something too.

OK, I promise not to sleep with Monty.

Good, that's a relief.

Cara, I hope after Renk finally seduces you that you cease to be such a prude. I can't believe we have exactly the same genes.

*Chapter 10*

"They've got the fall campaign all plotted out," said Howard, picking at a tiny lambchop bone.

We were dining outdoors on the deck on Flunch family china. Arranged on real dishes the child-sized portions seemed almost plausible—like those dainty entrees served at trendy restaurants.

"They're going to make Greer look like the Antichrist," said Renk despondently. "They're planning to play the race card, the anti-immigrant card, the anti-welfare card, the family values card, the crime card, the anti-homosexual card, and a host of others."

"Sounds like we'll be playing with a full deck," I said brightly.

"Essex Kennard is writing some devastating campaign commercials," said Howard. "We're going negative from day one."

"Uh-oh," hissed Renk, "here comes the future First Lady."

"Antonia, Carissa," said Mrs. Flunch, smiling graciously as she approached, "I'm scheduling you after the baton-twirling tonight. Mindy says your performance makes her nervous. Forest has had to cancel his saxophone solo, but Dola has some new poems, and we have a surprise finale I think you'll all enjoy. Antonia, I'm receiving positive reports from the kitchen about your friend. Thank you for recommending him. In the future, though, you might suggest to him that he not appear at job interviews in swim attire. A nice jacket and tie would be more appropriate, even for a minimum-wage position. In normal circumstances, I might have selected another candidate more suitably dressed."

"I'll mention that to Thom, Mrs. Flunch," I replied. "By the way, how does one go about obtaining seconds of these lovely lambchops?"

"Why, Toni, I'm surprised at you," smiled Mrs. Flunch, clearly shocked. "Girls of your age should be more interested in impressing the young men with your birdlike appetites."

To our distress, she felt the need to express this musically:

> If a husband you hope to entwine,
>   You must curb your gluttonous urges;
> Nibble lightly and delicately dine,
>   Do not indulge in caloric splurges.
>
> Avoid all starches, eschew all sweets,
>   Rich foods your diet should be lacking;
> Eat portions small of the leanest meats,
>   And refrain from excessive snacking.
>
> Save your lips for kisses, avoid those blisses
>   Associated with epicurism,
> For girdles, loose dresses, and such artifices,
>   Cannot disguise a lost feminism.
>
> Heed not those clamoring pangs,
>   That rise from regions alimentary;
> Yield only to those heartfelt clangs
>   That lead on to vows nuptuary!

"But I'm only 15," I pointed out. "I don't want a husband. I want a lambchop."

Her jaw set in a grim smile, Mrs. Flunch ignored me and moved on to the next table.

"Fat selfish cow," I muttered. "And look at the boring husband she entwined."

* * *

The "surprise finale" to the evening's entertainment was a wrestling match in the grass between Hamler Flunch and Thom Kirkwood. My ex-boyfriend, still garbed in his arrival Speedos, was escorted from the dish room by Columbus and made to remove his greasy apron and rubber gloves. The combatants circled each other in their bare feet, then grappled and grunted as the audience howled. Mrs. Flunch cheered loudest of all, lustily shouting encouragements to her firstborn son. The burly youths, evenly matched in size and oafishness, gripped and pulled, slapped and gouged, strained and heaved, tumbled and rolled, then broke free, leaped to their feet, and lunged at each other anew. Again and again they tripped and scrambled across the grass. At last, a panting Hamler locked an arm around Thom's neck, pushed his face into the ground, then rolled him on his back, and pinned his shoulders against the turf. The crowd roared. Score: Ruling Class: 1, Proletariat: 0.

Mrs. Flunch clapped wildly, Cara and I sighed in disappointment, Gilboa McComb rushed out and kissed the victor, the weary combatants shook hands, and Thom plodded back to the dish room to resume his monumental task.

OK, I admit it. I feel a little sorry for the lug. Maybe I'll reconsider his invitation to the homecoming dance.

※ ※ ※

Another night. Another adventure groping about in the dark.

"Who's there?"

"It's me, Thom. Toni."

"Toni, darling, I knew you would come!"

"Don't jump to conclusions, Thom. And don't paw at me. I only dropped by to ask if you'd seen my sister."

"I want to see you, Toni," he said, switching on a lamp. "And hold you!"

"I know what you want to hold. Why aren't you sleeping in the kitchen?"

"The accommodations are full up over there. Besides, I wanted to be close to you."

"Forget it, Thom. How's your job?"

"Terrible. But the guys in the kitchen are OK. You can't imagine the working conditions over there. Here, I sneaked you out a couple of left-over lambchops."

"Thank you, Thom! I'm famished as usual."

"I ran into that Howard twink in the bathroom, Toni honey. He loaned me a toothbrush—not his, he had an extra one. I was nice to him and didn't pound his puny ass."

"I appreciate your sacrifice, Thom. I'm sorry you had to fight Hamler."

"I enjoyed it, Toni. We have a rematch tomorrow. I think I can take that dude. Just think, I'm wrestling the son of a guy who might be elected President. He's going to show me how to make one of those neat loincloths. Kiss me, babe."

"Sorry, Thom. Duty calls. Thanks for the chops."

"I like you a lot, gal."

"Keep up the good work, Thom."

※ ※ ※

"At last I found you, Toni," said Cara, clutching her fuzzy robe and hurrying toward me from the other end of the dimly lit hallway. "Where have you been? Who were you visiting in the Herbert Hoover room? And what's in that bag?"

"Uh, it's Thom's room. I was just tucking the boy in. He's quite exhausted. And these are his socks. I said I would launder them."

"That's odd, Toni. Thom wasn't wearing socks when he arrived. The bag appears to be grease stained. And I detect the distinct aroma of rosemary-braised lambchops."

"OK, you win. I'll share. Why were you looking for me?"

"Oh, you have a phone call. Long distance!"

\* \* \*

Ma Bell herself might have once placed a call in the ancient oaken phone booth.

"Hello, this is Toni."

"Hello, Toni," said a faint but hearty voice. The line crackled with static. "Maximo Flunch here. I was talking to my baby brother Claude this evening, and he mentioned you were asking for me. What can I do for you, little lady?"

"Mr. Flunch! Where are you? Everyone's looking for you."

"Call me Max, Toni. Press have their tits in a wringer again, do they? Well, just between you and me and the bartender here, I'm down in sunny Montevideo, Uruguay on a little secret mission."

"What kind of mission, Max?"

"Hell, it wouldn't be much of a secret if I told you!"

"You can trust me, Max. My father is Senator Horace B. Mason."

"Never had much use for preachers. Always skittish in the woods and a guaranteed downer on a booze barge."

"Max, we're on the same team. You can tell me."

"Have to tell someone, girlie. I'm 'bout to bust my britches with excitement. I just bought me a battleship."

"You what?"

"I bought a battleship, all 52,314 metric tons of her. *The Fructuoso Rivera*, 879 feet of fighting warship. Pride of the Uruguayan fleet 'til the bozo brass at the top let 'em run an honest election. Their new tin-pot president is selling her off to build schools for bare-assed peasant brats."

"And you bought it?"

"Wrote out the check yesterday. Bought me the fanciest gunboat on the block. Originally the *San Cristobal*, built in Madrid back in '51 for Franco's navy. With a suite for the dictator himself paneled in satinwood and Madagascar monkey wood. Gold-plated seat in the head for the Generalissimo's well-kissed behind. Armor plating fourteen inches thick at the water line. Whole batteries of five-inch antiaircraft cannon. And the sweetest sixteen-inch guns that could blast that damn Indian right off the Capitol dome from Baltimore harbor. The Uruguayans spent a fortune refitting and modernizing her in '78. Now I'm picking her up for a song—less than scrap value, not that I'll ever let 'em break her up. She's my baby now, Toni."

"What are you going to do with your, uh, baby?"

"Sail her straight up the coast and down the St. Lawrence Seaway. Me and my shooting buddies. Anchor her right beside my dock at Bag Island. Anybody wants to say something about it, they'll have to look down the barrels of my sweet sixteens. I got my Second Amendment rights. You savvy, chiquita?"

"Right, Max. It sounds like quite the boat. How's the roof?"

"Not a leak on her. I double-checked that. Four galleys and twenty-eight tons of refrigeration for the potted shrimp too. Quite the party barge. Well, got to go, missy. I'll give you a tour in six weeks or so. Now no reckless chin-wagging in the meantime. This is top secret."

"You can rely on me, Max. Thanks for calling. 'Bye."

I hung up and immediately deposited a quarter. "Operator, I'd like to make a collect call. Yes, to a satellite phone. It's urgent!"

* * *

We're in the shower. Female readers only may join us for another intimate twins conversation.

I don't think I'll ever get used to this frigid water, Cara. Can I borrow your shampoo?

Sure. Here, catch.

Got it, thanks. What are we wearing today?

Howard specified the periwinkle poodle skirts and tan saddle shoes. Toni, guess what? I talked to Mother this morning.

Already? What time did you get up?

Dawn. Mom leaves for the shelter so early.

How did she sound?

You know Mother, Toni. She tried to downplay the weekend in Toronto, but I could tell she had a good time.

What did she say about Special Agent Pulaski?

She said Troy spent most of the time in conferences with the Mounties. Vice President Greer is visiting there next week. But they had a nice dinner Saturday night at a Greek restaurant downtown.

And after dinner?

She wasn't very specific about that.

That's promising.

I thought so too, Toni. She sounded very upbeat. She wasn't even too upset that Lizzie moved back—it didn't work out with her and Ed.

But there's no room, Cara.

I know. Lizzie's making a temporary bed for herself under the Ping-pong table in the family room. Mother was amazed to hear Thom was here. She requested me to remind you of your safe-sex vows.

Really, Cara, I got the message! Not that I plan on sleeping with the lout. I don't dig guys with dishpan hands. Which reminds me, your pal Renk seems quite down in the dumps.

His parents are giving him a difficult time, Toni.

The guy could use a morale booster, Cara.

What are you suggesting?

It's time to take a dive off the high board, Cara. It's time to make a man out of your boyfriend.

Why do you care how Renk feels, Toni? You don't even like him.

Well, he is proving moderately useful. A person gets accustomed to having a publicist. At least the press isn't ignoring us totally. Sam Donaldson actually waved to me yesterday. And it's always good to have a competent media spokesperson should one elope suddenly or be discovered in a compromising position.

I hope you're not planning to do either, Toni. But what about Forest? I'm thinking about him more and more. He's quite attentive.

Forest is just a flirt. He's been all over me too.

Really? I hadn't noticed that.

Cara, I suggest you go to Renk's room tonight.

Just walk in, unannounced? What if he's undressed?

So much the better. Go heavy on the perfume and take along plenty of condoms.

That seems so calculating, Toni.

Believe me, Cara, he won't mind. Say, I wonder what all the excitement is about out there?

* * *

After breakfast (one-quarter grapefruit, two slices of dry toast, one spoonful of marmalade, and hot tea), Governor Flunch held a news conference on the deck to deny the blockbuster CNN world media scoop that his reclusive brother was buying a South American warship. He called the story a "heinous lie" and a "damnable calumny," and said it was a "vicious smear against my entire peace-loving family." He said if they did not receive a retraction and apology by 4 p.m., they would have no recourse except to file suit against CNN.

Governor Flunch petulantly refused to recognize Monty Bellefontaine during the question-and-answer period, forcing the reporter to hold his own follow-up press conference on the beach. Monty declared their information came from an "unimpeachable source" at "the highest level." He insisted they were standing by the story, adding that Adena Zoar had just arrived in Montevideo and would be interviewing Maximo Flunch live via satellite as soon as she located his hotel. He then passed out photos CNN had obtained of the original Battlefield Flunch, including the liquor bar, mounted caribou head, and militaristic pinball machine.

"It's high time Governor Flunch came clean about his brother," said Monty. "The whole world wants to know."

At that moment Dad strode down to the beach on a mission of damage control. Calling Monty a "scandal monger," a "yellow journalist," a "media louse," and "a tool of Hanoi Jane," he tried to pull the plug on Monty's microphone. They struggled, two special agents leaped to intervene, and a trench-coated reporter was pushed into the lake, possibly inundating a fortune in concealed cash. Mrs. Flunch cheered from the deck and waved her fist—a defiant gesture that was beamed live over the airwaves around the world, subsequently causing her personal popularity ratings to soar and giving a much-needed boost to the Flunch campaign. The cameras then swung around to Cara and me, looking on in astonished disbelief, sparking a brief but widespread revival of the poodle skirt.

* * *

As the weather continued sunny and warm, Toni and I accepted an invitation to go for a sail with Hamler in his little boat. We changed into our sunflower suits, and brought along Dola as a stabilizing influence. The fiberglass boat has a single aluminum mast; a cramped, untidy cockpit; and a tiny forward cuddy cabin jammed with fishing poles, crudely sharpened wooden spears, tangled nets, eel snares, tackle boxes, bait cans, and slimy bits of dismembered marine life.

"This boat is filthy," said Toni, as the wind filled the two dingy sails and the hull charged briskly across the blue water. "And it reeks horribly."

"You take off tops now," replied Hamler, leaning back and gripping the tiller with his long, prehensile toes.

"Hammy, they can't take off their tops," pointed out his sister. "They're wearing one-piece bathing suits. I'd take off mine, but Mom would kill me."

"No sun on lungs, bad for health," said Hamler, beating his sunburned chest with his fists.

"Your friend Gilboa must be very healthy," noted Toni. "How's your affair going?"

"Mighty swell. She some good lay. Better than you, I bet big dolla'."

"Sorry, Hamler," said Toni. "I don't think we'll be taking you up on that bet. Will we, Cara?"

"Highly unlikely," I agreed. "Say, what are those boats out there?"

"Yuppie tourist scum," said Hamler, steering toward the pack of speedboats and cabin cruisers drifting just beyond the two-mile exclusion zone. "They snap photos. We beg for snacks."

"Oh, cool," said Dola. "It's the barter system."

Fifteen minutes later we were gorging on potato chips, cheese curls, corn chips, canned sardines, ham sandwiches, macaroni salad, candy bars, cupcakes, handmade maple fudge, sodas, beer (Hamler), and cigarettes (also Hamler). One family was so thrilled to capture us live on their camcorder, they presented us with a whole watermelon. We rolled it gratefully into the cramped cockpit, and waved and blew kisses as we sailed away.

"Now I know how the natives felt when Captain Cook arrived," said Dola, carving into the bulky melon with Hamler's knife.

"Me too," said Toni. "When those cute fellows in the fishing boat handed over their lunch buckets, I felt the strongest urge to give myself to them."

"That's funny," said Dola, "I felt exactly the same way. Should we go back?"

"Look!" I exclaimed. "It can't be! Hamler, turn the boat! To the right! To the right!"

Hamler yanked the tiller toward him, and swung the boat around northward.

"What is it?" asked Dola.

"Some damn kayacker," replied Hamler, peering into the distance. "With insulting sign."

"Dan!" I called. "Dan, is it really you?"

"My God!" exclaimed Toni. "It's Dan Wyandot."

"Who's he?" asked Dola. "He's cute!"

"Dan's our own personal Sierra Club picketer," replied Toni, waving.

"Hi, Cara!" shouted Dan, waving his large plastic-wrapped cardboard sign. "Hello, Toni!"

Hamler expertly circled beyond the kayak, tacked, and drifted up alongside the low, one-man craft. Dan smiled and clutched his hand-lettered placard. It read: "Say No to Another Corporate Bag Man in the White House."

"Dan, what are you doing out here?" I asked, overwhelmed with feelings at seeing him so unexpectedly. He was dressed only in black swim trunks; sunlight reflecting off the water lit up the golden wool on his bronzed, muscular chest.

"The Coast Guard says I can't come any closer, Cara. They stopped me twice this morning."

"You're completely insane, Dan," said Toni. "No one pickets in the middle of Lake Michigan. Meet Dola and Hamler Flunch."

Hamler and Dan nodded guardedly to each other. Dola smiled and held out a large wedge of watermelon.

"Thank you, no," said Dan. "I'm not hungry. I just had a granola bar."

"Dan, you must come back with us," said Toni. "Bag Island is ever so much fun. The eats are crummy and the accommodations are the pits, but there's always room for one more. We'll sneak you on shore."

"Yes, Dan," I implored. "Do come! You can ride in our boat and we'll tow your kayak. The Coast Guard won't stop us."

"Him outside agitator," protested Hamler. "Him no welcome on Bag Island."

"Yes he is, Hamler," said Dola. "I'm sure he's a member of the liberal wing of the party. Dan, you can picket me any time. Here, we'll make room for you."

Dola heaved the watermelon overboard, Toni reached for Dan's sign, and I helped him pull himself into the boat. I gazed into his magnetic blue eyes and felt the powerful presence of his sun-warmed body next to mine. Hamler reluctantly tied the kayak to the stern, grabbed Dan's sign from Toni, and flipped it into the lake.

"Hamler, that's called a tan," said Toni, pointing at our new passenger. "That's what you're supposed to do in the sun—not get broiled like a psoriasitic lobster."

"I wrestle you tonight, agitator," said Hamler. "I crush your jerking liberal knees."

"Fine," replied Dan. "I did a little wrestling in high school."

"Yes, Dan, we know," said Toni, patting his tanned thigh, "with Cheryl, your peppy Pom-Pom Queen."

## Chapter 11

When you are the victim of vile treachery, many emotions roil within your breast. There is outrage, of course, and embarrassment at having been duped. And anger at one's stupidity. And a black bitterness as you reproach yourself for the overlooked signs and misread intentions. Looking on the bright side, if there is a bright side, and I think usually there is, even in the worst disasters, you also experience the not inconsiderable satisfaction of having acquired a great and formidable enemy against whom you are now compelled to plot a terrible revenge.

"Hi, Toni. You missed dinner."

"Oh, hi, Dola. I'm not hungry."

"Wow, that's incredible. Why are you sitting by yourself under this tree?"

"I'm thinking."

"It's not good to think on an empty stomach. Did you hear the news? They can't find Uncle Max in South America and the Uruguayan navy says they never owned a battleship—ever. CNN has issued a formal retraction and apology. Dad's still mad though. They banished Monty from the island. Too bad. What a hunk."

"Yes, Dola. I've heard."

"We had chipped beef on toast for dinner. It's Mom's new strategy. Nobody asks for seconds of that."

"Dola, do you know anything about the geography of Spain?"

"A little. We go to private school."

"Is Madrid on the coast?"

"No, it's inland—in the middle of the country. Why, Toni?"

"Oh, just wondering. Your brother, Forest, he's good with electronics?"

"The best. Don't tell anyone, but he's now jamming the Secret Service communications band with the recorded speeches of Bob Dole."

"Dola, could your brother make a phone sound staticky? And disguise a voice?"

"Easy. I tell you the guy is very bright, for a Flunch. Last summer he was always calling up Hamler and pretending to be a foxy girl hot to date him. Now Hamler gives passwords to his real girlfriends. Thom says chipped beef is a dishwasher's worst nightmare. He looks sensationally cute in his apron and new loincloth. Not as cute as Dan, though. What a dreamboat. I like that all these new boys on the island have hardly any clothes to wear. I just hope Thom doesn't get scabies like Hamler. Do you think rubber gloves are sexy?"

"Dola, where's your uncle Maximo? Please tell me!"

"Honest, Toni, I don't know. I'd tell you if I did. Dad and Mom might know, but they're not saying."

"Dola, if you find out where your uncle is for me, I'll help you get together with Thom."

"Gee, you mean it? You won't be like, insanely jealous?"

"No, I told you: I broke up with Thom. He's just a friend."

"He doesn't think so. He told me he's taking you to the Rocky Pike homecoming dance. The rat."

"No, he's not—believe me. Dola, can you help me find your uncle?"

"I'll do my best, Toni. You can count on me, hon."

※ ※ ※

Wrestling is a despicable sport; I think it must have been invented by sadists. I shall refuse to play the accordion again if these sordid contests continue. Hamler proved he is a most detestable brute, winning both matches this evening. I couldn't bear to watch him thrashing about like a crocodile and overpowering poor Dan. I think Hamler had an unfair weight advantage, and I know he resorts to underhanded tactics. I felt like slapping his face and his gloating mother's. What I can't understand is how Dan and Thom can say afterwards that they enjoyed wrestling with that beast. Perhaps some misguided macho impulse prevents them from revealing their true feelings. That wouldn't surprise me from Thom, but I expected more candor from Dan. Men can be so disappointing, as I experienced again this evening on a stroll along the shore with Renk.

"How pretty the waning moon looks reflected in the still water," I said. "The lake is like a mirror tonight."

"Cara, I can't believe you brought Dan to the island."

"I didn't bring him, Renk. We all brought him. He was invited by Dola, as a matter of fact."

"Maybe I should wrestle Hamler. Maybe then you might notice me."

"What are you talking about, Renk?"

"I watched you, Cara. I saw the way you looked at him. You're stuck on that guy."

"I am not. Dan is much too old for me."

"Uh-huh. Well, Cara, let me tell you it's all an act with that guy. That 'save the earth' business is just a pose. He was grinning like an idiot when he shook Governor Flunch's hand."

"He was only being polite, Renk. Dola introduced him to his parents, and he stood by his principles. He refused Mrs. Flunch's offer of a job weeding the flower beds."

"He's a real martyr to the cause. I suppose you'll be sleeping with him tonight? He's in the Joseph McCarthy room."

"Actually, Renk, I had been planning to come to your room tonight."

"What?"

"That's right. I discussed the idea with my sister only this morning."

"I suppose she tried to talk you out of it."

"Quite the contrary, Renk. She suggested it."

"She did? Why?"

"She thought you looked unhappy. And she knew I was considering it."

"You were?"

"Yes, I had been at the time."

"Cara, darling!"

"It's late, Renk. We better get back. Please withdraw your arm from my shoulder."

I removed his hand and sang this heartfelt lament:

> Boys are a fixation of girls my age,
>     Or so it's often stated;
> But though teen love is all the rage,
>     I've found it's overrated.

> Despite the subject's reputed appeal,
>     It palls in application;
> Experimentations with boys reveal
>     A cause for enervation.

> One soon uncovers a hallowed truth,
>     A poignant revelation:
> Romance involving a callow youth
>     Is a form of self-flagellation.

> I doubt if love is at all present
>    When my person he is pawing;
> I have a tip for that adolescent:
>    My reserve he is not thawing!

> My steadfastness he'll not unnerve,
>    Nor surmount my rigidity;
> His blandishments can only serve
>    To buttress my virginity.

> Of boys' caresses I've had a satiety—
>    One more and I shall throw up;
> These eroticisms induce no gaiety,
>    I'll wait until they grow up!

"But, Cara," protested Renk, "I love you!"

"Well, you have an odd way of showing it, Renk Pohlsohn. Good night!"

* * *

The stars were blazing again at maximum wattage above Big Bag Bay—as was my companion's libido.

"Thom, please remove your hand from under my blouse."

"Geez, Toni baby, I washed 3,000 dishes today just to be with you. Besides, it's not like it's any place it hasn't been plenty of times before."

"Behave yourself, Thom. I didn't bring you out here to be groped for old time's sake."

"What did you bring me here for? This is a very private spot, baby. Want to see how my loincloth works?"

"No, thank you. Thom, I want you to swim out to that big boat over there and hand this note to Monty Bellefontaine. I've taken the trouble of wrapping it in plastic, but try not to get it too wet. And only give it to Monty."

"What's it say?"

"None of your business."

"Is it a love letter?"

"Of course not, idiot. It's just a publicity matter. Now take it out there, and try to bring back some food if you can. I'm starving."

"Gee, you should have said something, babe. I could have smuggled you out some chipped beef."

Thom obediently gripped my apology letter in his mouth and splashed out into the calm water. A few minutes later Mr. Tiro shuffled over the dune, followed by Forest, Howard, Dan, and Dola.

"Ah, a Mason sister," said Forest. "Now which one do you suppose it is?"

"She's here by herself, Thicket," said Howard. "It must be Cara."

"She looks kind of serious," said Dola. "It's probably Cara."

"Cara, is that you?" asked Dan.

"You're wrong," said Forest. "It's not Cara, it's Toni. I can always tell."

"How can you be so sure, Forest?" I asked. "We look the same, we dress the same, and we talk the same."

"True, but your emanations are quite distinctive."

"Our emanations?"

"Your spiritual vibrations. Antonia is vibrating at a high frequency these days. It's detectable even in the dark. Besides, I saw Cara strolling off with Renk a while ago."

"OK, guys," said Dola. "Get stripped and bring us back some grub."

"Dola, we're wearing our swim trunks tonight," Howard pointed out. "We don't have to take off our clothes."

"Yes, you do, honey," she replied. "Mom's always saying it's not healthy sitting around in a damp bathing suit at night. Besides they're more generous on the boats when you show up buck naked."

The boys shrugged, stepped out of their trunks, and waded into the water.

"Boy, that Dan has a lot to offer some lucky girl," said Dola, gathering up the swim trunks and burying them in the warm sand. "I only wish it was me."

"Sorry, Dola. You're welcome to Thom, but I've got dibs on Dan."

"Oh, hell, I might as well take off my swimsuit too. Do you mind, Toni?"

"Not at all, Dola. It seems to be the fashion on this beach."

※ ※ ※

"I feel very uncomfortable eating raw oysters in front of a fully clothed woman," slurped Howard.

The Tupperware was overflowing with media delicacies; the bottle being passed around was a 12-year-old scotch.

"We could strip her," suggested Forest.

"My outraged screams would bring the press," I replied, helping myself to a turkey drumstick. "What a front-page story that would be: Minister's Daughter Violated by Flunch Scion at Bag Island Orgy."

"I feel pretty exposed being the only naked girl here," commented Dola, wiping cream cheese off an ample breast.

"You're doing good, Dola," said Thom, patting her bare back. "Toni can't help it that she's uptight. She's from Ohio."

"Oh, all right," I said, handing my turkey leg to Dan and quickly shedding my clothes. "There, I hope you're satisfied."

They seemed to be, judging from the leers and slobber.

"Gee, I hope your sister doesn't look that good," said Dola. "I'd hate to think there were two girls on this island with a body like that. Nobody would ever come to my room. By the way, I'm in the Margaret Chase Smith room, in case anyone is wondering."

"I'll keep it in mind," said Thom. "What do you say to that, Toni?"

"I'd say it's without a doubt the best offer you'll get tonight."

"Hey, I hear voices," said Dan.

Howard tipsily lowered the bottle. "It sounds like it's coming from the other side of that dune."

We put down our snacks, crept nakedly up the dune, and peered over the top. Across an inlet two figures were splashing in the shallow water.

"O-o-oh, somebody's skinny-dipping," said Dola, resting a warm hand and breast on Thom's bare back. I did the same on Dan's.

"That's Hamler," said Forest. "Who's the chick?"

"It must be Gilboa," said Howard.

Forest clearly was shocked. "Let's, let's give them some privacy. And let's put on our damn clothes."

"Uh-oh," said Howard. "Your Republicanism is showing."

I knew boys made up fanciful names for it, but I'd never heard it called a "Republican" before.

\* \* \*

One feels such a sense of anticipation slipping into strange bedrooms at night. Have you noticed that?

"Who's there?" asked a sleepy voice.

"It's me, Dan. Cara."

"Oh, hi, Cara. Here, let me turn on the light."

"Don't bother, Dan. Push over, these beds are absurdly narrow."

"Cara, what are you doing?"

"Shhh. We have to be quiet, Dan. There's very little soundproofing in these walls. What are you wearing?"

"My swim trunks. They're all I have. Thank God, Dola finally dug them up. Cara sweetheart, you have removed your nightie."

"Kiss me, Dan."

"I can't."

"Why not? Are your lips on strike?"

"Cara, you're only 15."

"Who says?"

"You did. Remember?"

"Oh right. I would say something like that. Well, what of it?"

"Cara, you're under age. I could be prosecuted. It's not right."

"Dan, you're saying one thing, but your body is communicating a different story. It's safe. I brought condoms. No one will ever know."

"I'm sorry, Cara. I think I'm in love with you. That's why I came all the way here. I had to see you. It's terrible. Your father's politics are appalling. Our relationship is philosophically untenable. And I'm four years older than you. Yet I love you. We'll have to wait until you're older. Please don't kiss me like that."

"You really love me?"

"Of course I do. You're all I think about. I'm even being pleasant to those despicable Flunches to be near you."

"They're not that bad, Dan. Except for Forest. He's a slime-bag. You don't like Toni?"

"No. I always liked you. From the first moment I saw you."

"Then why did you go out for lunch that time with Toni? And to the movies?"

"Because she asked me. I thought she would make my concerns known to your father. And I wanted to be near you."

"OK, Dan. You win. I'm leaving."

"Cara, you're not angry are you?"

"No, Dan. You're a nice person. You're right. It's better to wait. Good night."

"Good night, Cara darling."

* * *

The room was very dark and I was very nervous. My throat was so constricted I could barely swallow and my legs were shaking with every step.

"Who's there?"

"It's me, Dan. Cara."

"Oh, hello, Cara. Would you like me to turn on the light this time?"

"No, Dan. Do you mind if I sit on a corner of your bed?"

"Of course not, darling. I'm glad you're not upset."

"I am upset. . . terribly . . . Dan, you called me darling."

"Yes, Cara. I hope you don't mind. I told you how I feel about you."

"Did you? Oh, Dan, I'm so confused."

"We can wait, honey. It's not so long."

"Wait for what, Dan?"

"Cara, sweetheart, I do desire to have . . . to have a physical relationship with you. But it's better to wait until you're older."

"Oh, I agree, Dan. I wasn't coming here to seduce you, if that's what you thought."

"No, of course not."

"I was going to sleep with Renk tonight. I was on my way to his room."

"Cara, that seems rather vindictive."

"Does it?"

"Yes, very much so. Considering how I feel about you."

"Now I'm more confused. Do you like me, Dan?"

"I love you, Cara. I wish you could believe me."

"I do believe you, Dan. It's just, so sudden. How long have you loved me?"

"Since the first moment I saw you!"

"You didn't like Toni?"

"No! I liked you!"

"Don't get angry, Dan. Why did you have lunch with my sister? And take her to the movies?"

"You know why. To be near you!"

"Wow. Is that true?"

"Do you want me to write it in blood?"

"This is awful, Dan. I don't want to be in love at age 15. I want to have a nice educational affair with someone like Renk."

"Renk is very fortunate he has not been the victim of a cruel assault."

"You're jealous, Dan?"

"Seething, Cara."

And then he sang these words in a clear and manly tenor:

> Cara, the fair, a
>     Girl who's one of two;
> Yes, I care a
>     Lot for only you.
>
> Cara, so rare a
>     Feeling that you drew,
> That I'll bear a
>     Dealing with this zoo.

Yes, I beware a
    Divergency of view;
Dare we pair a
    Dogma so askew?

Cara, I declare a
    Love so very true
Can outwear a
    Division or two.

Though I despair, a
    Lust we must subdue;
Lest this affair a
    Censure to accrue.

Cara, I swear a
    Love may be taboo,
But we'll share a
    Future rendezvous!

"Oh, Dan, I hope so," I sighed. "Would you mind kissing me?"

"Not at all."

Somehow we found each other in the dark. I was surprised that he was trembling as much as I was.

"That was extremely marvelous, Dan. I felt that down to my toes. Would you mind if I ran my fingers through your chest hair? I've been wanting to do that all day."

"Be my guest, Cara. It's odd, your lips feel a little different."

"Different from Cheryl's?"

"No, silly. Different than before."

"Before what, Dan?"

"When I kissed you before."

"Dan, that was the first time I ever kissed you. I think I would remember."

"Don't be ridiculous, Cara. You were all over me 15 minutes ago."

"That wasn't me, Dan. Fifteen minutes ago I was in my room having a nervous breakdown."

"Oh, Jesus."

"How does my sister kiss, Dan? You seem to be in an ideal position to make the comparison."

\* \* \*

I woke with a start. Something terrifyingly large was looming before me in the blackness of my room.

"Who's there?" I demanded, recoiling in fright and tugging up the covers. No reply. Just painfully labored breathing. I heard a lighter flick open and saw a flash of flame as a cigarette was lit. The apparition breathed in, then noisily exhaled.

"Mr. Kennard," I gasped. "What are you doing here?"

"You're a smart kid, Toni," he wheezed. "I think maybe I need your help."

"What, what kind of help?"

"Bad news. We've got a rat in our midst."

"Oh?"

"I want you to keep your eyes open. You see anything, hear anything, you come to me."

"Oh, uh, OK, Mr. Kennard."

"I'm used to winning. That's why people hire me. I don't let anything stand in my way—nothing."

"I, I believe it," I stammered, watching the glowing end of his cigarette retreat as he moved silently toward the door.

"Good night," he called. "Sleep tight."

"Er, good night. Thanks for visiting."

Then he was gone—the odor of his cigarette lingering menacingly in the air.

Damn, what a scary guy.

Of course, it's too bad for him that I'm used to winning too. Still, in this league a girl had better watch her back.

# Chapter 12

Dan has been expelled from Bag Island!

He's been railroaded you mean, Toni.

During the night someone spray-painted in cursive red letters across the front of the main house "Bag the Flunches!"

And without a shred of evidence the Secret Service detained Dan, searched his room, interrogated him for two hours, and put him and his kayak on the Coast Guard cutter for a fast trip back to the mainland. It's so unfair!

It may all be for the best, Cara.

I don't think so, Toni. And what were you doing in Dan's room last night? Why were you passing yourself off as me?

I was just trying to find out how Dan feels about you, Cara. And believe me, he's only lukewarm.

Dan loves me, Toni. And I love him. I don't want to, but I do.

OK, fine, just don't mention it to Renk.

I'm not going to sleep with Renk, Toni.

Don't worry about it, Cara. You already did.

What?

Let's just say that Renk has been pacified. He's still on our team—for the time being, at least.

Are you telling me you slept with him, Toni?

Well, someone had to. And don't think I enjoyed it—much.

You mean Renk is walking around today thinking he and I are lovers?

Well, you could put it that way.

Toni, you're out of your mind. Why did you sleep with him? And don't tell me it's because you appreciate his work as our publicist.

Hey, you try guzzling a bottle of scotch and hanging out on a moonlit beach with four naked guys. OK, so I was feeling a little randy.

So you went to Dan's room and he refused you. Why didn't you go to Thom's room?

I did. He wasn't in.

Where was he?

With Dola, I assume, judging by the expressive way she was spooning up her Cream of Wheat this morning. I expect we'll be hearing all about it in her poetry tonight.

This is insane. I'm going to lose my mind!

I don't know why it is, Cara. All the guys seem to be falling your way lately. I'm getting the short end of the stick.

It doesn't sound like it to me! Toni, did you have any access to spray paint?

Now you are jumping to ridiculous conclusions, Cara. It's not like you to be so suspicious.

I'm learning quickly, Toni. Who do you think painted it?

Cara, you have to admit scrawling slogans on walls is not that dissimilar to picketing.

You couldn't be more wrong, Toni. One is an act of cowardly stealth. The other is a noble act of forthright expression.

* * *

I think Cara may be right about islands. Something definitely seems to be chipping away at a girl's inhibitions here. Perhaps all those watery vistas cause a subtle narrowing of moral perspective. What the hell was I doing in Renk's room last night? Sure, I was a little tipsy, but on the mainland I wouldn't touch that guy with sterile latex gloves if he begged me. OK, Dan rejected me—is that any reason to stoop to consorting with the rabble?

I feel so retroactively violated. And when you think about it, Renk had no right taking advantage of an inebriated minor—even if he did swear he loved me (well, actually Cara) 37 times. Really, the whole odious episode makes my skin crawl. I only wish I'd stayed a little longer so I could have missed Mr. Kennard's visitation—or did I dream that? Fortunately, the fact that Renk believes it was my sister he was pawing somewhat lessens my revulsion. I feel the only practical solution is to cleanse oneself as soon as possible by sleeping with someone truly attractive like Special Agent Ryan Holgate.

While mulling over these and other matters, I ran into my Fashion Czar on the path to the big house.

"Toni, you're wearing your sash on the wrong side. Only lesbian Girl Scouts wear their sashes like that."

"Thank you for bringing this faux pas to my attention, Howard," I replied, hastily rearranging my attire. "I wouldn't want anyone to get the wrong idea. Say, I've been meaning to ask, are you still gay?"

"Of course, Toni. One doesn't change one's sexuality like one changes one's politics. Being gay is something one makes a sincere commitment to."

"I admire your determination, Howard. Are you having an affair with Forest?"

"No. Are you?"

"Of course not."

"Well, someone is, Toni. I'd sure like to know who."

"Howard, I've noticed you spend a lot of time with Forest. And you were sitting rather close to him at the picnic last night."

"I was sitting close to an attractive nude boy on the beach. That is one of the things you try to do when you're gay. It's lesson 23 in the *Gay Handbook*."

"You could have sat close to Dan. He's more attractive than Forest."

"That may be, Toni. But as I recall you were practically in his lap already."

"What do you and Forest do together?"

"I'm teaching him to lose graciously at chess. Someone told him I was a beginner, so I'm letting him believe that. I've found the Flunches as a group can benefit from lessons in humility. I only wish Hamler played chess, or Thom was a better wrestler."

"What do you talk about during your matches?"

"Not much. I say 'check' and then I say 'mate' and then he sighs attractively. Maybe we're just sublimating. Why?"

"Does Forest ever talk about his uncle Maximo?"

"Certainly not. Who talks about their uncles when they're playing chess? People have been disqualified from tournaments for much less."

"Howard, I know for a fact you're a sneaky person."

"Thanks, Toni. That sort of testimonial means a lot coming from you."

"I want you to find out from Forest the current location of his uncle Max."

"And if I do you that small favor?"

"I'll tell you the name of the person with whom your chess partner is currently entangled."

"A tempting offer, Toni. I'll think about it. Too bad the Girl Scouts don't offer a merit badge in political intrigue. You'd be earning another dazzler for your sash."

※ ※ ※

Howard was right. It was 112° in the dishroom.

"Hello, Toni. Are you here selling Girl Scout cookies?"

"Very funny, Thom. I came to see how you were doing."

"You caught me at a low ebb, Toni. Did you ever try washing dried-on Cream of Wheat? The stuff sticks like glue."

"You're doing a splendid job, Thom. Your future mother-in-law couldn't be more pleased."

"I went to your room first last night, Toni. You were gone. I got pissed and kept on walking. Where were you?"

"I was having a nice chat about our Scout troop with Cara in her room."

"That's a lie. Her room was empty too."

"Thomas Kirkwood, you stay out of my sister's room. So how was Dola?"

"Not bad. Pretty enthusiastic actually. She reminded me of a beagle puppy I had when I was a kid. It wiggled a lot too."

"Thom, the girl you slept with may someday be residing in the White House."

"I know, Toni. It's an awesome responsibility."

"I didn't realize washing dishes involved so much sophisticated technology. What are all these sinks for?"

"Well, this is my dishwater sink. It has the flame under it, so if I stick my rubber gloves in too far the boiling hot water runs down inside, burning off the top layers of my skin. And this sink is my clear rinse, and this third sink is the sterilizing iodine rinse. Then I put the dishes in the rack, and that old fan there blows on them. It also blows on me so I don't pass out from the heat. When the dishes are dry, I stack them in the kitchen. Then I get 10 minutes off for fun, and we start over again on the next meal."

"You could go home, Thom."

"Nah, I promised Dola I'd go for a swim with her tonight. And I have to wrestle her brother again. I'm going to beat that dude this time."

"That's what you said yesterday."

"I know I said it, but I didn't really believe it. I do now. Coach Granger says winning is ninety percent mental attitude."

"Is that so? Say, I was wondering, Thom, are all the meals you fellows prepare served at the house and at the lab?"

"I guess so. What do you mean?"

"The cook doesn't prepare any extra meals that are taken someplace else?"

"No, Toni. I can't think of any. Except for that meal on the tray."

"Oh, really? Who gets it?"

"I don't know. Columbus takes it up the back staircase. The one off the kitchen that goes to the upper floors."

"And you don't know who it's for?"

"Nope, I never asked. I assumed it was for Granny Flunch or somebody. Why?"

"Oh, just asking. Is the person on the second floor?"

"Not from the way Columbus comes puffing down the stairs. I'd say they're up higher. 'Course the guy really should give up those discount CrumpPak cigarettes."

"Thanks, Thom. You've been a great help."

"Toni, you're still my babe. It's just physical with me and Dola."

"That so, Thom? Is love ninety percent mental attitude too?"

"Yes, I believe it is."

* * *

On the path to the main house I ran into the one person I was hoping to avoid.

"Why are you standing at attention and saluting me, Renk?"

"I always salute women in uniform, Cara."

"It's Howard's latest fashion fantasy, Renk: Girl Scout uniforms."

"Did you really earn all those merit badges, Cara?"

"No, Howard's sister Tallmadge did. She must have been quite the industrious teen. Please, I don't feel like kissing anyone this morning, Renk. I didn't sleep well last night."

"I did. You were fantastic in bed, Cara. I only wish you'd stayed longer."

"I'm glad I lived up to your expectations, Renk."

"How was I?"

"You were, you were fine."

"Cara, you don't have to worry. I haven't lost respect for you."

"That takes a load off my mind, Renk. I haven't lost respect for you either— yet. Did you paint that message on the front of the house?"

"Of course not, sweetheart. What do you take me for? OK, I'll admit I'm not too broken up that your pal got thrown off the island. But I wouldn't do anything like that. You know me."

"I hope so."

"Besides, you proved to me who you really care about."

"Yes, I suppose I did."

"Cara honey, that uniform looks sensational on you. My meeting doesn't start for another twenty minutes. Let's go find a private spot up in the woods."

"Oh, Renk, put a sock on it!"

\* \* \*

I waited until Columbus and Ottokee, the cook, came out for a cigarette break, then slithered in through the kitchen door. Thom in the dish room was still busy at his sinks. I looked around, spotted a doorway, and darted up a narrow staircase. The unpainted pine treads, worn concave by generations of Flunch servants, wound steeply and unevenly upward. I came to a small locked door, which I assumed opened somewhere on the second floor. I continued upward and came to an identical door. This one, much to my relief, was unlocked. It opened on a narrow hallway, with walls and low ceiling crudely sheathed in wide, rough-sawn boards turned gray with age. Doorways off the hall opened on abandoned, cell-like rooms dimly lit by small grimy windows. Glamorous calendar girls from decades past displayed faded pink nipples as they gazed down from the board walls onto piles of broken paper furniture.

Following the footprints in the dust, I walked cautiously down the hallway—the old wooden floor bouncing like a trampoline with every step. At the end of the passageway the hallway turned left down the center of the building. From its opposite end, I could hear what sounded like a radio playing. I walked as quietly as I could toward the sound, and came at last to the final doorway on the hall. Reaching out, I pushed open the unpainted door and peered around it. A portly middle-aged man with a shiny bald head looked up from where he was fanning himself in a molded paper rocker.

"Oh, the Girl Scouts have arrived," he said amiably. "The Tigers are ahead three to two."

"Greetings," I said, "Maximo Flunch, I presume."

*Chapter 13*

The bald man turned down the volume on his small plastic radio.

"Sorry, Miss, you got the wrong fellow. I'm Pasco Tawawa, Lima Flunch's brother."

"Really?" I said, naturally skeptical. "Uh, I'm Toni Mason, Senator Mason's daughter."

"Yes, I know. I heard about your famous bake sale on the radio. You look like Doris Day. I hear you singing sometimes, and that whistler. Boy, he's really something."

"Are you sure you're not Maximo Flunch? You look very familiar, like a potential Flunch."

"Please, I've had a hard life. Don't tell me that. Here, I'll show you my I.D."

The man put down his cardboard fan and laboriously extracted a fat, damp wallet from his back pocket. He flipped it open to the plastic window displaying his Michigan driver's license.

"It does say Pasco Tawawa," I said, disappointed. "And that picture does look somewhat like you."

"It's me," he affirmed. "My hair, what's left of it, has since gone white from stress. Say, what's all that shouting down there? Is the house on fire? Have you come up to rescue me from a fiery death?"

"No, it's just another staff meeting on the campaign's abortion position. Father is standing firm, I'm afraid."

"Too bad—I mean about the house not being on fire. I could use an airing."

"What are you doing up in this room, Mr. Tawawa?"

"I'm staying out of sight."

"Yes, I can see that. Any particular reason?"

"I'm a failure, Toni."

"How so?"

"The worst way. I'm a business failure. My company went belly up."

"Well, that's no disgrace."

"It is when your sister has her eyes on the White House. Lima's afraid the reporters will find out about me. The Flunches are pretty touchy about their relatives—as well they should be with all the dingbats in their family. The Tawawas are mostly respectable folk: cherry farmers, wholesale fudge brokers, unemployed machinists, that sort of thing. Anyway, I'm hiding out until after the elections."

"That's awful. You have to stay cooped up in this stuffy room until November?"

"Yep. Lima's orders. Could I offer you an orange sour?"

"Yes, please."

We removed the cellophane from our candies and sucked pensively on the tart sweets.

"What sort of business did you have, Mr. Tawawa?"

"Call me Pasco. I had a dunk tank rental business."

"A what?"

"Dunk tank rentals. You know, hit the bull's-eye with a baseball, and down splashes the celebrity into the tank. Very popular with your Jaycees and your Kiwanis groups. I had 45 tanks all over the state."

"What happened?"

"Lima got me a big write-up in *Inc.* magazine. Good for the family's image, she said. Inside of a month I had four competitors undercutting my rates. Pretty soon you could hire a nice dunk tank for about the same rental as a pair of hedge clippers. Before I knew it, my business was in the tank."

"And now you're exiled to the attic. That is so unfair. And what about your family?"

"My wife left me. Ran off with one of those celebrity radio DJs we used to dunk. I'm not bitter though. I've got the Detroit Tigers to keep me company. And Columbus stops by and chews the fat when he can. He's an Indians fan though."

"Doesn't your sister visit you?"

"Not if I can help it. Another sour orange, Toni?"

"Yes, please. Thank you, Pasco. Do you know Maximo Flunch?"

"Yes, that is one of my biggest regrets. I always wanted to get that pompous gasbag up on one of my dunk tanks. The one with the piranha fish in the water. I wouldn't miss with the baseball either, except to bean him in the head once or twice first. He's the dolt that recommended the dunk tank business in the first place. One of his drunken gun freak buddies makes them. Never take business advice from a Flunch, Toni. If Claude gets elected, I'm buying a one-way ticket to Tasmania. This country will be finished. In the bag, so to speak."

"Do you know where Maximo is?"

"Well, Toni, I'm kind of out of the loop up here. But I heard a rumor a couple days ago through the floorboards."

"What was it?"

"All I know is one thing. Now don't pester me for any of the dirty details, I don't have them. The rumor is that Maximo Flunch is over there hobnobbing with the ex-reds and has-been Commies."

"You mean. . ."

"Yep. Ol' Max is in Russia!"

\* \* \*

Lunch was somewhat strained. Renk was furious with me because I asked Hamler if we could go out in his boat this afternoon to look for Dan in his kayak. Observing Renk's distress, Hamler naturally agreed—causing Gilboa to yank the marigold from her hair and stomp angrily off the deck.

I asked Toni to accompany us on the boat as our chaperon, but she said she had "important fish frying on the front burner." Dola likewise demurred, citing a desire to loiter near the dishroom. Howard declined out of loyalty to his friend Renk. Forest refused, mentioning a long-standing aversion to his brother. I thought of asking Renk, but decided that sailing alone with Hamler might be the lesser of two evils.

I changed into my swimsuit, doused myself liberally with sunblock, and stepped warily into the little boat with the rustic sailor. He cast off, unfurled his grubby sails, and eyed me lasciviously across the cockpit.

"You look mighty, mighty fine, Cara baby," he said, fondling the end of the tiller in a suggestive way. "Hamler like babes all oiled up and slippery."

"Someone should write a book about you, Hamler," I replied. "They could call it *The Dirty Old Man and the Sea*."

"You like Hemingway? Him some boffo writer. Spent summers as youth sailing on lakes of Michigan. Him fish and camp, be one with nature. Win Nobel Prize."

"I haven't read him, Hamler. Have you?"

"Sure, baby. Him big favorite of Uncle Max too. But we like Tom Clancy best."

"When do you read, Hamler? I never see you with a book."

"Hamler read when moon is high, and much satisfied babe lies contented beside him."

He edged a scaly foot toward my leg; I inched away.

"That reminds me, I saw you on the dock making eyes at Mindy."

"Her some gorgeous babe. Have big artificial bosom. Science march on."

"She's very attractive in her own way."

"Her mighty hot for Hamler too."

"I'm sure Mindy is completely faithful to my father."

"Monogamy big myth. Time to sow wild oat. It nature's way. You want too."

"I want no. Well, maybe someday with Dan. I love him, Hamler."

"Phhh. Hamler out-wrestle that boy. Hamler bigger and stronger. Hamler rich too. Make plenty paper bag. Better you love Hamler. Him an expert. Babes always come back to Hamler for more."

"You are a sexist pig and completely conceited."

"Hamler speak truth."

"You are the strangest boy I've ever met."

"You meet too many boring Ohio boy, Cara. Too many!"

\* \* \*

Someone pushed open the door to my room. Hoping it was Ryan or Monty, fearing it might be Mr. Kennard again, I looked up from my magazine and frowned at Howard.

"Toni, could I have a word with you?"

"Certainly, Howard. OK, I confess. I've cut the little flouncy skirt off my bathing suit without your permission, but I had to. That awful yellow rickrack was affecting my sense of self-worth. Now I feel like a new woman. If only I could get rid of these horrid sunflowers and cone-like breast molds."

"I'm sorry, Toni. You give me no option but to rustle up some retired bathing suits of Dola's for you and Cara."

"Don't bother getting two. One should do nicely for us both."

"I have some vital intelligence for you, Toni. I got Forest to spill the beans. His uncle Max is in Russia!"

"Big deal, Howard. I knew that much already."

"You did?"

"Yes. Where is he in Russia? And what the hell is he doing over there? That's what I want to know."

"Er, I can't answer that."

"Well find out. Snoop! Sneak around. Get some dirt on Forest and make him come clean."

"It might help if I knew with whom he was sleeping."

"Forget it, Howard. It's time you soloed. You've got to earn your wings as a spy. And who said you could cut the legs off your purple pants?"

"Sorry, Toni. I got hot. How do I look in aubergine cutoffs?"

"They're awfully short, Howard. You look kind of faggy."

"Do you really think so, Toni? Gee, thanks."

* * *

Hamler cruised along the line of tourist boats in the hazy afternoon heat. He posed for photos, flirted with girls, gave misleading directions to phantom fishing spots, and trolled voraciously for snacks like one of those pan-handling bears in Yellowstone Park. Hamler is just as omnivorous, devouring a lime-and-pimento molded salad, two pickled eggs, half a coconut cake, a bunch of concord grapes, a bag of candy corn, two yards of red licorice, a cheese taco, and several other unappetizing handouts. I nibbled from a damp box of stale pretzels and scanned the choppy waters for my love.

A middle-aged couple in a shiny new cabin cruiser donated a bag of Amish dinner rolls and a celery stalk. Hamler eyed his prizes and grunted in thanks.

"We're heading in," said the man. "Coast Guard's posted small craft warnings. Radio says they're forecasting thunderstorms and 60 knot winds."

Along the western horizon, gray clouds were piling up.

"Have you seen anyone in a kayak?" I asked.

"Saw some fruitcake radical waving a sign," replied his wife. "He's lucky we didn't run him down."

"Where was he?" I asked urgently.

"Oh, mile or two south," called the man, motoring away. "Be one less voter for Greer if he drowns."

I was frantic. "Hamler, we have to find Dan!"

"Bad blow coming," he replied calmly, chewing on a piece of unwashed celery. "Bag Island to north."

"Hamler, we must sail south! We must!"

"OK, Cara. But Hamler expect mighty big favor in return."

"Anything, Hamler! We have to find Dan!"

* * *

"Hello, Dola. Why are you staying here in your room?"

"Oh, hello, Toni. I'm feeling poetical. I think I'm in love."

"I talked to Thom, Dola. He told me he liked you a great deal."

"He did? You're not just saying that, Toni?"

"Of course not, Dola. He's washing all those dishes so he can stay here and be with you."

"Wow, I've got to express that in a poem. What rhymes with dish?"

"Er, fish, wish, squish, uh . . . establish."

"You can't use establish in a love poem. It sounds like the Gettysburg Address. I know, how about: Splish, splash, splish. My lover is washing a dish?"

"A promising beginning, Dola. Say, I met your uncle Pasco."

"You weren't supposed to. Mom is hiding him."

"I know, Dola. I think it's disgraceful. He's such a nice man too. We had a friendly chat up in his room. He told me your uncle Max was in Russia."

"Don't tell anyone, Toni. Mom will really be pissed if that gets out."

"Dola, I thought you said you didn't know where your uncle was?"

"Well, I didn't know for sure, Toni. I didn't want to spread any more false rumors."

"Dola, I believe I am being rather accommodating about you and Thom. All things considered."

"You are, Toni. I'm very grateful."

"Where in Russia is your uncle?"

"I don't know."

"What's he doing there?"

"I'm not sure, Toni."

"Well, what have you heard?"

"Forest thinks he's there buying something. He told me not to tell anybody though."

"Buying what?"

"Something big. And expensive. That's all I know."

"I'm not falling for any more of those shopping for battleship stories, Dola."

"Uncle Max loves guns, Toni. Maybe he's buying some guns."

"Dola, you must find out for me what it is your uncle is doing there. Otherwise, I'll have to reconsider Thom's invitation to the homecoming dance."

"Why don't you ask Forest, Toni?"

"Forgive me for saying this, Dola, but I have found your brother to be less than trustworthy and consistently deceitful."

"Sounds like Forest. OK, Toni, I'll see what I can dig up. Oh, Howard mentioned that you wanted to borrow one of my swimsuits."

"Howard is not entirely trustworthy either, Dola. In fact, very few boys are. I take everything they say with a grain of salt."

"That seems rather confining, Toni. What if they say they love you?"

"Oh, I always try to stretch my credulity to accommodate flattery, Dola, however calculating or insincere. It's very nourishing to a girl's self-esteem."

\* \* \*

The storm overtook us with frightening speed. The ashen sky darkened to black, lightning flashed from cloud to cloud, thunder boomed, and a gusting wet wind churned the once blue water into a sickening grey-green foam. Our little boat bobbed like a cork on the pitching swells. Hamler struggled to reef the sails and made me tie a rope around my waist. Of course there were no life jackets in the boat. Each time we ascended the crest of a wave I peered anxiously across the heaving waters and called out for Dan.

A gray curtain advanced toward us from the west. Big drops splattered down on the boat, then the wall passed over us, and we were enveloped in pounding rain. A wave swept heavily over the bow, sending Hamler's bait boxes crashing about in the flooding cuddy cabin. Hamler calmly tossed me a plastic bucket and told me to bail. I scooped bucket after bucket, as the soggy sails fluttered wildly and the boom jerked against the lines in the wind.

How inconvenient to have to sing a song in the middle of a raging storm:

> As we ride the tail
> Of a cyclone's gale,
> And toss and turn
> In the bucking stern
> Of a too-small boat
> In a zone remote
> Far beyond all help,
> My heart doth yelp
> At the thought of him
> In that craft so slim!

Hamler lustily sang the chorus:

> *Roll on mighty waves!*
> *Do not send us to our graves!*
> *My wee boat do not dismast her!*
> *Please forestall this Flunch disaster!*

I sang as I bailed:

> I must scan the lake
> O'er our awesome wake,
> And 'tween the gaps
> In the foamy caps
> For the welcome sight
> Of a kayak light
> And its occupant;
> May God him grant
> A safe refuge
> From this damn deluge!

To which Hamler amended:

> *Roar on mighty storm!*
> *But no capsizings perform!*
> *With your waves do not engulf us!*
> *Such an end could only repulse us!*

⁑ ⁑ ⁑

"Dola, what's that horrible din?"

"Rain on the lab's tin roof, Toni. Looks like a pretty bad storm. I better go find Mr. Tiro. He's terrified of thunder."

"Me too. I like to be comforted in the arms a big strong boy."

"Sorry, Toni. They're all in meetings or washing dishes. We better make sure all the windows are closed."

"OK. You take the girls' side and I'll take the boys'."

I closed Forest's window and casually inspected his room. Nothing was out of place. His clothes in the dresser drawers were folded as compulsively as Cara's; under his neatly made bed, his shoes were lined up with military precision. Something in a chess strategy book on the table caught my eye: a torn piece of paper with what looked like latitude and longitude coordinates, followed by an equal sign, and the word Vladivostok. I folded it twice and slipped it down the front of my bathing suit. In a foot locker under the bed were some neatly soldered electronic boards and a half-empty can of red spray paint.

"Oh, Cara," said a voice. "You're back, thank God."

I looked up and casually replaced the bedspread. "No, Renk," I replied, "I'm Toni. Where's my sister?"

Renk paled. "Oh, Jesus. I'm going to murder that asshole Hamler!"

*  *  *

"It's no good," yelled Hamler, struggling to control the tiller and sails.
"Dan's out here somewhere!" I screamed. "We have to find him!"
"We can't see 100 feet in this gale," he shouted. "I'm going to beach her."
Ahead of us loomed a tiny island—a sliver of sand, a black rock, and a dozen writhing pine trees. A surge drove us toward the island, Hamler yanked up the centerboard, the hull scraped against the shore, he leaped into the water, stumbled, and slipped under a wave. Several dreadful seconds later he reared up, spewing water, and pulled the boat up on the sand. I jumped out, felt the forgotten rope painfully pinch my waist, and tugged and pulled in the blinding rain. With each heave, the water-filled hull slid another notch up the beach. Then another figure was beside us pulling on the boat. I looked up in surprise.

"Dan!"
"Cara! Or is it Toni?"
"It's Cara. Oh, Dan, you're safe!"
"Pull!" shouted Hamler.

We pulled, the boat lurched up the bank, and Hamler wrapped the forward line around a stout pine tree and deftly tied a sailor's intricate knot. Dan helped me free the rope from around my waist. Lightning flashed overhead, punctuated immediately by a deafening crash. Dan put his arm around me, and we followed Hamler into the thicket of trees. In the center was Dan's kayak and a rustic lean-to made from pine branches. We ducked under the shelter, but its porous roof scarcely abated the torrents of cold rain.

"Cara, you're shivering," said Dan, pulling me close to him.
"Your roof needs work, Dan," I said, feeling safe and happy in his arms.
"It's not mine, Cara," said Dan. "I just moved in ten minutes before you showed up."
"This my camp," said Hamler, digging in the sand. He uncovered a blue plastic tarp, which we unfolded with difficulty in the gale and draped over our heads.
"Where are we, Hamler?" I asked as the rain turned to hail. Lemon drops of ice hurtled down among the trees and clattered against our tarp.
"Fig Island," he said. "Six miles south Bag Island."
"I don't see any fig trees," I said.
"First Flunch in Michigan grew fig," he replied. "Got plenty rich."
"Then you own this island too?" I asked.
"You betcha. Flunches own all island. Us mighty rich fellas. Us kick Dan

off when storm pass. Him lousy trespasser."

"What were you two doing out on the lake in this storm anyway?" asked Dan, politely ignoring Hamler's bad manners.

"Looking for you, Dan," I replied. "I thought you were drowned. Promise me you'll go home when this is over."

"I'll think about it," he said, smiling.

"Him go home," said our host. "Hamler punch out Ohio boy's face. Him go home to mama."

"Your threats don't bother me, Hamler," said Dan. "I'm a pacifist."

"You wrestle like pacifist," agreed Hamler.

My bare toes dug up something in the clotted sand. It was a foil-wrapped condom.

"Hamler brings his women here!" I exclaimed.

"You betcha. Many sweet virgin look up at pretty pine tree. Have plenty good time. Hamler make it extra nice for first time. You see."

"You're not going to lay a hand on her," warned Dan.

"Ohio boy in quandary," taunted Hamler. "Him face mighty big test of pacifist ideals!"

*　*　*

From the satellite positioning beacon the Secret Service had concealed in Hamler's sail locker the Coast Guard determined the boat was six miles south of Bag Island, probably at one of the small islands in the area. While the wind blew and hail thundered down, we sat at the metal tables in the lab common area and waited for news from the cutter fighting its way through the storm toward the islands. The hail drummed down on the metal roof, the overhead lights flickered off and on, then blinked out. Forest lit several candles. Mr. Tiro whimpered in Dola's arms and cried out at every crack of thunder.

"The ground looks like it's covered with snow," said Renk, peering out a front window. "The hail must be an inch thick."

"Hard to believe I was sweating from the heat only two hours ago," said Howard. "Now I wish I hadn't cut off my pants."

"This is the worse storm in years," said Dola. "Uncle Max says sometimes in bad summer storms one of those big ore carriers will break up and sink in the monster waves. The lake gets as wild and fierce as any ocean."

"Thanks, Dola," I said, "that's very comforting."

"Hamler's boat is pretty unsinkable," said Forest. "Fiberglass is strong and every cranny is filled with flotation foam. And Hamler's an experienced sailor. Even if they haven't reached an island, they'll still be safe—assuming they haven't been swept out of the boat."

"I'm going to kill your brother, Forest," said Renk.

"Be my guest," he replied. "The deed is long overdue."

"Someone's running this way," called Howard. "Toni, it's your dad."

The door opened, hail swirled around, and the candles blew out as Dad bundled in with his shredded umbrella. He stomped his feet and brushed ice off his grey plastic raincoat.

"The Coast Guard found them," he announced. "They're safe. They were on some island with that agitator fellow who vandalized the Flunches' house."

"Oh, Dad, that's wonderful!" I exclaimed.

"That's great!" said Renk, clapping Howard on the back.

"We have much to be thankful for after this trying day," said Dad, warming up.

I recognized that timbre in his voice.

"We must give thanks for this propitious rescue and the wonderful story of deliverance to recount to the press," he continued.

"It's PR from God," muttered Howard.

"Renk," said Dad, "would you like to lead us all in a prayer of thanksgiving?"

*Chapter 14*

Someone knocked on my door as I was changing into my nightgown.

"Come in, Howard," I called.

"How did you know it was me, Toni?" he asked, entering in his flannel robe and floppy slippers.

"You have a distinctively tentative knock, Howard."

"Perhaps it reflects a deep-seated sexual ambivalence. Toni, I've had some success with my sneaking around."

"It's about time. What have you discovered?"

"Well, I ducked into the house when the rain started—I was looking for Timber Line—and I happened to overhear a conversation between Claude Flunch and Essex Kennard. The name Maximo was mentioned."

"What did they say? And what have you got on under that robe?"

"Well, as I was preparing to go to my lonely bed, where as you know I sleep in the nude, I have nothing on under this robe. Why do you ask?"

"I merely like to be fully informed as to the state of dress of the boys who visit my room at night. Howard, should you have any serious doubts about your being gay, you are welcome to come to my bedroom later."

"Really, Toni? That's awfully nice of you."

"Don't mention it. Now what did you hear?"

"Well, I couldn't hear very well over the thunder and rain, but I distinctly heard them mention Russia and Vladivostok. That's a city in Siberia on Golden Horn Bay. It's lousy with great chess players—there's not much else to do there if you're not interested in zinc smelting."

"Hmmm, that's intriguing. And what else did you hear?"

"Not much, except for two words that came through quite clearly: foxtrot class."

"Foxtrot class? Are you sure?"

"I'm sure. Both men sounded gravely concerned. And did you notice Essex left with his suitcase on the Coast Guard cutter that was hauling Dan back to Petoskey?"

"I did notice that."

"Why would Essex leave so suddenly? And in the middle of a violent storm?"

"Good question, Howard. And here's another one: Why would a presidential candidate's nutty brother go all the way to Siberia to take dancing lessons?"

\* \* \*

Another twins conversation, this one in our jammies:

Toni, I've got a problem. It's Hamler.

You're in love with him? That adventure on the boat has opened your eyes to the man beyond the loincloth?

Hardly, Toni. He's the weirdest boy I've ever met. The problem is I owe him several enormous favors.

That's bad, Cara. What sort of favors?

Well, first of all he took me out in his boat to look for Dan. Then, at great risk to his personal safety, he agreed to search for Dan in the raging storm. Then, at my whispered suggestion, after we were safely aboard the Coast Guard cutter, he tossed Dan's kayak overboard. I can't have my love paddling about Lake Michigan in that unsafe craft. And just now I have prevailed upon him to decline Renk's challenge to meet him at the swimming beach at midnight for a no-holds-barred wrestling match.

Renk must be out of his mind. Hamler outweighs him by at least 50 pounds.

You should never have slept with Renk, Toni. He's been impossible ever since.

I do sometimes have that effect on boys. Sorry, Cara.

Anyway, I am severely in Hamler's debt. And I have reason to believe he will be dropping by my room late tonight to collect.

No problem, Cara mia. We'll switch rooms tonight. I'll take care of Hamler Flunch for you.

You're not going to sleep with him are you? Toni, I wish sometimes you were slightly more discriminating in your relations with the opposite sex.

No one is going to sleep with anyone, if I can help it.

He's big and strong, Toni. I believe he is capable of resorting to force.

I am prepared for that eventuality, Cara. As Mother has shown by her inspiring example, we women are not helpless in the face of male oppression.

* * *

"Hello, Monty, this is Antonia Mason. Thank you for accepting my collect call. . . I'm sorry about that small misunderstanding over the battleship. I hope you got my note. . . Monty, you sound rather odd. . . No, Monty, you're not an international laughing stock, and even if you were, that's no reason to ruin your liver with drink. . . Hell, Monty, I'm embarrassed too. . . Yes, I know. Really? I'm sorry you got seasick during the storm. . . That's not fair that all the other reporters got to ride it out on land. . . Well, you shouldn't have drunk all that gin. . . Listen, Monty, I know where Maximo Flunch is. . . No, this is not another sick practical joke on the media. I've had three independent sources confirm his location. . . He's in Vladivostok, Russia. . . No, I don't know where in Vladivostok. Probably at the five-star hotel if they have one . . . I'm not sure exactly, Monty. He may be there taking dancing lessons . . . No, I'm not drunk, Monty. I'm serious. He may be enrolled in a foxtrot class. . . Yes, foxtrot as in Fred and Ginger. . . I don't know why. I'm trying to find out. . . I'm handing you a worldwide exclusive, Monty. . . Well, at least you can send your man in Vladivostok around to check it out. . . Oh, Monty, go sleep it off. Is Adena there? Let me speak to her."

* * *

As I was exiting the lab phone booth, I ran into Dola in revealing pink baby-dolls.

"Hi, Toni. Who were you calling?"

"Oh, hi, Dola. I was, uh, talking to my mother."

"She must keep late hours."

"Yes, she heard about the storm and was worried about us. Where are you off to, Dola?"

"Thom's room. He's upset that the rain forced a postponement of his wrestling match with Hamler. To cheer him up, I suggested he wrestle me instead. I hope you're not jealous, Toni."

"So far so good, Dola."

"Well I am. It bothers me now to think that my precious honey did it with you too. If I fall much more in love with him, my emotions may take over entirely. In which case, I may no longer be able to speak to you, Toni."

"I hope it doesn't come to that, Dola dear. It could lead to some social awkwardness on the campaign trail."

"I'm trying my best, Toni honey. I regret now we talked you into taking off your clothes on the beach. Now that I know what you look like naked, it's just that much easier for me to imagine you two in bed together. I suppose you enjoyed it tremendously?"

"Hardly at all, Dola. We were incompatible sexually."

"I'm not sure that makes me feel better. No, I'm not sure at all."

＊　＊　＊

I lay in the dark, waiting for the visitation by the Beast of Bag Island. He didn't knock.

"Who's there?"

"Your dream guy, Cara."

"That's odd. It smells like Hamler Flunch."

"I took a shower, Cara babe. I've come about that whopping humongous favor you owe me."

"Ommpf! Gee, Hamler, you didn't have to jump on me."

"Sorry, Cara. I tripped in the dark."

"You're being awfully polite for an opportunistic rapist. What happened to your Tarzan act?"

"I can't be my Man in a State of Nature now, Cara. I've removed my loincloth."

"Oh, so you have. Goodness, it's so big."

"Don't be frightened. I'll take it slow."

"I was referring to your butt. Hamler, could you move over? You're crushing me. That's better. May I ask what you think you are doing?"

"Collecting my debt. How many buttons does this damn nightgown have?"

"Forty-eight. It's the latest style."

"Damn, they're so small too."

"Please, Hamler, I couldn't possibly owe you enough to have to kiss you as well."

"Cara, I'm a great kisser. Everyone says so."

"I'd have to rate you slightly below Mr. Tiro. Now what are you doing?"

"What the hell is this?"

"I believe it is my chest."

"What's on it?"

"A corduroy jumper. Too bad it unzips so inconveniently in the rear. Darn, you shouldn't have pulled so hard. Now the zipper's jammed."

"Fuck!"

"I doubt that very much. Now you've torn it, Hamler. Cotton doesn't grow on trees, you know. You'll have to pay for this dress."

"OK, OK. What's that?"

"Why are you asking me, Hamler? I'm the virgin in this bed. I thought you were the one with the experience in these matters."

"What is this clothing item, Cara?"

"Oh, it's my Grandmother Drucker's gabardine jodhpurs. I packed them along in case you had horses on the island. I suppose your uncle Max shot them all. You won't find a zipper there, Hamler, although I confess that feels rather stimulating. No, the zipper is on the side."

"It won't unzip."

"Of course not, silly. First you have to undue the snap. Or is it a button? I forget. Hamler, do you like to dance?"

"No way, babe. Dancing is for sissies. Why won't it come down?"

"I don't know. Did you unclip the suspenders? How about your uncle, Hamler? I understand he's quite the dancer."

"Ouch! That damn clip pinched me. Uncle Max hates dancing too. He doesn't like to touch people unnecessarily—except to roll the occasional babe. Now what's the fucking holdup?"

"I don't know, Hamler. Things are becoming quite confused down there in the dark. We seem to be approaching a state of fashion chaos. Do you suppose your uncle has fallen in love with someone—perhaps a Russian woman who likes to dance?"

"Cara, my uncle is not the kind of guy who falls in love. He's very unemotional—except about his right to bear arms. What the hell is that?"

"What? Oh, that's a Butt Buddy. And don't think it's a girdle, Hamler. Personally, I wouldn't be caught dead wearing a girdle. No, it's just that sometimes a modern woman appreciates a little discreet shaping. How about foxtrots, Hamler? Has your uncle ever expressed an interest in learning to dance the foxtrot?"

"Never. And he'd probably deck anyone crazy enough to suggest it to him. Cara, this Butt Buddy isn't budging."

"Darn. And Toni warned me to get a larger size too. Sorry, Hamler, looks like that avenue is closed off."

"Damn. Say, Cara, would you like to learn how to perform oral sex on a guy?"

"I better not, Hamler. Not that I'm squeamish, mind you, but I have a frightfully nervous stomach. I get violently ill at the least provocation."

"Damn."

"I'm sorry I'm such a dud in bed, Hamler. Though I believe it's a common problem with us virgins. In fact I can't understand why men put such a high premium on sleeping with us."

"What should I do?"

"Well, Hamler, I could loan you a hankie and you could do it yourself."

"Cara, I couldn't do that. It wouldn't be right. Especially in front of a virgin."

"Thank you for considering my delicate sensibilities, Hamler. Well then, why not pay a nocturnal call on your friend Gilboa?"

"I don't know, Cara. She's looking for emotional commitment. I guess I could fake it though."

"Why not, Hamler? I understand these small deceptions are common between the sexes. Wait! Who's there?"

"Cara, darling, it's me. Renk."

"Beat it, Pohlsohn," hissed my bedmate. "Three's a crowd."

"Cara! You and Hamler!"

"Renk, it's not what you think."

"Oh, Cara. How could you? How could you!"

* * *

I had just gotten comfortable when I was startled to hear the door open.

"Who's there?"

"Hi. It's me, Howard."

"Hello, Howard. Is something wrong? Howard, what are you doing? You've removed your robe. And your pajamas!"

"I don't wear pajamas. You know that."

"Howard, why are you kissing me? And caressing my chest? I thought, I thought you were gay?"

"I decided to take you up on your offer. How many buttons does this damn nightgown have?"

"Forty-eight. It's the latest style. Howard, there's something you should know."

"There's something you should know, Toni. Preliminary signs indicate I could be decidedly bisexual."

"Howard, wait a minute! I'm Cara. Toni and I switched rooms tonight."

Howard removed his moist lips from my left breast. "Toni, this is no time for jokes. You could traumatize me for life."

"I'm sorry, Howard. It's true."

"Oh well, pardon the intrusion, Cara," he said, pulling my nightgown closed. "If you excuse me, I'll just hop on over to the other room now."

"You can't, Howard. Toni's in there with Hamler. She's trying to prevent him from forcing himself on me."

"Toni's making it with Hamler?"

"I hope not. Howard, don't leave. Stay here and let's talk."

"Cara, I don't want to talk. I want to fondle a nice warm body. I want to have sex!"

"I know exactly how you feel, Howard. Well, sort of. I want to make love too. In the worst way."

"Then why aren't you in Renk's room, Cara? He told me he had slept with you."

"That incident was private. He did not have my permission to discuss it with other parties. Anyway, it wasn't me."

"It wasn't? Cara, is your sister a nymphomaniac?"

"Of course not. She's only sleeping with all these boys to help me and assist Father's campaign."

"It's true: politics makes for strange bedfellows. Cara, I have an idea. Why don't we have sex?"

"You mean perform the act merely for educational purposes, Howard?"

"That's right. For mutual enlightenment. Look at it this way: we're past all the most nervous-making parts. We've met. We've gone out—in a manner of speaking. We're in bed together. I'm naked. You're practically naked. I've kissed you. I've fondled you intimately. Let's face it, we've generated considerable momentum toward sexual congress here."

"Well, it's true I had been contemplating having a therapeutic affair. Being a virgin can be so irksome at times. The trouble is I've fallen in love with Dan."

"I know how you feel, dammit. I'm in love too."

"How wonderful for you, Howard. Who's the lucky, er, person?"

"Promise me you won't tell anyone?"

"I promise."

"It's one of our hosts, believe it or not—Forest Primeval. I only beat him constantly at chess because I long so for his rubescent Flunch lips."

"Why don't you tell him, Howard?"

"I can't, Cara. I'd be mortified if he rejected me. Anyway I'm pretty sure he's straight. I have reason to believe he may be sleeping with a girl—your sister in fact."

"I don't believe it, Howard. What makes you say that?"

"Well, I know he's sleeping with someone. And when it comes to illicit carnal affairs, your sister always has to rank as a prime suspect."

"That could be. Wait! I heard the door open. Who's there?"

"It's me, Toni," said a voice in the darkness. "Forest."

"Hello, Sylvan Glade," drawled Howard. "Fancy meeting you here."

\* \* \*

Howard dressed us this morning in our cowgirl sheriffs' outfits: western blouse with tin star and red bandanna neckerchief, wraparound denim skirt, leather boots with twirling German silver spurs, tall white Stetson hat, faux pony-skin jacket with fringe trim, and toy sixguns in tooled leather holsters. On our beaded Taiwan Navaho belt each of us carried real working handcuffs. Despite our festive garb, breakfast (limp cherry popover, four mini cantaloupe balls, one cup of Flunch java) was more than usually somber. Renk is not speaking to Cara, Howard and Forest were observing a frosty silence, I'm cutting Forest dead as usual, Gilboa was pointedly snubbing me and my sister, Hamler bolted his food with his back to everyone, and Dola stared at me with pensive, hostile eyes as she idly stroked my ex-boyfriend's naked thigh. Only Thom, dining in his dishwater-stained loincloth, seemed cheerful and unpreoccupied despite the mountain of crockery that awaits his rubber-sheathed touch.

"They've got some new poll numbers," announced Forest to no one in particular.

"What are they?" asked Renk with profound lassitude.

"Fifty-eight percent for Greer, thirty-seven percent for Flunch, and five percent undecided. A gain of two percentage points for us since last week."

"That still seems such a long way to go," observed Cara.

"It is," agreed Forest, "but the Greer people are starting to look less confident. The smart money is moving our way."

"Money talks," sighed Renk. "Democracy walks."

"The elites always call the shots," said Howard. "It's a historical fact. Get used to it."

"I can't get used to it," muttered Dola vacantly. "I just can't!"

We all stared at her.

"Time to saddle up, Cara," I said, corralling my last melon ball. "Let us leave these gloomy depressives to their morose musings."

\* \* \*

Toni and I strolled over the hill in the storm-freshened sunshine, and were interviewed live on the Today Show by vivacious Anna Swanders. My sister told a nationwide television audience that she was proud to have been named honorary co-chair of the Christian Cowgirls for Flunch Committee, a statement which appeared to have no foundation in fact.

Then she drew her six-shooters and stated that she believed strongly that the Second Amendment also guarantees the right of minors to bear *toy* arms. Still smiling, Ms. Swanders pointed the microphone at me and asked me to comment on my dramatic rescue from the storm-lashed lake. I said it was a terrifying but valuable experience, and I expressed my sincere appreciation to Hamler Flunch and the U.S. Coast Guard for saving my life. Ms. Swanders then broke for a commercial and was playfully handcuffed to her sound man by Toni, who remembered too late she had left the key back in her room.

"We'll go get it," said Toni to the panicking media personality. "Don't go away, Ms. Swanders."

Toni took my hand and we dashed down the hill toward the main house as the manacled technician attempted to duck out of camera range behind Ms. Swanders' fashionably short skirt.

"But Toni," I protested, "the key is back at the lab!"

"That's OK," she said, slowing at last as we approached the back of the house. "Network people love incidents like this. It's what makes live television so stimulating. Besides, Anna has always seemed a little too plastic for my tastes. She reminds me of Mindy in that respect."

We walked into the kitchen where Ottokee and Columbus were enjoying a post-breakfast coffee break.

"Look, Columbus," said the cook. "The posse has arrived."

"Lunch smells delicious," commented Toni, pointing to a large aluminum pot bubbling on the stove. "What is it?"

"That's the filters from the ventilation hood," replied Ottokee. "I'm boiling them in lye."

"Soup stock?" inquired Toni.

"Maintenance," replied the cook. "I don't have no grease fires in my kitchen."

Toni waved hello to Thom in the dishroom and led the way toward a narrow staircase.

"Now just where are you two ladies going?" asked Columbus sharply.

"Oh, up to see Pasco," Toni replied, pausing on the steps.

"I don't know if Mrs. Flunch would like that."

"It's OK, Columbus," Toni assured him. "I visited him before. He's our friend."

We found Mr. Tawawa standing before a cracked mirror in his stark wooden room. He was humming to himself and adjusting a bushy grey hairpiece.

"Oh, it's the Mason girls," he exclaimed, turning around. "Don't you look fresh as daisies. I thought I heard the rattle of spurs in the passageway. I wondered if Clint Eastwood was paying a call. One of you I know already, now which one should I introduce myself to?"

"Me," I said, extending my hand. "I'm Cara."

"My pleasure," he said, shaking my hand warmly. With his other hand he caught his sliding hairpiece. "I don't suppose you have any double-sided tape?"

"No, sorry."

"Too bad. I thought I'd give my toupee an airing. Would you believe I bought this rug secondhand in 1983? All hand-tied human hair. It formerly graced the head of a socially prominent muffler manufacturer in Flint."

"It looks very natural and becoming," lied Toni. "Now I know who you look like, Pasco. With a full head of hair, you're the spitting image of Vice President Greer. The resemblance is striking."

"Do you think so, Toni? Other people have said that too, but I don't see it. Still, I think that's another reason Lima has me squirreled away."

"Is it terribly lonely for you, Mr. Tawawa?" I asked.

"Cara, you're only as lonely as you feel. And right now I feel very humanly connected. Sour orange?"

"Yes, please," we replied.

We unwrapped our candies and sat on Mr. Tawawa's battered black footlocker. He settled heavily into his Flunch paper rocker.

"What day of the week is it?" he asked.

"Wednesday," replied Toni.

"Ah, Wednesday," he sighed, rocking. "A busy day. Many people reserve their weekend dunk tanks on Wednesday. The phone used to ring off the hook."

We all sucked our fruit balls and sighed.

"Pasco," said Toni, "I found out Maximo Flunch is in Vladivostok, Russia."

"Yes, I know. I just heard it on the radio."

"You did!" exclaimed Toni. "Was it a CNN report?"

"No, Reuters. A stringer of theirs happened to spot him at a disco there."

"Was he dancing the foxtrot?" I asked.

"They didn't say," he replied. "But I doubt if Russian discos are quite that far behind the times. Max told the reporter he was just there seeing the sights—an obvious lie. The only sight Max likes to view is animal life trembling in the cross-hairs of his gun. Columbus told me something interesting about my brother-in-law."

"What?" asked Toni.

"Now Columbus is no teller of tales," whispered Mr. Tawawa, leaning forward, "but he is very well-informed. He sees all, hears all, and knows more than all the rest of us put together. He said Max has been selling stock for over a year and accumulating cash. He says ol' Max has an ammo box filled with bundles of $100 bills. And he hasn't seen hide nor hair of that box since Max left."

"How expensive can Russian dance classes be?" wondered Toni. "We heard he might be over there taking a foxtrot class."

"Foxtrot, huh?" said Mr. Tawawa, adjusting his toupee. "Seems like I heard Max mention that word, but he wasn't talking about dancing."

"What was he referring to?" asked my sister.

Mr. Tawawa scratched his head, causing his toupee to slip sideways again. "Damn, I don't remember. I never made it a practice to pay much attention to what that idiot said."

* * *

Mrs. Flunch was boiling mad. Toni and I had been called onto the carpet—an oval braided rug frayed slightly at the edges from Mr. Tiro's puppy teething days—in Mrs. Flunch's square sitting room. She sat at her faux rosewood paper desk and glared up at us over her gold-rimmed bifocals.

"This is an inexcusable breach of my hospitality," she declared, red-faced. "I gave strict orders that my brother was not to be disturbed by anyone during his convalescence."

"We didn't know he was ill, Mrs. Flunch," said Toni. "He looks fine."

"He is not fine. He has been under tremendous mental strain due to unforeseen business reverses. He requires complete quiet and total bed rest."

"I'm sorry, Mrs. Flunch," I said. "We thought he might be lonely and would like some company."

"He is not lonely, I can assure you. I spend as much time as I am able to spare with him. Neither of you had any business snooping about on the third floor. That area is closed off and unsafe. Had you been injured, my family would have been held financially responsible for your criminal trespass."

"You're quite right, Mrs. Flunch," said Toni abjectly. "Our behavior is inexcusable. Only it seemed like such a good idea of Hamler's."

"Hamler? What does my son have to do with this?"

"Well, Hamler happened to mention he had this uncle who, when he put his toupee on, looked very much like Vice President Greer."

"My brother is much better looking than that scoundrel—with or without his toupee."

"Oh, I agree," said Toni. "Anyway, Hamler mentioned that this uncle is in the dunk tank rental business."

"Was in it, you mean," she said. "His tanks are in receivership."

"Right," said Toni. "But that's what makes Hamler's idea so brilliant. It turns the whole unfortunate situation around."

"How?" asked Mrs. Flunch, intrigued.

"Hamler thinks we should make a campaign commercial featuring your brother dressed up as the Vice President sitting on one of his dunk tanks. As the announcer recites the administration's shortcomings, your husband tosses baseballs at the target. Finally, the announcer says, 'They raised your taxes to pay for welfare chiselers,' the ball smacks into the target, Uncle Pasco plunges into the water, and your husband turns to gaze sternly but compassionately at the camera as the announcer says simply, 'Dunk Greer. Elect Claude Flunch President of the United States'."

Mrs. Flunch looked up unblinking. "It's good."

"It's perfect for television," insisted Toni. "It's so visual and graphic. It could be the central image of the campaign. In fact, the campaign committee could get all of Uncle Pasco's tanks out of hock and use them at rallies and public appearances."

"Was that Hamler's idea too?" asked his mother.

"Of course," said Toni, "the boy is a genius."

"My son is quite brilliant," agreed Mrs. Flunch, rising from her paper chair. "That idea is ten times better than 'Your Change Is in the Bag.' Your little friend Howard is not so smart. Excuse me, girls, I must go see my husband immediately."

"Was that really Hamler's idea?" I asked, after she had bustled from the room.

"It will be," replied my sister, "as soon as you go and tell him. Meanwhile, I'm going to track down Howard."

❊ ❊ ❊

The lab was deserted except for Renk, sitting at a metal folding chair. He was ripping a Flunch media handout into long thin strips and staring moodily into space.

"Hello, Renk," I said coldly. "Have you seen Hamler?"

"Your boyfriend is down at the pier, Carissa. Patching up his love boat."

"Hamler is not my boyfriend."

"Oh, I get it. You just sleep with the lummox."

I sighed and sat down beside him. "OK, Renk. I'll tell you something if you promise to keep it confidential."

"I'm very discreet, Carissa."

"Right, except for bragging to Howard that you and I were lovers."

"It slipped out. Sorry, Cara. What is it you wish to tell me?"

"The person you discovered with Hamler last night wasn't me. I knew he was going to come to my room to collect on the 'favor' I owed him for rescuing Dan. So Toni and I switched rooms."

"That was Toni? Then what were Howard and Forest doing with you in Toni's room?"

"Renk, are you spying on everyone? You're so suspicious. We were just chatting."

"Then you didn't sleep with anyone, Cara?"

"Of course not."

"What about Dan?"

"I haven't slept with him either, if you must know."

Renk reached over and embraced me. "Oh, Cara, darling!"

I pushed him away. "Renk, as long as I'm being completely candid, there's something else you should know. That wasn't me in your room the other night."

Stunned, Renk collapsed backwards in his chair. "It wasn't! But, but why?"

"Toni thought you looked miserable. She did it to cheer you up."

"Toni doesn't even like me!"

"OK, so my sister is a nicer person than you imagined. I hope you will be more pleasant to her in the future."

"Cara, it must have been you. The person I was with was so loving. So, so generous!"

"I'd rather not hear the nitty-gritty details, Renk, if it's all the same to you."

"This is so embarrassing, Cara. I've told your sister I love her. I've poured out my heart to her!"

"That's OK, Renk. I'm sure she won't hold it against you."

❖ ❖ ❖

I located Howard in some bushes overlooking the Secret Service encampment.

"Howard, I've been looking everywhere for you. I even had to speak to Forest to ask where you were."

"Shhhh, Toni. Special Agent Ryan Holgate is walking around down there with his shirt off."

"Oh, let me see. Very nice. Howard, my sister informs me you may be bisexual."

"That issue is unfortunately unresolved at this point in time, Toni. We were interrupted at a critical juncture by Piney Patch, who—I might point out—was looking for you. Why do you suppose he came into *your* room late at night?"

"I'm sure his motives were entirely innocent. Perhaps he was looking for you."

"No, he was quite surprised to find me there. He canceled our game this morning, the prick."

"It's just as well, Howard. I need your assistance. Did you hear the news? Reuters has confirmed that Maximo Flunch is in Vladivostok."

"Yeah, Big Trees mentioned it. He didn't seem too concerned though."

"Howard, it appears Uncle Max has gone to Russia to buy some sort of big gun or weapon. He's taken oodles of cash. When you were in Russia, did you hear of a gun called the Foxtrot?"

"I didn't hear of any guns, Toni. Chess players don't need guns. They battle with much more formidable weaponry called knights and bishops and rooks and queens."

"How do I find out if Russia has a military weapon called Foxtrot?"

"Well, we could go search the Internet on Woodpile's computer."

"Great! Let's go do it."

"But we'd need his on-line password to get connected."

"Damn!"

"Of course, I happen to know his password, which I would be willing to share with you in exchange for one small piece of information."

"What?" I demanded.

"The name of Cedar Grove's lover."

"OK, Howard. You win. I've only been withholding it from you to spare your feelings. It's Cara."

"Cara! Damn, I should have known. I've seen him making eyes at her, the beast. But why did he come to *your* room?"

"You know why, Howard. Cara and I switched rooms last night. Forest must have seen us."

"Damn. Cara is so attractive—for a girl. And nice too. No doubt she's much too considerate of my feelings to have told me herself. Now I wish I'd made it with her. I could have had sex with the person who had sex with the person I'm infatuated with. Intercourse through an intermediary: it's the next best thing to being there."

"Howard, you are a seriously deranged person."

"It's my celibate lifestyle, Toni. It's unhinged my reason."

*Chapter 15*

Howard typed in "Russia Foxtrot" and clicked on Search. The modem chattered busily as our electronic quest roamed the virtual globe.

"That's what I hate about computers," I said. "They're advertised as being faster than God, but you spend so much time waiting around for them to do something."

"We could kill some time, Toni," leered Howard. "We could fondle each other's erogenous zones."

"Not in a room filled with the trappings of Mindy Mason. It might put a permanent crimp in my libido. Howard, do all stepchildren wish to murder their stepmothers?"

"Yes, Toni. That is the most typical reaction, especially for girls. You see her as a rival for your father's love."

"But I don't particularly like my father, Howard."

"Most people don't. Let's face it, few straight guys are capable of coping with the emotional demands of fatherhood. Only gay men can bring the necessary sensitivity to the task."

"But gay men seldom have children," I pointed out.

"Yes, that's one of nature's ironies. For example, I noticed your father hasn't been going out of his way to spend much time with you girls. Of course, this neglect makes your relationship with Mindy that much more competitive. The subconscious never takes a day off."

"I hate her. I'm only participating in Dad's campaign because she didn't want me to. I'd like to see her run over by a large bus. Is that sick?"

"Only if you are actively pursuing your bus driver's license, Toni. Oh good, we've had some hits. We're getting a list."

Howard read down the list on the screen. "OK, foxtrot recordings, foxtrot lessons, foxtrot and the balalaika, foxtrot—Stalin's purge of, foxtrot as a tool of Western imperialism. Oh, here: Foxtrot class—status of Russian naval fleet."

"The navy!" I exclaimed.

"Sounds intriguing, Toni," said Howard, clicking the mouse. "Let's call up that page."

We looked at each other silently as the modem churned and buzzed. Then, finally the screen filled with dense type.

"OK, what have we got here?" said Howard, reading. "Foxtrot class—diesel attack submarine."

"It's a submarine!"

"Looks like it, Toni." He read on, "Uh, built between 1958 and 1971 at Sudomekh (Leningrad). A follow-on of the Zulu class. Military men are so fanciful, Toni. Why do you suppose that is? Uh, a total of 60 were completed. This class is now being progressively withdrawn from frontline service. You know, now that I think of it, Vladivostok is the home port of Russia's Pacific fleet."

"Uncle Max is buying a submarine! But why?"

"Have you ever looked closely at those torpedoes, Toni?"

"You think so, Howard?"

"It's the ultimate bragging rights, Toni. Guys are hauling out their guns for show and tell. Uncle Max can say: 'Hey, let me show you my Type 53 dual-purpose torpedo with pattern active/passive homing up to 20 kilometers at up to 45 knots with a 400 kilogram or low-yield nuclear warhead'."

"Nuclear warheads!"

"Let's hope the Russians aren't tossing those in with the deal. Looks like Uncle Max will be sailing home in a 299.5-foot sub powered by three 5,956 horsepower diesel engines and three 5,400 horsepower electric motors. Bet it gets lousy gas mileage. Fortunately, fuel capacity is 360 tons. Boy, those fill-ups must put a dent in your American Express card."

"Now I get it, Howard. That battleship story was just a diversion to throw people off the scent."

"It appears that way, Toni. I hope Admiral Maximo gives us a ride in his new boat. Submarines are extremely Freudian—all that penetrating murky depths in cigar-shaped vessels. I've heard it's technology's ultimate thrill ride."

"You men are so strange, Howard."

"We're jungle savages with computer chips. And thermonuclear weapons."

Some people have no talent for singing, but that didn't stop Howard:

> Come listen to my tale
>   Of men who must prevail:
> In any arms display

Their might must rule the day.
(It's a form of therapeutic play.)

It seems that their libidos
    Are fired by their torpedoes;
In some deep-seated way
    Their guns hold them in sway.
It's ballistically risque!

They really start to sizzle
    When fon - dl - ing a missile,
And go off like a rocket
    With a mortar in their pocket.
But who are we to mock it!

They sing a lovely serenade
    To some enchanting, fair grenade;
And never take the floor to dance
    Unless they're packing or - d - nance.
Do I hear "Give War a Chance?"

A bludgeon, a lance, a pike
    Are what they truly like,
Or smuggle out a musketoon
    And watch the grizzled fellows swoon.
It's like a martial honeymoon!

And when they sigh, "Wow, it's her,"
    They're speaking of their howitzer.
And higher prized than sweatered lasses
    Are lethal stocks of mustard gases.
Oh, do inhale, you silly asses!

"My piece," "my heater," "my gat,"
    Doctor Freud could identify that;
The inference seems quite exact to me,
    The reference here is to anatomy.
There's something amiss, it's clear to see!
    But nothing that can't be fixed in an armory!

\* \* \*

I followed the sounds of whistling to a meadow behind the lab. Renk was practicing "Bag of My Heart," a potential Flunch theme song.

"Renk, have you seen Hamler?"

Renk paused in mid-trill. "Hamler is in a committee meeting, Cara."

"It's Toni."

"Oh," he said, blushing. "Uh, they're discussing some sort of commercial about a dunk tank. It's top priority. You might as well know, Cara has told me everything. Toni, may I ask why you slept with me?"

"You're delusional, Renk Pohlsohn. I have never even touched your skinny and—just to set the record straight—highly repulsive body."

"But, but Cara said . . . it was you."

"Renk, have you ever heard of post-virginity denial syndrome?"

"Uh, no."

"I'm surprised. There was a big cover story about it in *Seventeen* magazine a few months back. Renk, sometimes a young woman is incapable of handling the emotional implications of her first sexual experience."

"I could understand that. It's a big step."

"So, she simply denies the act ever took place."

"Then it was Cara! That is such a relief. I knew it must have been. What should I do, Toni?"

"Just be patient. The authors of the article stressed that confronting the PVDS person is the worst thing you can do."

"Oh, I won't. I'll be very understanding and loving. Toni, your sister has me tied up in emotional knots."

"Glad to hear it. Since Hamler is indisposed, I'm sure you won't mind doing me a small favor. I need help with some inflatable boat portage."

\* \* \*

"Oh, Dan, it's so wonderful to hear your voice. I was worried sick. Where are you?"

"Back in Cleveland, Cara. I slept in my van in Petoskey, then drove back today. I miss you, darling."

"Oh, I miss you, Dan darling."

"Has Hamler been behaving?"

"Reasonably for him. We're all tremendously disappointed. He beat Thom again at wrestling tonight after dinner. And Thom was so confident too. Dola is consoling him now."

"Hamler's a good wrestler. It helps to be oblivious to pain—yours and the other guy's."

"Oh, Dan, let's not talk about Hamler."

"Cara, I miss you. I was thinking of you the entire drive back."

"I miss you too, Dan."

"When are you coming home?"

"We should be back in Rocky Pike by dinner time tomorrow."

"I'll be there picketing."

"Will you write something nice about me on your sign?"

"No, Cara, but I hope you won't take personally my public demonstrations against your family."

"I'll try not to. Oh, Dan, I must go. I have to find my sister. I haven't seen her in hours and we're due up next. Mrs. Flunch has arranged a lavish entertainment program to celebrate our leaving. Renk has already whistled nine songs."

"OK, Cara, I'll let you go. By the way, I'm in big trouble with my friend Cheryl."

"Why, darling?"

"It was her kayak your Tarzan heaved into the lake."

"Good. I only wish your Miss Pom-Pom Queen had been in it."

* * *

I had removed my Stetson. Monty Bellefontaine's mustache was tickling my upper lip; his face powder was flaking off on my cheek. We were sipping gin fizzes in the grey leather and polished teak flying bridge of Ted's anchored yacht. Monty was giving me a tour of the boat and his tongue. Jane, looking confident and fit, was gazing down at us from a gold frame on the wall. Somehow I could sense she did not approve of my being there.

"Monty, I don't think we should be doing this," I said, removing his hand.

"Why not?" he whispered, moving it back.

I removed it again. "Because I would not wish to cloud your journalistic objectivity."

"I'm impartial toward your father, Toni. I think he's no worse than the rest of those clowns. But, like any reporter worth his salt, I have a strong bias toward attractive horsewomen."

On camera Monty looks tremendously sexy smoking his little cigars, but in real life only a corporate tobacco lobbyist could appreciate his breath.

"Shouldn't you be earning your salt now, Monty? Not to mention your reputed six-figure salary."

"Seven figures, Toni. Adena makes six figures and she's only a woman. What could be more important right now than getting to know you better?"

"How about following up on that potentially Peabody-winning Foxtrot story?"

Monty frowned and gulped his drink. "Oh yes, that bizarre alleged submarine purchase. Why exactly would the Russians want to sell a diesel attack submarine to Maximo Flunch?"

"For the money, of course. Or Howard thinks they could have more sinister motives. Perhaps they're doing it to influence the presidential election."

"Maybe they're doing it to sabotage my career. Have you considered that possibility, Toni? Maybe the Russians want me to go on the air with this story so I can look like even more of an ass than I did with the battleship report."

"My information is reliable this time, Monty. It's a worldwide exclusive in your lap."

"I'd rather have you on my lap, Toni. Is that real pony-skin?"

"Call Atlanta, Monty. Phone in this story while it's still hot. Wasn't I right about Max being in Vladivostok? Think how pleased Ted would have been if you'd followed up on that lead. You've got to trust me on this, Monty."

Monty drained his cocktail. "OK, Sheriff Mason. You've got the draw on me. But I'm really putting my neck in the noose for you this time."

\* \* \*

I was very late getting back. When I reached the spotlight-illuminated deck, Howard was singing "Fools Rush in (Where Angels Fear to Tread)" in his wobbly tenor and Cara was glaring at me as she squeezed her accordion. I grabbed a microphone and joined Howard in an impromptu duet. Despite our ragged finish, the audience clapped and cheered. Encouraged, we worked our way through a medley of 1950s dating imperatives: "Remind Me," "Close Your Eyes," "Give Me Time," and culminating in the inevitable "Control Yourself."

"Toni, where were you?" demanded my sister, as we walked off to tepid applause. "Mrs. Flunch was furious at the delay. She made me start without you. I had to lasso poor Howard and drag him on stage."

"I was taking a farewell stroll around the island," I lied. "I'll miss this place. Gilboa was right. I've never been so thin." Just then Dola burst through the doorway from the house.

"It's CNN," she cried. "They're saying Uncle Max is buying a submarine!"

I looked over at Dad sitting beside Claude Flunch. The candidates were white as sheets. Behind them stood Forest, grimacing and mouthing a silent imprecation.

Sorry, Dad. This hurts me more than it hurts you. But really it's for your own good.

* * *

To foil unwanted visitors, I pushed my bed against the door and refused to acknowledge nighttime knocks, of which there were several. This morning in the shower Toni also reported gratefully that she had passed a similarly solitary night. We were fortunate not to have been disturbed. The Bag Island prowler has been at work again. When Columbus arrived with the breakfast cart, he broke the shocking news that someone had scrawled in red spray paint across the front of the laboratory "Flunches Go Home!" Within two minutes of his discovery the lab was swarming with Secret Service agents.

"But we are home," said Dola, perplexed. "Bag Island is where we live."

"Maybe they want you to clear out for Kalamazoo," speculated Thom.

"I think she meant home as in absent from the political arena," explained Howard.

"What makes you think it was a she?" demanded Toni.

"It's apparent from the girlish handwriting," he said. "The perpetrator was obviously a female."

"The young man you unfairly accused the last time is hundreds of miles away in Cleveland," I pointed out to Special Agent Smyrna Bradford. "I spoke to Dan Wyandot yesterday by phone. I knew he could never be involved in this sort of vandalism."

"You can search my room if you like," volunteered Toni. "I have nothing to hide."

"We're going to search everyone's room," said Smyrna, grim-faced. "Nobody leave the premises."

"No one's searching my room," declared Forest. "Unless they have a warrant."

"Search his room first," she commanded.

The special agents dispersed to begin their violent ransacking.

"I hope they don't disturb my bag," said Toni. "It was all I could do to get everything packed."

"By the way, Toni," said Special Agent Bradford. "What are you wearing?"

"It's their mod '60s traveling apparel," explained Howard. "Shimmery chartreuse blazer with velvet collar, loden turtleneck, animal-print hip-hugger skinny pants, and black patent leather boots with lethally pointed tips. Extremely Julie Christie."

"I love the emerald eye shadow," added my sister.

A door banged open down the hallway and a tall agent emerged with an object wrapped in his handkerchief. "Got something," he said, trotting toward us. He flipped back a corner of the white cloth—revealing a can of red spray paint.

"Where did you get it?" demanded Smyrna.

"Found it in the Thomas E. Dewey room," he replied. "Under the bed."

Dola and my sister gasped.

"Whose room is that?" asked Smyrna.

"It's, it's Hamler's room," said Dola.

"It can't be!" cried Toni.

"What do you know about this?" demanded the agent.

"Not a thing," said Toni. "It's, it's just I can't believe Hamler could do such a thing."

"Where is he?" asked Smyrna.

"He's in my room," blushed Gilboa. "He's resting."

Smyrna listened intently as her earpiece buzzed. "OK, folks, breakfast is postponed," she announced. "They want everybody over at the main house as soon as possible."

"What's happening?" asked Dola.

"It's your uncle," replied Smyrna. "He's about to give a press conference in Vladivostok."

※ ※ ※

Hamler's crimes were temporarily forgotten. Everyone crammed into the Flunches' square living room to watch the press conference live via satellite. As cameras whirled and flashed, several Russian trade officials, smiling broadly, strode into the auditorium of the Vladivostok Port Ministry, followed by Essex Kennard, also smiling, followed by Maximo Flunch, not smiling. An older, fatter, and balder caricature of his brother, he was dressed in a wrinkled khaki leisure suit suggesting a slovenly South American colonel in repose. Perhaps to deter impertinent questions, he had strapped a pistol to his hip and was carrying a riding crop.

Without any preliminaries, Essex Kennard made the explosive announcement. All reports to the contrary, Maximo Flunch was in Russia for one reason only. With the cooperation and consent of the Russian government and local business leaders he was purchasing the *Oblako v Shtanakh*, the first and only product of a former Soviet aeronautical consortium. One of the beaming trade officials held up a large color photograph. The audiences in Vladivostok and on Bag Island gasped.

"The gas bag is buying a gas bag!" exclaimed Pasco Tawawa.

Howard and I exchanged shocked glances. Across the room vile Forest chuckled to himself.

"The *Oblako v Shtanakh* is a helium-filled airship of advanced design," continued Essex. "Mr. Flunch will employ it for inspecting his extensive forest holdings and patrolling for fires. It has no weapons and no military utility of any kind."

"What happened?" I whispered to Howard.

"Looks like Essex Kennard arrived in time to put the kibosh on the deal. Probably the Russians refused to hand back the cash. So the rube Yankee got stuck with the sucker prize: a white elephant dirigible."

"Does Uncle Max really want a 600-foot blimp?"

"He doesn't appear to be too thrilled. No torpedoes, alas, but it's still the biggest phallic symbol on the block."

"Monty's going to kill me."

"Hard cheese for Monty," agreed Howard. "I hope they don't fire Adena too."

"My airship runs good and was an excellent buy," declared Maximo. "I intend to fly it personally to Michigan. No, I won't tolerate any interference from the damn bureaucrats at the FAA."

"Was it ever your intention to purchase a submarine?" asked a reporter.

"That's a damn lie," snapped Maximo. "Absolutely not. What would I do with a goddam submarine?"

"What are you going to do with a blimp?" asked another reporter.

"It's a semi-rigid airship, dammit," replied Maximo. "It has over forty-four tons of lift and sleeping accommodations for 29. I may use it for running big-game hunting safaris to Africa."

"For hunting with *cameras*," Essex hastened to add. "Mr. Flunch is opposed to the killing of endangered species."

"Yeah, as long as they stay out of rifle range. Of course, an airship makes a very stable and vibration-free aerial gun platform. And the Bosch used them extensively for bombing ground targets in World War I."

"Mr. Flunch hopes to demonstrate the peaceful uses of airship technology," stressed Essex.

"Totally peaceful," agreed Maximo. "Just keep out of my damn way."

❖ ❖ ❖

"I'll miss Bag Island," said Cara, fastening her seat belt. "We made so many friends here."

Handsome Kent Stow pulled back on the stick, the engines roared, the big pontoons bounced across the waves, then the quivering seaplane parted from the blue water. Kent swung around low over the island and tipped his wings to the small crowd waving at the dock. I recognized Dola, Thom, Forest, Mrs. Flunch, Pasco, and Mr. Tiro.

"Don't kid yourself, Cara," I said. "Most of those happy faces down there are smiling with relief at seeing us go."

Gaining altitude, the plane turned south over the press fleet in Big Bag Bay. I thought of poor Monty having to turn in his trench coat to a wrathful Ted. I hoped he was going easy on the gin.

"It will be good to get back to the real world," commented Renk.

"Why exactly?" asked Howard.

"I can answer that," I said. "To eat actual food again. I intend to stuff myself."

"I'm too depressed to eat," sighed Howard. "Lumber Pile didn't even offer to shake my hand."

"That reminds me," I said, lowering my voice. "What do you know about that paint can?"

"The spray can that Hamler denied ever having seen? The mystery can that is now on its way to Washington for fingerprint analysis?"

"Uh-huh, that one."

"Well, Toni, as you know I keep a sharp lookout on Forest's room. This morning I couldn't help but notice that someone had entered his room while he was taking a shower. I waited until the intruder had left, then discovered the incriminating can under Forest's bed. Preferring to have suspicion fall elsewhere, I took it upon myself to move the can to Hamler's room."

"They're going to find your prints on it, Howard," I replied. "The Secret Service will be hauling you in for interrogation. I hope they don't get too rough."

"I don't think so, Toni. Fortunately for me and that other party I had the foresight to wipe the can down thoroughly."

"Your friend Forest is a double-crossing liar, Howard. He's going to get it. And get it soon."

"I hope so, Toni. And confidentially I hope I'm the fellow who gives it to him."

*Part Three*

*Chapter 16*

Well, the Secret Service officers are still with us in our modest raised ranch in Rocky Pike, Ohio. They're so attentive and anxious to please, I keep thinking of them as houseguests. Now, after nearly three months of visiting, it's time to load up their car, give them farewell hugs, wish them a safe journey, and wave with relief as they pull out of the driveway. But no, here they remain: swigging orange juice at the kitchen island, lounging in the family room, peering longingly out the windows at the great outdoors, urinating with gusto in my bathroom.

Of course, their presence has necessitated some lifestyle changes. For example, one must now devote considerably more effort to one's appearance. Mother, always a model of fastidious middle-age grooming, is now rarely seen without full makeup. Coarse language is completely out of place, I've had to straighten up my room, and God help the person who has to sneeze, belch, or worse. If this is what it's like to live with men, I may have to reevaluate my marriage plans.

It's the day after the much-anticipated homecoming dance, and you can imagine how much my sister and I have to discuss:

Good news, Cara. Howard said last night on the way home from the dance that we have achieved media ubiquity.

I believe it, Toni. You can't turn on the TV without seeing our commercials for Dad or Flam Cola—not to mention our profile on 60 Minutes and that infomercial we did for TrudgeTread Support Shoes. I felt so conspicuous wearing them to the dance. We looked like lumberjacks in matching pink formals.

We're setting new fashions in footwear, Cara. And the support was marvelous. My arches have never been so high. And neither have our bank balances.

Do we really have to wear them all the time, Toni? It's like strapping on ungainly leather boulders. And the hand-stitched buffalo hide digs cruelly into my ankles.

Only when we appear in public, Cara. Renk explained the terms of the contract before we signed. Don't forget, he and Howard are wearing them too.

I wonder if they dance that poorly in normal shoes?

I expect so in the case of your boyfriend Renk. He dances like some sort of pick-and-place industrial robot.

Please don't call him "my boyfriend," Toni.

Why not? He kissed you after the dance, didn't he?

Yes, but there were two Secret Service agents in the room with us.

No doubt your intimacy has already been reported to Washington. Did Renk feel you up?

Of course not, Toni. Did Howard make any advances toward you?

No. I sensed he wanted to, but was constrained by some inner turmoil. Special Agent Ryan Holgate was with us in the back seat, and you know how Howard's always flirting with him.

Yes, you both seem to share that inclination. I thought Dola looked very nice, Toni.

I can't believe the Governor and Mrs. Flunch permitted their only daughter to attend an out-of-state dance in the company of their former dishwasher. She said exactly two words to me the entire evening: "Nice shoes."

I don't think she was being catty.

Don't you? Well, she's going to get hers, believe me.

Please don't do anything rash, Toni. We have to be nice to the Flunches for the sake of the campaign. The election is less than two weeks away.

I'm well aware of that, Cara. Can I bring you a Flam Cola? It's "The Cola To Slam When You Need a Wham Bam."

No, thank you, Toni. I don't feel in need of a "wham bam" at the moment. I must get Howard to explain what he means by that peculiar slogan. I can't believe they paid him $250,000 for it.

Cara, you haven't drunk a Flam Cola in days. Need I remind you we have

112 cases stacked in the garage?

Dan says Flam Cola is marketed heavily in the third world. Poor peasants spend a quarter or more of their income on it—money that should be going to buy food for their families.

Why do they buy it if they can't afford it? I mean, it's not like the taste is anything special.

It's a status symbol, Toni. Flam Cola is advertised heavily as the modern luxury beverage. So people buy it to serve to guests; they don't drink it themselves.

Those Latin cultures are so inscrutable. Hey, I thought you weren't speaking to Dan.

He isn't speaking to me. He says I've sold out. He doesn't even picket us any more. He only communicates by sending me very painful and upsetting notes.

Tear them up unread, Cara. This Flam Cola deal of Renk's has secured our financial futures. We won't have to marry wealthy men—although being well off now virtually assures our making dazzling liaisons among the affluent elite. And we were able to buy Mother a new family-room sofa for Lizzie to sleep on. Don't forget, Cara, it was Flam Cola that bought that fancy new rhinestone-encrusted strap for your accordion. And paid back the Pom-Pom Queen for her wrecked kayak.

I'm aware of that, Toni. I'll endorse Flam Cola. I'll hold up the distinctive green can in commercials and say, "Thanks, Flam, for the wham bam," but I refuse to drink it.

How about a Diet Flam? We have 36 cases of that.

No, thank you.

Cherry Flam?

I think not.

Tropical Flam?

No, nothing.

Suit yourself, Cara, but Mother isn't going to like it if she has to park her car outside in the snow all winter. Taking a strong ethical stand is not always practical in the Rust Belt.

* * *

I don't know why anyone wants to be famous. Once the novelty of being mobbed in public wears off, personal notoriety is mostly an annoying inconvenience. People stare and point as you walk by, your friends grow awkward and distant, teachers grade you severely to avoid any signs of favoritism, complete strangers walk up to you on the street and start telling you what they think of you and your family. Suddenly you're adrift in a world in which all the normal rules of social intercourse are suspended.

I'm finding it all quite a burden, but Toni doesn't seem to mind. She enjoys being fawned over, which I fear can turn one's head if you're not careful. Two days ago she went to the mall with Howard and came home with over fifteen hundred dollars worth of fancy lingerie. She now has her own personal sales representative in the Intimate Sleepware department. I believe a prolonged overexposure to this sort of obsequiousness is a primary cause of the many bizarre behaviors manifested by celebrities. I hope my sister doesn't start sniffing cocaine, creating disturbances in nightclubs, getting her body pierced, or hanging on the arm of balding middle-aged business tycoons.

For example, I needed a few things this morning for our upcoming campaign trip. But instead of making a quick run to the mall for some light, anonymous shopping, I had to give my list to Mother and Special Agent Pulaski. Fortunately, they were willing to interrupt their busy Saturday to run errands for me. Toni and I often suggest to them these small joint expeditions. Last week we sent them out for more envelopes for our fan mail replies, and they were gone for nine hours. We speculate they have to conceal their romantic feelings so Troy won't be transferred to another assignment by his superiors. It's so endearing to observe their businesslike conversations, when as Toni puts it, "you know they just want to rip each other's clothes off."

We were leery of Special Agent Pulaski at first, but he is not, as my sister suspected, a two-faced adulterer. His engraved gold ring, Toni discovered, was a gift from former President Nixon. The ornate inscription is a grateful message from the late president, thanking Troy for guarding Pat and him at their retirement estate.

Dan says no man of character would wear a gift from the pardoned leader of a criminal conspiracy to subvert the U.S. Constitution, but I am not prepared to judge him so harshly. I heard Troy tell Mother that Dick Nixon was the most considerate ex-chief executive he ever guarded. Mr. Nixon was always sending out sandwiches to the men on duty, or insisting they come in to warm up on freezing New Jersey nights. According to Troy, next to Ronald Reagan, Nixon was the most popular president among Secret Service agents, most of whom couldn't stand Jimmy Carter (even Smyrna disliked him). Of course, Mother herself despised Richard Nixon, and once suffered the ignominy of being photographed with him in the banquet hall of a Marriott Hotel when Father was a young congressman. She may have expressed those feelings to Troy on a recent shopping errand, as the ring seems to have disappeared from his hand. I hope he hasn't presented it to her privately as a token of his affection!

\* \* \*

My wealthy chum Howard Archbold dropped by after lunch to consult on our wardrobe for the campaign trip. He has new contact lenses, a flattering $125 haircut, a dusky tanning-booth tan, modish Italian sport clothes, custom-made TrudgeTread Support Elevator Shoes, and attractive new transportation. His parents refused to let him buy a new car, so he compromised on a flame red 1963 Corvette Sting Ray. Yes, under my careful tutelage we have wrought a complete and total Howard Archbold image make-over.

"*Ciao*, Toni," he said, presenting a bronzed cheek for me to peck. I kissed the air in its immediate vicinity, heavily scented by an expensive cologne.

"Hello, Howard. You're looking frightfully stylish and tall. Thank you for a lovely time at the dance last night."

"Don't mention it, baby. Did you see the way Ryan looked at me just now? I think he was checking me out."

"That's his job, Howard. Special Agent Holgate checks every visitor out."

"Yes, but his eyes smoulder so when he visually examines me."

"No more than they smoulder when he looks at me. Ryan is not interested in men, Howard."

"That's OK, Toni. I've decided I prefer straight men anyway. I find his South Carolina accent devastating. I wish I was from the South."

"I doubt you would be much of a chess player if you grew up in Dixie, Howard."

"That's true, but I probably wouldn't be an anguished sexual basket case either. All those southern boys engage in a great deal of erotic horseplay among themselves, you know. It's those long muggy summers. Folks just can't keep their clothes on."

"You mean, Howard, that to attract Special Agent Ryan I should turn the furnace up full blast?"

"I'm surprised you haven't thought of that already, Toni. Seems to me you've tried everything else."

"I still have a few maneuvers in reserve, Howard. Can I offer you a Flam Cola?"

"I thought you'd never ask, Toni. There's nothing like an icy, bubbling Flam Cola when you're contemplating carnal relations with an agent of the U.S. Government."

"You're ready to slam down a cold one?"

"I suppose, Toni. Though personally I'd prefer to slam down a warm one."

*  *  *

Special Agent Smyrna Bradford was watching Lizzie apply metallic silver polish to her toenails in the family room when Renk came over with the papers for the CrumpPak deal. Our boarder has been despondent since she broke up with her boyfriend Ed and was furloughed by Chrysler. According to a friend of hers in the plant, she was replaced on the line by a 32-bit microchip that cost $15.07.

"Lizzie, would you mind if we all came in here to discuss business?" I asked. "Special Agent Holgate is watching a football game in the living room. Alabama is leading by three points, much to his distress."

"Come on in, Cara," said Lizzie. "Smyrna was just explaining the qualifications needed to become a Secret Service agent. I'm thinking of going into police work when my unemployment runs out. Boy, Howard, how did you get to be so tall?"

"Flam Cola," he replied, sipping from his tinkling glass. "It's the secret effervescent formula."

"I see you're limping, Renk," observed Smyrna. "I told you those shoes would give you bunions."

"I am *not* limping," insisted Renk. "It's just this briefcase is so heavy."

"Oh, I see," she said. "They payin' off in cash now?"

"Nothing of the kind," he retorted.

"Don't keep us in suspense, Renk," said Toni. "What's their final offer?"

"Well, you have to understand it would have been higher if you'd been willing to model their clothing."

"No way we're going to been seen in public in a wardrobe from CrumpPak," said Toni. "These shoes and Howard's retro fantasies are bad enough."

Renk opened his bulging briefcase and spread out some papers on the Ping-pong table. "OK, I've been meeting with your lawyers and their lawyers. These are the numbers that have been agreed upon, subject to your approval. They're offering a one-year contract, with three one-year renewals, cancelable by either party, for print and media endorsements of hard goods only. First year 1.8, second year 1.8, third year 1.5, fourth year 1.2."

"And if Dad gets elected?" asked Toni.

"There's a $500,000 bonus, first year only," he replied.

"So we get $2.3 million in the first year?" I asked.

"Right, sweetheart," said Renk, "assuming current trends hold and your father is elected. Our negative ads are bleeding Greer badly, especially among high-school educated blue-collar workers in the south, west, and mountain states. The spots with Uncle Maximo at the firing range are especially effective. Right now, we're looking at a near sweep in the electoral college."

"How come the dollars go down in the later years?" asked Howard.

Renk shrugged. "CrumpPak figures the public is fickle and will be looking for new faces by then. I had to fight to get that much."

"Where do we sign?" asked Toni, clicking open her green Flam Cola ballpoint pen.

"Toni, shouldn't we wait until Mother comes home?" I cautioned.

"Hey, Cara, $2.3 million is going to save Mom some serious money in weekly allowances. Where do we sign, Renk?"

"I've highlighted every place in yellow," he replied. "Of course, your mother as legal guardian will have to sign too, but I understand that is no problem."

My sister finished signing with a flourish and passed the pen to me.

"One other thing," said Renk. "The contract contains a strict morality clause. CrumpPak is concerned about upholding its family image."

"That's why they fire any employee they suspect of being gay," observed Howard. "They're known to be quite ruthless."

"No hanky panky?" asked Toni.

"None whatsoever," said Renk, "or CrumpPak gets every cent back."

"I wouldn't be cashin' that check any too fast if I were you," commented Smyrna.

"Give it some thought, Cara," said my sister. "Your love for Renk might have to remain on a higher plain for years."

I signed my name without hesitation.

"Of course," said Renk, "the contract only mentions immoral acts which become publicly known. CrumpPak is not interested in micro-managing your private lives."

Our new-found affluence put Toni in the mood for a song:

> I hope you don't get churlish,
>     If I express a tender girlish
> Enthusiasm for being rich—
>     From poverty it's such a switch.

> We've had a wealth infusion,
>     A sudden cash transfusion
> That's left us rather rich—
>     Satisfying our material itch.

Alas, we have not billions,
　　But must scrimp by on mere millions,
So though not colossally rich,
　　We can indulge without a glitch.

Our holidays will be gleeful,
　　Of gifts we'll have a tree-full;
My extravagance will be truly rich,
　　My old stuff I'll have to ditch.

Some jewels I'll be acquiring,
　　My person I'll be sapphiring,
The look will be very rich,
　　For those boys I need to bewitch.

My wardrobe I'll be augmenting,
　　Some envy perhaps fomenting
Among girls not quite so rich—
　　Compared to me, they'll have not a stitch.

I'll wave to those poor ladies
　　As I motor by in my Mercedes;
The sheen will be luxuriously rich—
　　A swank ride they'll long to hitch.

And when I inspect a painting,
　　At the price tag I'll not be fainting;
My collection will be tastefully rich,
　　With none of that offensive kitsch.

And after long days of shopping,
　　My heart won't be flipflopping,
At the bills I'll give not a twitch,
　　For you see, I'm delightfully rich!

"And I hope," amended Howard, "money doesn't make you a bitch."

"This is so unfair," complained Lizzie, recapping her polish and admiring her glittering feet. "Everyone's getting wealthy and I'm the only one here who's actually been in a CrumpPak store."

"Alas, that won't be true for long," said Howard. "All the stores on our itinerary are installing giant hooks in their parking lots."

✻ ✻ ✻

Dan telephoned as we were dressing to go out for a celebratory dinner. "I don't think you should go tomorrow, Cara."

"Dan, we've been through this before. The FAA has certified it as safe. The campaign spent over $300,000 refitting it."

"Then why won't the Secret Service let the candidates ride in it?"

"They're just being overly cautious. That's their job. I'm looking forward to the trip. I think it will be very educational. And we get a two-week sabbatical from school."

"How much are you receiving from CrumpPak?"

"How did you hear about that, Dan?"

"Knowing Mr. Pohlsohn, I just put two and two together."

"Well, you have to keep it a secret. We're getting several million dollars. But we don't have to wear their clothes."

"Cara, CrumpPak has been a disaster for hundreds of communities across the country."

"They're a very successful retail chain, Dan. They got a medal from the government."

"They wipe out local small retailers and pay their employees peanuts."

"It's free enterprise, Dan. The market rewards firms that are best able to compete. You can't fight progress."

I heard what sounded like a deep sigh.

"How was the dance, Cara?"

"It was very nice. Renk is a wonderful dancer."

I regretted that lie as soon as it passed my lips.

"Cara, you have the power to affect the course of our country's future.."

"Dan, be reasonable. We're just a minor sideshow. I'm going to play my accordion and Toni's going to sing. Howard's written some neat new campaign songs."

"You underestimate yourself, Cara. Give it some thought. Don't be dazzled by the hype and the money."

"Dan, I know what I'm doing."

"I hope so. What did you think of your father's performance in the debate?"

"I feel he did fine overall. I feel that incident where he got flustered and misspoke about stoning women who have abortions has been blown out of proportion by the media."

"I counted 37 lies and distortions, Cara."

"Dan, you're hardly an unbiased observer. Really, I don't think this conversation is getting us anywhere."

"Cara, darling, you hold the key."

"Good night, Dan."

Chapter 17

The campaign van arrived right on the dot at 6:30 a.m.; Howard and Renk were already on board. The latter's parents finally seem resigned to his assisting our campaign. Perhaps it helped that Renk was paid $50,000 for providing background whistling for Flunch-Mason TV ads—media exposure that resulted in his new album, "Pohlsohn Astride the Prairie," currently rocketing to seventh place on the Country & Western charts.

As directed by our Fashion Czar, Cara and I had dressed for travel like nomadic tribeswomen. We were garbed in flowing silk caftans the color of a Saharan dawn, matching harem pants, gold silk turbans, and mirrored TrudgeTread Support Sandals adorned with tiny brass bells.

"Good morning," called Cara, tinkling softly as she loaded in her accordion and modest bag. "The weather promises to be warm and glorious."

"I can't speak for the rest of the world," I said, as Special Agent Holgate trundled down the walk with my bags, "but global warming has certainly improved the climate of northeastern Ohio."

"My father says it should prove a great boon to local property values if all the retirees have to move back up from Florida," said Renk.

"Toni," observed Howard, "you appear to have packed for a grand expedition up the Nile."

"Just the necessities," I replied. "As instructed, I pared my luggage down to the bone. Where's Smyrna?"

"Here I am," said Special Agent Bradford, carrying a large blue Secret Service duffle bag. "I think I should get hazard pay for going up in that thing."

"I'm looking forward to it," said Ryan. "We're fortunate to have this assignment."

"We're fortunate to have you with us," smiled Howard, flirting shamelessly.

"Now, you girls be careful," said Mother, giving us both farewell hugs. "If anything goes wrong—even minor—make them land it. And don't go up in it again until you're satisfied it's safe."

"Don't worry, Mother," said Cara, straightening her turban. "We'll be fine. We won't take any chances."

"Special Agent Pulaski," I said, "I hope you will guard our mother while we're away."

"I'll do my best," he said, shyly scratching his nose.

Mother glanced at him and smiled. Love among older people can be so charming and sweet. Then we were waving good-bye as the van pulled away and drove down the deserted street in the soft early-morning light. To my surprise we did not get on the interstate heading south, but proceeded to the familiar red brick home of Thom Kirkwood, where the thick-necked defensive end was waiting by the curb with his gym bag. He tossed it on the pile in the back, was frisked for old time's sake by Ryan, and pushed in beside me.

"Thom," I exclaimed, "where are you going?"

"Hi, Toni. I'm coming with you guys. I was specially recruited by the Flunch campaign."

"But what about your Rocky Pike football schedule, Thom?" asked Cara. "Aren't you on the varsity?"

"Sure am," he replied. "I'm a starter. But Coach Granger excused me. He says electing the leaders of our country is more important than winning football games."

"And what will you be doing for the campaign?" asked Howard.

"Washing dishes," replied Thom. "They love my work."

"It's nice that you're coming along, Thom," I said, grasping his big bruised hand. "I've missed you terribly."

"Gee, Toni, have you really? You look nice. Is that a preview of your Halloween costume?"

❄ ❄ ❄

Despite the earliness of the hour, several hundred dignitaries, campaign volunteers, and reporters were milling about on the tarmac when we pulled up in front of the immense Akron Airdock, where the *Oblako v Shtanakh* had been refitted (and rechristened *Liberty or Death*, after the stirring Patrick Henry speech). Its original Russian name, according to Howard, was the title of a Mayakoffski poem, which he translated loosely as "A Cloud in Trousers."

Renk said the hangar-like airdock was so large it had its own weather (with real indoor rain clouds), and could easily accommodate two dirigibles side-by-side. The great doors had been rolled open, and the silvery nose of

"Flunch's Folly" (as Democrat detractors called it) loomed high above us. I gazed anxiously beyond the crowd for a familiar picketer, but did not see that person.

"*Liberty or Death*," commented Toni, "what an unfortunate name for an experimental aircraft. It's even worse than those New Hampshire license plates. How ironic to perish in a car wreck in that state."

At that moment we were thronged by dozens of shouting reporters, including Monty Bellefontaine, newly appointed campaign correspondent for SKNN (Southern Kentucky Network News). Naturally, we answered only Monty's questions as impatient campaign aides shouldered the media representatives aside and hustled our party toward an aluminum staircase extending down from the airship's grand gondola car.

"Yes, we're looking forward to our trip," I beamed.

"No, we're not afraid," scoffed Toni. "I only hope there's enough refreshing Flam Cola on board."

"Yes, we're very heartened by the polls," I said, walking up the stairs.

"Father and Governor Flunch are doing a wonderful job of communicating their message of hope to the American people," added my sister. "We are marching to victory in our TrudgeTread Support Shoes, available now at your local CrumpPak store."

At the top of the steps we paused to pose for pictures with Maximo Flunch himself and Captain Yevgeny Mingov, veteran of the Afghanistan war and pilot of our aircraft. Not tall but obviously fit, he bore his fifty years with an intimidating military correctness. He had a thick brow, heavy beard, and dark, flinty eyes. Toni commented later that he looked exactly like a Communist. In person, Mr. Flunch seemed older, shorter, stouter, and balder than he did on TV. Both men gave evidence of not having bathed recently. They brusquely shook hands with us as camera strobes flashed, and Forest, neatly dressed in a brown wool suit, made the introductions.

"Whose goddam luggage is that?" demanded Mr. Flunch, pointing. "This is an airship, not the goddam *Queen Mary*."

"It's luggage from all of us," lied Toni, smiling as she adjusted her turban. "It was carefully weighed according to your written instructions. I myself am bringing barely more than a brassiere and a change of panties. Would you care to inspect my bag?"

Mr. Flunch colored. "You look like Doris Day of the Arabian Nights."

"You look like Ernest Hemingway," she replied. "Do you mind if I call you Papa Max?"

Mr. Flunch beamed. "Not at all. Welcome aboard."

"Hello, Dwindling Forests," said Howard, climbing the stairs with several more of Toni's bags. "You're looking very corporate."

"Howard, is that you?" replied Forest. "You're so tall, so dark."

"You left out handsome. How's your chess game?"

"Excellent. I'm ready to kick some butt."

A body pushed its way past us. "Oh, Thom!" shouted Dola, fighting her way down the stairs. "Oh, Thom, my dear sweet honey!"

"Don't tell me Dola's coming on this trip," said Toni. "I thought they were enforcing a strict weight limit."

* * *

The entrance from the stairs opened on the grand salon—a spacious room about the length of a railroad car and over 20 feet wide. Arrayed along both sides were delicate-looking silvery metal armchairs that swivelled to face large windows canted outward at the top. A door in the forward wall opened on the navigator's compartment, which led to the pilot's bridge: a large window-lined room bristling with impressive-looking instruments, gauges, levers, and switches. Standing near this door were the now-celebrated Pasco Tawawa, wearing his toupee, and a handsome young man in a trim blue blazer.

"Hello, Toni," said Pasco. "Let me help you with your bags."

"I'm Cara," I replied, smiling. "It's nice to see you again, Mr. Tawawa."

"Please, Cara," he said, "the whole country calls me Pasco."

"Hi, Cara," said the young man, placing an arm familiarly on my shoulder and kissing me on the lips. "Those sandals look ridiculous."

"Hamler, is that you?" I asked, greatly startled.

"I should have wrestled some sense into your pal Renk. He's selling you out too cheaply."

"TrudgeTread Shoes is a very lucrative connection," said Renk, entering behind me and gazing about with interest. "Cara and her sister will never have to work."

"That's fortunate," replied Hamler, "because soon they may no longer be able to walk."

"Follow me," said Pasco, hoisting my accordion case. "Dola worked out all your cabin assignments. Everybody's got their own private stateroom on the upper deck."

We walked through the salon behind Pasco and Hamler. Arranged down the center of the cabin were a half-dozen lightweight tables, each with six chairs. All furnishings featured the same perforated silvery metal construction as the armchairs, including a bar with four stools in an aft nook and a small upright piano in a forward corner. On the floor was a beautiful tapestry carpet depicting an aerial view of blue rivers winding among forested green hills.

"The ship seems quite stable," remarked Toni, carrying only her purse.

"It should," replied Forest. "It's still resting on its wheels."

My sister scowled and turned her back on him.

A corridor off the salon led to a galley on the right and what looked like a pantry on the left. In this small room Columbus and Ottokee were busily unpacking boxes, including several cartons of Scotch whiskey. They looked up, smiled, and returned our waves. Past several more closed doors labeled in Russian, we came to a rear emergency escape door and a steep staircase leading up.

"The upper deck is larger," said Hamler, leading the way. "It's built within the superstructure of the ship."

Up the narrow stairs, we came to a long, wide corridor extending forward under two immense beams fashioned from silvery spars riveted in complex, interlocking triangles. Down the center of each beam ran an array of pipes, cables, and bundles of multicolored wires. Several feet above the beams stretched a vast fabric ceiling, stitched with thick, uniform seams and interrupted at regular intervals by a cat's cradle of metal cables anchored to the beams. Exposed lightbulbs in metal cages under the beams illuminated the corridor, lined on both sides with low hollow metal doors. Taped on each door was a handwritten name card.

"Cara," said Forest, "you and your sister are aft here. Renk, you're next to Cara. Howard, you're here across from me."

Thom trooped up the stairs with four bags clutched in his arms and Dola clenched affectionately around his waist. Behind them came Special Agents Holgate and Bradford.

"We're up front, honey," said Dola. "I've given you the best view." She glanced up at my sister's turban. "What's with the head bandage? Did you forget to wash your hair or are you recovering from brain surgery?"

"Thom, darling," said my sister, ignoring the query, "you can take my bags into my room."

"Sure, Toni." Thom disengaged himself from Dola, opened the door, and carried his load inside. Dola stared straight ahead down the corridor; Toni examined the overhead mechanical systems with feigned interest.

"Secret Service, you're in the middle of the corridor," said Hamler, directing Ryan and Smyrna.

Pasco carried the accordion case into my room and set it down at the foot of a narrow metal bed that reminded me of our Bag Island accommodations. The room was larger than I had expected. There was a small closet just inside the door, a built-in bureau with eight crimped tin drawers, and a tiny metal shower behind a floral plastic curtain. Opposite the bed was a small metal table and an odd metal lounge chair that looked like it might recline if you knew how to manipulate its many levers. The room was illuminated by a long, low window set into the angled far wall about a foot above the floor. The walls and ceiling were upholstered in a light grey fabric, and the tiles on the floor appeared to be tawny cork. The window drapes and matching bedspread were a bright May Day red.

Pasco showed me how to work the complicated Russian plumbing. By turning a knob and pulling down on a handle, a small stainless steel sink folded down out of the wall. You pushed another handle to swivel the sink back up, then pressed a foot lever and pulled a cable to unfold a matching stainless steel toilet with integral molded seat and tissue dispenser. Very ingenious, if not particularly clean. Then you reversed this elaborate operation to wash your hands in the sink. The shower was more straightforward, except for the timer.

"You push this red button by the door," Pasco said, pointing. "Then you have two minutes of water in the shower."

"Two minutes, right," I noted. "Is that all?"

"Well, you can get out and push the button again. That gives you one more minute of water."

"They make you get out of the shower?" I asked. "That's not very convenient. What happens if you press the button a third time?"

"Then a bell goes off in the pilot car, and Maximo comes up and screams at you for wasting water."

"Is there a shortage of water, Pasco?"

"Water is very heavy, Cara. Maximo would rather devote his expensive helium to lifting alcoholic beverages, T-bone steaks, his shotgun collection, and his freeloading poker buddies."

The room lurched. We had begun to move.

\* \* \*

Howard, Forest, Renk, and I hurried down to the grand salon to observe the preparations for our departure. The exterior stairs had been folded away, the door secured, and the airship towed out into the bright October sunshine by a small tractor. In the pilot's room Captain Mingov and two other uniformed officers were monitoring instruments and adjusting controls. At the bar Maximo Flunch and three disreputable-looking men were hoisting glasses of celebratory champagne. They glanced toward us as we passed, but Forest did not stop to introduce us. I waved to Gilboa McComb chatting with Hamler by an aft starboard window. We sat at armchairs near the piano along a forward port window, and shared salted peanuts from a gold-rimmed white china bowl set into an indentation in the metal window ledge.

"Forest, those men with your uncle, are they reporters?" I asked.

"Hardly, Cara," he replied. "Uncle Max is still pissed about the battleship and submarine stories. He's banned all reporters from the airship. That's his personal retinue of Michigan lackeys—or part of it. The tall guy in the plaid shirt is his driver Meeker Chuckery. The skinny guy with the thinning flat-top and tattoos is Geyer Wabash. The big-nosed guy missing three fingers on his right hand is Kirby Belmore. His hobby used to be making pipe bombs."

"A festive bunch," said Howard.

"I've been around those guys all my life," said Forest. "They're part of the scenery now. Nobody pays them much attention. I couldn't believe it this morning when reporters were trying to interview them."

"What did they say?" asked Renk.

"Not much," replied Forest. "Dad's got everyone on a short leash, including Uncle Max, who is certainly making the most of his moment in the spotlight. Did you see that big profile of him in *Newsweek?*"

"Oh, there you are," said Toni, jangling harmoniously as she approached. "Is it just me, or is this carpet positively vertigo-inducing? I've discovered an enormous propeller outside my cabin window. Does everyone have that sort of view obstruction?"

"I don't," said Howard.

"Me neither," said Renk.

"I see," said Toni, sitting in the armchair beside me and helping herself to a handful of nuts. "Now I know why thoughtful Dola assigned me to that cabin. Cara, I've hung a few of my things in your closet. These Russians have very odd notions about travelers' accommodations. I believe a monk in a cave has more storage space. And the bathing facilities look positively medieval. When do we take off? I notice Mindy outside has concluded her speech, or perhaps someone has mercifully unplugged her microphone."

"Any minute now," replied Forest. "They've fired up the burners."

"Is the *Liberty or Death* steam powered?" asked Toni.

"We call her the *Lod* for short," noted Forest.

"No, the technology is quite up-to-date," said Howard. "Instead of jettisoning ballast to get airborne, they generate additional lift by heating the helium with computer-controlled propane burners."

A low rumble vibrated through the ship.

"They've started the engines," said Renk.

Almost imperceptibly, the airship began to rise.

"Praise the *Lod*," said Howard. "We're moving."

We peered eagerly out the windows as the airship rose sedately over the vast landing field, turned slowly toward the northeast, and sailed above the modest homes and shuttered rubber factories of east Akron. A grimy river glittered in the late morning sun, then blinked out as our bulbous shadow crossed its surface. We could see people lounging in their back yards, children playing in a park, a dog barking furiously at us from the end of its tether. Here and there across the brown autumnal landscape, a few malingering trees still wore threadbare reds, oranges, and yellows.

"When do we start accelerating?" asked Toni.

"I think we're pretty close to cruising speed now," replied Forest.

"We're crawling!" exclaimed my sister.

"Oh, our ground speed is probably 75 or 80 miles an hour," said Howard. "Depending on the winds."

"But you can drive that fast in a car," noted Toni.

"Sure," said Renk, "but you can't drive a 30-room hotel down the turnpike."

\* \* \*

Considering our previous experience with Ottokee's cooking, lunch was much better than we had dared hope. Uncle Max is certainly less niggardly with the provisions budget than his thrifty sister-in-law. He can afford it. Forest revealed that Max is billing the Flunch-Mason Campaign $2,000 a day per passenger! Ottokee and Columbus laid out a lavish buffet, including something Howard speculated might be roasted pheasant. We filled our gold-rimmed *Oblako v Shtanakh* china plates, and dined at the light-as-a-feather metal tables in the grand salon. Several tables away, Ryan and Smyrna lunched with two Secret Service agents I vaguely remembered from Bag Island.

Dola clung to my ex-boyfriend all through lunch, casting frigid glances in my direction and interfering with poor Thom's food intake. Forest was surprisingly amiable toward me. I hope he has not forgotten how much we detest each other. At the owner's table Uncle Max and his low pals switched from champagne to beer and grew quite boisterous. Forest said Maximo received a severe dressing down this morning from Captain Mingov for fiddling with the controls. He and his cohorts have been banned from the pilot's bridge.

I observed Columbus carrying three trays into the pilot's car, but none to the upper regions of the *Lod*. I am told this airship is crawling with unseen Russian crewmen. Where do they dine? I hope we will be able to meet some of them. I was disappointed to learn that the not-very-attractive copilot and shockingly middle-aged navigator are experienced blimp aviators from Ohio.

Despite our torpid pace, the slate green waters of Lake Erie came into view as lunch was concluding. We circled leisurely above the modest skyline of Erie, Pennsylvania—our first scheduled stop—greatly exciting the populace below (we hoped). Thom pried himself free of Dola, strapped on an apron, and began gingerly busing the dishes. He was informed by Columbus that each hand-painted porcelain plate has an appraised value of $600.

"Forest, you'll be making a brief speech," said Gilboa, checking her clipboard. Besides her arduous role as companion to Hamler, she is in charge of campaign logistics on this trip. "Dola, you'll be reading a poem—not the one about Thom. Pasco, I've been assured the water will be nicely warmed this time."

"I hope so," said the presidential-candidate look-alike, straightening his silk power tie.

Gilboa continued. "Toni and Cara, you'll be greeting the mayor and 37 Protestant ministers. No songs on this stop—not enough time. You'll also be posing for photographs in the garden department. They have snowblowers on sale this week. I suggest you change out of those sandals. Too summery for snow."

I appealed this outrageous edict to Howard, but the wimp acceded without a murmur to the desecration of his fashion vision. We retired reluctantly to our cabins to change into our horrible, horrible support shoes. I tried to follow Renk's suggestion and think only of the money. This was far from easy as—bells silenced, feet imprisoned—we clomped painfully back down to the salon.

Descending in a mild breeze, our airship lumbered stately toward a huge CrumpPak store set amid a profusion of fast food eateries and franchise outlets on a suburban strip street. A large crowd was gathered in front of the bunting-draped store. I also spotted several TV news vans and what looked like a high-school band garbed in purple and gold. Mobile barricades held the eager throngs back from a square section of blacktopped parking lot that had been cleared of cars and lamp stanchions.

Instead of having 200 CrumpPak shoppers tug on ropes to bring us down, the captain lowered a hook on a steel cable. A man on the ground grabbed the swaying hook and fastened it to a metal ring anchored in the center of the cleared area. Then a winch under the gondola was activated, and *Lod* reeled itself smoothly down until its four large outrigger wheels made contact. The crowd roared; the band launched into a militant fight song. We had survived our first flight!

*  *  *

Maximo Flunch was the first one out the door. He waved, called to the cheering crowds, pointed proudly up at his airship, and raised both hands in a victory salute. I hope someone takes him aside soon and informs him that he is not the candidate. Gilboa had to prod him down the steps to get the proceedings underway. She runs a tightly paced campaign appearance. After Mayor McKean's welcoming address, Forest gave a two-minute speech of bland platitudes, Dola recited her dreary poem, Hamler read a "telegram" from Governor Flunch to the citizens of Erie County, and Renk in a rhinestone-studded white leather vest whistled "Tumbling Tumbleweeds." Then Pasco was dunked with dispatch in his trademark red, white, and blue tank, and the legion of grinning ministers filed by for affable well-wishing.

Improbably, all 37 men of the cloth had worn their tap shoes. Pulling out gold-tipped canes and black top hats, they began to dance and sing:

> We're making this a better world,
>    By preaching in this manner;
> To liberals damned this gauntlet hurled:
>    Desist and furl your banner!
>
> Our cause answers to a higher force—
>    To us He delegates authority;
> We must pursue His faithful course,
>    And proceed to legislate morality.
>
> Congress must be swiftly purged
>    Of the blight of secular humanism,
> And our judges regularly scourged
>    By the light of scriptural dogmatism.
>
> *Repent! Repent!*
> *Of your left-wing demonolatry!*

*Assent! Assent!*
    *To our rightist ideology!*

The bedroom we must also invade—
    Not to pry, but merely for probing;
Our edicts no citizen may evade,
    Banned will be all but marital disrobing.

And decency we'll restore to the arts,
    Where so much smut and slime are;
And clothed will be those disgusting parts
    Now bared as in some Republic Weimar.

*Repent! Repent!*
    *Of your fervent criminality!*
*Assent! Assent!*
    *To our reverent Christianity!*

Heretics, apostates, and backsliders
    From public life will be excluded;
Also feminists, queers, and welfare idlers,
    And the rest of the wickedly deluded.

Flags unburned, dope unsnorted,
    Guns at hand and laws that allow use,
Kids at prayer and not aborted,
    This is our vision of family values!

After the ministers withdrew to polite applause, we circulated among the awed crowd for two additional minutes of handshaking (unsanitary and unpleasant), were introduced to the manager and assistant-managers of the store, posed for photos with the assembled aqua-smocked staff, trooped *en masse* to the garden department, examined heavily discounted snowblowers with feigned enthusiasm while cameras flashed, autographed a TrudgeTread Support Shoes point-of-sale poster, gave a 15-second interview to the local newspaper, accepted stained jumbo bags of imitation-buttery CrumpPak popcorn from an elderly clerk, waved to the crowd, hugged a flower-bearing majorette (spilling popcorn down her bare back), hurried up the gondola steps, turned and waved farewell. Then the steps powered up, the door was closed, the hook was released, and we were airborne again. Total elapsed time: 27 minutes.

"Good job," said Gilboa, checking her watch. "But let's try not to dawdle next time. Pasco, how was the water?"

"A bit on the hot side," he replied, clutching his red satin "Hell to the Chief" robe around his dripping grey suit. "I'm afraid it melted my toupee adhesive. I don't like being photographed without it."

"My uncle's hairpiece must remain in place," insisted Hamler. "It's crucial to my dunk-tank media strategy."

"OK, Hamster," said Gilboa, "I'll phone ahead to our next stop to have the water adjusted."

"Don't bother, girlie," said Max. "We'll get some vodka into Pasco and I'll have my rigging man sew that goddam rug to his scalp. Whatd'ya say, Pasco?"

"I think first, Max, he should sew your chin to your scalp. It might help your looks and it would certainly improve your conversation."

*Chapter 18*

Our brief stop in Erie was my first opportunity to get a full view of our airship. I was stunned by its awesome size. It is magnificent: the length of two football fields (according to Thom), and taller than a twelve-story building. Hard to believe, as Renk points out, that some pre-war German Zeppelins were considerably larger. Huge fins extend out from its tail, and two engine cars hang fore and aft on each side. Painted in immense blue letters on its silvery skin are the words "FLY WITH FLUNCH." Under this, much smaller red letters spell out "AND MASON." Toni says this is a preview of the sort of billing we can expect when father is elected Vice President. I feel it is a tremendous honor just to be mentioned at all.

* * *

While we were cruising toward Buffalo, loathsome Forest gave Howard and me a tour of *Lod's* mechanical regions. A small door at the rear of the upper deck led to a narrow catwalk snaking aft beneath the twin triangular beams of the "keel." Sunlight glowed through the translucent silver fabric; the still air was heavy and warm. The airship creaked softly, and overhead we could hear the gurgle of unseen propane burners.

"I'm sure I would feel quite nervous on this catwalk if we weren't enclosed," I said.

"It's a false sense of security, Toni," said Forest. "If you slip, you'll fall about 2,000 feet. That thin fabric beneath us won't stop you."

"That's a pleasant thought," said Howard, gripping the flimsy railing.

We made our way several hundred feet toward the tail, then followed Forest along a branching catwalk to a ladder leading down through a fabric-skinned tube. This long, narrow, scary ladder terminated in a cramped noisy room where a thin young man was reading a magazine called *Double D-Cup* beside a throbbing orange diesel engine the size of a small car. He dropped his magazine behind his stool and welcomed us in voluble Russian, barely audible over the deafening rumble. He pointed out the features of his engine, indicating with dramatic flourishes the levers and buttons we mustn't touch. Then he raised a flap and let us take turns peering out a small, greasy window at the great propeller spinning at the end of the engine shaft.

"Yes, it's nearly as good a view of the mechanism as the one from my cabin," I noted.

Smiling, we thanked the crewperson for the tour; he wiped his hands on a rag and shook our hands. We ascended the ladder and continued aft on the main catwalk.

"Is there a crewman in every engine car?" I asked.

"Yes, a two-man rotating crew is assigned to each engine," replied Forest. "They change shifts every six hours."

"Where do they hang out when they're not on duty?" asked Howard. "This place is deserted."

"I'm told there are modest crew quarters forward on the third deck," said Forest. "They have their own mess hall and cook."

"Can we visit there?" I asked.

"Sorry, Captain Mingov declared it off-limits. He doesn't want the crew fraternizing with the passengers."

"And vice versa," noted Howard.

The catwalk terminated in another steep ladder. Howard grasped its rails and peered up doubtfully.

"Wind in Your Willows, this thing goes on forever. What's up there?"

"The elevator room," said Forest. "I think you'll find it interesting."

"Why isn't there an elevator to the elevator room?" I demanded.

"Different type of elevator," explained Forest. "These elevators are the big horizontal fins outside that move up and down to keep the ship flying on a level plane."

Forest led the way. Howard and I followed behind, laboriously hoisting our heavy TrudgeTread shoes up the endless rungs. At last, puffing from exertion, we came to a tiny platform such as trapeze artists might swing from in the circus. From this precarious perch, a small door opened on a sunny room shaped like a sideways flattened cone. We were in the very tail of the airship. A ring of windows framed a brilliant blue doughnut of sky—split vertically by the great fabric-sheathed rudder extending backward from the ship. At a control panel under the windows sat a young man wearing headphones. He looked up from his instruments and smiled. It was the most breathtaking vision I had ever seen.

* * *

I gasped, Howard gasped.

"*Zdrastviytye*," said the young man, brushing back soft cascades of golden hair from his noble brow. His eyes were the color of luminescent jade. A carpet of blond bristles sprouted evenly from his perfect jaw. In one electrifying motion, he pulled off his headphones and slid a cigarette behind his right ear. I had never witnessed a more sensual act.

Forest introduced us. "This is Dimitri Batovo, the elevator man," he said. "As far as I can tell, Dimitri doesn't speak a word of English."

"Who needs language," I said, holding out my hand. Dimitri rose, wrapped his warm fingers around my yielding digits, and squeezed with immense delicacy. He smiled, pointed at my turban, and spoke Russian phrases of enrapturing musicality. Of course I understood every word, except I didn't quite. I cursed myself for all those months wasted in Italian class.

"What did he say, Howard?" I asked anxiously.

"I don't know, Toni," said Howard, needlessly prolonging his handshake. "Maybe he wants to know if you're a Cossack."

"Tell him I'm very pleased to meet him."

"Toni, my Russian is extremely rudimentary. I was only in that country for three weeks, and I spent 90% of my waking hours in silent chess matches. Besides, I think he can tell you're pleased to meet him. You're practically swooning at his feet."

Dimitri gestured for us to sit. The only guest seating was a low bench beside his console. We squeezed onto it, and Dimitri returned to his stool. His tall, slim body was garbed all in grey: heavy duck trousers, military-style tunic open at the neck, scuffed leather boots laced halfway up.

"This is a very pleasant room," said Howard, looking around and gesturing. "Much nicer than the engine room."

Dimitri smiled. No plaque germs had dared sully his gleaming white teeth.

Howard made explanatory engine-like rumbling sounds and stuck his fingers in his ears.

Dimitri looked puzzled, then held out a pack of Marlboros. Only I accepted one.

"Toni, you detest smoking," Howard reminded me.

"I'm not going to smoke it," I replied. "I'm going to treasure it always."

Dimitri lit a kitchen match and held it out to me. I smiled, leaned forward, and blew it out. "Save for later," I said, slipping the cigarette sexily (I hoped) under my turban.

Dimitri pondered these actions, then smiled. The guy was obviously bewildered. The girls of Russia probably smoke like chimneys. I was suddenly overwhelmed by a wave of hatred toward every nicotine-addicted Slavic floozy who had ever laid an overly familiar hand on him.

Dimitri idly stroked the cigarette behind his ear and glanced at my shoes. I could sense his keen Russian mind was trying deduce the fashion concepts behind TrudgeTread Support Shoes.

I pointed at my footwear and rubbed my fingers together. "Big bucks," I said. "Endorsements."

Dimitri smiled and looked impressed. "Extra cool."

"What do you know," said Forest. "He knows two words of English."

"The man has odd opinions on shoes, though," said Howard. "Is that why he's locked away up here instead of starring in the latest Hollywood blockbuster?"

"Dimitri is a redundant system," explained Forest. "The elevators and rudder are controlled hydraulically from the pilot's bridge. Dimitri is the manual backup in case of system failure. He has to man these controls whenever we're airborne."

"Who relieves him at night?" I asked.

"Wouldn't you like to know," said Howard.

"No one," replied Forest. "It's a tricky job keeping an airship level. He's the only one with the training."

"But we'll be flying for days," I pointed out.

"Dimitri's used to it," said Forest. "He takes catnaps. According to Captain Mingov, Dimitri's accustomed to waking immediately if the ship tilts out of plane."

Dimitri smiled and pointed to his control board. "Extra cool."

"And definitely worth the climb," I added.

※　※　※

"Where have you been?" inquired Renk, when we returned to the grand salon. At the owner's table, Maximo Flunch and his cronies were cleaning their shotguns—an operation Smyrna and Ryan were observing with some nervousness. I hope they've had the sense to confiscate the bullets.

"We were seeing the sights," I replied. "We visited an engine room and met the elevator man."

"Those catwalks are dangerous," said Ryan. "I think it would be best if you all remained on the public decks. Or ask an agent to escort you on the catwalk."

"That's right," said Smyrna. "And preferably not me."

"You missed Buffalo," said Cara.

"Oh, did we stop there?" asked Howard.

"Of course not," said Dola. "We just circled the downtown area at a low altitude so the voters could see us."

"I'm told that's the best way to visit Buffalo," I said.

Dola ignored me. "Then we flew over Niagara Falls. It was awesome."

"Where are we now?" asked Forest.

"Heading toward Rochester," said Renk. "The terrain is still pretty flat. Farmlands and small towns. Sometimes you can make out the names on the municipal water towers or spelled out on airport hangars. We just passed over our second Akron of the day."

"You can see so much more at this altitude than you can flying in a jet," said Dola. "I love it when little kids run out and point up at us. I wish we could drop them a little note."

"You could tie it to a little brick," I suggested.

Dola gave me her most frigid look.

"How do like my Ruskie balloon?" asked Max, sighting down a swabbed-out gun barrel.

"It's wonderful," said Cara. "I'm very grateful for the opportunity to participate in this flight."

The tall cretin known as Meeker Chuckery giggled lasciviously.

"I think, Papa Max, it's ever so much more interesting than riding in, for example, a submarine," I commented.

"That could be, girlie," replied Max. "But the weight limits are a damn nuisance. We're the biggest target in the sky for any radical nut packing anything larger than a Daisy air rifle. We've got four Federal agents on board, who are reporting on our every move. There's a goddam Soviet military officer manning the stick. And the armaments frankly suck."

"Cocktails are served," announced Columbus, entering from the galley with a tray of martinis.

"Yes, but the refreshments are great," I said, helping myself to a glass.

"Are we allowed to drink booze?" asked Dola.

"Help yourself," said Max. "I dumped those goddam cases of Flam Cola in the parking lot at Erie. Captain Mingov says somebody went way over their luggage allotment. He almost had a goddam hernia getting us off the ground this morning."

\* \* \*

Ever the sneaky person, Howard slipped stealthily into my cabin.

"Toni, may I speak with you?"

"You may if you are able, Howard. How many martinis have you consumed?"

"Three. All on an empty stomach too. Is my speech impaired?"

"I detect some slight slurring. What is that large body of water out there? Are we over the Atlantic already?"

"That is Lake Ontario, Toni. Spread out at our feet, as it were, is Rochester."

"Rochester, Minnesota? We *have* drifted off-course. And with an American navigator too."

"I believe it is Rochester, New York. Yes, that is unmistakably the Xerox Building. Toni, I've been observing Forest and your sister."

"A delightful occupation, I'm sure."

"Not entirely. Toni, given their long period of separation, they do not appear particularly overjoyed at being reunited."

"They are being discreet, Howard. You should try it sometime."

"Toni, I have confided to Piney Patch that Cara went to the Rocky Pike High School homecoming dance in the company of Renk."

"A reckless move on your part, Howard. How did Forest take that distressing revelation?"

"He appears to be holding his jealousy in check."

"And did he appear happy to see you, Howard?"

"I can't tell. Forest is so damn unemotional. How can you tell if an unemotional person likes you?"

"I wouldn't know, Howard. I'm not attracted to unemotional people."

"I seem to be. The colder the better. I'm probably destined to have a long-term relationship with a sociopath. I wonder if Dimitri Batovo is emotional?"

"I'll let you know in the morning."

"Toni, you heard Ryan. That catwalk is dangerous."

"Everything pleasant in life is dangerous, Howard. All the rest is boring. Shall we go have another martini?"

"I don't mind if I do."

\* \* \*

The setting sun gilded the salon with an amber light as we sat down to dinner. To the south, one of the Finger Lakes mirrored a long sliver of the darkening sky. Columbus served, assisted by Thom in a crisp white jacket and black sweat pants. Ottokee had prepared a delicious Chicken Kiev. I didn't drink any of the wines, which Toni reported were superb. They must have been. Gilboa and Hamler, I noticed, polished off several bottles between them.

During dessert Howard tested the stability of the airship by attempting to balance a nickel on the tabletop. The coin remained on its edge for more than three minutes, but Howard fell out of his chair. I think he may have had too much to drink. That is not surprising; there are no soft drinks to be had. After several requests Columbus finally consented to bring me a small glass of tepid foul-tasting water. Thom reports he is permitted only the barest puddle of water in his dishpan. The glasses, I noticed, were not as clean as one might wish.

That oafish fellow Geyer Wabash told a crude, racist joke that cast a pall over the entire room—except for the owner's table, where Maximo Flunch led the hearty laughter. That sort of male behavior infuriates me, and makes me want to have nothing at all to do with men. It did not help that Renk became boorishly affectionate and spilled his after-dinner brandy down my front. I fear I was less than tactful in rebuffing his slobbering advances.

The salon overhead lights came on as it grew dark outside. Tiny lights began to twinkle charmingly here and there in the carpet—almost as if the floor had disappeared and we were floating magically above a moonlit landscape. Out the canted windows, the eastern horizon began to glow with the lights of a large city. As we sailed over the outskirts, demarcated by a uniform grid of purplish streetlamps, we could see in the distance eight brilliant shafts of light streaming straight up into the night sky.

"What are those strange lights?" asked Dola.

"I think they're searchlights," said Forest, sipping his brandy. "By the way, Uncle Pasco has passed out."

"He never could handle his liquor," remarked Hamler, staggering over to the window. "He's worse than Mother."

"It looks like the Nuremberg Rally of 1934," slurred Howard. "The great cathedral of light created by Albert Speer's massed searchlights. My God, it is Nuremberg! We've passed through a time warp! So that's why the Germans were monkeying around with Zeppelins."

"I don't think so, Howard," I said. "I just saw a neon sign for the Syracuse Bank and Trust. That must be Syracuse down there. Yes, there's the Carrier Dome."

"It's almost like they're welcoming us," said Dola. "Look, we're flying into the center of the lights."

Intense white light stabbed across the walls and ceiling as we passed through the beams.

"The lights are coming from some kind of shopping plaza," said Renk. "Oh, it's a CrumpPak store. Fancy that. They must be having a sale on searchlights this week."

"It feels like we're descending," said Toni, holding her turbaned head. "Or else my stomach is rising."

"Did you say Syracuse?" gasped Gilboa. "Oh, my God! We *are* landing! We're meeting the governor of New York. And a bunch of other big-shots. Holy shit! Where's my clipboard?"

Uncle Pasco woke with a start. "The floor!" he screamed. "It's fallen out!"

\* \* \*

Our campaign appearance in Syracuse did not begin badly. Governor Pompey, gallantly putting his convention disappointments behind him, delivered a rousing endorsement of the Flunch-Mason ticket that brought the vocal crowd to its feet (or perhaps they were standing already—details at this point were beginning to lose their crisp definition). Forest gave a fairly coherent two-minute speech, sounding only slightly more woodenly sibilant than usual. Dola launched into her approved poem, then lurched off into uncharted territory. I remember a murmur going through the audience at the reference to "muscular buttocks." The following stanza rhymed "my venus gap" with "Thom's jock strap," causing Hamler to collapse in convulsive snickering and Dola to terminate abruptly her recitation.

As Hamler proved unable to read his telegram, the program moved on to Renk, who got most of the way through "Doney Gal" before succumbing to the infectious giggles. Cara stepped bravely into the fray, squeezing out the first chords of "Responsible Flunch" (lyrics by Howard Archbold) that I was supposed to sing to the tune of "Impossible Dream." I got as far as "To vote for the responsible Flunch, to reject the incumbent Greer," when I too regrettably lost my composure.

"Shut up, Renk," I giggled into the microphone. He and Hamler howled. Cara determinedly played on. Rising to the occasion, I segued into an impromptu tap dance—difficult but not impossible in TrudgeTread Support Shoes. Inexplicably, this enraged my nemesis. Dola swung a drunken punch and knocked off my turban. I gave her a (slight) push, she fell against Governor Pompey, he instinctively grabbed for her, and she executed a noisy George Bush down the front of his blue suit and yellow power tie. Simultaneously, Pasco Tawawa toppled forward off his dunk tank perch and had to be rescued from drowning by two CrumpPak stock boys. I expect that is why the red-faced store manager canceled our photo session in the sporting goods department.

After Pasco was resuscitated, he was carried aboard the *Lod* and we immediately departed. I thought I'd rest a few minutes in my cabin before venturing back to visit Dimitri, but when I awoke sunlight was streaming in, my head was throbbing, and outside my window I could see a large revolving propeller and the Chrysler Building.

*Chapter 19*

"I was just thinking," remarked Howard over breakfast. "You know, we're among the few people in history who can say they've taken a shower at an altitude of 2,000 feet over Manhattan."

"Some shower," said Renk, nibbling a piece of dry toast. "I'd describe it more as a heavy mist. I've been wetter than that on muggy days in Ohio."

"Did you get out for the bonus round?" asked Dola.

"Yes, but I still feel sticky. How does my hair look, Cara?"

"Very nice, Renk," I lied. I was not feeling very talkative. I had had to expel Hamler from my cabin last night after he broke the lock on my door and forced his way in. Fortunately, the cad was falling down drunk and unable to put up much of a fight. Underneath the trim suit and Ivy League haircut, he was still the same lecherous boor I had grown to dislike and fear on Bag Island.

"Oh, look," said Dola, "here comes the other nurse."

My sister entered looking sweet and fresh in her red-and-white striped dress, opaque white hose, and white TrudgeTredge Nurse's Support Shoes—accessorized with a prim white cap and stainless steel stethoscope. Howard dressed us as hospital candy-stripers this morning to help accelerate our recovery from last night's unfortunate image-tainting events. He says Americans feel an unconscious need to be taken care of. Though our party platform stresses individual self-reliance, he believes the voters will respond positively to our nurturing apparel.

"I feel rotten," said my sister, pouring a cup of coffee. "My damn shower's broken. The water just dribbles out, then stops. I dropped my toothbrush down that bizarre toilet. I hope it doesn't plug up the works. Is that the Statue of Liberty?"

Forest glanced out the window. "Seems to be. It's a large copper-clad figure of a woman holding up a torch."

"So what's happening with the powers that be?" asked Toni, buttering a slice of cold toast.

"They've been partially appeased," said Howard. "Renk got his ass chewed by Mr. Crump himself."

"My first cellular phone conversation with an irate billionaire," said Renk. "It's fortunate he appreciates my whistling. I managed finally to get him calmed down."

"The deal's still on?" asked Toni.

"Yes, assuming your conduct is above reproach from now on. And Gilboa's smoothed things over with Essex Kennard, Governor Flunch, and your dad. She's been on the phone for hours coordinating damage control with our PR people. The official explanation is giddiness caused by a helium leak, combined with food poisoning. Ottokee's not too happy about that though."

"I thought breakfast seemed rather meager," said Toni. "For a frightening moment I thought I was back on Bag Island."

"In some ways it was fortuitous that Dola threw up," said Forest. "It lends credibility to the story."

"I always get a little queasy when I'm starting my period," she confessed.

"Your period of public drunkenness?" inquired my sister.

"Look who's talking, Nurse Ratched," Dola retorted.

"It's fortunate that newspapers aren't delivered up here," said Howard. "And the only TV is in Maximo's cabin. Like it or not, we must remain blissfully ignorant of the present media feeding frenzy."

"In some ways, I blame myself," sighed Renk.

"As well you should," said Toni. "You're supposed to be looking after our interests, not boozing it up like some coarse Maximo Flunch flunkie. Cara was extremely disappointed in you. I doubt seriously she will be coming to your cabin this evening."

"Toni, please!" I protested.

"Oh, there you are, Thom," said Toni, taking our waiter's hand. "Bend down, honey, I want to check your vitals." While Dola fumed, Toni placed her stethoscope against his broad, T-shirted chest. "My goodness, Thom," she said. "You're either having a massive coronary or you're very excited to see me."

✳ ✳ ✳

Once you get past the sprawl of Newark and the chemical complexes of Elizabeth, the state of New Jersey is surprising verdant and rural. I don't know what Dan is complaining about. The trees seem to go on forever down there. I'm sure they must be hiring forestry majors by the droves. Our first stop of the day was Trenton. We sailed over the sluggish Delaware River, circled the golden-domed State House, and landed in a comfortingly familiar suburban shopping district, where the CrumpPak manager greeted us with cautious cordiality. More than 50 eager reporters shouted questions at us as Cara and I toured a large display of garage door openers.

"Yes, they've patched the helium leak," I said. "It's quite a relief. We were feeling dreadfully light-headed. Fortunately, our TrudgeTread Support Shoes kept us at least partially grounded in reality."

"No, we never drink anything stronger than Flam Cola," replied Cara. "We're too young, and our parents strongly disapprove of teenage drinking."

"You mean just by pressing this little button your garage door will go up and down by itself," I exclaimed. "How marvelous!"

Our family has had an automatic garage door opener for years, but Howard has stressed that we must reach out to the less affluent voters as well. His advice on wardrobe selection was equally astute. Our candy-striped apparel proved both sobering and soothing to the media. They quickly realized they would have to look elsewhere for scandal.

Before departing, I was able to grant an exclusive interview to Monty Bellefontaine, who had driven all night from Ohio in the SKNN news van (a rust-eaten 1958 Ford panel truck), and looked quite the worse for wear. I hope he is getting enough to eat. The imported little cigars have disappeared, and he is now rolling his own cigarettes. His makeup looks like he purchased it on sale at CrumpPak. I told Monty's viewers that should Father be elected, one of his highest priorities will be the economic revitalization of southern Kentucky. "He's determined to get the mines reopened," I avowed. "Jobs must come before the environment. The meddling bureaucrats at the EPA must be restrained."

By the time we reached our next stop (suburban Philadelphia), Maximo and Hamler had dragged themselves from bed, performed their ineffectual ablutions, and were ready to face the public. Hamler read his standard tele-gram with a straight face, Uncle Pasco dropped soberly into his tank, and Papa Max declared to the press that the reputed helium leak was a "damned and vicious lie," causing Gilboa to pale visibly. At our third stop (outside Baltimore), Max grudgingly corrected this "misstatement," explaining that though he personally had never smelled any gas, he had just been informed that helium was colorless and odorless.

An emergency supply of Flam Cola was waiting for us in Baltimore; only our host and his poker sycophants had beer with lunch. To punish the overly intrusive Federal bureaucracy, Max insisted that we bypass Washington—depriving entrenched officialdom of the thrilling sight of our magnificent airship in flight.

Autumn returned as we sailed over pastoral Virginia. The brown landscape gave way to patchy undulations of orange and red, recalling to Howard the shag carpeting in his parents' bedroom. Since we were now over firmly Republican territory, fewer stops were scheduled and we had more free time. Max and his pals played with their firearms, Hamler changed into shorts and went for a jog through the upper and lower decks, Thom toiled over his precious dishes, Howard and Forest broke out the chess board, Dola mooned out a window and awaited poetic inspiration, Uncle Pasco groomed his damp toupee, Renk plumbed our financial futures with his pocket calculator, Cara penned a letter to Mother, and I announced I was going to my cabin for a short rest.

* * *

"Dimitri?"

The handsome elevator man did not look up. He was sitting at his control panel, a cigarette behind his ear, with his eyes closed.

"Dimitri?"

He made a darling face and brushed his cheek with his hand. His breathing was slow and regular. Apparently Dimitri had mastered the art of sleeping while sitting upright on a small stool. I know this is difficult to believe, but I found him even more irresistibly desirable in this unconscious state. I felt a mad impulse to disrobe one or both of us. I tiptoed over and touched him lightly on his shoulder, evidently disturbing his delicate equilibrium. He toppled over backwards and crashed to the cork floor.

"Dimitri! Are you all right?"

The fallen aviator curled his hands under his head and slumbered on.

"Goodness, you Russians can certainly sleep." I leaned over and sniffed his breath. I could detect no alcohol. This close, his pale sensual lips looked impossibly inviting. Recklessly, I kissed him. Muscles immediately tensed beneath me, arms locked around me in a powerful embrace, and surprised green eyes stared into my own.

"Eva?"

"No, actually. It's Toni Mason. We met yesterday."

Dimitri released me and scrambled back onto his stool. He brushed back his hair in embarrassment, and made what sounded like polite entreaties for forgiveness in Russian. To show that I was not offended, I sat on his lap, put my arms around his broad shoulders, and kissed him again. Long thin fingers wrapped themselves around my left breast as he kissed me back. Then the hand crept inexorably under my candy-striped skirt like a red tide; I shuddered as it crossed into American territory.

With gentle deliberateness Dimitri removed first my clothing, then his. Interestingly, Russians don't wear socks; they just wrap large handkerchiefs around their feet. Darling Dimitri needed a bath, but then don't we all? We lay back on a dusty mat under the round window. Only a thick white scar across his abdomen marred the perfection of his body. I traced its jagged course with my fingers, then reached for its logical conclusion. Dimitri closed his eyes and moaned. He said something sweet in Russian. I fumbled through my piles of clothes, pulled a condom from a pocket, and handed him the foil-wrapped package. He pushed it away.

"*Nyet.*"

"Oh, Dimitri darling, you must."

"*Nyet.*" Dimitri tossed the prophylactic aside and kissed me passionately. My mind raced. How long had it been since my last period? About two weeks. Damn! Dimitri tenderly stroked the insides of my thighs. His technique was quite advanced. I bet Eva liked that too. I tried to think. What, what would Mother do in a situation like this?

*       *       *

To gain a new perspective on the beautiful countryside, Renk and I descended 900 feet in *Lod's* bullet-shaped observation car. Housed in one of the chambers behind Ottokee's galley, it was lowered on two steel cables through a hatch in the floor. The car was a lightweight tubular metal pod sheathed in fabric, with a narrow bench for a seat, a large plastic window across the front, and an intercom for communicating with the pilot's car.

"It's not too chilly for you, is it, Cara?"

"No, Renk, it's lovely. I feel like we're soaring silently above the ground like the birds. It's almost like riding a magic carpet."

"You do get a better sense of our relative groundspeed at this lower altitude."

"I think it's thrilling. Look, you can see the airship far above us. It's wonderful."

"You're wonderful, Cara."

Renk put his arm around my shoulder.

"Thank you, Renk," I said, straightening my nurse's cap. "I hope that position does not impair the circulation to your hand."

"Cara, I love you."

"I wonder what that river is down there? Are we still over Virginia do you suppose?"

"Cara, you're the most wonderful person I've ever met."

"You're only 16, Renk. You haven't met that many people."

"I'll never love anyone like I love you."

"You shouldn't jump to hasty conclusions, Renk. What are you doing?"

"Kissing you."

He did. I had to admit it was not unpleasant. As Renk began to sing (and yodel), I understood why he had taken up whistling.

> Cai-ee-ai-yo-ai-yay,
>     I long to drive away
> The cares that makes you trifle
>     With my love you say to stifle.
>
> Cai-ee-ai-yee-ai-yo,
>     I longed for us to go
> To a cabin in the sky
>     Where I could look you in the eye.
>
> Cai-ee-ai-yo-ai-yai,
>     We're a floatin' by and by,
> We're a soarin' in the air,
>     And I'm a nuzzlin' at your hair.
>
> Cai-ee-ai-yo-ai-yum,
>     I hope you're not so glum,
> When I take you in my arms
>     Just to know your womanly charms.
>
> Cai-ee-ai-yo-ai-yay,
>     I got to up and say
> That you're the only one—
>     To no other am I gonna run.
>
> Cai-ee-ai-yo-ai-yup,
>     I'm as frisky as a pup,
> Just a waitin' for a sign
>     That your heart's a joinin' mine.

Cai-ee-ai-yo-ai-yes,
    I hope you can sorta guess
I got feelin's I must express,
    It's just somethin' I can't suppress.

Cai-ee-ai-yo-ai-yee,
    I'm a singin' with sincerity,
That my lovin' ain't incidental,
    But a passion transcendental!

Cai-ee-ai-yo-ai-yum,
    I guess I'm just a bum,
But my love runs mighty deep,
    With you I'm a hankerin' to sleep!

Cai-ee-ai-yo-ai-yees,
    Well, I guess I sang my piece,
This I'm a wishin' to discover:
    Darlin', am I to be your whistlin' lover?

I sighed and looked out across the landscape.

"Cara, I've waited very patiently."

"I appreciate that, Renk."

"I'd like to come to your cabin tonight, sweetheart."

He kissed me again.

"Tonight, Renk? But the final presidential debate is tonight. Maximo Flunch is bringing his TV down, and we're all going to watch it in the salon."

"After the debate, Cara, I'm going to come to your room."

"The bed is frightfully narrow."

"We'll manage somehow. Cara, I love you."

"Renk, what was that noise?"

"It sounded like gunshots!"

"There it goes again!"

Our tiny car lurched and began to move rapidly upward.

❊ ❊ ❊

When I threw on my clothes and raced down to the salon, Maximo Flunch and his men had been disarmed and were being held at gunpoint by the four Secret Service agents.

"Never point a goddam gun at me unless you intend to use it," said Max, calmly lighting a cigarette.

"I'll use it if I have to," said Smyrna. "Discharging a firearm from an aircraft is a violation of FAA regulations."

"I have a right to defend my property," insisted Max. "And I am prepared to defend that right by any means necessary."

"What the hell were you firing at?" demanded Ryan. He looked attractively intimidating with his revolver drawn.

"The black helicopter," replied Max's crony with the deformed hand. "It was following us."

"I'll handle this, Kirby," said Max. "I do not intend to be shadowed by unknown federal agents in helicopters. You can tell that to your goddam bosses in Washington."

"Anybody see any helicopters?" asked Smyrna.

The other Secret Service agents shook their heads.

"I saw something," said Dola. "I'm not sure what though."

"It was a helicopter," insisted Kirby. "It backed off when we fired at it."

"I would have drilled it too if I'd had my telescopic sight," drawled the ever-repulsive Meeker Chuckery.

"There's an Air Force base at Goldsboro, North Carolina," said one of the Bag Island agents. "We're probably within 50 miles of there. They might have had a copter in the area."

"Well, no harm was done," said Gilboa cheerily. "I suggest everyone put away their guns, and we all get ready for our appearance in Raleigh."

"Mr. Flunch, since you lied to us when you said you'd handed over all your ammunition," said Smyrna, "this time we'll have to confiscate your weapons. They will be returned to you at the conclusion of the trip."

"Well, lady, you've got the drop on me," smiled Max. "Take our goddam guns. I just hope you find them all. For your sake."

Max's pals smirked and snickered.

What a loutish bunch. But such a timely interruption!

* * *

The sun was low in the west as we floated over Raleigh's historic Greek Revival State House, manicured golf courses, tidy pocket lakes, and bustling red-brick cigarette factories. The largest and most enthusiastic crowd of our trip so far turned out to welcome us at the suburban CrumpPak store. While we twirled the dials of elaborate boomboxes displayed in the home electronics department, a dozen Secret Service agents, assisted by the North Carolina State Police, conducted a discreet but thorough search of the *Liberty or Death*. Howard said later that he saw them carry out numerous long, narrow objects wrapped in black plastic. I think we all feel safer knowing that Maximo Flunch has been disarmed. Captain Mingov especially seemed relieved. Maximo sulked all through dinner after we were again airborne, and much angry muttering was heard at his table. "Wait 'til we cross the Rio Grande," I heard that vile Kirby Belmore whisper.

Papa Max's spirits seemed to revive during the televised debate. He was able to laugh heartily at many of his brother's statements. I thought Governor Flunch did as well as could be expected, but I couldn't help but notice Forest wincing, Renk grimacing, Gilboa biting her nails, and Howard squirming in his chair during the Governor's more fanciful analyses of U.S. foreign policy (tonight's topic).

"It's not fair," said Dola, at one point. "Vice President Greer's had eight years to get all his answers down pat. He thinks he's so articulate."

"Well, he is," pointed out Renk.

"Why is that?" asked Dola.

"I think it has something to do with possessing a lively and informed intelligence," said Howard. "Fortunately, voters are seldom impressed by that."

"Father looks very comforting," remarked Dola proudly. "Like an old shoe."

"Is Liberia a terrorist nation?" asked Cara.

"Only to its own citizens," said Forest. "I think Dad meant Libya."

"Oh dear," said my sister.

"Claude's a pantywaist," declared Max. "He's been one for 53 years. It's the plague on second-born male Flunches. Right, Hamler?"

"You know it, Uncle."

Everyone looked at Forest. He appeared unruffled by these familial barbs.

"What exactly is a pantywaist?" asked Thom. "I mean, what's the legal definition?"

"A pantywaist," expounded Max, "is a person without the balls he was born with. He's your basic ball-free wonder."

"It takes a lot of courage to run for president, Uncle," said Forest evenly. "This country is full of crazy people with guns. In my opinion confronting the daily risks of being President is a true test of bravery."

"A classic pantywaist statement," said Max.

How unnerving. I actually felt myself sympathizing with Forest Flunch!

\* \* \*

We were stunned by a news report that came on after the debate. A protester has climbed the large sycamore in front of our Rocky Pike home and tied himself to an upper branch. (He has fastened the ropes in such a way as to prevent injury to the tree.)

"It's Dan!" cried Toni.

"Oh no!" I exclaimed.

Dan is refusing all nourishment. More alarming still, temperatures in Ohio are expected to fall into the low 30s tonight. It may even snow!

"The guy will do anything for publicity," sneered Renk, "even catch pneumonia."

"He's extremely sincere in his beliefs," I retorted.

The TV news cameras spotlighted a dim figure far overhead among the naked branches. A crowd had gathered on the sidewalk; I recognized little Amy Czerkoffski from next door. Disturbingly, Toni thought she spotted Cheryl the Pom-Pom Queen holding a Thermos bottle. Dan, thank goodness, appeared to have dressed warmly in thick gloves, a woolen cap, and a down jacket. Tied at his feet was a handwritten sign reading "Protect our Natural Heritage. Reject Flunch-Mason Environmental Extremism."

"Look who he's calling an extremist," scoffed Dola.

"There's Mom!" called Toni.

Mother appeared in a taped segment saying she respected "young Mr. Wyandot" for "acting on his principles," and would take no action to have him evicted from her property. "This is a free country," she told the reporters. "Let his message be heard."

"Father's not going to like that," said Toni.

"He's going to be furious," I agreed.

"At this moment Mindy is probably having what we in the medical profession term a coronary thrombosis," noted Toni, twirling her stethoscope.

"You're *not* in the medical profession," said Dola. "And your mother is just as nutty as you are."

"At least my mother knows where Libya is," Toni retorted.

"I got an idea how to drag down that damn tree-hugger," said Maximo.

"Toss him one of Kirby's pipe bombs?" suggested Meeker Chuckery.

"One shot from a .357 Magnum?" volunteered the loathsome Kirby Belmore.

"Nope," said Max. "Chain saw."

"I got a better way, Max," said Geyer Wabash, chortling repulsively. "We build a bi-i-i-g bonfire at the bottom of the tree."

I could listen to no more; I got up and hurried from the salon.

* * *

As I walked down the dim, shadowy passageway toward my cabin, I had an unsettling feeling of being observed. I looked around but could see no one. As I undressed for bed I thought of my dear friend whose principles had compelled him to retire for the night on an empty stomach in a frigid tree. I felt a flush of admiration for Dan, and prayed Renk would have the good taste not to come to my room this evening. It was not to be. A half-hour after retiring, I heard my door open and close softly. I did not switch on the lamp.

"Renk, I'm feeling very tired."

He only grunted in reply. Apparently, he was determined to have his way. He silently shed his garments and pushed his way into my narrow bed. His body had an unusually strong aroma which I attributed to the inadequate bathing facilities. He brushed a lock of hair from my cheek and kissed me with great tenderness.

"Renk, you might have at least shaved."

He grunted and kissed me again. In spite of myself, my body began to respond to his soft caresses. Frankly, his passion took me by surprise. He boldly pulled down my nightgown, and I felt his hot mouth on my breasts.

"Oh, Renk, darling . . ." I stroked his hair and encountered a foreign object behind his right ear. To my curious fingers it felt like a cigarette.

"Renk, honey, with your asthma, I hope you haven't begun smoking. You know, according to the Surgeon General. . ."

I was startled to hear the door open and close softly. I froze.

"Renk, someone is in the room!"

"Yes, Cara," I heard Renk's voice say from across the cabin, "it's me."

Then who . . .? I screamed and pushed with all my strength. The unknown assailant toppled out of the narrow bed, pulling the covers off with him. He shouted something in a foreign language.

"What the hell is going on?" Renk cried. Then I heard what sounded like a scuffle, following by a punch, and then a body thudded heavily against the floor. I screamed again, and tugged up my nightgown. More foreign-sounding shouting. Then the door flew open and someone switched on the cabin light. It was Special Agent Smyrna Bradford brandishing her service revolver. Renk, apparently unconscious, lay sprawled on the floor, his pajamas torn. An extremely handsome blond-haired man I had never seen before broke off his unintelligible expostulations, released the red wool blanket he was clutching to his naked torso, and raised his hands in panic. Both Smyrna and I checked him out.

"Who's your boyfriend, Cara?" she asked calmly.

"I, I've never seen him before."

Toni burst in through the doorway behind Smyrna. "Dimitri!" she cried.

The man stared wonderingly at my sister, glanced over at me, muttered to himself, and slapped his forehead with the palm of his hand.

## Chapter 20

Renk ordered a porterhouse steak for breakfast, which he is presently holding over his black eye. I feel terrible. He also has a torn lip, which much to everyone's consternation will prevent him from performing for several days at least. Howard is concerned that this whistling shortfall might cost the ticket 100,000 votes in the South alone. I hope not. The nude elevator man, Dimitri Batovo, has received a stern dressing down from Captain Mingov, and my sister has been forbidden to associate with him. She is outraged because she claims, much to Thom's distress, that Dimitri is the only man she has ever truly loved. I hope she will do as she is told for once.

"Cara, what on earth are you wearing?" asked Renk, beef blood rolling down his arm. "You look like Scarlett O'Hara."

"Howard feels this is appropriate southern belle attire for our present location over Georgia. The frilly pantaloons are fun, but I haven't quite mastered the art of sitting down in this hoop skirt. It wants to billow up, as you can see. At least when I am standing it fully obscures my TrudgeTread Support Shoes. This low neckline seems rather disturbing. What do you think?"

Renk studied my bodice with interest. "I think you should lose the Shirley Temple wig. Those blond curls do not look very fashionable."

"Howard says we must appeal to the voters' longing for a return to a more genteel and gracious era. He says Southerners resent fashion trendiness even more than our Yankee accents. It's fortunate that we are Southern Baptists at least. Howard says it's a tremendous handicap pursuing a southern strategy without an actual Southerner on the ticket."

Gilboa rushed breathlessly into the salon and handed me her cellular phone.

"Hello?" I said cautiously.

"Good morning, Cara," said my father, his familiar resonant voice fading in and out of the ether. "I understand you're over Georgia."

"Yes, Dad. We were circling the skyscrapers of Atlanta at sunup, but we seem to have left the metropolitan area behind. One of our Secret Service agents was disappointed that we passed entirely over his home state of South Carolina in the dead of night. He wanted to point out the Congaree Swamp and Stock Car Hall of Fame."

"Did you watch the debate last night? I thought Governor Flunch did a superb job."

"Yes, Father. And so did you in your debate. We're all quite proud of you both."

"Thank you, Cara. Uh, Mindy informs me that you may be acquainted with that person who has occupied the tree in your mother's yard."

"Yes, his name is Dan. You met him briefly on Bag Island, if you recall."

"I'm afraid I don't. Cara, you know the elections are just a week from today."

"Yes, Father, I know. Next Tuesday."

"Cara, at this late date, we can't afford any negative publicity. I'd like you to call that fellow and ask him to come down out of that tree."

"I'm not sure he'd listen to me, Father. And I'm not sure he has access to a telephone."

"The Secret Service will take a phone up to him. Give him a call, Cara. I'm counting on you."

"Yes, Dad, of course."

Carrying a pink parasol under her arm, Toni swished into the room. "Good morning all," she drawled, fluttering her hand-painted silk fan. "How oppressive is this torrid Georgia sun that blazes down upon our esteemed kinfolk. Columbus, a glass of chilled orange juice, if you please. I'm fairly fainting from the heat."

"Yes, Miss Daisy," he replied.

※ ※ ※

Cara, can you help me recapture my sink from this toilet?

Sure, Toni, you just pull this lever here. *Voila!*

Thanks. I thought perhaps Dola had sabotaged it. No, it was just the inherent sadism of Russian plumbing.

Toni, if it's 8:20 in the morning in Georgia, what time is it in Ohio?

Let's see, that's a toughie. It's uh, 8:20.

That's what I thought. Do you think it's too early to call Dan?

Another difficult question, Cara. As far as I know, the rules of etiquette have not yet been established for telephoning people residing in trees.

I think I'll wait another half-hour in case he's sleeping in.

Cara, I meant to ask you about your interlude with my boyfriend Dimitri last night. Did you, uh . . . ?

No, Toni. Renk interrupted us before things had progressed very far, thank God.

It's fortunate for you, Sister mia. Dimitri, though extremely modern in most of his thinking, takes a regrettably backward view toward birth control. He refuses to wear protection.

Toni! You haven't . . .?

Absolutely not, Cara. But I had a rather close call.

Toni, how on earth did you progress to the point of actually sleeping with the guy? He speaks no English!

Cara, in most cases language is a hindrance to love. Look at you and Renk. All you've ever done is talk. No, we've simply eliminated a lot of superfluous chatter. Since words are so inadequate in explicating these matters, I shall now resort to song:

> If his kiss you are longing for,
>     You must not become a bore;
> Pursuing a discussion
>     Is no way to woo a Russian.

> You will find that long discourse
>     Merely sets you off your course;
> And earnest elocution
>     Fosters male irresolution.

> If to him you will be clung
>     You must manacle your tongue;
> And curb all inclinations
>     Toward impromptu declamations.

> A pregnant moment cannot be had,
>     When you're chatting up the lad,
> And launching disquisitions
>     On your marital ambitions.

> A gravid silence will announce
>     Your wish for him to pounce;
> With relief he'll take the bait,
>     And then quietly you'll mate.

> At this point it is permitted
>     That some phrases be emitted

Of an exclamatory sort,
With an amatory import.

Though a timely reticence
Should undo his hesitance,
You may vocalize your needs
As the situation proceeds.

Forgive me, Toni, if I don't take your advice.

I didn't expect you would. Oh, Cara, you have to help me figure out a way for Dimitri to defect.

Toni, Russians are free now, they can't defect. They have to join the queue with the millions of other aspiring immigrants. Anyway, what would he do for a living? He's trained to be the elevator controller on a semi-rigid airship. How many openings do you think there are in that field?

Cara, I'm madly in love with him.

It's simple infatuation, Toni. You like him because he's so good looking, has a fabulous body, and is unusually adept in bed.

I thought you said things hadn't progressed very far with you two.

Well, I did get a brief sample.

And I suppose it's not simple infatuation with you and Dan, Cara?

I don't know, Toni. I wish it were. Oh, how I wish it were!

＊　＊　＊

Mother said Dan had accepted a cup of herbal tea this morning from Special Agent Pulaski, but had refused a granola bar. She also divulged that he is having difficulty answering the call of nature, what with two dozen news-camera telephoto lenses trained constantly on him. Mother asked me if Toni had been drinking, and I said not since Syracuse. She asked me if my sister had gotten into any mischief, and, answering truthfully, I said no more than usual. We discussed the high points of the trip, then I heard her ask "Troy darling" to take her cellular phone up to Dan. A minute later, I was speaking with the person who continues to monopolize my innermost thoughts.

"How are you, Dan? Were you cold last night?"

"More uncomfortable than cold, Cara. This tree limb is inclined to cut off circulation to my legs. Where are you?"

"Over Georgia. We're heading toward Macon. Were you able to sleep?"

"A little. The reporters and spectators made quite a lot of noise. I can't complain. At least I'm not being ignored. I'm sorry for the inconvenience this is causing your mother."

"Dan, you've made your point. Why not come down?"

"I can't, Cara. I've pledged to fast and remain up here until the election."

"Dan, it would mean a great deal to me if you would reconsider."

"I'm sorry, Cara. In my own small way, I'm trying to undo some of the damage you're causing."

"Dan, all we're doing is touring the country in Maximo Flunch's blimp and making a few campaign stops. We're trying to help our father. Is that so terrible?"

"You know your father's positions, Cara. You know you should be opposing him."

"Dan, what you ask is impossible. My father is an idiot sometimes, but his intentions are good. And he needs his family's support."

"I need your support as well, Cara."

"Dan, a week in that tree without food could damage your health for life. I won't think less of you if you come down now. No one will."

"Sorry, Cara. I'm determined to persevere up here."

"Oh, Dan, this is most upsetting. I, I care about you."

"I care about you, darling. I have your picture in my pocket. That is, I think it's you. It could be Toni, I guess. I clipped it from the local paper. I take it out and think about our night together on Bag Island."

"I think about that too. Constantly."

"I love you, Cara."

"I love you, Dan. Stay warm if you can. Do what you feel you must do, darling."

"You too, Cara. Remember, you have the power."

"Really, Dan, sometimes you sound like a George Lucas movie."

\* \* \*

Our approach to Macon took us over the Indian mounds of the Ocmulgee National Monument and the busy zipper factories of industrial Bibb County. We landed in a shopping plaza near the sprawling Westgate Outlet Mall, visited by numberless Florida-bound travelers on Interstate 75. I would love to have gone over there with some of my Flam Cola mad money, but Gilboa insisted we keep to her rigidly inflexible schedule. We did our usual dog and pony show, except that the injured Renk—now wearing dark glasses—was obliged to whistle-sync a selection from his CD, and Dola modestly put aside her own wretched poetry to recite "Song of the Chattahoochee" by Macon-native Sidney Lanier. The crowd, I regret to say, loved it.

In the local CrumpPak store we visited the pet department, where a professional canary model sat on my finger and chirped on cue like an avian Renk Pohlsohn. Then, unnerved by the crush of photographers, it unprofessionally panicked, taking refuge under Cara's hoop skirt. Despite much coaxing by its embarrassed manager, the recalcitrant bird refused to come out. Flustered, Cara retired to the ladies' room, where the trespasser was extracted at last by its manager's wife. Soon both my sister and the canary had regained their composure. As we were walking up the airship steps, I overheard Hamler tell Cara that the incident confirmed his long-held opinion that one in the skirt was worth two in the blouse. Smiling and waving to the crowd, she told him he was a disgusting degenerate.

⁜ ⁜ ⁜

"Good news, Toni," said Howard, slipping into my cabin with his usual exaggerated stealth. "Renk reports that in the last ten miles of our descent toward Tallahassee, we have flown over the towns of Cairo, Reno, Amsterdam, and Havana."

I gazed into the too-small mirror and adjusted my Dixie Belle wig. So far I wasn't having any more fun as a blond. "Well, Howard, they say world travel is broadening. Is that the Gulf of Mexico down there?"

Howard flopped down on my bed and peered out the low window. "Not quite, Toni. I believe that is Lake Miccosukee."

"Try to keep your mind out of the sewer, Howard."

"Toni, I've been keeping an eagle eye on your sister's cabin. Thus far she has received nocturnal visitations from Hamler, Dimitri, and Renk."

"Yes, I find her popularity extremely depressing."

"Toni, at no point has Forest made any move toward her door."

"Perhaps, Howard, he is deterred by the constant foot traffic in that area. Has he made any moves toward your door?"

"None. And I've beaten him eight straight games in chess too."

"He should be in a highly submissive state by now. Howard, there's only one thing for you to do."

"Kill myself? I've considered that."

"You have to launch the lunge, Howard. You have to go for the grope. Proceed with the pass."

"Toni, you are proposing a monumental step. A monstrous leap into the dark. And just when my tan is fading."

"No one likes a coward, Howard. Or, more to the point, loves them. Do you have a condom?"

"Yes, I've got dozens."

"Expecting a busy time, were you?"

"Well, I've heard that airship travel can be highly erotic. All that sensual motion and floating about. I know Thom and Dola are doing it almost continuously. Ottokee is always grumbling about the dishes stacking up."

"It's the only way Dola can distract him enough to keep him away from me, poor thing."

"Airships *are* romantic, Toni. I must say, I've taken heart from your split-second seduction of Dimitri."

"It was not quite that fast. I'm deeply, deeply in love. Howard, I want you to have a talk with Dimitri—man-to-man. You must convince him that it is acceptable for a modern, passionate Russian to don a condom."

"And if I do you this small favor, Toni?"

"Howard, you are so reciprocity minded. OK, I'll have a chat with Forest. I'll see if I can elicit any indications of an inclination in your direction."

"Toni, we may soon resolve these troublesome issues."

"That may be, Howard. But first we must dazzle the good citizens of Tallahassee. I just saw another tiresome State Capitol breeze by outside the window."

❖ ❖ ❖

After a successful visit to Tallahassee, we crossed the Chattahoochee River, set our watches back one hour, ate a hearty lunch, and sailed on toward Mobile, Alabama. Our route is designed to take us to as many important states as possible, while avoiding mountainous regions. Renk says we are proceeding over a flat, fertile plain of cattle ranches and cotton and peanut farms. We have come a long way from Ohio, and, in truth, I am beginning to feel pangs of homesickness. I am missing one person in particular, whose picture appeared on the front page of today's *Tallahassee Democrat*. I read the story eagerly. The AP mentioned that Dan plays the trombone, a fact which I never knew. I wonder if any music has been written for trombone and accordion? How silly I've become. I was just trying to decide what instruments our children should study to fill out a family musical ensemble. I must continue to remind myself that I am only 15. Early marriages have such a low success rate, and I am sure that Dan and I have much growing and changing to do before we are sufficiently mature to marry responsibly. I can only hope my future husband, whoever he may be, possesses many of the sterling qualities I admire in Dan. Now I have made myself quite sad, and I think I'll go to my cabin for a therapeutic lie-down and cry.

❖ ❖ ❖

"What's that town down there, Forest?"

"I believe, Toni, that may be De Funiak Springs. There along the southern horizon you can just make out the waters of Choctawhatchee Bay. They probably have a better view from the airship."

"But this observation car is so much more fun," I exclaimed, waving my fan. "I feel, I feel like a bird soaring on a breeze. All you hear is the sound of the wind and the trucks directly below us on Interstate 10."

"Yes, Captain Mingov is following that route west. We'll soon be passing the perimeter of Eglin Air Force Base. I hope Uncle Max isn't planning any more provocations. You look very nice with blond curls, Toni. I like the ribbon in your hair too."

"Thank you, Forest," I replied, startled by this unexpected flattery. I coughed and pushed down my upwelling skirt. "I hope my gown isn't crowding you."

"No, it's very becoming." He boldly put his arm around my shoulder.

"Forest, I suppose you realize it wasn't Cara who came to your room that night on Bag Island?"

"Yes, Toni. I never believed it was. You caught me by surprise. You are always doing that."

"Such as suggesting a ride together in this cozy observation car?"

"A good example of your capacity to startle."

"Forest, why did you plant that story with me about your uncle buying a battleship in Uruguay?"

"I think you can guess why, Toni. I knew you were looking for Max and were friendly with Monty Bellefontaine—a reporter as dim as he is photogenic. I thought if that false story came out, Max might be dissuaded by the press uproar from pursuing the Russian submarine. I hadn't counted on his colossal pig-headedness. Fortunately for all of us, resourceful Essex Kennard saved the day. I came to your room one night on Bag Island to apologize, but you were occupied with Howard."

"That wasn't me, Forest. That was Cara; we had switched rooms to foil your randy brother. Why did you spray-paint anti-Flunch messages on your own house? Were you jealous of Dan's attentions toward Cara?"

"No, I regretted his expulsion from the island. I did it to shake up the Secret Service. I thought if they were more watchful, Hamler might be forced to be a little more discreet in his pursuit of your stepmother."

"Wait a minute. Hamler was after Mindy?"

"Didn't you know? That wasn't Gilboa we saw skinny-dipping with my brother that night on the beach. It was your stepmother."

"Oh my God! So that's why you didn't want us to spy on them. And I thought you were just being a prude."

"No, Toni, I was afraid the press would get wind of their affair."

"Now I know who was hiding up in the loft of Uncle Max's battleship that day. I thought I recognized her tacky perfume."

"Yes, it was Mindy. I think she was up there spying on my brother and Gilboa. One of the broken portholes looks directly out on the old power house."

"And, of course, you were too discreet to tell us."

"Well, I didn't want you to think badly of your stepmother."

"Forest, we despise our stepmother. We love hearing dirt about her. I suppose I should thank you for not ratting on me to the campaign bigwigs for all those terrible leaks to Monty. If you'd squealed, I'm sure Essex Kennard would have had me rubbed out by now."

"I assumed you had your reasons. What was all that about anyway?"

"Uh, it's complicated. But I'm on your side now. You can trust me, Forest."

"I hope so," he replied.

"One more question," I said.

"What, Toni?"

"What do you think of Howard?"

Forest withdrew his arm and looked at me warily. "Howard Archbold?"

"No, Howard the Duck. Yes, Howard—author of 'CrumpPak: Taking Low Prices to a New Low'."

Forest pondered this question. "He's, he's a magnificent chess player."

"Forest, do you like him?"

"How do you mean?"

"You know how I mean."

Forest gazed out the window. "What difference does it make, Toni? Howard's in love with you, or, I guess with your sister."

"No, he's not. He likes you. He told me so."

"Really?" Forest applied his logical mind to this unexpected news. "How interesting. But there's a slight complication."

"What?"

Forest reintroduced his arm about my shoulder and looked into my eyes. "Because, Toni. . . I like you as well. A great deal."

He pushed away my fluttering fan and kissed me. I remembered those warm pliant lips and experienced fresh waves of emotional turmoil.

\* \* \*

I was awakened from my nap by the sound of my cabin door opening and closing. I looked up in surprise. Standing by my bed was Maximo Flunch— smiling a disquieting smile and holding two crystal glasses and an opened bottle of champagne.

"Yes, Mr. Flunch," I said, sitting up in alarm and yanking a blanket over my pantaloons. Why had I ever removed my skirt? "Can I help you?"

"Cara, I think it's time we got to know each other better." The bed creaked as he sat down heavily beside me. "I understand from Hamler we have a mutual interest in the works of Ernest Hemingway. Did you know I once went hunting with the great man himself? Down at Tarpon Springs. A grand day." He paused in his champagne pouring and studied my lace-trimmed bodice.

"Mr. Flunch, I believe it would be best if you left my room now." His bulk and body odor were oppressive at such unwanted proximity.

He smiled and handed me a bubbling glass. "Actually, Cara, I believe this is my room. I own the lot of them, you know." He smiled and clinked his glass against mine. "May you live fast and watch your enemies perish slowly." He noisily gulped his wine. I pondered what Mother would do in such a situation, and emptied my glass in his lap. He did not react as I expected.

"You girls are always doing that sort of thing," he sighed, idly brushing the foaming liquid from his khaki trousers. "That's why I never go into a duck blind or a lady's bedroom without my waterproof pants. The tightly woven cotton twill is impregnated, you'll pardon the expression, with a synthetic wax. Care for a refill?"

"Mr. Flunch, if you don't leave immediately, I'll scream."

"Cara dear, all we're doing is having a friendly little drink. There's no cause for these childish and unbecoming protests. Be sociable with your Uncle Max."

"Mr. Flunch, I am not of age to drink and legally too young to do anything else you may be contemplating. If you persist, you will be facing disgrace and a long prison sentence."

"Cara, my brother will soon be President of the United States. Something of a joke, I admit. Whoever would have believed it—Claudie Flunch in the White House? But you know as well as I do how these things work. No, they won't be tossing the nation's First Brother into the slammer on a morals charge. That would prove disruptive to the social fabric. At worst, these little affairs are quietly hushed up, and in time the young woman comes to see that she has acquired an impressive benchmark for evaluating future lovers."

He downed his second glass of champagne and poured a third. I scowled at him and wondered if anyone would hear my screams.

"Hamler said you were fun. He's right. I like your spirit, Cara. This is excellent French champagne. It's a shame you're making me drink it all by myself."

I heard a knock on my door. "Come in!" I shouted.

Pasco Tawawa looked in. "Excuse me, Cara. Max, you're wanted down below."

"Who wants me?" he demanded.

"Captain Mingov. He says it's urgent."

"Damn this infernal Russian balloon! I should have sued those bastards when they stiffed me on my submarine. Out of my way, buffoon!"

Maximo lumbered unsteadily from the room. Pasco stood by the door, watched him go, and smiled at me. "Captain Mingov isn't looking for anybody, Cara, but I figured you could use a break from Max's tiresome company."

"Oh, thank you, Pasco," I said, leaping up from the bed. "He wouldn't leave. Can you fix my door lock? Hamler broke it."

"Wouldn't do any good, Cara. Max has a passkey to all the doors. But I'll keep my eye on him. I won't let him bother you again. And you might have a chat about Max with Special Agent Bradford. She'd love to nail him breaking into your room."

"Thanks, Pasco. I'll talk to Smyrna. You're a lifesaver."

"My pleasure, Cara. We have to stick together. As near as I can figure it, these Flunches have been out of control for 200 years."

※ ※ ※

Howard was picking out notes on the featherlight piano in a corner of the salon.

"Oh, there you are, Howard. Is that Mobile down there?" I sat down beside him on the narrow metal bench.

"No, Toni. I think that's Pensacola. We're about to leave Florida—a state I will never forget."

"Really, why's that?"

"Uh, it's kind of personal."

"Whatever you say, Howard. Did you talk to Dimitri?"

"Uh, yeah, I did talk to him. Uh-huh. That is, I tried talking to him. My Russian is at best rudimentary—you have to understand that, Toni."

"Howard, you're acting very strange. What happened?"

"Well, uh, actually, I don't think the guy had ever seen a condom before. They're not that common in Russia, you know."

"So?"

"So, it was fairly obvious I wasn't making myself clear. The guy was looking pretty confused. I think he was still partly asleep. It took me forever to wake him up."

"Let's back up here, Howard. You showed Dimitri a condom?"

"I did, yes. A lubricated nipple end in a festive shade of tangerine orange. I unwrapped it. The guy was looking, well, clueless. I unrolled it down my finger. Not a spark of comprehension in those sleepy green eyes. So, I, well . . ."

"Well what?"

"So I remembered a demonstration we had in health class . . . where we practiced putting it on the anatomically correct plastic model. I didn't have a model, so I, well, I put it on . . . myself."

I gave him a severe look. "How could you, Howard? I mean, didn't you have to be, uh, excited?"

"Actually, that wasn't a problem, Toni. It wasn't a problem either . . . for Dimitri . . . when he tried one on."

"Howard, are you telling me that you got naked and made it with my boyfriend?"

"Not entirely, Toni. Actually, he sort of made it with me. He was pretty enthusiastic. I felt very flattered, after getting over my initial nervousness."

I was stunned. "Howard, are you saying that Dimitri is gay?"

"I don't know, Toni. For all I know he may like girls too. I think the guy's been stuck away in a room by himself too long. Gee, and I thought I was horny. Come to think of it, he could be gay—he wears the most peculiar socks."

I was speechless; I turned and stared numbly out the window. I knew in my heart I would always loathe Pensacola, Florida.

"Toni, did you talk to Cedar Rapids?"

"I did actually, Howard. I have some good news to report and some bad news. The good news is that Forest confessed to having strong romantic feelings toward you."

"That's wonderful!" he exclaimed.

"The bad news is your friend just seduced me in the observation car. You can't imagine how difficult it was consummating the act in a hoop skirt in that cramped seat."

\* \* \*

After hovering long and lovingly over the retired battleship *USS Alabama*, berthed at Pinto Island in Mobile Bay, we cruised on to a suburban CrumpPak store, where disaster engulfed us. A wave of reporters descended on Cara and me as we stepped from the *Liberty or Death*.

"Miss Mason," shouted one reporter, "is it true you think your father is mentally deficient?"

"Carissa!" screamed another, "how long have you been lovers with the protester in the tree?"

"Are you a supporter of extremist eco-terrorism?" demanded another, thrusting his microphone toward us.

"How soon will you be announcing wedding plans?" inquired an unshaven, bleary-eyed Monty Bellefontaine.

"Are you expecting his love baby?" bellowed a distinguished grey-haired reporter who had once served as Paris correspondent for a major television network.

"Are you considering an abortion?" yelled a fat woman in a purple hat.

Jostled mercilessly by the press of reporters, our hoop skirts trampled, our blond curls awry, we fought our way behind Smyrna and Ryan to a Flunch-Mason charter bus, where Gilboa and Renk were being briefed by grim-faced campaign aides.

"What's happening?" I demanded, as Smyrna closed the bus door on a reporter's hand—the clamor of the crowd nearly drowning out his piercing screams.

"Somehow Cara's cellular conversation this morning with that tree-sitter was monitored," explained Gilboa. "The audio tape was just played to a national TV audience on In Your Face."

"Oh, dear," I sighed, "not that sensationalist tabloid TV show. Cara mia, what on earth did you say?"

"Nothing," mumbled my sister, stunned. "I just, I just asked Dan to end his protest. That's all. I can't believe they would eavesdrop on a private conversation."

"Cara, you boasted openly of spending the night together," Renk said bitterly. "How am I supposed to explain that to Mr. Crump?"

"You called Senator Mason an idiot," charged one of the campaign aides, who I vaguely recognized from Bag Island. "How are we supposed to explain *that* to the American voters?"

Everyone stared at my pale, stricken sister. She collapsed in a seat and began to sob. Somewhere, a cellular phone chirped. An aide answered it and announced ominously, "It's Mindy Mason."

"I'll take it," I said. "Hello, Mindy. How nice to hear your voice. Hamler was just saying how much he missed you."

*Chapter 21*

I am struggling to remain optimistic. The good news is we are in Texas and a cold rain is falling. The tour is continuing by the grace of Essex Kennard, who says a cancellation under a cloud would be disastrous. Mindy is still hysterical. Cara has apologized to Father for her ill-chosen words. Renk has prostrated himself cellularly at the feet of Mr. Crump. Cara has given her personal assurances to the incensed billionaire that she remains chaste; similar declarations of unsullied purity have been released to the media, and Dan has gone firmly on record from his treetop perch that his physical relationship with Senator Mason's underage daughter has progressed no further than a platonic kiss.

"I love her," he shouted to the ever-burgeoning mob of reporters gathering from all corners of the globe, "and she loves me. But that is not the important issue here. As I stated in my written manifesto . . ." Here, thankfully, the media news coverage switched away.

Last night *Lod* made its scheduled stop at Plaquemine, Louisiana—outside Baton Rouge—but Cara and I were advised to remain on board. We watched from a window as the Plaquemine High School Girls Pep Club unfurled a large banner made from bed sheets scrawled with the letters "S-H-A-M-E!" in scarlet paint. According to Gilboa, photos of it appeared this morning on the front pages of many of the country's leading newspapers. Surprisingly, the most encouraging show of support so far has come from Vice President Greer, who paused on an early morning campaign jog through Encino, California to remark that he didn't see what all the fuss was about. "They seem like nice young people," he said. "But let me add I am not yet privy to all the facts."

Howard feels extreme countermeasures must be taken. He has banished all makeup, confiscated our jewelry, forbidden any styling of our hair, and dressed us in grey sack-like tunics of plain boiled wool. No stockings either.

"We look like Joan of Arc!" wailed Cara.

"Joan of Arc enjoyed very good PR," Howard replied.

"She was burned at the stake," I pointed out.

"Martyrdom can be a savvy career move," he replied. "People admire sincerity. It's such a rare quality in public life. And you girls do look sincere."

"This wool is like a medieval hair shirt," I protested, scratching furiously.

"Don't complain," replied our Fashion Czar. "At least I've finally achieved a look that coordinates nicely with your shoes."

* * *

What a horrible, miserable night; I am praying for better times in Texas. This misunderstanding distresses me so, and I feel acutely the embarrassment it must be causing Dan. I couldn't sleep last night for thinking of him alone and famished in that freezing sycamore. Thank goodness Toni consented to stay with me in my cabin (we made up a tenuous bed for her on the odd metal lounger). We were visited in succession by Hamler, Maximo, Meeker Chuckery, and Renk. I think only the last one came to talk. Toni forcefully ejected them all. And what shocking news about Mindy and Hamler! If things weren't confused enough, my sister mentioned casually at two this morning that she had had relations the previous afternoon with Forest Flunch—a person I would have said she was adamantly shunning. Toni says she is fairly sure she doesn't love him, but is undecided whether she actively dislikes him.

"Are you going to sleep with him again?" I asked, aghast.

"I think so," she replied. "I do like that part. It depends on whether I can find it in my heart to forgive Dimitri."

"For having sex with Howard?"

"No, for making no effort whatsoever to contact me in the past 24 hours."

"But he's not allowed to leave his post, Toni."

"A puny excuse. I thought these Russians were revolutionaries. Not even a phone call."

"Men are such a bother, Toni. It's no wonder Mother did without them all those years."

"She's happier now though. Men do add a certain spice to life, Cara. I hope you will be able to experience intimately at least one of them soon from the army presently volunteering."

We heard footsteps in the hallway.

"Who do you suppose that was?" I asked.

"A stranger in search of love," speculated Toni.

"I don't think so," I replied. "They passed right by your door."

Then at breakfast I had to face my disappointed suitor.

"You look like a nun," Renk said coldly. "What are those dark circles under your eyes?"

"Howard drew them on with mascara," I replied.

"Oh," he said, "I thought perhaps you were overcome with grief and remorse."

"I am, Renk. I regret everything that's happened. I appreciate your helping me placate Mr. Crump. I know how much I've disappointed you."

"Cara, your friend up in the tree has done nothing but hinder this campaign."

"I know that, Renk."

"I, on the other hand, have swallowed my principles in order to assist you and your father as much as I can."

"I appreciate that, Renk. And I know your commissions and recording contract are small recompense for all your efforts."

Renk stared moodily at his oatmeal. "OK, I've profited too, I admit it. But I've given you my heart and soul. Cara, you've got to repudiate that guy. The nation demands it!"

"It certainly doesn't look much like the Old West down there," said Howard, carrying a plate of hushpuppies in from the galley. "The flat countryside is as green as Iowa and dotted with Minnesotan lakes. The cowboys down there must wage a constant battle against trench foot. Cara, go easy on the cereal. I want you looking gaunt and ephemeral for the cameras. Have any of you seen Elm Disease?"

"No, Howie," said Renk. "Forest hasn't come down yet."

"Good," said Howard. "He's sparing me the trouble of not speaking to him. I spotted him leaving his cabin last night at 2:30 a.m."

"Where did he go?" asked Renk.

"That's what I'd like to know!" said Howard.

✻ ✻ ✻

Another difficult cellular conversation. I'm not sure all this modern technology is such a blessing.

"Hello, Dan."

"Good morning, Cara darling."

"Dan, we should assume this conversation is being monitored."

"Yes, I suppose so. Perhaps everyone who's listening in will take a few moments to ask themselves if clean air and water are important to them and their children. Where are you, Cara?

"Approaching Houston. Oh, Dan, how are you?"

"Very well, Cara. You know we can only ravage nature so far, before nature strikes back. It wasn't as cold last night. You won't believe how many reporters are here now. Studies prove that acting responsibly toward the environment actually produces a net *increase* in jobs."

"Dan, have you eaten?"

"I had some tea and fruit juice. It's foolish public policy to let the polluters rewrite the nation's pollution control laws. I'm sorry my protest is inconveniencing so many of your neighbors. The Czerkoffskis have moved into a motel. How are you coping, Cara?"

"Well, enough. I'm worried about you though."

"I'm OK, except for the stiffness in my legs. The property rights movement means *less* control over development by local citizens, and *less* power to oppose the intrusion of large corporations such as CrumpPak Stores. We may get some rain today, but I have my rubberized tarp."

"Dan, that night on Bag Island . . ."

"All we did was kiss, Cara. Citizens who are sexually repressed create a society that is politically repressive. We must open our hearts to nature and to each other."

"Dan, honey, they're just going to edit all that out."

"I love—if everyone who valued this small, fragile planet would vote, we could turn this nation around—you, Cara."

* * *

Damage control continued when we landed at suburban Humble, near our refueling stop at Houston Airport. The advance staff had marshaled our own banner-waving supporters to counter the prudish protesters. Christian seniors in sequined tutus tapped out a welcoming dance. And waiting in CrumpPak's snack bar for a live interview with Cara was Texas's biggest radio talkshow host, Brady Streeter—all 475 affable pounds of him. He once good-naturedly suggested that if any drivers spotted the President or Vice President out jogging, they should "faint from delight and steer to the right." Since Cara was nervous about speaking on the radio, Howard suggested I temporarily assume her identity.

"They're here! They're here!" bellowed Brady into his microphone. Our earphoned host filled one side of an orange plastic booth; we slid in opposite him. "Better late than never," he bubbled. "Big relief to CrumpPak too. I could see those guys getting fidgety. They were scared ol' Brady was gonna demand another free caramel pecan roll. Welcome to Texas, girls!"

"Thank you, Brady," I said, returning his smile. He was intimidatingly massive. His black string tie, I noticed, stretched almost horizontally across his iridescent cranberry shirt.

"I'm seeing double, folks. I do that often, but not usually this early in the morning. OK, help me out, girls. Which one of you go-o-r-rgeous twins is Miss Carissa Mason?"

"I am," I lied. "This is my baby sister Antonia. We call her Toni."

"Nice to meet you both, girls. I just got one small complaint."

"What's that, Brady?" I asked.

"I just wish you all hadn't gone and tied up your blimp to my leg!"

Brady roared, the crowd howled, Cara and I glanced at each other and smiled politely.

"Now, I got to tell you," he confessed to his listeners, "these girls aren't lookin' exactly the way I expected. Tell me, Cara—now be honest—did your granny make that dress out of a potato sack or a flour sack? Which was it, huh?"

The crowd convulsed again.

"We don't spend a lot of money on clothes, Brady," I replied. "Father believes you can't balance the national budget unless you first balance your household budget."

The audience applauded.

"Very true, very true, Cara," he affirmed. "And if you have to dress like an Arkansas sharecropper's hired girl, so be it! At least you're not spendin' Uncle Sam's welfare checks down at Neiman Marcus."

More sympathetic laughter.

"Actually, Brady, we always feel well-dressed when we step out in our TrudgeTread Support Shoes."

"Just don't step on my corns, Cara!"

Only a titter of laughter; Brady moved on. "Now, Cara, what we want to know is, what has that ca-ray-zee tree-hugger been hugging besides trees? Time to eat some good ol' Humble, Texas pie. Has that uppity boy been messin' with the preacher's daughter?"

"Not this preacher's daughter," I answered truthfully.

The crowd cheered.

"Anyway, I think Dan's more interested in politics than girls," I added. "He's always trying to indoctrinate me with his liberal beliefs."

The audience gasped.

"And what do you say to him?" demanded Brady.

"I tell him that I'm interested in boys who want to build up this country, not tear it down."

The biggest applause yet. Cara winced.

"And do you think he should be allowed to trespass on your mama's private property?" inquired Brady.

"He's, he's not hurting anyone," interjected my sister.

Brady looked shocked. "And maybe we should just let him stay warm up in that tree by burning the American flag. How would that be?"

"No one's burning any flags," insisted Cara.

A disquieting murmur rumbled through the audience.

"Not yet!" railed Brady. "Not yet! But who knows what those people are planning? Do you, Cara?"

"I don't know," I laughed. "But I'm sure whatever it is, it will be very boring. And ineffectual."

Brady chuckled, the crowd laughed, the CrumpPak manager smiled, Howard and Gilboa beamed. The campaign was back on track!

* * *

It's amazing how quickly one adapts to a new routine. It seems like we've been touring in an airship forever. I've even gotten used to feeling unwashed and having stringy hair and offensive body odor. Howard says the pheromone count in the passenger quarters must be astronomical, whatever that means. Airship travel is very educational. We're all becoming experts on American roofing materials and regional variations in backyard pool shapes. Presently we're headed northwest toward Dallas at our usual sedate pace. In the war between the farmers and the cowhands, it appears that in Texas victory went to the former.

Not being fascinated by agriculture, I thought I would sneak back and beard Dimitri in his den. To my surprise, I found the door to the catwalk locked. So I complained privately to Papa Max, who very nicely gave me one of his passkeys. I now have the run of the ship! I also asked him to lay off my sister, explaining that she was under a great deal of stress. He said sure. These wanna-be swashbucklers are manageable if you know how to handle them.

I took a detour on the catwalk to hunt for the fabled lost crew quarters. It turned out to be a sparsely furnished, windowless room lined with tiers of narrow bunkbeds. No one was home except a tiny man prone on the floor in a bloody chef's uniform. He looked up with a start and scrambled to his feet.

"Good night," he said, saluting. He was well under five feet tall, the uppermost four inches comprising greased black pompadour. "You are Cara?"

"I am Toni. What were you looking at?"

"Nothing, sir!"

I knew embarrassed prevarication when I saw it. I got down on my knees and peered through a hole in the floor. A broad athletic back was moving rhythmically above a squirming torso. I put my lips near the hole and sang in a low voice, "The time has come to repent your sins!"

"What the hell was that?" I heard Thom say.

I pulled a grimy rug over the hole and stood up.

"I Ivan," smiled the little man. "They stop never never."

"Yes, I know, Ivan. It's an appalling scandal."

Ten minutes later I discovered that Dimitri was not alone. I found him sleeping contentedly in the repellent embrace of a snoring Geyer Wabash! My illusions were shattered. Howard I could see in a moment of madcap abandon, but scrawny, tattooed Geyer Wabash required a complete suspension of all critical faculties. Nor could I detect any evidence that the act had been committed under duress. Another bitter disappointment in love. I silently closed the door and let the lying dogs sleep.

✤ ✤ ✤

At cosmopolitan Arlington (between Dallas and Fort Worth), we cruised over the sinuous roller coasters of a giant amusement park and landed at the CrumpPak store in the middle of a noisy demonstration by militant Dan Wyandot sympathizers. They shouted and booed all through our program, and even jeered when dedicated Pasco selflessly hit the water. The embarrassed CrumpPak manager explained they were "radical fringe agitators from U of T."

Fortunately, the campus Young Republicans also turned out in force to lend moral support to our cause. I just wish they weren't so uniformly dweeblike and relentlessly clean-cut. Loosen up guys, I felt like saying, you *are* in college after all. At least Cara and I didn't feel out of place signing autographs for them in our Mother Teresa tunics. And their cloying cologne removed any cause for olfactory self-consciousness on our part. Speaking of which, I had a brief chat with rumpled, red-eyed Monty Bellefontaine, who related a harrowing tale of blowing an engine in his panel truck and having to hitchhike all the way from Eunice, Louisiana.

When we had refueled and left Big D and Big FW behind for more relentless farmland (now dotted with the occasional oil derrick and lonely cow), Forest took me aside for a feverish kiss and skillful grope. He alone retains a pleasant odor I would describe as "old currency in neat wrappers."

"Forest honey, have you talked to Howard?"

He sighed. "He's apparently not speaking to me."

"Well, he saw you leave your cabin in the middle of the night. Where did you go?"

"Toni, there's something I've got to show you."

\* \* \*

Gilboa just handed me her cellular phone again. We must be running up a tremendous bill.

"Hello, Father. How nice to hear from you again so soon. Where are you?"

"I'm up in Sitka, Alaska, Cara. Governor Flunch felt it was important that I visit all 50 states."

"How is it there?"

"Awful. I'm snowed in. Cara, that friend of yours is still up in that damn tree."

"I know, Father. I'm sorry. As you may know from the tape they just played on the radio, I asked him again this morning to come down."

"I heard his disgusting left-wing propaganda. Cara, this is exactly the kind of publicity we don't need."

"It's an act of conscience, Father. I think we should accept it with Christian charity."

"I'm planning on doing no such thing. Our polling people say he's potentially disastrous. His favorability ratings are scary."

"He's quite an admirable person, Father. I think you'd like him."

"Cara, I want him out of that tree. That's an order!"

"But, Father, what can I do?"

"You've got to persuade your mother to have him evicted."

"Father, she would never agree to that. And neither would I."

"You've got 24 hours, Cara. That's it."

"But, Dad . . ."

I heard the phone click. He had hung up.

\* \* \*

Resourceful Forest also had his own private key to the catwalk door. I followed him to the end of a metal passageway that snaked through a narrow, claustrophobic space between two enormous gas bags. Forest reached up behind a panel and flipped a hidden switch. Somewhere overhead a motor droned, and an aluminum ladder powered down before us.

"It's a long climb, Toni. Are you up for it?"

"Not if there's a cute, lonely Russian waiting at the top. I've had it with those guys."

"Don't worry. You're safe."

"Too bad. Lead the way."

We climbed the ladder to a tiny perch, where another electrical switch—this one unconcealed—raised the ladder back up. A fixed ladder led to even more ladders, seemingly without end. We were both puffing noisily when we came at last to a narrow platform beside a metal wall with a small door stenciled in Russian. I could tell from the curvature of the visible spars that we were near the top of the ship.

"How did you find this place?" I asked.

"I trailed Max and Geyer Wabash to that catwalk last night and watched them let down the ladder. I didn't dare follow them, so I waited until they came down, then went up after they'd gone." Forest removed a purloined screwdriver from his flannel trousers. "We've got to try and pry this door open."

"Allow me," I said. My passkey turned the lock; I pushed open the door.

"Damn, my key didn't fit," grumbled Forest, following me into the room. Stacks and stacks of cardboard boxes. So many, it was hard to get a sense of the room's actual dimensions. A narrow ladder in the center extended up to a transparent plastic hatch revealing a square of grey Texas sky.

"Uncle Max's private stash," I said, running a hand over the boxes. "Of what exactly?"

Forest lifted a flap. "This one's filled with ammunition clips."

"Here are the guns," I said, recoiling from a box full of lethal-looking weaponry.

Forest peered over my shoulder. "Russian AK-47s. Or maybe Bulgarian. Looks like Uncle Max had some spare cash after he bought the airship."

"Forest, your uncle is creepy."

"Tell me about it, Toni. Here's something interesting."

"What?"

"It's some sort of literature. A whole pallet of it." From a bound bundle Forest removed a sheet of bright orange paper. At the top were printed the words: "CITIZEN CALL TO ARMS! DECLARATION OF THE REPUBLIC OF MESILLA!"

Somewhere below us a motor droned.

"Damn!" whispered Forest. "Someone's coming."

* * *

You get a new perspective on air travel riding a semi-rigid airship bareback in a bone-chilling 70 mile-per-hour wind. Lying flat on our stomachs, Forest and I clutched small metal handholds. Sloping away from us on both sides, like the back of an enormous whale, stretched acres of silvery fabric. Up ahead, along the western horizon, sunlight streamed down through fissures in the clouds. Far below, revolving pipes quilted the brown treeless plain with giant green circles. At least the rain had stopped.

"Don't let go, Toni. The fabric is slippery, and you'd have a lot of time to think about things before you hit land."

"You're so cheery, Forest. I hope my dress doesn't blow off. Can you see who it is?"

Forest inched forward and peered cautiously into the hatch. He ducked back down. "It's Kirby Belmore. He's doing something with what looks like a white tablecloth."

"Forest, for being a wacky gun nut your uncle Max is awfully domestic."

"Toni, things could get dangerous. I think when we land in Abilene, you and your sister should stay behind—withdraw from the tour."

"No way, Forest. How could we explain that? Maybe we should alert the Secret Service to the weapons stash."

"We can't, Toni. The press would go nuts. The scandal might cost our fathers the election."

"What a predicament," I sighed, gripping the cold metal as my scratchy Joan of Arc dress beat wildly against me like a penitent's lash. A loss by Father would prove disastrous to my finances. It's not that I'm mercenary, mind you. It's just that suddenly I have an overwhelming compulsion to own a buff-brick Tudor mansion bigger than Mindy's.

* * *

Dear Mother,

I have enclosed a note with this letter. Please give it to Dan if he is still occupying the tree when you receive this. We both appreciate your forbearance in permitting him to take his moral stand on your property. I hope it is not excessively inconveniencing you and the neighbors. I also appreciate your permitting me to talk to Dan on your cellular phone, even if the entire world is listening in.

Both Renk and Gilboa have had long conversations today with Essex Kennard and other campaign officials trying to persuade them not to take any precipitous actions against Dan. Howard also believes it is the worse thing they could do, and I know his opinion carries much weight. If Father or Mindy calls you again from Alaska, I hope you are able to calm them down. It's unfortunate the snowstorm there is not abating.

We've had a busy day with stops in Abilene and Odessa. The

latter has a reproduction of Shakespeare's Globe Theatre—an unexpected sight on the Western plains. There is also a famous meteor crater nearby. I wanted to stop and buy you a postcard of it, but Gilboa said there wasn't time. I snapped a photo of it out my window.

The landscape is quite dramatic now, with isolated mountains jutting up from the lonely plain. Such a change from the placid countryside of Ohio. I feel that we are at last entering the real West. I have a sense of the trepidation the early settlers in their covered wagons must have felt approaching these forbidding mountains. Like them, we have only limited climbing abilities, so Capt. Mingov must choose our route carefully. But don't worry, our airship is performing splendidly and everyone is very comfortable.

I must end here. It's late and Howard is anxious to discuss our dress for tomorrow (Halloween). Toni says every day seems like Halloween with Howard in charge of our wardrobes! She and I miss you so much. Hope you are well. Please get Dan to eat something if you can. Regards to Lizzie and Troy.

Your loving daughter,

Cara

❊ ❊ ❊

Chilled to the bone, we retreated to Forest's cabin and got warm together under the May Day bedspread. I can only attribute Forest's improbable adeptness in the sack to his many years of proximity to a saxophone. Somehow it must have stoked a small blaze of passion in his white Republican soul. Afterwards, lingering in bed, we shelled salted peanuts filched from the galley and discussed his wacky uncle.

"Forest, what's this 'citizens call to arms' business?" I asked, cracking a nut with my teeth.

"It's one of Maximo's obsessions, Toni. He's been talking about it for years. I never imagined he would try something as stupid as this."

Not surprisingly, Forest brought his usual methodical precision to the shelling of peanuts. After neatly extracting the nuts, he carefully deposited all husk remnants in a paper bag. I, by contrast, tossed my ravaged shells all over his bed and room.

"As what?" I asked.

"Toni, did you ever hear of the Gadsden Purchase?"

"No, I go to public school, remember?"

"Well, the Gadsden Purchase happened sometime back in the 1850s. The

U.S. bought some territory in the Southwest from Mexico. About 30,000 square miles of what is now the southern quarter of Arizona around Tucson and a sliver of New Mexico—the Mesilla Valley. Price was $10 million dollars."

"Sounds like a fair deal for desolate sagebrush and future trailer park sites."

"Many Mexicans didn't think so at the time. Anyway there are some people today in this country who believe that the treaty was illegal. There *were* plenty of irregularities. The original deal was for $15 million, but the U.S. Senate arbitrarily knocked off a third."

"Father would be proud."

"No doubt. Well these people contend the sovereignty of that land is still in dispute. There's been a movement of certain groups to the area. Militant groups."

"Oh dear. But, Forest, if the United States doesn't own the land, wouldn't it belong to Mexico?"

"Sure, and these people are willing to concede that. They intend to fight Mexico for it, just as U.S. settlers fought Mexico for Texas and California."

"My God, Forest. Your uncle is involved in this?"

"Toni, my uncle has a Napoleonic complex."

"But, but the whole idea is absurd."

"So it may seem to us. Anyway, it also dovetails neatly with what I think is Maximo's other agenda."

"What's that?"

"Keeping his brother out of the White House. A firstborn Flunch could never accept a second-born Flunch rising to such heights. Max had a hard enough time accepting my father as the governor of Michigan."

"Boy, you Flunches take your sibling rivalry seriously. Is Hamler in on the scheme?"

"I don't know. He might be. He's been acting strange lately."

"How can you tell?"

"I'm attuned to the subtleties of his weirdness. His indices have been high recently, even for him."

Running his fingertips sensually over my neck and shoulders, Forest kissed me again with his expert, goober-scented lips. I wondered if he found me as attractive as Howard. Was it me or the impending political crisis that was turning him on? God, what a screwy family!

*Chapter* 22

Abraham Lincoln.

We didn't believe it either when Howard announced it last night, but it was true. He had brought all the necessary accouterments in his executive garment bag. He had the ungainly, ill-fitting black suits, the collapsible stovepipe hats, the fake beards. This morning Toni and I climbed into our Halloween costumes and felt, well, ridiculous.

How does my beard look, Cara?

Rather artificial, Toni. The stick-on cheek mole looks authentic though. You look like the father of the Republican Party—with breasts. Toni, are you by any chance wearing a push-up bra?

You noticed, huh? It was a small gesture of appeasement demanded by my femininity. Cara, did you ever want to be a man?

Not recently. Boys do have more freedom, but let us not forget they can never bear children.

A lot of annoying discomfort I hear. And almost as ruinous to one's figure as this suit.

Toni, I feel so noble dressed as Lincoln.

This is no time for nobility, Cara. We're trying to get Father elected. I hope Howard knows what he is doing. I don't quite see how appearing as the Great Emancipator fits in with the key wedge issues of our southern strategy.

* * *

We created a minor sensation at breakfast. Happily, Renk refused to kiss me through my beard; I must remember to wear one more often. He had dressed in the rough uniform of an 1830s Ohio Canal mule skinner—a look Howard described approvingly as "extremely butch." Our Fashion Czar himself resembled a smokestack in faux brick turtleneck and pants, elaborate mortar-like makeup, and tall fake-brick hat with battlements around the top.

"What are you?" asked Dola, disguised as a brown paper Flunch shopping bag. "A fifth-degree Mason?"

"I'm a chess piece," he replied. "I'm a rook: quietly formidable and able to go both ways."

Hamler entered dressed all in black with a headlight stuck to his chest and chrome handlebars mounted on his head.

"Not a 1948 Indian Scout motorcycle again, Hammy," complained his sister. "Aren't you getting sick of that costume? We are."

"Bag it, toadlife," said her brother. "What's with the bearded ladies? Shouldn't you girls be dressed as *vice presidents?*"

"That's what I told them," said Dola.

"They're very inspiring," replied Gilboa, a fairy princess in pale, revealing lemon chiffon. I wondered if she also was sporting an engineered brassiere. "I know the press will love them. Howard, you're a genius."

"A terrible burden," he admitted. "Oh, here comes Walk the Plank."

Forest was dressed in the shattered ocher and brown planes of a Picasso painting. He had applied a second realistic nose to his right cheek and another mouth to his chin. Additional lifelike eyes gazed out from his forehead, temple, and cheek. Unnervingly, all of his multiple eyes moved and blinked in unison.

"Not the Prince of Cubism again," sighed Dola. "I swear my brothers have no imagination."

"Forest, that's gross," said Toni. "It's enough to put a brooding President off her poached eggs."

A tall African-American, carrying a tray of bacon and dressed as a Rocky Pike defensive end, entered from the galley.

"Thom!" cried my sister, "you're black!"

"It was Columbus's idea," he said. "I feel weird."

"You look weird," laughed Smyrna from the Secret Service table. On duty as always, she and her fellow agents had not been able to alter their customary conservative attire.

Columbus entered with a pot of coffee on a silver tray.

"Columbus!" cried my sister, "you're white!"

Our unexpectedly pale-faced steward wore a brown wig parted down the middle and a jumble of clashing plaids.

"Halloween is for frightening folks, Miss Abe," he replied. "This is the scariest look I know. Care for a cracker?"

\* \* \*

"Hello, Dan darling."

"Good morning, Cara."

"Dan, you sound so far away."

"I'm pretty bushed. There was an chilly fog last night. What day is it?"

"Thursday."

"Only Thursday? Time is slowing down. Must be the cold. Where are you?"

"Still in Texas. They reduced our speed last night because of the mountains. We're traversing the Apache Mountains now. They're quite stark and desolate. . . Dan, are you there?"

"I'm here, Cara." My love sounded terribly fatigued.

"Dan, Mother said it was raining there. Why don't you come down and get warm and dry in the house? Then you could go back up when the rain stops."

"No can do, Cara. I'm under my tarp. It's OK."

"Dan, you sound so faint. I'm worried about you."

"Don't worry about me, Cara. Worry about the future of this country."

"Dan, this is a secure Secret Service phone line now. They scramble it somehow. You don't have to give any speeches. No one's listening."

"I wasn't giving a speech, darling. I was talking only to you."

✳ ✳ ✳

"Come in, Howard," I called.

"Ah, Toni, I see you still recognize my knock. What are you doing?"

"Trimming my mustache. Forest says it tickles."

"Toni, I must insist you cease all intimacies with that person at once. He and I made tremendous progress last night."

"Don't be greedy, Howard. Forest has more than enough lips to go around. I thought I heard someone bustling about late last night in the passageway. If Cara hadn't insisted I remain in her room, I would have gone out to investigate. What were you doing?"

"Toni, Oak Grove came to my cabin at last."

"No doubt after finding mine deserted. What did he want?"

"He requested I come with him. And bring any marking pens I might have. Oh, he's into kinky stuff, I thought. It was more than I dared hope."

"Where did you go?"

"Well, after climbing about 14 ladders, we came to a small locked door."

"I know that door."

"Yes, only now somebody had installed a big shiny new padlock on it.

And the key you lent Forest didn't open it."

"Damn, they must have known somehow we'd been there."

"Forest speculated you might have dropped a hairpin."

"I didn't have any hairpins! I was dressed like Joan of Arc. What did you do then?"

"Well, Forest looked so acutely distressed, I naturally kissed him."

"What did he do?"

"He kissed me back, thank God. I didn't know quite what to expect. It was all quite stimulating. Not in Dimitri's class, of course, but nice. He has very active lips. Then he said we were in very grave danger."

"What did you say?"

"I said it wasn't that serious, I had plenty of condoms."

"Did you, uh, proceed?"

"No, he was too distracted. Probably worried about the wiring of his many Cubist eyes. Have you noticed he's glued little wires all over his face? Not a look I'd strive for."

"I'm not sure your running-bond brick is that much more attractive."

"That scraggly beard doesn't do much for you either, Toni."

"I knew you had an ulterior motive in dressing us this way. Howard, you're a very sneaky person. Why did Forest want to get back in the room?"

"He was planning to monkey with the guns, extracting vital bits, while I penned 'Just fooling!' on 25,000 seditious leaflets. Talk about a romantic evening. I figure that padlock saved me from terminal writer's cramp."

"We've got to stop Maximo Flunch, Howard. He's out of control!"

"You don't know the half of it, Toni."

\* \* \*

We're in a crisis. Maximo Flunch and his three henchmen have appeared in shocking Halloween costumes—the white robes and hoods of the Ku Klux Klan! They refuse to take them off. We're outraged, the kitchen staff has threatened to quit, even the scrupulously nonpartisan Secret Service agents appear repulsed. Hamler alone has defended his uncle's right to parade in these notorious symbols of hatred and racial bigotry.

Gilboa has been on the phone most of the morning with Essex Kennard and other distraught campaign officials. They canceled our scheduled stop in El Paso, but Max ordered Captain Mingov to land there anyway. We've been hovering above the CrumpPak parking lot for at least a quarter of an hour. So far, the ground crew has made no move to secure our dangling hook to the ring.

"Mr. Flunch," pleaded Gilboa to the hooded figures lounging against the bar in the main salon, "your appearance in El Paso dressed like that would be a disaster for the campaign."

Max's defiant, squinty eyes glared at her through the slits in his hood. "Miss McComb, you are a guest aboard my airship. Do not presume to tell me what to do. May I point out that however objectionable you may find my costume, I shall always defend your right to walk about with half your tits exposed."

Coloring, Gilboa raised a hand over her plunging fairy princess neckline.

Suddenly, the standoff took an even more ominous turn as Maximo began to sing:

> A robéd we shall go,
>     Marching manly to and fro,
> In hoods of snowy white
>     Just to give the folks a fright.
>
> Upholding are we a tradition
>     Of ol' Confederate sedition,
> And of midnight incendiarism
>     Through applied vigilantism.
>
> Inspired by Thomas Dixon
>     And latterly Richard Nixon,
> We are exalting the place
>     Of God's most favored race.
>
> We are glorying in the pallor
>     Of our epidermal color,
> Unsullied by tonal gradation
>     From careless miscegenation.

Max stepped back to let his hooded cohorts sing the chorus:

> *Oh, it's fun to ride at night*
>     *Like a bold avenging knight!*
> *'Round obstacles dim tiptoeing*
>     *'Cause we can't see where we're going!*

Max stepped forward to resume his song:

> Yes, a robéd we shall stroll
>     In our ivory camisole—
> So thoroughly de-hued
>     Like a nude albino viewed.

No one sneers that you're effete
When you're modeling a sheet;
Or dares to give you trouble
When you've donned a fitted double.

Tho' with raiments so pure and pale
Liquor stains can be a travail;
And care must be taken with torches,
Lest you get some nasty scorches.

All in all I'm proud to say
That it's swell to dress this way;
Too bad we can't so preen
Except on Halloween!

*Oh, it's fun to ride at night*
*In a gown so frightfully white!*
*Staring out through slits quite tight,*
*Doing mischief by the bright moonlight!*

"Uncle, perhaps we can agree on a compromise," suggested Forest, his many eyes gazing evenly at the men.

"Compromise," observed Max, "the first impulse of the second-born Flunch. What do you propose, Nephew?"

"That you keep the robes, but you take off the hoods."

"What are we supposed to be?" sneered a voice that sounded like Geyer Wabash's. "Choirboys?"

"And if I agree to your compromise?" said Max.

"You'll get permission to land," said Forest, "and you can continue the tour. CrumpPak Stores would not wish to be associated with the KKK, you know that."

"Uh-oh," called Toni, "helicopter approaching!"

"It could be the press!" shouted Renk.

"What do you say, Uncle?" asked Forest.

Max stood motionless as the pulsing whirl of the helicopter grew louder, then slowly reached up and pulled off his hood. His companions reluctantly did the same.

"We're angels, boys," said Max. "Beautiful angels. Only we've lost our wings."

\* \* \*

While we were wowing the patient crowds in suburban El Paso with our festive costumes, Ottokee and Columbus packed their bags and quietly left the airship. Thom said they were planning to catch a bus back to Kalamazoo.

"I could see where Ottokee might be sensitive," commented Max after we had departed, "but I don't understand why Columbus as a white person should object."

Ivan, the short Russian chef with the tall pompadour, has been put in charge of the galley. As we followed the Rio Grande up a scenic valley under a cloudless blue sky, Thom served a lunch of gristly grey meat with tainted gravy and boiled cabbage.

"This really takes me back," said Howard, scraping off the fetid, congealed gravy with an archeologist's finesse. "I can almost hear the balalaikas strumming and the vodka glasses slamming against the walls."

"Now I know why Russians drink," said the shopping bag, picking at her food.

I put down my fork and looked out the window. "We're not actually going to cross the river, are we? I mean, that would put us in Mexico. Right?"

"No, Toni," said Forest. "The Rio Grande is the international border only in Texas. We're in New Mexico now. We'll cross the river after our stop at Las Cruces."

"What are those lovely mountains over there?" asked Cara.

"Those are the Organ Mountains," replied Renk, chewing his cabbage. "And beneath us is what they call the Mesilla Valley. I think those might be pecan orchards down there."

※ ※ ※

Our appearance at Las Cruces was not a success. The crowd was small and unenthusiastic, the water was so cold Pasco emerged uttering profanities that a footsore but alert Monty Bellefontaine captured on video, several protesters from New Mexico State were arrested for attempting to occupy CrumpPak's frail parking lot trees, and Howard was detained by a store security guard for allegedly shoplifting a hacksaw from the hardware department. Fortunately, Gilboa intervened in time to quash the budding scandal.

Relations with CrumpPak were strained further when Maximo Flunch hired the snack bar cook (23-year-old Virden Hatch) at the unheard of wage of $12 a hour. Leaving his burgers sizzling on the grill, Virden handed his paper hat to the indignant store manager and climbed on board without so much as a toothbrush. Ivan the Truly Awful (as Toni called him) was sent back to the crew galley, and soon we were airborne again, across the Rio Grande, and heading west. An hour later we had crossed the Continental Divide and were approaching Lordsburg near the Arizona border.

"Oh shit!" I heard Gilboa exclaim into her cellular phone. "Oh damn!"

"What is it?" asked Renk. "What's wrong?"

I felt a sense of dread. Had something happened to Dan?

"It's the *El Paso Times*," said the white-faced fairy princess. "They just published a photo on their front page of four Klansmen having coffee and donuts in this airship!"

Maximo Flunch looked up nonchalantly from his card game. "That photographer wouldn't have got within a thousand yards if we'd had our rifles."

"Yeah," said Geyer Wabash, "I'da blasted that spyin' copter right out of the sky."

* * *

Dimitri Batovo was doing push-ups in his dingy underwear when I entered from the ladder. The circular window behind him framed a Maynard Dixon view of improbably hued mountains. My former love leaped to his feet, stared at me in surprise, and exclaimed incoherently in Russian. He was heartbreakingly attractive as usual. How, I wondered, did he always appear not to have shaved for exactly three days? I removed my stovepipe hat and shook down my hair. Dimitri laughed, stroked his chin, and pointed at my beard. Then he frowned.

"Extra cool?" he asked, pointing to me and then beside me as if to another person.

"Yes, extra cool," I nodded. "I'm Toni. Extra cool."

Smiling, Dimitri embraced me, we kissed, and I locked my arms around him. "Got him!" I shouted. Forest and Howard rushed in from the door, Dimitri tried to break free, I held on with all my might, Forest tripped him, we fell to the floor in a heap, and Forest and I restrained the struggling elevator man while Howard bound his hands behind his back with a length of CrumpPak-brand nylon cord, then tied his legs. That done, Forest knotted a cloth around his mouth to muffle his shouts. I felt a twinge of pity; the gag was one of Dimitri's own less-than-pristine handkerchief/socks. Howard and Forest dragged our prisoner across the floor and leaned him against a wall in a corner. I smoothed his disheveled hair and tried to comfort him as his green eyes glared at me in angry bewilderment.

"Damn, he wrecked my brickwork," said Howard, picking up his badly crumpled cardboard hat.

"Quick. Let's get that ladder cut," said Forest, handing Howard a small battery-powered circular saw.

In less than a minute the carbide blade had screeched through the silvery metal, and the uppermost 12-foot section of ladder had been hauled up into the room.

"Where did you get that cool saw?" I asked.

"He stole it," replied Howard. "While I was getting nabbed in the hardware department, Forest Gimp here was committing major grand theft in CrumpPak's power tool department."

"I was lucky to get it," said Forest, training his battery of eyes on Dimitri's control board. "It was a demo model and fully charged up."

"We already used it to sabotage the ladder to the gun room," said Howard.

Forest flipped a switch and pulled back on a control stick. A buzzer blared a warning as lights began to flash on the instrument panel. The bound elevator man strained against his ropes and let out muffled protests. Outside the window, the great rudder fin swung slowly over to the right.

*Chapter* **23**

"Yes, Uncle, I'm here," said Forest, occupying Dimitri's stool and wearing his headphones. He flipped a switch below a speaker so we could listen in on the conversation.

"Forest, I'm in the pilot car with Captain Mingov," said Max calmly. "He tells me you have activated the manual override on the steering system. That is not a very intelligent thing to do in mountainous terrain. We are wondering what the hell you think you are doing?"

"Uncle, I'd prefer that we not continue on to Tucson today."

"I see. You have some objection to that city?"

"I think you know why, Uncle."

"What are you proposing we do, Nephew?"

"Nothing, Uncle. I'm content to cruise in circles for a while. We seem to be safely away from the mountains. Let me know if we get close to any."

"And how shall I explain this unexpected development to our Secret Service friends?"

"Just tell them there's a minor problem with the steering, and your mechanic is working on it. We wouldn't want them to get concerned and learn about your secret storage room."

"No, ah, we wouldn't. Nephew, you might as well stop this nonsense before you kill us all. Captain Mingov says he can regain control of the rudder from the bridge. He's working on it now."

"Nice bluff, Uncle, but I've studied the control lines. They all go through this console. Just maintain this altitude. If the ship shows any sign of descending, I'll have to start experimenting with the elevator controls."

"Don't touch those elevators!" cried Max, losing his cool.

"I don't want to, Uncle," said Forest. "Let's keep everything on a nice even keel."

\* \* \*

There's some sort of glitch in the rudder controls. The engines have been throttled back and we're sailing slowly in a circle above the Arizona desert. Renk says we're somewhere between Safford and Bowie near Route 666. It's probably just as well we've been delayed. I don't think any of us—with the possible exception of Maximo Flunch—are looking forward to facing the mob of reporters in Tucson.

Twenty minutes ago Essex Kennard went on CNN and declared the El Paso photo a fake. "It's obviously been doctored," he said. "I'm sure the American people will not be taken in by this desperate ploy and heinous smear."

Governor Flunch in Cutbank, Montana told reporters the Ku Klux Klan was anathema to every Flunch and all decent Americans, implying as Renk points out that these were two separate and distinct groups. Dola took offense, castigating him for "inappropriate hairsplitting." Father has not yet expressed his opinion, as all communication has been lost to snowbound Sitka.

I wonder what Toni is up to? I haven't seen my sister for some time, and we were supposed to rehearse our act for Tucson. Our last performance of "Responsible Flunch" was a disgrace.

\* \* \*

Fearing that Dimitri might be suffering from acute nicotine withdrawal, we removed his gag and lit a Marlboro for him. He refused it. Howard speculates that he doesn't actually smoke, and only wears cigarettes as ear ornaments. It's true that none of us has ever seen him light up.

We have rifled Dimitri's personal locker for foodstocks, finding only a two-liter bottle of vodka, a six-pack of Flam Cola, and a half-gnawed piroshki. Worse, it appears that Max has peevishly turned off the water to Dimitri's modest toilet stall. I don't see how we can possibly last until Tuesday. Forest had planned to secure rations from Ottokee, but the galley walkout scuttled that.

We've been passing the time by looking out the window and gazing admiringly at our prisoner. Perhaps we should have permitted Dimitri to dress before trussing him up. You can't imagine how those tight ropes coiling about his lithe, nearly nude torso add to his already prodigious erotic appeal—especially combined with his current expression of smoldering anger. Already I have worked through most of my resentment toward him for sleeping with vile Geyer Wabash.

"I wonder how Dimitri got that scar?" I said.

Howard glanced toward the prisoner. "Probably a possessive lover wanted something to remember him by. They settled for a spleen."

"Howard, did you tell Forest that you'd made it with our friend?"

"No, Toni," said Howard sourly, "but you just did. Thank you very much."

"Are you jealous, Forest?" I asked.

Forest's many eyes looked at me and then at his friend. "Jealousy is a waste of psychic energy, Toni. If Howard and Dimitri gave each other pleasure, why should I feel resentful?"

"For that matter, why bother having feelings at all, Forest? You seem to get along fine without them."

"I have feelings, Toni. I like you. And I like Howard."

"Second billing again," said Howard. "My destiny in life."

"Forest, girls don't want to be liked by guys who like guys," I pointed out.

"That's right," confirmed Howard. "And guys don't want to be liked by guys who like girls—unless they're desperate."

"That's so limiting," said Forest. "I don't see why we can't all be cool and do what we feel like with each other."

"Forest Ranger, that's breathtakingly advanced thinking for a Republican," said Howard. "If you're going to be so flexible, I think we should be fair and include Dimitri too. He has a lot to give."

"Yes," said Forest, adjusting his false nose, "I know."

\* \* \*

"Toni has a headache," I announced, taking my seat at the table. "She's going to have her dinner in her cabin."

"Forest and Howard are locked in a close chess battle," added Renk, nonchalantly unfolding his napkin. "They're planning to grab a bite later."

Smyrna glanced over from the Secret Service table and shrugged. "Well, they're not missing much."

I think it's extraordinarily brave of my sister and Forest and Howard to have seized control of the airship's guidance system. I'm not sure why they've done it, but Renk speculates they may have acted to foil some nefarious scheme by Maximo Flunch. Renk heard about the true cause of our delay from Gilboa, who received only the sketchiest report from Maximo. We are endeavoring to keep the Secret Service in the dark, which may prove difficult. So far, thankfully, they look more bored than suspicious. And I am hopeful this fat-laden meal will cause a further ebbing of their mental acuity. For dinner our new cook made Durango chicken nuggets, deep-fried onion rings, coleslaw, pickle chips, and chocolate milkshakes. I noticed a similar meal on special this week at CrumpPak for $4.39.

We have switched on Maximo's little TV in the salon. You cannot believe the wild speculations in the media concerning our delay in reaching Tucson. Essex Kennard had to go on CNN to deny that the airship had been taken over by knights of the Ku Klux Klan. The editor of the El Paso paper admitted to ABC that the photograph had been "slightly retouched" to heighten "defining contours," but denied that it had been altered materially.

Several news helicopters have been buzzing around us for the past hour, putting everyone on edge and causing Maximo and his men to chafe visibly. One copter from CNN has been hovering so close, we can now watch ourselves dining on live TV. Maximo just raised his bottle to the camera and chug-a-lugged an entire beer. When the camera zoomed in close, I was embarrassed to see I had a piece of chicken nugget stuck to my beard.

* * *

We've had to move our prisoner to the opposite wall. Some nosey helicopter just shined its searchlight in through our window. We waved and held up our cans of Flam Cola. I trust the company appreciates these valuable media plugs.

Howard is upset with Forest for having slept with Dimitri; I am irritated with him for being so obstinately Flunch-like. I've decided I can only take Forest in small doses—preferably horizontally and with a minimum of conversation.

"It's almost dark," I said. "What time is it?"

Forest looked at his watch. "Six thirty."

"I'm hungry," I said. "Forest, you think you're so smart. Get us some dinner."

Forest flipped a switch on his console. "Captain Mingov, Forest Flunch here. I'd appreciate it if you'd tell my uncle that we'd like some food and water, or I'll have to start adjusting the elevator flaps. We'll lower the ladder and send Miss Mason down in 10 minutes. And don't try anything foolish . . . OK, thanks."

He flipped off the switch and looked at me. I glanced at Howard.

"Don't you just want to kill him?" asked Howard.

* * *

"What's this supposed to be?" Howard wondered.

"It's supposed to be a Durango chicken nugget," I replied, feeding docile

Dimitri a spoonful of sweet coleslaw. I figured his Russian palate would appreciate the cabbage.

"It tastes like it's already been chewed," commented Forest.

"That's the Durango part," explained Howard. "They pulverize the birds with stampeding horses."

"Did you hear any news, Toni?" asked Forest.

"I spoke briefly with my sister when she passed me the food package on the catwalk. She said the media are still going bonkers over the KKK photo."

"Damage assessment, Howard?" requested Forest.

Howard bit thoughtfully into an onion ring. "It could be trouble for our team if Greer exploits it skillfully, as he probably will. They've been trying to paint your father as an extremist. This plays right into their hands."

"Damn my uncle," muttered Forest.

"Here's something I don't understand," I said, sharing a nugget with Dimitri; he seemed to like them. "Why did your uncle want a submarine in the first place? His new republic wouldn't have a coastline. Would it?"

"My uncle—like certain military-minded novelists—believes that the foundation of a modern nation is a strong navy. I think they may have designs on parts of Mexico as well. Puerto Peñasco on the Gulf of California is less than 50 miles from the Arizona border."

"They're crazy," I said.

"They're boys playing soldier games," said Forest. "Max probably has been plotting this for years. God knows what he's cooked up for when we get to Tucson. I'm sure Max thinks if he can only keep the plot secret until we get there, the success of their uprising is assured. They're not too rational. They've all got gun fever."

"I've got something worse," groaned Howard. "Indigestion."

* * *

I'm outraged! The Rocky Pike police SWAT team just arrested Dan!

The entire nation watched on live TV as five officers dragged my love down out of the tree at gunpoint, handcuffed him, and drove him away. According to CNN, Father swore out a complaint against Dan via an emergency satellite hookup from a Snow-Cat in Alaska. He's been arrested on a charge of statutory rape!

"Now, Cara, try to stay calm," said Renk soothingly.

"But why? Why!" I demanded.

"They had to, honey," explained Gilboa. "I just got the whole story from Essex Kennard."

"What's he got to do with it?" I demanded.

"It was his call," she replied. "He made the decision. It was for the good of the campaign."

"But why? Dan was demonstrating peacefully! He never, we never, did anything!"

"They had to do it, Cara," said Gilboa. "They had to distract the media from focusing on the KKK photo."

"And arresting an innocent boy and charging him with a crime is better?" I asked, incredulous.

"Essex believes it is," she said. "He says this way we'll be perceived as occupying the moral high ground."

"The moral high ground! The moral high ground! This campaign has no morals! It's morally bankrupt!"

"It's not that bad, Cara," pleaded Renk. "Please, don't rock the boat, honey. We're close, Cara. We're close to winning big."

"Winning big," I said. "Yes, we've got to win. We've got to win big."

## Chapter 24

"Four more days of this tedium," sighed Howard. "What a thought. I'm sure we're missing some fabulous Halloween parties."

"We could have our own party," I suggested.

"OK," said Howard. "I'm inviting Dimitri. He's free tonight—in a manner of speaking—and he's already in costume. He's going as Harry Houdini."

"I thought he was a calf roper on a bad night," I said. "My date is the vodka bottle."

"No drinking," said Forest. "We have to remain alert."

"What a party pooper," said Howard. "Chestnut Tree is annoyed because I invited Harry first."

"What was that sound?" asked Forest.

"Don't be so jumpy," I said. "It was just the win—"

The round window behind us exploded into the room as a dark figure swung in on a rope. A blinding light blazed in the center of his chest. Forest and Howard rushed him. They grappled and kicked. Grunts and thuds, curses, shouting. I grabbed the nearest object—a vodka bottle—and swung. It thudded against walls, flesh, bone. A shattering sound. Someone screamed, I felt a push, an arm clutched at the broken window frame, the tangled bodies lurched, a light flashed across my eyes, another scream.

"It's Hamler!" cried Howard. "He's fallen!"

"Cut the rope!" shouted Forest. "Cut the rope!"

"He's your brother!" I screamed.

"Cut the rope!" shouted Forest, scrambling wildly for his knife. Howard dived on top of him.

"Forest, no!" he screamed. "It's murder! It's cold-blooded murder! We have to help him!"

"Quick!" I shouted. "Before the helicopters come back! Pull up the rope! Pull up the rope!"

* * *

I don't care if I am only 15. I don't care!

I love Dan Wyandot and he loves me. If uptight Mr. Crump doesn't like it, he can take his lousy money back. I don't want it. His stores are tacky. His popcorn is stale!

I'm so proud of Mother. Walking out of the women's shelter, she told news reporters that she was shocked and appalled by Dan's arrest. She said she had "complete faith" in my judgment, and would have tried to prevent the execution of the warrant had she been home at the time. I'll bet the police waited until they saw her leave! Some brave shelter residents have marched down Euclid Avenue to picket the Flunch-Mason campaign headquarters. More power to them!

I came up to my cabin to try and think, and was immediately spotlighted by a hovering helicopter. So I grabbed a bar of soap from the shower and scrawled FREE DAN!!! on my window. I hope my darling sees it, wherever he is. I pray he has not been locked up with other sex offenders.

* * *

Hamler lay gagged and bound on the floor beside Dimitri. Forest and Howard have tied him up with the rope he had swung from (and fortuitously had knotted around his waist). He has ugly rope burns on his chest and a frightening, oozing gash on his left arm. His motorcycle headlight and handle-bars have disappeared.

"Forest, I can't get the bleeding to stop," I said. "He needs immediate medical attention."

"Hamler isn't going anywhere," said Forest. "If Tarzan bleeds to death, it's his own tough luck."

Hamler grunted and glared at his brother.

"Come on, Forest," said Howard. "All this blood is going to spoil our party. At least phone up Uncle Max and ask for a first aid kit. And tell him to send back some party refreshments too."

* * *

This twins conversation took place in the middle of the catwalk:

Cara, there was a terrible fight! I thought for sure someone was going to be killed.

I heard, Toni. How's Hamler?

Not so good. Thanks for bringing the first aid kit.

Toni, I'm going to take it up there myself.

That's OK, Cara. I studied first aid, remember?

No, Toni, I'm going up there. You go back to the salon.

Cara, what's wrong?

Nothing. You just go back to the salon, Toni. I'm taking over now.

Cara, don't be silly. Give me that medical kit.

Toni, I'm going up there. Stand aside please. This catwalk is dangerous.

Cara, you're acting strange. You're not going anywhere.

How are you going to stop me, Toni? Are you going to try and kill me again?

Cara, you knew!

Of course I knew, Toni.

But, but why didn't you say anything?

We're sisters, Toni. Twin sisters. Like it or not, we're stuck with each other.

Cara, you hate me. You want Father to lose the election. All right, so did I once. But don't you see—he has to win. Cara, be reasonable. We'd have to give back all the money!

The money isn't important, Toni.

Oh, I get it. You're doing this out of spite. Because you hate me.

I don't hate you, Toni. Sometimes I think you're loud and unfeeling and selfish. But I don't hate you. You're my sister. Now don't make me push you off this catwalk.

You'd really do that, Cara?

Yes, I would. Now get the hell out of my way.

*  *  *

"What took you so long, Toni?" asked Howard.

"Sorry, I had a little difficulty with Cara. She's upset about something. I think I've got everything I need. Hamler, are you still alive?"

Hamler looked up and grunted indifferently.

"That cut is deep," said Forest. "You'll have to sew it up. Use a big needle, it'll hurt more."

I removed a needle from its sterile wrapping and set to work. Hamler didn't flinch as I stabbed in the point and tugged the thread through his torn flesh as blood pulsed from the wound.

"How do you suppose he got up there?" asked Howard.

Forest pondered the shattered window. "Probably bypassed the damaged ladder somehow and went out through the hatch in Max's secret room. There's a narrow track along the top outer spine of the ship. He made his way back, then rapelled down along the tail."

"Like a human fly," said Howard.

"Like human fly shit," said Forest.

"Do you think your uncle will try anything else?" asked Howard.

"Probably," Forest replied. "Keep your eyes peeled for Kirby Belmore heaving a homemade bomb."

I cut the thread and applied gauze to Hamler's sutured wound. I taped the bandage in place, cutting the white surgical tape with a scalpel from the first aid kit. Then I swiftly severed the ropes that restrained Hamler. He pushed me aside, leaped to his feet, and swung his entire body behind a punch that sent his brother sprawling. Blood gushed from Forest's torn mouth as he tried to rise from the floor. Hamler ripped off his gag and kicked his brother in the stomach.

"Fly shit!" raged Hamler, kicking him again. "Fly shit, is it?"

"Don't hit him!" screamed Howard, lunging at him. "He saved your life! He saved your fucking life!"

Hamler pushed Howard, who fell back heavily on Dimitri's stool. Forest moaned and rolled into a ball on the floor, his many false eyes dangling and blinking wildly.

"Why Toni? Why?" demanded Howard. His eyes widened. "You're not Toni. You're Cara!"

"Thanks, Cara babe," said Hamler. "I owe you one. Hey you, brick shithouse, untie that guy."

Howard hastened to obey, scuttling over to Dimitri and glancing back at me reproachfully. "That was a very deceitful act, Honest Abe."

Forest turned his head painfully and stared at me. "She's not Cara," he gasped. "She's Toni."

"It's true," I admitted. "Forest can always tell."

"But why, Toni?" demanded Howard.

"Why? I did it for my sister. Because she asked me to."

Dimitri smiled in gratitude as Howard undid his ropes. He rubbed his chafed wrists, reached for the vodka bottle, took a virile swig, smacked his lips, carefully replaced the cap, and brought the bottle down hard on Hamler's head. The thick Russian glass remained intact as Hamler's eyes rolled up like a snapped window shade and he crumpled untidily to the floor. Howard and I were too stunned to speak.

Exclaiming in Russian, Dimitri bent down and helped Hamler's brother to his feet.

"Thank you, Dimitri," mumbled Forest, pressing a corner of his shirt against his bleeding lip.

Hamler moaned.

"Howard, tie up my brother before he comes to," commanded Forest. "And tie up the traitorous Miss Mason."

"Really, Forest," I protested, "I hardly think that will be necessary!"

"Tie her up."

"And what about Dimitri?" asked Howard.

Forest smiled at his solicitous Russian friend, who was attempting unsuccessfully to reattach his many dangling eyes. "Better tie him up too, Howard. We can't be too careful."

"I must say, Thicket," replied Howard, eagerly lashing his yellow CrumpPak rope around the supine wrestler, "this Halloween party is rapidly degenerating into a complete bondage scene."

* * *

I tiptoed down the hallway and darted through a door.

"Who's there?"

"It's me, Renk. Cara."

"Cara, you've come to me at last. Of your own free will!"

"Oh, Renk, why are you incapable of entertaining more than that one selfish thought? I can't believe you're that shallow."

Renk switched on the lamp and sat up in bed. Printed wagon wheels and cactuses decorated his rumpled flannel pajamas. "Cara, that's not fair. You know I love you."

I sat tenuously on a corner of the metal lounge chair. "Then help me, Renk. I'm worried sick. I haven't heard from my sister. We had an agreement, and I think she may have betrayed me. Renk, I think we should inform the Secret Service about what's going on."

He gasped. "Cara, we can't! They must be kept in the dark at all costs!"

"But why?"

"Cara, I just had a long discussion with Pasco. He's afraid Max and his stooges have access to hidden weapons. If we tell the Secret Service, there could be an armed confrontation. People could get killed!"

"Then what should we do, Renk?"

"Pasco and Gilboa agree we should just play it cool. Whatever he's up to, Max is counting on the element of surprise. Pasco doesn't think he'll try anything until we get moving again. As long as we're flying in circles, everything should be OK. Who knows? If Forest succeeds, we could be here until after election day."

I pulled my robe tight around me and thought about this. I felt confused and very alone.

"Cara, darling, stay with me tonight. I, I won't try anything. We'll just be together."

"I can't, Renk," I said, rising. "I must go. Oh, do you by any chance have a needle and some thread?"

"Certainly, Cara. In my travel sewing kit."

"Somehow I thought you might. Can I borrow it?"

"Of course, darling."

When Renk got out of bed to open his suitcase, I spotted a metal object glistening under his pillow. It was an *Oblako v Shtanakh* silver steak knife.

\* \* \*

I'm dreadfully uncomfortable. These ropes are cutting off the circulation to my extremities. At least our sadistic captor is permitting his many shackled prisoners to partake of the vodka. Hamler has revived and appears to be getting quite inebriated. Worse, he has lapsed into his tiresome Nature Cretin persona. Dimitri has decided to overlook Forest's second treacherous act of the day and is leading us in jolly Russian drinking songs.

"More vodka!" shouted Hamler.

Howard scurried over and held the nearly empty bottle to Hamler's lips. He gulped greedily, then belched. "Thanks, Brick Shithouse. Kind Hamler decide to spare your life. Him only chop off all arms and legs. You be very smart torso boy. Play chess with nose."

"Thank you, Hamler," he replied. "You say the sweetest things. Wood Pile, how come your big brother got all the charm in your family?"

Forest gazed out the broken window and did not reply.

"More vodka, Toni?" asked Howard.

"Sure, but please wipe off the bottle. God knows where Hamler's lips have been."

Hamler strained against his ropes and edged even closer to me. "Hamler's lips like radar, Toni babe. They find all of Toni's secret buttons. Her shake like Mexican jumping bean. Her agree, Hamler's lips the best!"

"Hamler, you are so clueless," I retorted. "I suggest you undertake a prolonged make-out session with Dimitri. You could learn some valuable techniques. Now there's a guy who knows how to employ his lips, not to mention the rest of his magnificent body."

"Hamler not kiss Dimitri," he replied. "When Hamler finish with Commie ambusher, his lips not be so kissable. Him spit out all those pretty teeth too!"

Dimitri laughed and winked at his drinking buddy. "Extra cool."

"Gee, Forest Fire," commented Howard, "maybe you should have cut that rope after all."

*Chapter* 25

The door opened a crack as I was getting dressed. Somehow I had slept a few hours.

"Good morning, Cara."

"Oh, good morning, Smyrna."

"Sorry to disturb you. Have you seen Toni?"

"Oh, uh, I'm Toni."

"You're Toni? You answer to Cara in Cara's cabin, but you're Toni. You twins really like to keep people on their toes. Have you seen Forest? His bed hasn't been slept in."

"Why do you ask, Smyrna? Is something wrong?"

"Nothing's the matter, Toni. We're just trying to get a fix on everyone. They get upset in Washington if we lose people. You seen Forest?"

"Yes, uh, actually he was just here. He, uh, slept with . . . me."

"I see," she said, reining in her rising eyebrows. "And where did your sister sleep?"

"Cara? With Renk, I'd expect."

"How about Hamler? He's missing too."

"Hamler's probably with Gilboa."

"OK, one last question. How about Howard? I haven't seen him since yesterday."

"Howard, yes, hmmm. Maybe he slept with Dola."

Smyrna considered this. "Not likely, Toni. And I doubt that little bed is big enough for three. Any other ideas?"

"Well, I think he may be sweet on one of the Russian crewmen."

"OK, so he probably hasn't fallen out a window. Everybody's accounted for. I can go eat my crummy breakfast in peace. Say, what happened here? Your bedspread's all in pieces."

"Oh, uh, I got bored, Smyrna. I'd read all the books that I brought. So I started a small needlepoint project. I hope Maximo Flunch doesn't mind."

"Needlepoint, huh? You never impressed me as the artsy type, Toni. What are you making?"

"It's, uh, a surprise."

"Well, it's going to be a big surprise for Mr. Flunch. I bet he clips you $500 for that ratty red fabric."

"Oh, I don't think so, Smyrna. It's just a cheap synthetic."

"That's why he's not charging you $1,000. Are you all right, Toni? You don't look so fresh."

"I'm fine, Smyrna. I'll see you down at breakfast."

"Toni, I don't understand why you girls let Howard dress you that way. That dumpy grey dress doesn't do a thing for you. And that droopy brown sweater looks like it came straight out of Hamler's closet."

"It did, Smyrna. I borrowed it last night."

* * *

What a horrible night. After interminable sleepless hours, with Hamler snoring boozily into my ear, I awoke with a miserable hangover. The ropes are continuing to dig into my flesh, and most of my body has gone numb from lack of circulation—except my face, irritated by Abe's glued-on beard. The only way I could scratch it was by rubbing my chin against Hamler's vile head. In the midst of these discreet efforts, his eyes blinked open and the vulgarian leered at me.

"Toni baby want Hamler very, very bad."

"I was just scratching my face, you idiot. Get away from me! What are you doing?"

"Hamler pull off hair with teeth. Him no want to kiss bearded chick."

"Hamler stop that! Ouch, that hurts. Forest, get your repulsive brother off me!"

Forest sauntered over and pulled the obnoxious savage a few inches away. The cubist facial decorations were gone. During the night a dark purple mushroom of a scab had formed on Forest's swollen lower lip.

"Forest, I'll give you $50,000 of my CrumpPak mad money if you push your brother out the window."

"A tempting offer," he replied. "I'd take you up on it, Toni, but I may need him as a bargaining chip. My uncle is unnaturally attached to him, you see."

"Little Forest big expert on unnatural attachments!" growled Hamler.

"Let's kill him, Coppice," said Howard, his eyes aflame. "We're just the sort of calculating intellectuals who do occasionally commit thrill homicides. There are a great many precedents for it in the psychiatric literature. I know! Let's set him on fire."

Hamler squirmed uncomfortably and tugged against his ropes. He was about to reply, when a low vibration was heard.

"What's that sound?" asked Forest, alarmed.

"The engines!" exclaimed Howard.

"Look!" I called. "The rudder!"

Outside, the immense rudder swung over toward the centerline as the ship began to pick up speed. Forest leaped toward the control console.

"Damn! The controls are dead. All of them. Somehow they bypassed them."

"What a shock," said Howard. "Your deceitful uncle was telling the truth."

"You boys in bi-i-i-g trouble now," smiled Hamler.

"We've got to stop him," said Forest. "Howard, look and see if the catwalk is clear."

Howard opened the low door and peered out. "I can see Kirby Belmore, Pinetum. Way down at the other end. He's smoking a cigarette and holding a large machine gun."

"Damn," muttered Forest. "OK, we'll go out the window."

"Uh, how exactly?" asked Howard, alarmed.

"We'll go out the way my brother came in," explained Forest, tying one of Dimitri's handkerchief/socks around Hamler's mouth.

"But, Thicket, your brother had a rope. And a certain crazed indifference to danger."

"Don't worry, Howard," said Forest, pulling out his pocketknife. "We'll slash handholds in the fabric skin and climb up to the walkway. Just follow me."

"Forest," I implored. "Untie me! Don't leave me here like this!"

He paused. "I can't, Toni. This is too important. And you proved I can't trust you. Come on, Howard."

"Oh, Jesus," he sighed. "What a fellow does for love and the Republican agenda."

✻ ✻ ✻

Still no sign of my sister. Renk and I are eating breakfast in the salon with Dola. (They're eating, I'm pretending to.) Virden Hatch has made some sort of fried egg sandwich on a bun with corn chips and pickles on the side. I am very upset with Gilboa. She refused to let me use her cellular phone to call

Mother or the Rocky Pike police department. I must find out what's happened to Dan!

The helicopters are still buzzing around, but Maximo Flunch won't let anyone switch on his little television. He says too much TV-watching rots your mind. He and two of his henchmen are having some sort of noisy celebration at their table. Smyrna, Ryan, and the other agents look extremely on edge. I hope it's only from Virden's wretched coffee. At least we're underway again and heading west. I intend to exit this airship in Tucson and never set foot on it again. Meanwhile, I'm getting these unsettling twin-sense feelings. Almost as if some unseen force were binding my limbs.

※　※　※

"Oh, Kirby! Kirby Belmore!" I paused and listened. No reply. Oh well, I'm not sure I'd want to be tied up and defenseless in the same room with creepy Mr. Belmore. I scratched my bearded chin against my ropes and glanced over at my fellow prisoners.

"Well, Hamler, it appears your clever brother has bested you again."

Hamler chewed his aromatic gag and sullenly returned my gaze.

"Yes, it's quite a comedown for a vaunted firstborn Flunch. I'd say we can safely discard that myth of superiority."

Hamler grunted and strained against his tethers.

"If you were really as strong as you think you are, Hamler, you'd cast off those shackles like a real man. Look at him struggle, Dimitri. How pathetic."

Hamler lurched closer, then rolled over on top of me.

"Get off, you beast!" I shouted. I strained to bite his ear, but it was enticingly just out of reach.

Hamler ducked down and maneuvered his bound hands toward my chest. The cad was trying to grope me!

"Dimitri!" I called. "Help!"

With a single powerful motion, Dimitri ripped free from his cords, roared something terrifying in Russian, hauled off my manacled molester, and heaved him across the room.

I am happy to report that behind the former Iron Curtain, chivalry is not dead.

※　※　※

Forest just strolled casually into the salon and took a seat at our table. He appears quite haggard and has a discolored gash on his lip.

"Good morning, everyone," he said, unfolding his napkin.

"Good morning, Nephew," called Maximo. "What happened to you? Did you cut yourself shaving?"

"It's nothing, Uncle," he replied. "I see you were able to correct the steering problem."

"Yes, it was just a minor annoyance, Nephew. I told you it was nothing to worry about."

His tablemates snickered as they gulped their champagne.

"We'll be over Tucson in less than an hour," Max continued. "We have an exciting program planned for our friends there."

"Sorry to hear that, Uncle," said Forest, sipping his coffee. "Too bad you'll have to cancel it."

"Why would I want to do that?" asked Max mildly.

Forest turned toward the aft passageway. "OK, Howard," he called. "You can come in now."

Howard entered wearing earphones and holding what looked like a microphone on a pole. Following him and linked to him by electronic cables was Monty Bellefontaine, carrying a portable television camera. A blinding light glared from above the lens, and a spindly metal antenna rose over Monty's head from a bulging equipment pack on his back. The four Secret Service agents leaped immediately to their feet.

"How did he get in here?" demanded Smyrna.

"Don't worry," said Forest. "He's an accredited media reporter. We encountered him up on the top of the airship. Mr. Bellefontaine was dangling by a cable from a chartered helicopter."

Max was livid. "I demand that trespasser be ejected at once!"

Forest ignored his uncle. "Howard, are you picking up the sound OK?"

"Fine, Arboretum. Everyone is bellowing nicely."

Forest turned to face his irate relative. "Uncle, you should know that everything you say is being broadcast live to the world."

"Damn you," hissed Maximo. "Damn you!"

All heads turned as my sister, still bearded, raced into the salon from the passageway. "Oh, good," said Toni, catching her breath. "I haven't missed the excitement. Monty! How wonderful to see you."

* * *

Dear Monty smiled and returned my wave. I was happy to see his career was back on an ascendant course. I also waved at Thom, still in black face. Not wishing to intrude on the proceedings, I hurried over and took a seat beside Cara, who appeared even less appropriately dressed for an appearance on live national television than I did. My sister greeted me with cautious reserve.

Forest addressed the camera. "Good morning, everyone. And welcome to the *Liberty or Death*. We're just finishing up our breakfasts. Some of us are still in our Halloween costumes, but as you can see there are no members of the Ku Klux Klan on board. Right, Uncle?"

"That's correct, Nephew," replied Max, gritting his teeth.

"We've had a pleasant journey," continued Forest, "but now, regrettably, mechanical difficulties are forcing us to cut short our trip. My uncle has decided that it is necessary for us to land here in the Arizona desert. Isn't that so, Uncle?"

Max glared at his nephew.

"Isn't that so, Uncle?" repeated Forest, removing a folded sheet of bright orange paper from his pocket.

"I, I suppose so, damn it," he replied, turning even redder.

"In fact," added Forest, "my uncle is going to order Captain Mingov to land at once. Right, Uncle?"

"Yes, all right," croaked Max. He nodded toward the captain, who had just emerged from the pilot's bridge. "Captain Mingov, put her down. There are some unwelcome passengers who wish to disembark."

Forest smiled at the camera. "Well, I hope you've enjoyed this visit, and your minds are now at rest. Everything is fine on board our airship, and we're all solidly behind my father. We know Governor Flunch will make a great president, and we hope to have your support on Tuesday. Thank you and good day."

"Just a minute," said Cara, rising from her chair. "There is something I wish to say."

Forest glared at her. "Howard," he snapped, "turn off that microphone."

"Don't you dare turn it off!" I commanded, standing up beside my sister. Monty swung the beam of his camera light in our direction.

Torn between loyalty and principle, Howard hesitated, his hand poised over the switch.

"Turn it off, Howard," insisted Forest.

"The truth must prevail," I declared. "Howard, touch that switch and I shall direct Thom here to pummel the daylights out of you."

Swayed by my logic, Howard withdrew his hand.

"I, I don't think I have the words to say it," gasped Cara. "So I'll just show you."

My sister removed her sweater. Across the front of her grey Joan of Arc

dress, appliqued red letters spelled out, "ASK MINDY ABOUT HER AF-
FAIR WITH HAMLER!"

Forest groaned and collapsed in his chair.

"Good work, Cara," I said to the camera. "And while we're on the subject,
I would like to point out that Hamler Flunch just attempted to molest me.
And he twice tried to break into my sister's room."

"That's right," agreed Cara. "And Maximo Flunch invaded my cabin and
tried to force himself on me."

"That's a lie!" shouted Max.

"It's the truth!" affirmed Pasco. "I was a witness."

"Why you turncoat swine!" raged Max. He reached into a coat pocket
and drew out a revolver. Dola screamed. Pasco ducked. Smyrna's right leg
kicked out in a blur, Max's gun flew out of his hand, she whirled, her black
leather government wingtips crunched noisily into Flunch nasal cartilage. The
other agents drew their guns on Max's men as their leader spiraled down
toward the tapestry carpet amid a clatter of crashing $600 plates.

"This is awful!" screamed Dola, pointing an accusing finger at me. "And
it's all your fault!" She clutched a silver butter knife and came at me over the
table. I retreated behind Thom, who was obliged to subdue his girlfriend
with a crisp right to the jaw.

"Dola, darling!" he gasped, "I didn't mean it!"

"Holy shit!" exclaimed Virden the cook. He waved to the camera. "Hi,
Mom! Could you airmail me some socks to Tucson?"

"Speaking of feet," I said, "I would just like to state publicly that
TrudgeTread Support Shoes give me terrible corns. They're nothing but bun-
ion bait."

Renk turned white as a sheet and slumped back stunned in his chair.

Cara pushed her way through the tumult toward the camera. "Oh, Dan,
wherever you are, I love you, darling. I love you!"

It was all quite exciting, especially after Hamler arrived on the scene and
Kirby Belmore showed up with his machine gun. I only wish I could have
seen it all on live TV like many of my friends back in Ohio. But the video was
amazing. The networks must have replayed it a hundred times.

*Epilogue*

Mother chose to have her second wedding in a lovely sylvan picnic glade in Cuyahoga Valley National Park. It was a fine Saturday in June, sunny and warm, with only a 20 percent chance of rain forecast for the afternoon. She kept the guest list short: just the family, a few close friends, several dignitaries, four shelter volunteers, some of Troy's Secret Service buddies, and our new stepfather's mother and sister from Parma.

At the reception after the ceremony, Toni and I shared a table with Dan, Renk, Howard, and our very special guest, Forest Flunch. He has a small scar on his lower lip from that tumultuous night in Arizona.

"I think I'll have my second wedding outdoors too," said Toni, sipping the champagne she had poured into a Flam Cola can.

"I forget, darling," said Renk. "Am I to be your first husband or second husband?"

Toni kissed him. "I have you penciled in for number five, Renkums, assuming your albums continue to sell and you don't lose your hair."

"True love," sighed Howard. "It's so unpredictable."

"I wish Smyrna and the other agents could eat something," I said.

"They can't," explained Renk. "They're on duty."

"How are you getting on in Washington, Forest?" asked Toni.

"Very well, Toni," he replied. "I was able to obtain early admission at the university. Dad thought it would be wise to put some distance between me and my brother."

"Is there still bad blood between you two?" I asked.

"Tarzan never forgets, Cara," he replied. "You know my brother."

"Him mighty abominable boy, you betcha," said Toni.

"Dan, where's your sign?" asked Forest. "I'm surprised you're not picketing this wedding. Isn't that the First Lady and her son at the refreshments table?"

My love glanced over in that direction. "Oh, let them eat cake."

"Dan is picketing me privately," I said, patting his hand.

"Co-optation through sex," said Toni. "It's still our most insidious tactic. Forest, how's your charming uncle? I was pleased to hear they tossed out his suit."

"Yes, the Gadsden Purchase Treaty remains in force—thanks to the U.S. Federal District Court."

"Is he quite despondent?" asked Howard.

"Not really," said Forest. "The Feds gave him back all his guns. Last I heard Max was trying to swap his blimp for a small aircraft carrier."

"Oh, look!" cried Toni, "That cute Ryan Holgate is ejecting someone. It's Monty Bellefontaine! He was trying to sneak a shot of Bobby Greer shucking corn."

"I wasn't aware your family entertained the Greers socially," said Forest.

"We don't," I confessed. "But our nice new stepfather has been guarding the Second Family for years. The President himself almost made it. It was so gracious of Mrs. Greer to come all the way from Washington."

"That Bobby Greer is a dreamboat," said Toni. "Cara, we must meet him."

"Toni, he's 24 and married," I pointed out.

"That's OK, Cara," she replied. "It's only his first marriage."

"Forest's been talking to Essex Kennard about the elections," remarked Howard.

"I hope he didn't take the loss personally," said Toni.

"I'm afraid he did," replied Forest. "He's been analyzing the results obsessively. You know what he's concluded was the primary cause of Dad's defeat?"

"Your father's monumental ignorance of U.S. foreign policy?" proposed Renk.

"His scorched earth environmental record?" suggested Dan.

"No," said Forest, "it was Thom Kirkwood's Halloween costume."

"I don't get it," said Toni.

"It's simple," he replied. "According to Essex, our core voters didn't like the idea of my sister being involved with a black fellow."

"Dola lost the elections!" exclaimed Toni. "I'm sure her poetry didn't help either."

"And how's your father?" asked Forest. "I see his wife is expecting."

"Yes, they just found out it's a boy," I replied.

"Mindy denied everything, of course," said Toni. "Dad apparently is buying it. I just hope he can keep an open mind when our little stepbrother starts swinging from vines and groping his preschool classmates."

"Forest, will you be visiting here for long?" I asked.

"A few days," he replied. "Howard is kindly putting me up."

"My sister Tallmadge has been throwing herself at Cypress Swamp," commented Howard. "It seems to be a common Archbold trait."

"I'm returning to Seattle next Thursday," said Forest. "I'm enrolling in a summer program at the University of Washington. Howard's promised to visit in August."

"Now Tallmadge wants to come too," sighed Howard. "It promises to be a festive trip."

"Look!" exclaimed Toni. "Here comes the photographer. Hold up your Flam Cola cans everyone. This might get national exposure!"

"But, darling," said Renk, "Flam Cola canceled your contract."

"I know, Renkums," she replied, "but you can't let a little adversity get you down. That's what the American way of life is all about."

Hoisting the distinctive green can, my sister led us all in song:

> In school we did study
>> Our Constitution free,
> But skipped o'er the muddy
>> Bog of politics tawdry.

> Of civics we have learned—
>> Though we shudder to think:
> When high office is yearned,
>> To low depths must you sink.

> Now, the polling is over,
>> The voters have spoken;
> The winner's in clover,
>> The loser's heartbroken.

> Big dollars were raised,
>> Attack ads have been aired,
> The citizens are dazed
>> By the scandals thus bared.

> The candidates weren't credible,
>> Their managers were scum,
> Their tactics regrettable,
>> Their ideas humdrum.

In moral confusion
  We grope for our way:
Is democracy an illusion,
  And can we make it pay?

The idealist inspires:
  Future hope to foresee;
The realist inquires:
  Hey, what's in it for me?

Miss Liberty still stands,
  Though her gown is askew,
Goosed by savage hands—
  What an ordeal she's been through!

Here ends our tale humble
  Of bumbled deceptions,
Of love all a-jumble,
  And of sisterly affections.

Let us raise high our glasses
  As a marriage here begins,
Though no love surpasses
  The steadfastness of twins.

C.D. Payne was born in 1949 in
Akron, Ohio, the former "Rubber
Capital of the World" famed for its
tire factories. He shares a birthday
with P.T. Barnum, a fact which has
influenced his life profoundly. After
graduating from Harvard College in
1971, he moved to California, where
he's worked as a newspaper editor,
graphic artist, cartoonist, typesetter,
photographer, proofreader, carpenter,
trailer park handyman, and advertis-
ing copywriter. He is married and lives
in Sonoma County, north of San
Francisco. He collects toy travel trail-
ers, builds furniture in the Arts and
Crafts style, and believes humans
should be genetically altered so they
are only one-quarter their present
size.

# *FRISCO PIGEON MAMBO*

a new comic novel by

# C.D. Payne

*coming soon*

Read about it now at

www.nicktwisp.com

# *Frisco Pigeon Mambo sneak preview*

"Heard the latest rumor?" asked Petey, puffing placidly on the Drag-O-Matic. "The word is we're actually pigeons."

"I am *not* a pigeon," stated Honky with conviction, fluttering his wings. "Am I, Robin?"

"Of course you're not," I agreed. "And neither am I. I don't know where Petey gets such preposterous notions."

Petey coughed, expelling a millet seed, then spoke. "Robin, take your beak out of that sherry tube, and answer me this: If we are not pigeons, why do they feed us Hygienic Pigeon Chow?"

My I.D. band tinkled softly against my leg as I scratched at a nit. "They feed us Hygienic Pigeon Chow as part of a scientific experiment, I said. "We are explorers on the frontier of knowledge."

"Hmmphh," snorted Petey, puffing away. "An experiment designed to prove exactly what?"

"I suppose that humans can thrive on Pigeon Chow," I replied. "I find it quite satisfying, especially served with a nice dry sherry."

"Me too," agreed Honky.

"Besides," I noted, "why would Dr. Milbrene name a pigeon Robin? That would be too absurd."

"Why *did* he name you Robin?" asked Honky.

"I think he was inspired by the russet tinge of my feathers," I explained. "Robin is, I believe, Latin for red."

"And why was I named Honky?" inquired my pal. "Is it because my feathers are pure, stark, unadulterated white?"

"Exactly so," I replied. "Honky is Latin for 'white.' Just as Petey is a common colloquialism for 'grossly corpulent'."

"Your scholarship is as miserable as your puny physique," replied Petey, puffing sedately.

"Petey!" snapped Honky, "don't bogart the Drag-O-Matic!"

"OK, OK. Keep your feathers on." Petey edged his porcine bulk over on the perch. He is a broad, grey-feathered fellow with a prodigious appetite for tobacco, sunflower seeds, and (so he thinks) knowledge.

"What are we smoking today?" I asked, sipping from my sherry tube.

"Chesterbogs," answered Honky, blowing smoke rings at Petey's head.

"Damn, I prefer Kalms," I said. "I wonder what brand Sam Spade smokes?"

Lovely Maryanne, our favorite lab assistant, has been reading to us from *The Maltese Falcon*, a book she's studying in class. She's an English major, which Petey says is a British military officer of middle rank. She certainly looks wonderful in her uniforms. She has downy fine golden feathers, slender nearly nude wings, and an attractively prominent bifid breast.

Maryanne is reading to us to take our minds off Wallace, our cagemate who died recently. What a shock. We woke one morning and there he was down on the soiled litter paper—with his toes in the air, stiff as a cuttle bone. Later, I heard Dr. Milbrene tell Maryanne to dissect his cardiovascular system and centrifuge his liver. I imagine that is some sort of solemn funeral rite. I only wish we'd been invited to the services.

A shady character named Joel Cairo just offered Sam Spade five thousand dollars for a statuette of a black bird, then pulled a gun on him. Fortunately, Mr. Spade wrestled away the pistol and knocked the fellow unconscious. I'd love to pursue an exciting career as a detective, though I'm not entirely clear what such a vocation entails. Modern writers are so lax in defining their terms. What exactly is "five thousand dollars?" And how similar is "apartment 1001 at the Coronet" to a stainless steel laboratory cage? I hope the author intends to explicate these mysteries soon.

I'm feeling a little edgy today. Petey is monopolizing the Drag-O-Matic again. I can't understand why everyone has his own personal sherry tube, but we're forced to make do with just one Drag-O-Matic. Petey theorizes that Dr. Milbrene is trying to induce stress in our lives. But why would he want to do that? The man is like a father to me.

Dr. Eli Milbrene is a world-renowned professor of biology at the University of California at Berkeley. Petey, Honky, and I are elite volunteers assisting him with his research as part of Test Group C. We're obliged to smoke cigarettes, drink sherry, and consume regulated quantities of Hygienic Pigeon Chow. Group B residents, in the next row over, have to do their seed munching and smoking entirely sober. Group A subjects are even more deprived. All they're permitted to do is dine on Hygienic Pigeon Chow and go up on the roof periodically for something called "fresh air." I don't know why they're called the "control group." They have so little control over their own happiness.

Group D members are the real party animals. They smoke, booze it up, and dine on rich delicacies like deep-fried prawns, cocktail wieners, macadamia nuts, barbecued pork ribs, and chocolate cheese cake. Often we can hear them down at their end of the lab whooping it up.

Wallace, before he died, confided he'd heard rumors of a Group E, caged in another room. The same delightful lifestyle as Group D, with the further stimulation of mixed-sex cohabitation. Perhaps it was just wishful thinking on his part. Wallace was always sweet on Julie, a Group A experimenter who lives across the aisle with Darla and Blanche. All nice, plain-feathered girls, if a little controlled, but clearly not in the same league as my dear Maryanne.

Sitting on her lovely finger last night after our reading, while she softly stroked my head, I felt the most exquisite tingle suffuse my body. Pleasant but unnerving. Could this be love?

Honky just dropped a large sunflower seed on Petey's head, freeing up the Drag-O-Matic.

"I'm next in line after Honky!" I announced.

"Go pluck yourselves," grumbled Petey, theatrically daubing sherry on his ruffled noggin.

※　※　※

Honky says we're smoking Marlrubos today, a brand that often causes me to gaze with a steely glint toward the western horizon. This is not as easy as it sounds—especially when one's eyes are situated on opposite sides of one's head.

We all have our particular talents. I am also able to walk without bobbing my head excessively. Petey can empty an entire sherry tube while remaining upright on his perch. And Honky can decipher the labels on cigarette cartons. He used to read the profoundly obscure inscriptions on lab assistants' T-shirts, but gave it up to appease Petey, who—though illiterate—fancies himself the intellectual of our cage. It's hard for a self-acknowledged egghead to confess he is as perplexed as the rest of us by the phrase "Young Dickheads Total Pillage World Tour."

Dr. Milbrene just made his daily rounds through the lab. "Hello, men," he said, stopping at our cage and making notations on his clipboard. "How are we today? Any signs of a palsied tremor or hacking cough?"

Dr. Milbrene is so solicitous of our welfare. He's a true man of the people, even though he's on everyone's short list for the Nobel Prize. Every time the lab phone rings, I expect it's long-distance from Stockholm. Usually, though, it's Eldon, our flunky day-shift lab assistant, calling in to say he overslept.

I'm smoking heavily today; my nerves are on edge. Last night in Sam Spade's apartment that slimy Joel Cairo got into a fight with nice Brigid O'Shaughnessy. As the quarrel escalated into violence, two police detectives arrived and threatened everyone with arrest! Now Mr. Spade's being followed by a sullen youth with a gun.

Petey says adolescents are the price parents pay for the pleasures of pro-creation. I must weigh this carefully before making further advances toward Maryanne. Yesterday I sat on her shoulder and nuzzled her silken perfumed ear. Wonderful!

Damn, the butt got stuck in the ejector impeller. Now the Drag-O-Matic's jammed. If slothful Eldon doesn't shuffle by in the next two minutes, someone's going to get his rude anatomy pecked the next time he opens this cage!

"Hi, Robin," called a voice from the Control Group A cage.

"Oh, hi, Darla," I replied distractedly.

"You sound like you're sober today, Robin."

She's right. In my agitated state I'd been neglecting my sherry tube. I took an emergency swig.

"The roof was beautiful this morning," she continued. "A gray haze lifted, and you could see all the way to the Golden Gate."

"Was it open?" I inquired, making an effort to appear interested.

"Was what open?" she asked.

"There's no point talking to him, Darla," sniffed Blanche. "The fellow's drunk. They're all a bunch of cage-bound, inebriated, nicotine-breath rubes."

"The sweetest music on earth," noted Petey: "the prim condemnations of the self-righteous prude."

"Hear, hear," said Honky. "Can I buy you fellows a drink?"

We turned our backs on the ladies and bellied up to our beverage taps. Down the aisle the Group D gang was crunching noisily into a bag of fried pork rinds. I suppose there must be some sort of world out there beyond the walls of this cozy lab, but I think Honky's right. It really is no concern of ours.

We're in shock! Brigid O'Shaughnessy is missing! Last night she disappeared on the way to Effie Perine's apartment. Poor Mr. Spade: first his partner gets shot, then he falls in love with a client in distress, and now she disappears. And nearly everyone is trying to pin assorted murder raps on him.

After the reading, swept up in the emotions of the moment, I kissed Maryanne. She responded by pressing her soft voluptuous beak against my head. Never have I experienced such tumultuous emotions. It was all I could do to maintain my composure as she moistened a lab towel and daubed her scarlet beak-coloring from my feverish brow.

After lights out, I sat on my perch and thought of my future life together with Maryanne. Of course, we'll have to get a larger cage—one with a shelf for Maryanne's English books and a desk for my detective business. Honky and Petey can live in the cage next door and come over for sherry parties. Hey, I wouldn't be surprised if Dr. Milbrene gave us a transfer to Group D as a wedding present. Those fried pork rinds should taste pretty special shared with the woman I love.

Thank God the lab assistant stocked the Drag-O-Matic with unfiltered Cramels. There's nothing like a jolt of unexpurgated nicotine to clear the head and calm the nerves. Already Eldon, though hampered by a bandaged thumb, has had to reload twice. His grungy T-shirt, Honky informed me privately, reads: "Extra fries or the Nobel Prize. Have it your way."

"Extraordinarily opaque," whispered Honky.

"Virtually unfathomable," I agreed.

"What are you two cooing about?" demanded Petey.

"We were just remarking how attractive the ladies look today," answered Honky diplomatically.

Across the aisle, Darla and Julie smiled. Blanche studied us coldly through the bars of their cage.

"It's degenerates like you," she observed, "who put a permanent crimp in a girl's nest-building instincts."

"Glad to hear it," commented Petey, not withering under her icy glare. "Child-rearing is such a juvenile pastime."

"I'm feeling a bit on edge today," remarked Honky, sipping from his sherry tube.

"So am I," I whispered. "I feel anxious and restless. Very unsettling. It's worse when I gaze longingly upon dear Maryanne."

"She's very attractive," agreed Petey. "Except for her feet."

"I'm highly attracted to bright red feet," said Honky, admiring his own lumpy, carmine toes. "Maryanne has regrettably hideous feet. Did you see her yesterday in those open-toed sandals?"

I did, I must confess. Her feet were shockingly pale and smooth. Hardly a bump or nodule to captivate the eye. Then again, none of us is perfect. One must not dwell on the shortcomings of one's love. I myself am not as tall or broad-shouldered as one might wish. Nor am I as handsome as Zeb (short for Zebulon) of Test Group D, with his dark, shimmering feathers and film star good looks.

"Robin has very attractive feet," commented Darla. "They're wonderfully red and knobby. Very scaly too."

She's right, of course. How nice of her to notice. I only hope Maryanne is as observant.

* * *

Something is wrong, terribly wrong. The odious fat man Caspar Gutman had just given Mr. Spade a drugged drink when *CRASH*, the door to the lab flew open. Dropping her book in surprise, Maryanne leaped up as a half-dozen masked, black-garbed intruders swept into the room.

"Freeze right there!" shouted a burly man, waving what Petey informed me later was an automatic revolver.

"Who are you?" demanded my love, bravely standing her ground.

"ARF!" barked the invaders.

"Oh no!" exclaimed Maryanne. "Not Animal Rights Forever!"

"Yes!" affirmed the man. "We are liberating this lab!"

"You can't!" pleaded my sweetheart. "Six graduate students have their entire academic careers invested in this project!"

The man sneered under his bizarre gauze-like mask, later identified by Petey as a pair of lady's black fishnet pantyhose. "You're breaking my heart. Seize the animal torturer!"

Two women grabbed Maryanne; she struggled to pull away. Grappling fiercely, they fell back against our cage. Enraged, I leaped toward the bars and locked onto featherless flesh.

"AAIIYYYEEE!" shrieked one of the women. "Something's biting me!"

"Birdie, let go!" shouted her fellow thug, wrestling my dearest into a head-lock. "We're on your side!"

I bit down harder, tasting a spurt of warm saltiness.

"Help!" screamed the woman. "He's amputating my elbow! Shoot him, Ted!"

"No!" exclaimed Maryanne, suddenly ceasing to struggle. "Robin, let go!"

Exerting all my strength, I squeezed my jaws in one last ferocious bite, then released my grip. The woman sobbed and pulled away, clasping her injured wing.

"Damn, I'm bleeding!"

"Serves you right!" muttered my love, right before a male invader slapped a length of thick tape across her sweet beak. Rudely, the female thug bound Maryanne's silken wings behind her back with the Drag-O-Matic cord.

"OK, cover the cages," commanded Ted, the gun-toting leader. "Let's start moving them out."

"What's, what's happening?" whimpered Honky, cowering in a heap with Petey under the Pigeon Chow tray.

Before I could reply, a black cover descended over our cage, blotting out the light, as the only home we'd ever known began to swing and pitch violently.

"Earthquake!" shouted Honky, a whirlwind of panicked fluttering in the tumultuous, all-encompassing blackness.

"No, it's not," gasped Petey, rebounding heavily against the bars with every bounce. "They're taking us somewhere."

"This is an outrage!" shouted Zeb from the Group D cage. "We haven't finished our fried pork rinds!"

"I fear the worst," groaned Petey. "We're all going to be viciously slaughtered."

"Robin, where are you?" called a faraway voice that sounded like Darla's. "Robin!"

"Here I am!" I sang, receiving no reply. "Don't be afraid!"

Suddenly, we were enveloped in frigid air. Metal doors slammed shut, a rumbling mechanical sound roared, and we began to move.

"We're being kidnapped!" I shouted.

Yes, I realized with horror, we were being plucked from our loved ones— just as heroic Samuel Spade had been wrenched from his own dearest Brigid.